THE GOOD TERRORIST

THE GOOD TERRORIST

Doris Lessing

Alfred A. Knopf ✖ New York 1985

THIS IS A BORZOI BOOK
PUBLISHED BY ALFRED A. KNOPF, INC.

Library of Congress Cataloging-in-Publication Data

Lessing, Doris May
The good terrorist.
I. Title.
PR6023.E833G66   1985   823'.914   85-40214
ISBN 0-394-54339-4

Manufactured in the United States of America
FIRST AMERICAN EDITION

THE GOOD TERRORIST

The house was set back from the noisy main road in what seemed to be a rubbish tip. A large house. Solid. Black tiles stood at angles along the gutter, and into a gap near the base of a fat chimney a bird flew, trailing a piece of grass several times its length.

"I should think 1910," said Alice. "Look how thick the walls are." This could be seen through the broken window just above them on the first floor. She got no response, but nevertheless shrugged off her backpack, letting it tumble onto a living rug of young nettles that was trying to digest rusting tins and plastic cups. She took a step back to get a better view of the roof. This brought Jasper into vision. His face, as she expected it would be, was critical and meant to be noticed. For her part, she did not have to be told that she was wearing *her look*, described by him as silly. "Stop it," he ordered. His hand shot out, and her wrist was encircled by hard bone. It hurt. She faced him, undefiant but confident, and said, "I wonder if they will accept us?" And, as she had known he would, he said, "It is a question of whether we will accept them."

She had withstood the test on her, that bony pain, and he let her wrist go and went on to the door. It was a front door, solid and sure of itself, in a little side street full of suburban gardens and similar comfortable houses. They did not have slates missing and broken windows.

"Why, why, *why?*" asked Alice angrily, addressing the question, probably, to the universe itself, her heart full of pain because of the

3

capacious, beautiful, and unloved house. She dragged her backpack by its strap after her and joined him.

"Profit, of course," he said, and pressed the bell, which did not ring. He gave the door a sharp push and they went into a large shadowy hall where stairs went strongly up, turned at a wide landing, and rose out of sight. The scene was illuminated by a hurricane lamp that stood on the floor, in a corner. From a side room came the sound of soft drumming. Jasper pushed open this door, too. The windows were covered by blankets, leaving not a chink of light. A black youth looked up from his family of drums, his cheeks and teeth shining in candlelight. "Hi," he said, all his fingers and both feet at work, so that it seemed he was dancing as he sat, or was perhaps on some kind of exercise machine.

This smiling jolly black boy who looked like an advertisement for an attractive holiday in the Caribbean struck Alice's organ of credibility falsely, and she tucked away a little memo to herself not to forget a first impression of anxiety or even sorrow, which was the real message her nerves were getting from him. She found herself actually on the verge of saying, "It's all right, it's okay, don't worry!" But meanwhile Jasper was demanding, "Where's Bert?"

The black youth shrugged, nonchalantly, still smiling, and did not for one moment stop his energetic attack on his instruments. Jasper's tight grip on her upper arm took her out of the room into the hall, where Alice said, "This place smells."

"Well," said Jasper, in the clumsily placating way she knew was meant as love, "I suppose you'll put a stop to that."

At once, feeling her advantage, she said, "Don't forget you've been living soft for four years. You're not going to find it easy after that."

"Don't call me soft," he said, and kicked her on the ankle. Not hard, but enough.

This time she went ahead of him and opened a door she felt must be to the kitchen. Light fell on desolation. Worse, danger: she was looking at electric cables ripped out of the wall and dangling, raw-ended. The cooker was pulled out and lying on the floor. The broken windows had admitted rainwater, which lay in puddles everywhere. There was a dead bird on the floor. It stank. Alice began to cry from pure rage. "The bastards," she cursed. "The filthy stinking fascist bastards."

They already knew that the Council, to prevent squatters, had sent in the workmen to make the place uninhabitable. "They didn't even make those wires safe. They didn't even . . ." Suddenly alive with energy, she whirled about, opening doors. Two lavatories on this floor, the bowls filled with cement.

She cursed steadily, the tears streaming. "The filthy shitty swine, the shitty fucking fascist swine . . ." She was full of the energy of hate. Incredulous with it, for she had never been able to believe, in some corner of her, that anybody, particularly not a member of the working class, could obey an order to destroy a house. In that corner of her brain that was perpetually incredulous began the monologue that Jasper never heard, for he would not have authorised it: But they are *people*, people did this. To stop other people from living. I don't believe it. Who can they be? What can they be like? I've never met anyone who could. Why, it must be people like Len and Bob and Bill, *friends*. They did it. They came in and filled the lavatory bowls with cement and ripped out all the cables and blocked up the gas.

Jasper stood and watched her. He was pleased. This fury of energy had banished *her look*, which he hated, when she seemed, all of her, to be swollen and glistening, as if not merely her face but her whole body filled with tears, which oozed from every pore.

Without referring to him, she ran up the stairs, and he followed slowly, listening to how she banged on doors, and then, hearing nothing, flung them open. On the first-floor landing they stood looking into order, not chaos. Here every room had sleeping bags, one or two, or three. Candles or hurricane lamps. Even chairs with little tables beside them. Books. Newspapers. But no one was in.

The smell on this floor was strong. It came from upstairs. More slowly they went up generously wide stairs, and confronted a stench that made Jasper briefly retch. Alice's face was stern and proud. She flung open a door onto a scene of plastic buckets, topped with shit. But this room had been deemed sufficiently filled, and the one next to it had been started. Ten or so red, yellow, and orange buckets stood in a group, waiting.

There were other rooms on this floor, but none were used. None could be used, the smell was so strong.

They went down the stairs, silent, watching their feet, for there was rubbish everywhere, and the light came dimly through dirty windows.

"We are not here," said he, anticipating her, "to make ourselves comfortable. We aren't here for that."

She said, "I don't understand anyone choosing to live like this. Not when it's so easy."

Now she sounded listless, flat, all the incandescence of fury gone.

He was about to start a speech about her bourgeois inclinations, as she could see; but the front door opened, and against the sunlight was outlined a military-looking figure.

"Bert!" he shouted, and jumped down the stairs three at a time. "Bert. It's Jasper. . . ."

Alice thought maternally, hearing that glad voice ring out, It's because of his shitty father. But this was part of her private stream, since of course Jasper did not allow her the right to such ideas.

"Jasper," acknowledged Bert, and then peered through the gloom up at herself.

"Alice—I told you," said Jasper.

"Comrade Alice," said Bert. His voice was curt, stern, and pure, insisting on standards, and Jasper's voice fell into step. "We have just come," he said. "There was no one to report to."

"We spoke to him, in there," remarked Alice, arriving beside them, indicating the room from which came the soft drumming.

"Oh, Jim," dismissed Bert. He strode to a door they had not opened, kicked it open since it had lost its knob, and went in without looking to see if they followed.

This room was as near to normal as they had seen. With the door shut, you could believe this was a sitting room in an ordinary house, although everything—chairs, a sofa, the carpet—was dingy. The smell was almost shut out, but to Alice it seemed that an invisible film of stench clung to everything, and she would feel it slippery on her fingers if she touched.

Bert stood upright, slightly bent forward, arms at ease, looking at her. But he did not see her, she knew that. He was a dark, thin young man, probably twenty-eight or thirty. His face was full of black shining hairs, and his dark eyes and a red mouth and white teeth gleamed from among them. He wore new stiff dark-blue jeans and a close-fitting dark-blue jacket, buttoned up and tidy. Jasper wore light-blue linen trousers and a striped tee shirt like a sailor's; but Alice knew he would soon be in clothes like Bert's, which were in fact his normal gear. He had had a brief escapade into frivolity due to some influence or other.

Alice knew that the two men would now talk, without concerning themselves with her, and set herself to guard her interests, while she looked out of the bow window into the garden, where rubbish of all kinds reached to the sills. Sparrows were at work on the piles, scratching and digging. A blackbird sat on a milk carton and looked straight at her. Beyond the birds, she saw a thin cat crouched under a hydrangea in young green leaf and slim coronets of pink and blue that would be flowers. The cat was watching her, too, with bright, starved eyes.

Bert reached into a cupboard and took out a Thermos the size of a bucket, and three mugs.

"Oh, you do have electricity, then?" she asked.

"No. A comrade in the next street fills it for me every morning," he said.

Alice, watching the scene with half her attention, saw how Jasper eyed the flask, and the pouring of the coffee. She knew he was hungry. Because of the row with her mother he had slammed out of the house and not breakfasted. And he had not had time to drink the coffee she had taken up to him. She thought, "But that's Bert's supply for the day," and indicated she only wanted half a cup. Which she was given, exactly as specified.

Jasper drank down his cup at once, and sat looking at the Thermos, wanting more. Bert did not notice.

"The situation has changed," Bert began, as if this were a continuation of some meeting or other. "My analysis was incorrect, as it happened. I underestimated the political maturity of the cadres. When I put the question to the vote, half decided against, and they left here at once."

Jasper said, "Then they would have proved unreliable. Good riddance."

"Precisely."

"What was the question?" enquired Alice. She used her "meeting voice," for she had learned that this was necessary if she was to hold her own. To her it sounded false and cold, and she was always embarrassed by it; because of the effort it required, she sounded indifferent, even absent-minded. Yet her eyes were steadily and even severely observing the scene in front of her: Bert looking at her, or, rather, at what she had said; Jasper looking at the Thermos. Suddenly he was unable to stop himself, and he reached for the jug. Bert said "Sorry," and pushed it towards him.

"You know what the question was," said Jasper, sour. "I told you. We are going to join the IRA."

"You mean," said Alice, "you *voted* on whether to join the IRA?" She sounded breathless; Bert took it as fear, and he said, with loud, cold contempt, "Shit-scared. They ran like little rabbits."

Alice persisted, "How was it put to the vote?"

Bert said, after a pause, "That this group should make approaches to the IRA leadership, offering our services as an England-based entity."

Alice digested this, looking strained because of the effort it cost her to believe it, and said, "But Jasper told me that this house was Communist Centre Union?"

"Correct. This is a CCU squat."

"But has the leadership of the CCU decided to offer the services of the whole CCU to the IRA? I don't understand," she said fiercely, not at all in her "political" voice, and Bert said, curt and offhand, because, as she could see, he was uncomfortable, "No."

"Then how can a *branch* of the CCU offer its services?"

Here she observed that Jasper was seeking to engage Bert's eyes in "Take no notice of her" looks, and she forestalled him. "It doesn't make sense."

8

Bert admitted, "You are correct, in a way. The point was discussed. It was agreed that, while approaches could not be made as a group of the CCU, it would be permissible for a group of CCU members to make the approach, as associated individuals."

"But . . ." Alice lost interest. They are at it again, she was thinking. Fudging it. She returned her attention to the rubbish pile a yard beyond the dirty glass. The blackbird had gone. The poor cat was sniffing around the edges of the heap, where flies were crawling.

She said, "What do you do for food here?"

"Take-away."

"This rubbish is a health hazard. There must be rats."

"That's what the police said."

"Have they been?"

"They were here last night."

"Oh, I see, that's why the others left."

"No," said Bert. "They left because they got the shits. About the IRA."

"What did the police say?"

"They gave us four days to leave."

"Why don't we go to the Council?" said Alice, in an irritated wail; and as Jasper said, "Oh, there she goes again," the door opened and a young woman came in. She had short shiny black hair that had been expertly cut, black quick eyes, red lips, a clear white skin. She was glossy and hard, like a fresh cherry. She looked carefully at Bert, at Jasper, and at Alice, and Alice knew she was being seen.

"I'm Pat," she said. "Bert told me about you two." And then, "You are brother and sister?"

At once Jasper snapped, "No, we are not!"

But Alice liked it when people made the mistake, and she said, "People often take us for brother and sister."

Pat examined them again. Jasper fidgeted under the look and turned away, hands in his jacket pockets, as if trying to seem indifferent to an attack.

They were both fair, with reddish gleams in hair that wanted to go into little curls and wisps. Jasper's was cut very short; Alice's was short and chunky and serviceable. She cut it herself. They both

9

had pinkish freckled skin. Jasper's little blue eyes were in round white shallows, and this gave him an angelic, candid air. He was very thin, and wore skin-tight clothes. Alice was stocky, and she had a pudgy, formless look to her. Sometimes a girl of twelve, even thirteen, before she is lit by pubescence, is as she will be in middle age. A group of women are standing on a platform in the Underground. Middle-aged women, with carrier bags, gossiping. Very short women, surely? No, they are girls, of twelve or so. Forty years of being women will boil through them and leave them as they are now, heavy and cautious, and anxious to please. Alice could seem like a fattish clumsy girl or, sometimes, about fifty, but never looked her age, which was thirty-six. Now it was a girl who returned Pat's look with friendly curiosity from small blue-grey eyes set under sandy lashes.

"Well," said Pat, strolling to the window to stand by Alice, "have you heard that this happy little community is for the chop?"

She looked much older than Alice, was ten years younger. She offered Alice a cigarette, which was refused, and smoked hers needfully, greedily.

"Yes, and I said, Why not negotiate with the Council?"

"I heard you. But they prefer their romantic squalour."

"Romantic," said Alice, disgusted.

"It does go against the grain, negotiating with the Establishment," said Bert.

"Do you mean that this commune is breaking up?" said Jasper suddenly, sounding so like a small boy that Alice glanced quickly to see whether it had been noticed. It had: by Pat, who stood, holding her cigarette to her lips between two fingers and distancing them, then bringing them back, so that she could puff and exhale, puff and exhale. Looking at Jasper. Diagnosis.

Alice said quickly, her heart full of a familiar soft ache, on Jasper's account, "It doesn't go against my grain. I've done it often."

"Oh, you have, have you?" said Pat. "So have I. Where?"

"In Birmingham. A group of seven of us went to the Council over a scheduled house. We paid gas and electricity and water, and we stayed there thirteen months."

"Good for you."

"And in Halifax, I was in a negotiated squat for six months. And when I was in digs in Manchester—that was when I was at university—there was a house full of students, nearly twenty of us. It started off as a squat, the Council came to terms, and it ended up as a student house."

During this the two men listened, proceedings suspended. Jasper had again filled his mug. Bert indicated to Pat that the Thermos was empty, and she shook her head, listening to Alice.

"Why don't we go to the Council?" said Alice directly to Pat.

"I would. But I'm leaving anyway." Alice saw Bert's body stiffen, and he sat angry and silent.

Pat said to Bert, "I told you last night I was leaving."

Alice had understood that this was more than political. She saw that a personal relationship was breaking up because of some political thing! Every instinct repudiated this. She thought, involuntarily, What nonsense, letting politics upset a personal relationship! This was not really her belief: she would not have stood by it if challenged. But similar thoughts often did pass through her mind.

Pat said, to Bert's half-averted face, "What the fuck did you expect? At an ordinary meeting like that—two of them from outside, we didn't know anything about them. We don't know anything about the couple who came last week. Jim was in the room, and he isn't even CCU. Suddenly putting forward that resolution."

"It wasn't sudden."

"When we discussed it before, we decided to make individual approaches. To discuss it with individuals, carefully."

Her voice was full of contempt. She was looking at—presumably—her lover as though he was fit for the dustbin.

"You've changed your mind, at any rate," said Bert, his red lips shining angrily from his thickets of beard. "You agreed that to support the IRA was the logical position for this stage."

"It is the only correct attitude; Ireland is the fulcrum of the imperialist attack," said Jasper.

"I haven't changed my mind," said Pat. "But if I am going

to work with the IRA or anyone else, then I'm going to know who I am working with."

"You don't know us," said Alice, with a pang of painful realisation: she and Jasper were part of the reason for this couple's breakup.

"No hard feelings," said Pat. "Nothing personal. But yes. The first I heard of you was when Bert said he had met Jasper at the CND rally Saturday. And I gather Bert hadn't even met you."

"No," said Alice.

"Well, I'm sorry, but that's not the way to do things."

"I see your point," said Alice.

A silence. The two young women stood at the window, in an aromatic cloud from Pat's cigarette. The two men were in chairs, in the centre of the room. The rainlike pattering of the drum came from Jim beyond the hall.

Alice said, "How many people are left here now?"

Pat did not answer, and at last Bert said, "With you two, seven." He added, "I don't know about you, Pat."

"Yes, you do," said Pat, sharp and cold. But they were looking at each other now, and Alice thought: No, it won't be easy for them to split up. She said, "Well, if it's seven, then four of us are here now. Five if Pat . . . Where are the other two? I want to get an agreement that I go to the Council."

"The lavatories full of cement. The electricity cables torn out. Pipes smashed," said Bert on a fine rising, derisive note.

"It's not difficult to put it right," said Alice. "We did it in Birmingham. The Council smashed the place to a ruin. They pulled the lavatories completely out there. All the pipes. Filled the bath with cement. Piled garbage in all the rooms. We got it clean."

"Who is going to pay for it?" That was Bert.

"We are."

"Out of what?"

"Oh, belt up," said Pat, "it costs us more in take-away and running around cadging baths and showers than it would to pay electricity and gas."

"It's a point," said Bert.

"And it would keep Old Bill off our backs," said Alice.

Silence. She knew that some people—and she suspected Bert, though not Pat, of this—would be sorry to hear it. They enjoyed encounters with the police.

Bert said unexpectedly, "Well, if we are going to build up our organisation, we aren't going to need attention from Old Bill."

"Right on," said Pat. "As I've been saying."

Silence again. Alice saw it was up to her. She said, "One problem. In this borough they need someone to guarantee the electricity and gas. Who is in work?"

"Three of the comrades who left last night were."

"Comrades!" said Bert. "Opportunistic shits."

"They are very good, honest communists," said Pat. "They happen not to want to work with the IRA."

Bert began to heave with silent theatrical laughter, and Jasper joined him.

"So we are all on Social Security," said Alice.

"So no point in going to the Council," said Bert.

Alice hesitated and said painfully, "I could ask my mother . . ."

At this Jasper exploded in raucous laughter and jeers, his face scarlet. "Her mother, bourgeois pigs . . ."

"Shut up," said Alice. "We were living with my mother for four years," she explained in a breathless, balanced voice, which seemed to her unkindly cold and hostile. "Four years. Bourgeois or not."

"Take the rich middle class for what you can get," said Jasper. "Get everything out of them you can. That's my line."

"Yes, yes," said Alice. "I agree. But she did keep us for four years." Then, capitulating, "Well, why shouldn't she? She *is* my mother." This last was said in a trembling, painful little voice.

"Right," said Pat, examining her curiously. "Well, no point in asking mine. Haven't seen her for years."

"Well, then," said Bert, suddenly getting up from the chair and standing in front of Pat, a challenge, his black eyes full on her. "So you're not leaving after all?"

"We've got to discuss it, Bert," she said, hurriedly, and walked over to him, and looked up into his face. He put his arm around her and they went out.

Alice surveyed the room. Skilfully. A family sitting room it had been. Comfortable. The paint was not too bad; the chairs and sofa probably stood where they had then. There was a fireplace, not even plastered over.

"Are you going to ask your mother? I mean, to be a guarantor?" Jasper sounded forlorn. "And who's going to pay for getting it all straight?"

"I'll ask the others if they'll contribute."

"And if they won't?" he said, knowingly, sharing expertise with her, a friendly moment.

"Some won't, we know that," she said, "but we'll manage. We always do, don't we?"

But this was too direct an appeal to intimacy. At once he backed away into criticism. "And who's going to do all the work?"

As he had been saying now for fourteen, fifteen years.

In the house in Manchester she had shared with four other students she had been housemother, doing the cooking and shopping, housekeeping. She loved it. She got an adequate degree, but did not even try for a job. She was still in the house when the next batch of students arrived, and she stayed to look after them. That was how Jasper found her, coming in one evening for supper. He was not a student, had graduated poorly, had failed to find a job after halfhearted efforts. He stayed on in the house, not formally living there but as Alice's "guest." After all, it was only because of Alice's efforts that the place had become a student house: it had been a squat. And Jasper did not leave. She knew he had become dependent on her. But then and since he had complained she was nothing but a servant, wasting her life on other people. As they moved from squat to squat, commune to commune, this pattern remained: she looked after him, and he complained that other people exploited her.

At her mother's he had said the same. "She's just exploiting you," he said. "Cooking and shopping. Why do you do it?"

"We've got four days," said Alice now. "I'm going to get moving." She did not look at him, but walked steadily past him and into the hall. She carried her backpack into the room where

Jim was drumming and said, "Keep an eye on this for me, comrade."
He nodded. She said, "If I get permission from the Council for us
to live here, will you share expenses?"

His hands fell from the drums. His friendly round face fell into
lines of woe and he said, "*They* say I can't stay here."

"Why not?"

"Oh, shit, man, I'm not into politics. I just want to live."
Now he said, incredulously, "I was here first. Before any of you.
This was my place. I found it. I said to everyone, Yes, come in,
come in, man, this is Liberty Hall."

"That's not fair," said Alice, at once.

"I've been here eight months, eight months; Old Bill never
knew, no one knew. I've been keeping my nose clean and minding
my own business, and suddenly . . ." He was weeping. Bright tears
bounced off his black cheeks and splashed on the big drum. He
wiped them off with the side of his palm.

"Well," said Alice, "you just stay put and I'll get it on the
agenda."

She was thinking as she left the house: All those buckets of
shit up there; I suppose Jim filled them, nearly all. She thought:
If I don't pee I'll . . . She could not have brought herself to go up
and use one of those buckets. She walked to the Underground, took
a train to a station with proper lavatories, used them, washed her
face and brushed her hair, then went on to her mother's stop, where
she stood in line for a telephone booth.

Three hours after she had left home screaming abuse at her
mother, she dialled her mother's number.

Her mother's voice. Flat. At the sound of it, affection filled
Alice, and she thought, I'll ask if she wants me to do some shopping
for her on the way.

"Hello, Mum, this is Alice."

Silence.

"It's Alice."

A pause. "What do you want?" The flat voice, toneless.

Alice, all warm need to overcome obstacles in behalf of everyone, said, "Mum, I want to talk to you. You see, there's this house.

I could get the Council to let us stay on a controlled-squat basis—you know, like Manchester? But we need someone to guarantee the electricity and gas."

She heard a mutter, inaudible, then, "I don't believe it!"

"Mum. Look, it's only your signature we want. We would pay it."

A silence, a sigh or a gasp, then the line went dead.

Alice, now radiant with a clear hot anger, dialled again. She stood listening to the steady buzz-buzz, imagining the kitchen where it was ringing, the great warm kitchen, the tall windows, sparkling (she had cleaned them last week, with such pleasure), and the long table where, she was sure, her mother was sitting now, listening to the telephone ring. After about three minutes, her mother did lift the receiver and said, "Alice, I know it is no use my saying this. But I shall say it. Again. I have to leave here. Do you understand? Your father won't pay the bills any longer. I can't afford to live here. I'll have trouble paying my own bills. Do you understand, Alice?"

"But you have all those rich friends." Another silence. Alice then, in a full, maternal, kindly, lecturing voice, began, "Mum, why aren't you like us? We *share* what we have. We help each other out when we are in trouble. Don't you see that your world is finished? The day of the rich selfish bourgeoisie is over. You are doomed. . . ."

"I don't doubt it," said Alice's mother, and Alice warmed into the purest affection again, for the familiar comforting note of irony was back in her mother's voice, the awful deadness and emptiness gone. "But you have at some point to understand that your father is not prepared any longer to share his ill-gotten gains with Jasper and all his friends."

"Well, at least he is prepared to see they are ill-gotten," said Alice earnestly.

A sigh. "Go away, Alice," said Alice's mother. "Just go away. I don't want to see you. I don't want to hear from you. Try to understand that you can't say the things to people you said to me this morning and then just turn up, as if nothing had happened, with a bright smile, for another handout."

The line went dead.

Alice stood, in a dazzle of shock. Her head was full of dizzying shadow and light. Someone behind her in the queue said, "*If* you've finished . . . ," pushed in front of her, and began to dial.

Alice drifted onto the pavement and wandered aimlessly around the perimeter of that area, now fenced off with high, corrugated iron, where so recently there had been a market, full of people buying and selling. She had had a pitch there herself last summer; first she sold cakes and biscuits and sweets, then hot soup, and sandwiches. Proper food, all wholemeal flour and brown sugar, and vegetables grown without insecticides. She cooked all this in her mother's kitchen. Then the Council closed the place down. To build another of their shitty great enormous buildings, their *dead* bloody white elephants that wouldn't be wanted by anyone but the people who made a profit out of building them. Corruption. Corruption everywhere. Alice, weeping out loud, blubbering, went stumbling about outside the enormous iron fence like a fence around a concentration camp, thinking that last summer . . .

A whistle shrieked. Some factory or other . . . one o'clock. She hadn't *done* anything yet. . . . Standing on the long shallow steps that led to the public library, she wiped her face, and made her eyes look out instead of in. It was a nice day. The sun was shining. The sky was full of racing white clouds, and the blue seemed to dazzle and promise.

She went back to the telephones in the Underground and rang her father's office on the private number.

He answered at once.

"This is Alice."

"The answer is *no*."

"You don't know what I was going to say."

"Say it."

"I want you to guarantee our expenses, electricity and gas, for a squat."

"No."

She hung up, the burning anger back. Its energy took her to the pavement, and walked her up the avenue to a large building that was set back a bit, with steps. She raced up them and pressed a bell, holding it down until a woman's voice, not the one she expected, said "*Sí?*"

"Oh, fucking Christ, the maid," said Alice, aloud. And "Where's Theresa?"

"She at work."

"Let me in. Let me come in."

Alice pushed open the door on the buzzer, almost fell into the hall, and thumped up four flights of heavily carpeted stairs to a door where a short, dumpy dark woman stood, looking out for her.

"Just let me *in*," said Alice, fiercely pushing her aside, and the Spanish woman said nothing but stood looking at her, trying to find the right words to say.

Alice went into the sitting room where she had so often been with her friend Theresa, her friend ever since she, Alice, had been born, kind and lovely Theresa. A large, calm, ordered room, with great windows, and beyond them gardens . . . She stood panting. I'll tear down those pictures, she was thinking, I'll sell them, I'll take those little netsukes, what are they worth? I'll smash the place up. . . .

She tore to the telephone and rang the office. But Theresa was in conference.

"*Get* her," she commanded. "Get her at once. It is an emergency. Tell her it's Alice."

She had no doubt that Theresa would come, and she did.

"What is it, Alice, what's wrong, what is the matter?"

"I want you to guarantee expenses. For a squat. No, no, you won't have to pay anything, ever, just your signature."

"Alice, I'm in the middle of a conference."

"I don't care about your shitty conference. I want you to guarantee our electricity and our gas."

"You and Jasper?"

"Yes. And others."

"I'm sorry, my dear. No."

"What's the matter with Jasper? Why are you like this? Why? He's just as good as you are."

Theresa said, calm and humorous, as always, "No, Alice, he is not as good as I am. Far from it. Anyway, that's it. No, but I'll give you fifty pounds if you come round."

"I *am* around. I am in your flat. But I don't want your shitty fifty pounds."

"Well, then, I'm sorry, my dear."

"You spend fifty pounds on a dress. On a *meal*."

"You shared the meal, didn't you? This is silly. I'm sorry, I'm busy. All the buyers are here from everywhere."

"It's not silly. When have you seen *me* spend fifty pounds on a meal? If my mother wants to spend fifty pounds on food for all her shitty rich friends, and I cook it, that doesn't mean . . ."

"Listen, Alice, if you want to come round and have a talk tonight, you are welcome. But it will have to be late, because I will be working until eleven, at least."

"You . . . you . . . are a lot of rich shits," said Alice, suddenly listless.

She put down the receiver, and was about to leave when she remembered, and went to the bathroom, where she emptied herself, again carefully washed her face, and brushed her hair. She was hungry. She went to the kitchen and cut herself a lavish sandwich. Lisa followed her and stood at the door to watch, her hands folded around the handle of a feather duster, as if in prayer. A dark, patient, tired face. She supported her family in Valencia, so said Theresa. She stood watching Alice eating her salami and her pâté on thick bread. Then watched while Alice peered into every corner of the refrigerator and brought out some leftover spiced rice, which she ate with a spoon, standing up.

Then she said, "*Ciao*," and heard as she left, "*Buenos días, señorita*." There was something in that voice, a criticism, that again lit the anger, and she ran back down all the stairs and out onto the pavement.

It was after two.

Her thoughts whirled about. Jasper, why did they hate him so? It was because they were afraid of him. Afraid of his truth . . . She realised that she had walked herself to a bus stop, and the bus would take her to the Council. She got on, suddenly cold, concentrated, and careful.

She was rehearsing in her mind her previous successful negotiations. A great deal would depend, she knew, on whom she saw . . .

luck. . . . Well, she had been lucky before. And besides, what she was suggesting was reasonable, in the best interests of everybody, the ratepayers, the public.

In the great room filled with desks and people and telephones, she sat opposite a girl, younger than she, and knew at once that she was lucky. On Mary Williams's left breast was a "Save the Whales!" button, and the sprightly shape of the animal made Alice feel soft and protective. Mary Williams was a good person, like herself, like Jasper, like all their friends. She cared.

Alice gave the address of her house confidently, stated her case, and waited while the official turned to press a button or two, and the information arrived, to be set on the desk between them.

"Scheduled for demolition," said Mary Williams, and sat smiling, nothing more to be said.

This Alice had not expected. She could not speak. It was grief that filled her, transmuting, but slowly, to rage. The face that Mary Williams saw swelled and shone, and caused her to say uncomfortably, even stammering, "Why, why, what is the matter?"

"It can't be demolished, it can't," stated Alice, in a toneless, empty voice. Then, rage exploding, "It's a marvellous house, perfect! How can you demolish it? It's a bloody scandal."

"Yes, I know that sometimes . . ." said Mary Williams swiftly. She sighed. Her glance at Alice was a plea not to make a scene. Alice saw it, saw that scenes not infrequently occurred at this desk.

She said, "There must be a mistake. Surely they aren't entitled to destroy a house like this. . . . Have you seen it? It's a good house. A good place . . ."

"I think they mean to put up flats."

"Naturally! What else?"

The two young women laughed, their eyes meeting.

"Wait," said Mary Williams, and went off to confer, in her hand the sheet containing the vital statistics of the house. She stood by the desk of a man at the end of the room, and came back to say, "There have been a lot of complaints about the state of the houses. The police, for one."

"Yes, it's a disgusting mess," agreed Alice. "But it'll be cleared up in no time."

Here Mary nodded—Proceed!—and sat doodling, while Alice talked.

And talked. About the house. Its size, its solidity, its situation. Said that, apart from a few slates, it was structurally sound. Said it needed very little to make it livable. She talked about the Birmingham squat and the agreed tenancy there; about Manchester, where a slum scheduled for demolition had been reprieved, and became an officially recognised student residence.

"I'm not saying it couldn't happen," said Mary.

She sat thinking, her biro at work on a structure of cells, like a honeycomb. Yes, Alice knew, Mary was all right, she was on their side. Although Mary was not her style, with her dark little skirt and crisp little blouse, with her bra outlining the modest breast where the whale cavorted, tail in the sky, black on blue sea. All the same, Mary's soft masses of dark hair that went into curls on her forehead, and her plump white hands, made Alice feel warm and secure. She knew that if Mary had anything to do with it, things would go well.

"Wait a minute," Mary said, and again went to confer with her colleague. This man now gave Alice a long inspection, and Alice sat confidently, to be looked at. She knew how she seemed: the pretty daughter of her mother, short curly fair hair nicely brushed, pink-and-white face lightly freckled, open blue-grey gaze. A middle-class girl with her assurance, her knowledge of the ropes, sat properly in the chair, and if she wore a heavy blue military jacket, under it was a flowered pink-and-white blouse.

Mary Williams came back and said, "The houses are coming up for a decision on Wednesday."

"The police gave us four days to clear out."

"Well, I don't see what we can do."

"All we need is a statement, in writing, that the case is being considered, to show the police, that's all."

Mary Williams did not say anything. From her posture, and her eyes—which did not look at Alice—it was suddenly clear that she was, after all, very young, and probably afraid for her job.

There was some sort of conflict there, Alice could see: this was more than just an official who sometimes did not like the work she had to do. Something personal was boiling away in Mary Williams, giving her a stubborn, angry little look. And this again brought her to her feet and took her for the third time to the official whose job it was to say yes and no.

"You do realise," said Mary Williams, talking for her colleague, "that this letter would say only that the house is on the agenda for Wednesday?"

Alice said, inspired, "Why don't you come and see it? You and—?"

"Bob Hood. He's all right. But he's the one who . . ."

"Yes, yes," said Alice. "But why don't you both come and see the house?"

"The houses, yes—I think Bob did see them, but it was some time ago—yes, perhaps we should."

Mary was writing the words that would—Alice was sure—save the house. For as long as it was needed by Alice and the others. Save it permanently, why not? The piece of paper was slid into an envelope bearing the name of the Council, and Alice took it.

"Have you got a telephone in the house?"

"It was ripped out." It was on the tip of Alice's tongue to describe the state of the house: cement in the lavatories, loose electric cables, the lot; but instinct said no. Although she knew that this girl, Mary, would be as furious, as sick, as anyone could be that such deliberate damage could be done to a place, the damage had been done by officialdom, and Mary was an official. Nothing should be done to arouse that implacable beast, the bureaucrat.

"When should I ring you?" she asked.

"Thursday."

That was the day the police said they would be thrown out.

"Will you be here on Thursday?"

"If not, Bob over there will take the call."

But Alice knew that with Bob things would not go so well.

"It's routine," said Mary Williams. "Either they will pull the houses down at once, or they will postpone it. They have already postponed several times." Here she offered Alice the smile of their complicity, and added, "Good luck."

"Thanks. See you."

Alice left. It was only five o'clock. In one day she had done it. In eight hours.

In the soft spring afternoon everything was in movement, the pastel clouds, new young leaves, the shimmering surfaces of lawns; and when she reached her street it was full of children, cats, and gardeners. This scene of suburban affluence and calm provoked in her a rush of violent derision, like a secret threat to everything she saw. At the same time, parallel to this emotion and in no way affecting it, ran another current, of want, of longing.

She stopped on the pavement. From the top of her house a single yellow jet splashed onto the rubbish that filled the garden. Across the hedge from her, in the neighbouring house, a woman stood with a trowel loaded with seedlings, their roots in loose black earth, and she was staring at the shameful house. She said, "Disgusting, I've rung the Council!"

"Oh *no*," cried Alice, "no, please . . ." But, seeing the woman's hardened face and eyes, she said, "Look, I've just been to the Council. It will be all right; we are negotiating."

"And how about all that rubbish, then," stated, not asked, the woman. She turned her back on Alice, and bent to the fragrant earth of her flower bed.

Alice arrived at her door in a tumult of passionate identification with the criticised house, anger at whoever was responsible for the errant stream—probably Jasper—and a need to get the work of reconstruction started.

The door would not budge when she pushed it. The red heat of rage enveloped her, and she banged on the door, screaming, "How dare you, how dare you lock me out?," while she saw with her side vision how the woman gardener had straightened and was gazing at this scene over her neat little hedge.

Her anger went as she told herself, You must do something about her, soon; she *must* be on our side.

She offered the woman a quick little placatory smile and wave of the hand, rather like the wagging tail of an apologetic dog, but her neighbour only stared and turned away.

Suddenly the door opened and Jasper's fingers were tight around her wrist. His face had a cold grin on it which she knew was fear. Of whom?

As he dragged her in, she said, in a voice like a hushed shout, "Let me go. Don't be stupid."

"Where have you been?"

"Where do you think?"

"What have you been doing all day?"

"Oh, belt up," she said, shaking her wrist to restore it, as he released her on seeing that doors had opened and in the hall were Jim, Pat, Bert, and two young women dressed identically in loose blue dungarees and fluffy white cardigans, standing side by side and looking critical.

"We always keep this door locked and barred because of the police," said Bert, in a hurried, placating way, and Alice thought, Well, there's no need to bother much with *him*, as she said, "It wasn't locked this morning, when we came. And the police don't come at this hour, do they?" She said this because she had to say something: she knew her fit of rage outside the door was unfortunate.

The five were all staring at her, their faces shadowed by the dull light from the hurricane lamp, and she said, in her ordinary mild voice, "I've seen the Council, and it's all right."

"What do you mean, it's all right?" demanded Bert, asserting his rights.

Alice said, "Everyone's here, I want to discuss it. Why not now?"

"Anyone against?" said Jasper jocularly, but he was shielding Alice, as she saw with gratitude. The seven filed into the sitting room, which was still in full daylight.

Alice's eyes were anxiously at work on the two unknown girls. As if unable or unwilling to give much time to this affair, they perched on the two arms of a shabby old chair. They were sharing a cigarette. One was a soft-faced fair girl, with her hair in a ponytail, and little curls and tendrils all around her face. The other was a bulky girl, no, a woman, with short black curls that had a gleam of silver in them. Her face was strong, her eyes direct, and she looked steadily at Alice, reserving judgement. She said, "This is Faye. I am Roberta."

She was saying, too, that they were a couple, but Alice had seen this already.

"Alice. Alice Mellings."

"Well, Comrade Alice, you don't let the grass grow. I, for one, would have liked to discuss it all first."

"That's right," said Faye, "that goes for me, too. I like to know what's being said in my name." She spoke in a cockney voice, all pert and pretty, and Alice knew at once that she affected it, had adopted it, as so many others did. A pretty little cockney girl sat presenting herself, smiling, to everyone, and Alice was staring at her, trying to see what was really there.

This acute, judging inspection made Faye shift about and pout a little, and Roberta came in quickly with, "What are we being committed to, Comrade Alice?"

"Oh, I see," said Alice. "You're lying low."

Roberta let out a short amused snort that acknowledged Alice's acuity, and said, "You're right. I want to keep a low profile for a bit."

"Me, too," said Faye. "We are drawing Security over in Clapham, but better not ask how. Least said, soonest mended," she ended, prettily, tossing her head.

"And what you don't know don't hurt you," said Roberta.

"Ask no questions and get told no lies," quipped Faye.

"But truth is stranger than fiction," said Roberta.

"You can say that again," said Faye.

This nice little act of theirs made everyone laugh appreciatively. As good as a music-hall turn: Faye, the cockney lass, and her feed. Roberta was not speaking cockney, but had a comfortable, accommodating, homely voice with the sound of the North in it. Her own voice? No, it was a made-up one. Modelled on "Coronation Street," probably.

"That's another reason we don't want the police crashing in all the time," said Bert. "I am pleased Comrade Alice is trying to get this regularised. Go on with your report, Comrade Alice."

Bert had also modified his voice. Alice could hear in it at moments the posh tones of some public school, but it was roughened with the intention of sounding working-class. Bad luck, he gave himself away.

Alice talked. (Her own voice dated from the days of her girls' school in North London, basic BBC correct, flavourless. She had been tempted to reclaim her father's Northern tones, but had judged this dishonest.) She did not say that she had rung her mother and her father, but said she could get fifty pounds at short notice. Then she summed up her visit to the Council, scrutinising what she saw in her mind's eye: the expressions on the face of Mary Williams, which told Alice the house would be theirs, and because of some personal problem or attitude of Mary's. But all Alice said about this, the nub of the interview with Mary, was, "She's all right. She's on our side. She's a good person."

"You mean, you've got something to show the police?" said Jim, and when Alice handed over the yellow envelope he took out what was in it and pored over it. He was one whose fate, Alice could see, had always been determined by means of papers, reports, official letters. Jim's voice was genuine cockney, the real thing.

She asked suddenly, "Are you bound over?"

Jim's look at her was startled, then defensive, then bitter. His soft, open boyish face closed up and he said, "What about it?"

"Nothing," said Alice. Meanwhile, a glance at Faye and Roberta had told her that both of them were bound over. Or worse. Yes, probably worse. Yes, certainly worse. On the run?

"Didn't know you were," said Bert. "I was until recently."

"So was I," claimed Jasper at once, not wanting to be left out. Jasper's tones were almost those of his origins. He was the son of a solicitor in a Midlands town, who had gone bankrupt when Jasper was halfway through his schooling at a grammar school. He had finished his education on a scholarship. Jasper was very clever; but he had seen the scholarship as charity. He was full of hatred for his father, who had been stupid enough to go in for dubious investments. His middle-class voice, like Bert's, had been roughened. With working-class comrades he could sound like them, and did, at emotional moments.

Pat remarked, "It's getting dark," and she stood up, struck a match, and lit two candles that stood on the mantelpiece in rather fine brass candlesticks. But they were dull with grease. The daylight shrank back beyond the windows, and the seven were in a pool of soft yellow light that lay in the depths of a tall shadowed room.

Now Pat leaned her elbow on the mantelpiece, taking command of the scene. In the romantic light, with her dark military clothes, her black strong boots, she looked—as she must certainly know—like a guerilla, or a female soldier in somebody's army. Yet the light accentuated the delicate modelling of her face, her hands, and in fact she was more like the idealised picture of a soldier on a recruiting poster. An Israeli girl soldier, perhaps, a book in one hand, a rifle in the other.

"Money," said Pat. "We have to talk about money." Her voice was standard middle-class, but Alice knew this was not how Pat had started off. She was working too hard at it.

"That's right," said Jim. "I agree."

The only other person in this room, apart from Alice, with his own voice, unmodified, was Jim, the genuine cockney.

"It's going to cost more," said Bert, "but we will buy peace and quiet."

"It needn't cost all that much more," said Alice. "For one thing, food will be half as much, or less. I know, I've done it."

"Right," said Pat. "So have I. Take-away and eating out costs the earth."

"Alice is good at feeding people cheap," said Jasper.

It was noticeable that while these five outlined their positions, they all, perhaps without knowing it, eyed Roberta and Faye. Or, more exactly, Faye, who sat there not looking at them, but at anywhere—the ceiling, her feet, Roberta's feet, the floor—while she puffed smoke from the cigarette held between her lips. Her hand, on her knee, trembled. She gave the impression of trembling slightly all over. Yet she smiled. It was not the best of smiles.

"Just a minute, comrades," said she. "Suppose I like take-away? I like take-away, see? Suppose I like eating out, when the fancy takes me? How about that, then?"

She laughed and tossed her head, presenting—as if her life depended on it—this cheeky cockney as seen in a thousand films.

"They have a point, Faye," said Roberta, sounding neutral, so as not to provoke her friend. She was keeping an eye on Faye, unable to prevent herself from giving her quick nervous glances.

"Oh, fuck it," said Faye, really laying on the cockney bit, because, as they could see, she was afraid of her anger. "Yesterday, as far as I wuz concerned, everythink was going along just perfeck, and today, that's it. I don't like being organised, see what I mean?"

"And she did it her way," said Bert, in cold upper-class, smiling, as if in joke. He did not like Faye, and apparently did not care if he showed it.

Pat quickly covered up with humour. "Well, if you don't want to join in, then don't, have it on us!" This was said without rancour. Pat even laughed, hoping Faye would; but Faye tossed her head, her face seemed to crumple up out of its prettiness, and her lips went white as she pressed them together. The cigarette in her hand trembled violently, ash scattered about.

"Wait a minute," said Roberta. "Just hold your horses." This was addressed, apparently, to the five who were all looking at Faye. Faye knew it was meant for her. She made herself smile.

"Was anything said about how we were to pay?" asked Roberta.

"No, but I know of various ways they can do it," said Alice. "For instance, in Birmingham there was a flat sum assessed for the whole house, to cover rates. And we paid electricity and gas separately."

"Electricity," said Faye. "Who wants to pay electricity?"

"You don't pay at all, or you just pay the first instalment," said Jasper. "Alice is good at that."

"We can all see what Alice is good at," said Faye.

"Look," said Pat, "why don't we postpone this discussion till we know? If they make an assessment for rent and rates and put it on all our Social on an individual basis, then that would suit some and not others. It would suit me, for instance."

"It wouldn't suit me, see?" said Faye, sweet but violent.

"And it wouldn't suit me," said Roberta. "I don't want to become an official resident of this house. Nor does Faye."

"No, Faye certainly does not," said Faye. "Yesterday I was free as a bird, coming and going. I didn't *live* here, I came and went, and now suddenly . . ."

"All right," said Bert, exasperated. "You don't want to be counted in, all right."

"Are you telling me to leave?" said Faye, with a shrill laugh, and her face again seemed to crumple up out of its self, suggesting some other Faye, a pale, awful, violent Faye, the unwilling prisoner of the pretty cockney.

Jim laughed sullenly and said, "I've been told to leave. Why not Faye and Roberta, if it comes to that?"

Faye turned the force of her pale awfulness on Jim, and Roberta came in quickly, with, "No one is leaving. No one." She looked full at Jim. "But we have all to be clear about what we will or will not do. We have to be clear *now*. If a lump sum is assessed for this house, then we can discuss who is going to contribute what. If we are assessed individually, and our Social Security is adjusted individually, then no. No. No." This was kept amiable, but only just.

"I'm not going to contribute," said Faye. "Why should I? I like things the way they were."

"How could you like them the way they were?" said Bert. "Putting up with them is one thing."

And suddenly they all knew why it was Faye they had been eyeing so nervously, Faye who had dominated everything.

She sat straight up, straddling the chair arm, and glared, and trembled, and in a voice that in no way related to the pretty cockney, said, "You filthy bloody cuntish 'Itlers, you fascist scum, who are you telling what to do? Who are you ordering about?" This voice came out of Faye's lower depths, some dreadful deprivation. It was raw, raucous, labouring, as though words themselves had been a hard accomplishment, and now could only be shovelled out, with difficulty, past God knew what obstacles of mind and tongue. What accent was that? Where from? They stared, they were all silenced by her. And Roberta, putting her arm swiftly around her friend's shaking shoulders, said softly, "Faye, Faye darling, Faye, *Faye*," until the girl suddenly shuddered and seemed to go limp, and collapsed into her arms.

A silence.

"What's the problem?" asked Bert, who was refusing to see that he was the cause of this outburst from Faye's other self. Or selves? "If Faye doesn't want to contribute, that's fine. They always set the assessment very low, for squats anyway. And there'll be other people coming in, of course, to replace the comrades who left yesterday. We'll have to be sure they understand what arrangement we make with the Council."

Faye, half hidden in Roberta's arms, seemed to heave and struggle, but went quiet.

Alice said, "If we don't get this place cleared up, we'll have to leave anyway. We can clear it up, easy enough, but to keep it clean, we need the Council. There's been all the complaints. The woman next door said she complained. . . ."

"Joan Robbins," said Faye. "That filthy fascist cow. I'll kill her." But it was in her cockney, not her other, true, voice, that she spoke. She sat up, freed herself from solicitous Roberta, and lit another cigarette. She did not look at the others.

"No, you won't," said Roberta, softly. She reasserted her rights to Faye by putting her arm around her. Faye submitted, with her pert little toss of the head and a smile.

"Well, it *is* disgusting," said Alice.

"It was all right till you came," said Jim. This was not a complaint or an accusation, more of a question. He was really saying: How is it so easy for you, and so impossible for me?

"Don't worry," said Alice, smiling at him. "When we've got the place cleaned up, we will be just like everyone else in the street, and after a bit no one will notice us. You'll see."

"If you want to waste your money," said Faye.

"We do have to pay at least the first instalment of electricity and gas. If we can persuade them to supply us," said Bert.

"Of course we can," Alice said, and Pat said, "The meters are still here."

"Yes, they forgot to take them away," said Jim.

"And what are we going to pay with?" asked Faye. "We are all on Unemployment, aren't we?"

There was a silence. Alice knew that, if they were living on very low rent, there would be plenty of money. If people had any sense of how to use it, that is. She and Jasper, living with her mother and paying nothing, had about eighty pounds a week between them, on Social Security. But none of it was saved, because Jasper spent all his, and most of hers, too, always coming to demand it. "For the party," he said—or whatever Cause they were currently aligned with. But she knew that a lot of it went on what she described to herself, primly, as "his emotional life."

She knew, too, that in communities like this there were payers and the other kind, and there was nothing to be done about it. She knew that Pat would pay; that Pat would make Bert pay—as long as she was here. The two girls would not part with a penny. As for Jim—well, let's wait and see.

She said, "There's something we can do now, and that is, get the lavatories unblocked."

Roberta laughed. Her laugh was orchestrated, meant to be noticed.

Faye said, "They are filled with concrete."

"So they were in one of the other houses I knew. It isn't difficult. But we need tools."

"You mean tonight?" asked Pat. She sounded interested, reluctantly admiring.

"Why not? We've got to start," said Alice, fierce. In her voice sounded all the intensity of her need. They heard it, recognised it, gave way. "It's not going to be nearly as difficult as you think now. I've looked at the lavatories. If the cisterns had been filled with concrete, it would be different—they'd have cracked, probably—but it isn't difficult to get it out of the bowls."

"The workmen concreted over the tap from the main," said Bert.

"Illegal," said Alice bitterly. "If the Water Board knew. Are there any tools?"

"No," said Bert.

"You said you have a friend near here? Has he got tools?"

"She. Felicity. Her boyfriend has. Power tools. Everything. It's his job."

"Then we could pay him. He could get the electricity right, too."

"With what do you pay 'im," asked Faye, singing it. "With what do we pay 'im, dear Alice, with what?"

"I'll go and get the fifty pounds," said Alice. "You go and see your friend." She was at the door. "Tell him, plumbing and electricity. Plumbing first. If he's got a big chisel and a heavy hammer, we can start on this lavatory here in the hall. We really need a kango hammer. I'll be back," she cried, and heard Jasper's "Bring in something to eat, I'm starving."

On the wings of accomplishment Alice flew to the Underground, and on the train she thought of the house, imagining it clean and ordered. She ran up the avenue to Theresa. Only when she heard Anthony's voice did she remember Theresa would be late.

"Alice," she said into the machine. "It's Alice."

"Come in, Alice."

Anthony's full, measured, *sexy* voice reminded her of the enemies that she confronted, and she arrived outside their door wearing, as she knew, her look.

"Well, Alice, come in," said Anthony, heartily but falsely, for it was Theresa who was her friend.

She went on, knowing she was unwelcome. Anthony had on a dressing gown, and there was a book in his hand. An evening off was what he was looking forward to, she thought. Well, he can spare me ten minutes of it.

"Sit down, do. A drink?"

"No, Anthony, I never drink," she said, and went straight on, "Theresa said this morning I could have fifty pounds."

"She's not here. She's got one of her conferences."

"I thought you could give it to me. I *need* it." This was fierce and deadly, an accusation, and the man looked carefully at the young woman, who stood there in the middle of his sitting room, dressed in clothes he thought of as military, swollen with tears and with hostility.

"I haven't got fifty pounds," he said.

A lie, Alice recognised, and she was staring at him with such hate that he murmured, "My dear Alice, do sit down, do. I'm going to have to drink, if you won't." He was trying to make it humorous, but she saw through it. She watched, standing, while the big dark bulky man turned from her and poured himself whisky from a decanter. All her life, it seemed to her, she had had moments when she thought that he, and her *friend* Theresa, were naked at nights in bed together, and she felt sick.

She knew from her mother that the sex life of these two was vivid, varied, and tempestuous, in spite of Anthony's heavy, humorous urbanities, Theresa's murmuring, smiling endearments. Dear Alice, darling Alice, but *at night* . . . She felt sick.

And she thought, as she had done when she was little, And they are so old! Watching the man's broad back, grey thick silk, his smooth head—dark as oil, small for that body—she thought, They have been sexing all night and every night for all those years.

He turned to her in a swift movement, glass in his hand, having thought what he should do, and said, "I'll ring Theresa. If she's not actually in conference . . ." And he went swift and deadly to the telephone.

Alice looked around the big expensive room. She thought: I'll take one of those little netsukes and run out, they'll think it was the Spanish woman. But just then he came back and said, "They say they've called it a day. She's on her way home. Well, I'll get some supper on, then. Theresa's too tired to cook at conference times. Excuse me." Glad to be able to turn his back, she thought, and as he disappeared into the kitchen, the door opened. It was Theresa. For a moment Alice did not recognise her, thought it was some tired middle-aged woman, and then thought, But she looks so worn out.

Theresa stood heavily, her face in dragging lines, and she wore dark glasses, which left her eyes blinking and anxious when she took them off.

"Oh, Alice," she said, and walked fast to the chair near the drinks and collapsed. She fumbled as she poured herself a drink, and sat nursing the glass on her bosom, breathing slowly. Eyes shut. "Just a minute, Alice, just a minute, Alice dear," and as Anthony came in, moving his large bulk quickly to kiss her, she lifted her cheek to his lips, eyes shut, and said, "Thank God we closed early. Thank God, one more evening till eleven and I'd be done for."

He laid his hand on her shoulder and pressed down. She smiled, with small pouting kissing movements, eyes tight-closed, and he went back to the kitchen, saying: "I've done some soup and a salad."

"Oh, darling Anthony," said Theresa, "thank you—soup—it's just what I need."

What Alice felt then was a slicing cold pain—jealousy; but she did not know it was that, and she said, to be rid of the scene, rid of them, "You said I could have fifty pounds. Can I have it, Theresa?"

"I expect so, darling," said Theresa vaguely. And in a moment she had sat up, had opened her smart bag, and was peering inside it. "Fifty," she said, "fifty, well, have I got it? Yes, just . . ." And she fished out five ten-pound notes and handed them to Alice.

"Thanks." Alice wanted to fly off with them, but felt graceless; she was full of affection for Theresa, who looked so tired and done, who had always been so good to her. "You are my favourite and my best, and my very best auntie," she said, with an awkward smile, as she had when she was little and they played this game.

Theresa's eyes were open and she looked straight into Alice's. "Alice," she said, "Alice, my dear . . ." She sighed. Sat up. Stroked her deep-red skirt. Put up a white little hand to smooth her soft dark hair. Dyed, *of course.* "Your poor mother," said Theresa. "She rang me this morning. She was so upset, Alice."

"She was upset," said Alice at once. "*She* was."

Theresa sighed. "Alice, why do you stick with him, with Jasper, why—no, wait, don't run off. You're so pretty and nice, my love"—here she seemed to offer that kind face of hers to Alice, as if in a kiss—"you are such a good girl, Alice, why can't you choose yourself someone—you should have a real relationship with someone," she ended awkwardly, because of Alice's cold contemptuous face.

"I love Jasper," Alice said. "I love him. Why don't you understand? I don't care—about what you care about. Love isn't just *sex*. That's what you think, I know. . . ."

But the years of affection, of love, dragged at her tongue, and she felt tears rushing down her face. "Oh, Theresa," she cried, "thank you. Thank you. I'll come in to see you soon. I'll come. I must go, they are waiting. . . ." And she ran to the door, sobbing violently, and out of the door, letting it crash. Down the stair she pounded, tears flying off her face, into the street, and there she remembered the notes in her hand, in danger of being blown away or snatched. She put them carefully into the pocket of her jacket, and walked fast and safely to the Underground.

Meanwhile, back in the beautiful flat, they were discussing Alice. Anthony kept up a humorous quizzical look, until Theresa responded with, "What is it, my love?"

"Some *girl*," he said, the dislike he felt for Alice sounding in his voice.

"Yes, yes, I know . . ." she said irritably—her exhaustion was beginning to tell.

"A *girl*—how old is she now?"

She shrugged, not wanting to be bothered with it, but interested all the same. "You're right," she said. "One keeps forgetting."

"Nearly forty?" insisted Anthony.

"Oh no, she can't be!"

A pause, while the steam from the plate of soup he had brought her, and had set on the little table beside her, ascended between them. Through the steam, they looked at each other.

"Thirty-five; no, thirty-six," she said flatly at last.

"Arrested development," said Anthony firmly, insisting on his right to dislike Alice.

"Oh yes, I expect so, but darling Alice, well, she's a sweet girl— a sweet thing, really."

In Alice's little street the houses were full of lights and people, the kerbs crammed with the cars of those who had returned from work; and her house loomed at the end, dark, powerful, silent, mysterious, defined by the lights and the din of the main road beyond. As she arrived at the gate, she saw three figures about to go into the dark entrance. Jasper, Bert. And the third?—Alice ran up, and Jasper and Bert turned sharply to face possible danger, saw her, and said to the boy they had with them, "Philip, it is all right, this is Alice. Comrade Alice, you know." They were in the hall, and Alice saw this was not a boy, but a slight, pale young man, with great blue eyes between sheaves of glistening pale hair that seemed to reflect all the dim light from the hurricane lamp. Her first reaction was, But he's ill, he's not strong enough! For she had understood this was her saviour, the restorer of the house.

Philip said, facing her, with stubbornness she recognised as being the result of effort, a push against odds, "But I've got to charge for it. I can't do it for nothing."

"Fifty pounds," said Alice, and saw a slight involuntary movement towards her from Jasper that told her he would have it off her if she wasn't careful.

Philip said, in the same soft, stubborn voice, "I want to see the job first. I have to cost it."

She knew that this one had often been cheated out of what was due to him. Looking as he did, a brave little orphan, he invited it! She said, maternally and proudly, "We're not asking for favours. This is a job."

"For fifty pounds," said Bert, with jocular brutality, "you can just about expect to get a mousehole blocked up. These days." And she saw his red lips gleam in the black thickets of his face. Jasper sniggered.

This line-up of the two men against her—for it was momentarily that—pleased her. She had even been thinking as she raced home that if Bert turned out to be one of the men that Jasper attached himself to, as had happened before, like a younger brother, showing a hungry need that made her heart ache for him, then he wouldn't be off on his adventures. These always dismayed her, not out of jealousy—she insisted fiercely to herself, and sometimes to others—but because she was afraid that one day there might be a bad end to them.

Once or twice, men encountered by Jasper during these excursions into a world that he might tell her about, his grip tightening around her wrist as he bent to stare into her face looking for signs of weakness, had arrived at this squat or that, to be met by her friendly, sisterly helpfulness.

"Jasper? He'll be back this evening. Do you want to wait for him?" But they went off again.

But when there was a man around, like Bert, to whom he could attach himself, then he did not go off *cruising*—a word she herself used casually. "Were you cruising last night, Jasper? Do be careful; you know it's bad enough with Old Bill on our backs for political reasons." This was the hold she had over him, the checks she could use. He would reply in a proud, comradely voice, "You are quite right, Alice. But I know my way around." And he might give her one of his sudden, real smiles, rare enough, which acknowledged they were allies in a desperate war.

Now she smiled briefly at Jasper and Bert, and turned her attention to Philip. "The most important thing," she said, "is the lavatories. I'll show you."

She took him to the downstairs lavatory, holding the lamp high as they stood in the doorway. Since the day the Council workmen had poured concrete into the lavatory bowl, the little room had been deserted. It was dusty, but normal.

"Bastards," she burst out, tears in her voice.

He stood there, undecided; and she saw it was up to her.

"We need a kango hammer," she said. "Have you got one?" She realised he hardly knew what it was. "You know, like the workmen use to break up concrete on the roads, but smaller."

He said, "I think I know someone who'd have one."

"Tonight," she said. "Can you get it *tonight*?"

This was the moment, she knew, when he might simply go off, desert her, feeling—as she was doing—the weight of that vandalised house; but she knew, too, that as soon as he got started . . . She said quickly, "I've done this before. I know. It's not as bad as it looks." And as he stood there, his resentful, reluctant pose telling her that he again felt put upon, she pressed, "I'll see you won't lose by it. I know you are afraid of that. I promise." They were close together in the doorway of the tiny room. He stared at her from the few inches' distance of their sudden intimacy, saw this peremptory but reassuring face as that of a bossy but kindly elder sister, and suddenly smiled, a sweet candid smile, and said, "I've got to go home, ring up my friend, see if he's at home, see if he's got a—a kango, borrow Felicity's car. . . ." He was teasing her with the enormity of it all.

"Yes," she said. "Yes. Please."

He nodded, and in a moment had slipped out the front door and was gone. When she went into the sitting room, where Jasper and Bert were, waiting—as they showed by how they sat, passive and trusting—for her to accomplish miracles, she said with confidence, "He's gone to get some tools. He'll be back."

She knew he would; and within the hour he was, with a bag of tools, the kango, battery, lights, everything.

The concrete in the bowl, years old, was shrinking from the sides and was soon broken up. Then, scratched and discoloured, the lavatory stood usable. Usable if the water still ran. But a lump of concrete entombed the main water tap. Gently, tenderly, Philip cracked off this shell with his jumping, jittering, noisy drill, and the tap appeared, glistening with newness. Philip and Alice, laughing and triumphant, stood close together over the newly born tap.

"I'll see that all the taps are off, but leave one on," she said softly; for she wanted to make sure of it all before announcing victory to those two who waited, talking politics, in the sitting room. She ran over the house checking taps, came running down. "After four years, if there's not an airlock . . ." She appealed to Philip. He turned the main tap. Immediately a juddering and thudding began in the pipes, and she said, "Good. They're *alive*." And he went off to check the tanks while she stood in the hall, thankful tears running down her cheeks.

In a couple of hours, the water was restored, the three lavatories cleared, and in the hall was a group of disbelieving and jubilant communards who, returning from various parts of London, had been told what was going on and, on the whole, disbelieved. Out of—Alice hoped—shame.

Jim said, "But we could have done it before, we could have

done it." Rueful, incredulous, joyful, he said, "I'll bring down the pails, we can get rid of . . ."

"Wait," screamed Alice. "No, one at a time, not all at once; we'll block the whole system, after *years*, who knows how long? We did that once in Birmingham, put too much all at once in— there was a cracked pipe underneath somewhere, and we had to leave that squat next day. We had only just come." In command of them, and of herself, Alice stood on the bottom step of the stairs, exhausted, dirty, covered with grime and grey from the disintegrating concrete, even to her hair, which was grey. They cheered her, meaning it, but there was mockery, too. And there was a warning, which she did not hear, or care about.

"Philip," she was saying, "Philip, we've got the water, now the electricity." And, in silence, Philip looked gently, stubbornly at her, this frail boy—no, man, for he was twenty-five, so she had learned among all the other things about him she needed to know—and suddenly they were all silent, because they had been discussing, while she and Philip worked, how much this was going to cost and how much they would contribute.

Philip said, "If you had called in a plumber, do you know what you would have had to pay?"

"A couple of hundred," supplied Pat, tentatively, who, without interfering in this delicate operation—Alice and Philip and the house—had been more involved than the others, following the stages of the work as they were accomplished, and commenting, telling how thus she, too, had done in this place and that.

Alice took the fifty pounds from her pocket and gave them to Philip.

"I'll get my Social day after tomorrow," she said. He stood, turning over the notes, five of them, thinking, she knew, that this was a familiar position for him to be in. Then he looked up, smiled at her, and said briefly, "I'll come in tomorrow morning. I need to do the electrics in daylight."

And he left, accompanied not by his mate, Bert, who had brought him here, but by Alice, and she went with him to the gate, the rubbish malodorous around them.

He said, with his sweet, painful smile, which already tore her heart, "Well, at least it's for comrades." And walked off along the street, where the houses stood darker now that people had gone to bed. It was after one.

She went into the deserted hall and heard the lavatory flushing. Held her breath, standing there, thinking, *The pipes* . . . But they seemed to be all right. Jasper came out and said to her, "I'm going to sleep."

"Where?"

This was a delicate moment. In her mother's house, Jasper had had his own place, appropriating her brother's room, in which he curled himself up, a hedgehog, guarding his right to be alone at nights. She, daughter of the house, had slept in the room she had had all her life. She did not mind, she said; she knew what she felt; but what she did mind, badly, was the thoughts of others, not about her, but about Jasper. But they were alone in the hall, could face this decision together. He was gazing at her with the quelling look she knew meant he felt threatened.

Pat came out to them, saying, "The room next to ours is empty. It probably needs a bit of a clean; the two who were in it weren't . . ."

In the great dark hall, where the hurricane lamp made its uncertain pool, the three stood, and the women looked at Jasper, Alice knowing why, but Pat not yet. Alice knew that Pat, quick and acute, would understand it all in a flash . . . and suddenly Pat remarked, "Well, at any rate, it's the best empty room there is. . . ." She had taken it all in, in a moment, Alice knew, but it seemed Jasper did not, for he said heartily, "Right, Alice, let's go."

Pat said to them, as they silently went up, "Alice, don't think we don't think you aren't a bloody marvel!" And laughed. Alice, not giving a damn, went into the big empty room behind Jasper. His backpack had been undone; his sleeping bag lay neatly against the right wall at the end, as far away as it could get. Alice said, "I'll fetch my things," waited for him to repudiate her, but he stood, back turned, saying nothing. She ran down to the hall, hoping Pat would not be there, but she was, standing quietly by herself, as though she had expected Alice to come down, wanting to do what she then did, which was to advance, take Alice in her arms, and lay her smooth cherry cheek against Alice's. Comfort. Comradely reassurance. And a compassion, too, Alice felt, wishing she could say out loud, "But I don't *mind*, you don't understand."

"Thanks," she said to Pat, brief and awkward; and Pat gave a grunt of laughter, and waved as she went back into the sitting room, where—of course—the comrades were discussing Alice, Jasper, and this explosion of order into their lives.

Up in their room, it was dark. But some light came in from the sky and from the traffic. Alice spread her sleeping bag on its thin foam-rubber base, and was soon lying flat on her back, on her pallet, on the wall opposite to Jasper, who lay curled as he always did, in a fierce aloneness that made her ache for him. He was not asleep, but soon he slept, as she could see from a loosening of his body, as if he had been washed up on a shore and lay abandoned.

Too tired to sleep, she lay listening to how people were going to bed. Good night, good night, on the landing, and the corridor running from it. Roberta and Faye in one room, of course. Jim in another. And, in the room next to this one, Pat and Bert. Oh no, she did not want that, she did not want what she knew would happen. And it did, the grunting and whispering and shifting and moaning—right on the other side of the wall, close against her ear. It was too much. Love, that was; which everyone said she was a fool to do without; they were *sorry* for her. Theresa and Anthony, at it all night and every night, so said her mother, after years of marriage, grunting and panting, moaning and *wanting*. Alice lay as stiff as a rod, staring at the shadowed ceiling, where lights from the cars in the road fled and chased, her ears assaulted, her mind appalled. She made herself think: Tomorrow, tomorrow we'll get the electricity done. . . . *Money*. She needed money. *Where?* She'd get it. She wasn't going to cheat Philip. . . .

Philip, given the sack six months ago from the building firm— the first to be sacked, and Alice knew why, because of his build: of course any employer would think, This weakling—had set himself up. He was now a decorator and, he hoped, a builder. He had: two long ladders, a short ladder, a trestle (but needed, badly, another), paintbrushes, some tools; and could borrow from his friend, in

Chalk Farm. He had got the job of decorating a house, in spite of his frail appearance, perhaps because of it; had been paid only half, was told he was not up to it. He knew he would not be paid the rest; it would mean going to law and he could not do that. He was on the dole. He thought he would get a job doing up a pub in Neasden. He *said* he thought he would get this job, but Alice knew he didn't much believe it. He lived with Felicity (his girl-friend?) in her flat a couple of streets away. *He had to be paid.*

The noises through the wall, having died down, were starting off again. Alice dragged her pallet to the other wall, afraid of alerting Jasper, who would feel her being there so close to him as an encroachment. And sure enough, just as she was settling down, he started up and she could see him glaring at her, teeth gritting. "You are in my *space*," he said. "You know we don't get into each other's *space*."

She said, "I don't like that wall." This situation having occurred before, repeatedly, she did not have to explain. Leaning up on his elbow, his face clenched with fury and disgust, he listened to what could be plainly heard even from this wall; then lay tense, breathing fast.

She said, "I'm getting up early, to see if I can get hold of some money."

He did not say anything. Soon, the house became still. He slept.

Alice dozed a little. In her mind she was already living the next day. She waited for the light, which came in gloomily through dirty windows and showed the filth of this room. Now she ached for tea, something to eat. She crept down into the hall, which still belonged to night and the hurricane lamp, and into the sitting room, hoping that the Thermos might be there. But she drank cold water from a jug, then used, with pride but caution, the lavatory, thinking of the pipes left uncared for over an unknown number of winters. Then she went to the Underground, stopping for breakfast at Fred's Caff. There was room for eight or ten tables, set close. A cosy scene, not to say intimate. Mostly men. Two women were sitting together. At first they seemed middle-aged, because of their stolidity and calm; then it could be seen they were youngish, but tired. Probably cleaners after an early-morning job in local offices. At the counter, Alice asked for tea and—apologetically—brown toast; was told by—very likely—Fred's wife, for she had a proprietorial air, that they didn't do brown toast. Alice went to look for a place, carrying tea, a plate of white toast that dripped butter, a rock cake. As a concession to health, she went back to get orange juice. It was clear to her that in this establishment it would be best to sit with the two women, and did so.

They were both eating toast, and drinking muddy coffee. They sat in the loose, emptied poses of women consciously relaxing, and on their faces were vague good-natured smiles which turned on Alice, like shields. They did not want to talk, only to sit.

The salt of the earth! Alice was dutifully saying to herself, watching this scene of workers fuelling themselves for a hard day's work with plates of eggs, chips, sausages, fried bread, baked beans— the lot. *Cholesterol*, agonised Alice, and they all look so unhealthy! They had a pallid, greasy look like bacon fat, or undercooked chips. In the pocket of each, or on the tables, being read, were the *Sun* or the *Mirror*. Only lumpens, thought Alice, relieved that there was no obligation to admire them. Building or road workers, perhaps even self-employed; it wasn't these men who would save Britain from herself! Alice settled down to enjoy her delicious butter-sodden toast, and soon felt better. Not really wanting the cold sour orange juice, she made herself drink it between cups of the bitter tea. The two women watched her, with the detached attention they would give to the interesting mores of a foreigner, taking in everything about her without seeming to do so. She had quite nice curly hair, they could be heard thinking; why didn't she do something with it? It was dusty! What a pity about that heavy army jacket, more like a man's, really! That was dusty, too! Look at her hands: she didn't put herself out to keep her nails clean! Having condemned, and lost interest, they heaved themselves up and departed, with parting shouts at the woman behind the counter. "Ta, Liz." "See you tomorrow, Betty."

They came here every morning after three or four hours' stint in the offices. These men came in on their way to work. They all knew one another, Alice could see; it was like a club. She finished up quickly and left. Outside the newsagent's on the corner, the two women she had been sitting with had been joined by a third. They all wore shapeless trousers, blouses, and cardigans and carried heavy shopping bags. Their work gear. They stood together gossiping, taking up as little room as they could, because the full tide of the morning rush to work filled the pavements.

It was still too early. It was only just after eight. Her mother would be taking her bath. If Alice went there now she could quietly let herself in and make the coffee, to give her mother a surprise when she came down in her dressing gown. Then they could sit at the big table in the kitchen and eat their muesli and drink their coffee. Dorothy would read her *Times*, and she, the *Guardian*. To that house every day were delivered the *Times*, the *Guardian*, the *Morning Star*, and the *Socialist Worker*, the last two for herself and Jasper. Jasper said he read the *Worker* because one should know what the opposition was doing; but Alice knew that he secretly had Trotskyist tendencies. Not that she minded about that; she believed that socialists of all persuasions should pull together for the common good. In her mother's house, she read the *Guardian*. For years, that newspaper had been the only one to be seen. Then, one day, her mother dropped in to visit her great friend Zoë Devlin and found her wearing a *Guardian* apron; the word "Guardian" was printed in various sizes of black print, on white. This had given Dorothy Mellings a shock; she had a revelation because of this sight, she had said. That Zoë Devlin, of all people in the world, should be willing to put herself into uniform, to proclaim conformity!

It was the beginning of her mother's period of pretty farfetched utterances—a period by no means over. The beginning, too, of a series of meetings arranged between the two women for the purpose of re-examining what they thought. "We go along for decades," Alice had heard her mother say on the telephone, initiating the first discussion, "taking it for granted we agree about things, and we don't. Like hell we do! We're going to have to decide if you and I have anything in common, Zoë, how about it?"

Typical intellectual shit, Jasper had opined, meaning Dorothy to hear it.

Remembering Jasper, Alice understood she could not just turn up now, make coffee, and greet her mother with a smile.

She got on the train and found another café, where no one would think her remarkable. It was nearly empty; its busy time would not start for another two hours, when shoppers, men and women, came in. Now Alice ate wholemeal buns and honey and was restored to grace, and, with an eye on the clock on the wall, bided her time. Her mother would probably go out to the shops about nine-thirty, ten. She liked to get shopping over, for she hated it.

Alice had done the shopping for four years. She loved it. When she returned to the great kitchen with cartons full of food brought back in the car, she would carefully put everything away. Her mother would probably be there (if Jasper wasn't) and they would talk, getting on like anything! They always did! At home Alice was a good girl, a good daughter, as she had always enjoyed being. It was she who managed the kitchen. . . . Of course, her mother was pleased to have her do it. (There was an uneasy little thought tucked away somewhere here, but Alice chose to ignore it.) For the four years Alice and Jasper had been there, she had shopped and cooked. She had also cooked—sometimes commandeering the kitchen for two or three days at a time—the food she sold at the market.

Jasper used to come in quickly, taking his opportunity when Dorothy was not around, and fill himself with whatever she was cooking that day—"her" soup, for instance; cakes, good healthy bread. Or, if she was not cooking, might be at the market, he sneaked to the refrigerator and took anything there he fancied. Alice kept it well supplied with ham and salami and pickles for him. He cut himself great sandwiches and took them up to his room and stayed there, not coming down for hours. Dorothy, at the beginning, had used to ask, uneasy, "What does Jasper do up there all day?" "He studies," Alice always said, proud and forbidding. She knew that he did nothing at all, sometimes, all day. He might read the *Socialist Worker* and the *Morning Star*. Otherwise he listened to pop, through headphones, and sometimes danced to it quietly by himself, all over the room. He was very graceful, Alice knew; he hated to be seen, and this was a pity. He should have danced: done ballet, perhaps?

Then he would come down again, silently, to get more food. He would never willingly come into the kitchen if Dorothy was there. He never sat down to eat with them. When Alice had remonstrated, said her mother did not like it, he had said she did not like *him* (which was true, as it turned out, though Dorothy certainly had not said so at the start). For his part, he thought her a vulgar tart. This epithet, so far off any sort of mark, only stunned Alice's responses, so she said feebly, "But, Jasper, how can you say that?" At which he made loud rude noises, with his lips.

Of course, when Dorothy had guests, Jasper was not there. He really might just as well not have been in the house, except for that steady pilfering of food from the kitchen. Anyone would think that Dorothy grudged him the food! Alice had cried out often enough to him, and then, when he was merely abusive, to herself.

Now, sitting in this friendly, companionable café, where people coming in were likely to greet her; eating more buns, more honey (to fill in time now, not from hunger), Alice was thinking: Well, but she does hate Jasper, always did; people do. And she did grudge him his food, probably—if she hated him. Alice thought, at last, in something like a little panic: What must it have been like for her, never having her own kitchen, not even being able to come into it, for fear of running into Jasper? And then: I was simply doing everything, all the cooking. And she loves cooking. . . .

At half past nine, Alice left the café, calling good-bye to Sarah, who had served there for years. Once a refugee from Austria, she was now an elderly woman with photographs of her grown-up grandchildren stuck up on the wall behind the counter. Alice walked up, not too fast, to her mother's house. She stood outside for some time, then thought that any watching neighbour would find this peculiar. She let herself in with the key she had not handed her mother when she had left yesterday forever. Not a sound in the house. Alice stood in the hall, breathing in the house, *home*; the big, easy-fitting, accommodating house, which smelled of friendship. She went into the kitchen and her heart turned over. On the floor were tea chests full of dishes and plates, and, stacked all over the table, teacups and saucers and glasses, already tucked into newspaper. Oh, of course, now that she and Jasper had left, her mother would be giving the unnecessary china and stuff to jumble. Yes, that must be it. A small child, threatened, eyes wide and frantic, Alice stood looking at the tea chests, then ran upstairs to her own room. It was as she had left it yesterday. She felt better. She went up a floor to the room Jasper had used. On the floor was a rug, Bokhara. Once it had been in the sitting room, but it got frail and found a safe place under a table in this room, which, until Jasper commandeered it, was little used. The rug was beautiful. Alice tenderly rolled it up, and ran down with it to the kitchen. Now she hoped that she would not run into her mother. She looked around for paper and a biro, wrote, "I have taken the rug, Alice," and stood this note among the wrapped glasses. Again she was endangered by the sight of the tea chests. But she made herself forget them, and went out of the house. At the end of the street her mother was coming towards her under a canopy of bright green. She walked slowly, head down. She looked tired and old. Alice ran fast the other way, clutching the heavy rug, until out of sight of her mother, and then walked, increasingly slowly, to Chalk Farm. The carpet shop was only just open. A middle-aged woman sat at a desk, cup of coffee before her, and pushed down dark glasses to look over them at Alice.

"You want to sell?" she enquired. "Pretty!" as Alice unrolled the rug on the floor, breathing hard. Together they stood looking, captivated and quietened by the pool of soft patterned colour on the floor. The woman bent, picked it up, and held it against the light. Alice moved round to stand by her and saw the light prickling through, and in one place glaring. Alice's throat was tight at the back. She thought wildly: "I'll take it to the squat, it's so beautiful . . ." but waited as the rug was thrown down on the floor again, just anyhow, in folds, and the woman said, "It's badly worn. It would have to be mended. I couldn't give you more than thirty."

"Thirty?" moaned Alice. She didn't know what she had expected. She knew it was, or had been, valuable. *"Thirty,"* she stammered, thinking it had not been worth taking it.

"My advice is, keep it and enjoy it," said the woman, going back to her desk, letting the dark glasses fall back into place, and drinking coffee.

"No, I need the money," said Alice.

She took the three notes and, lingering to look at the rug lying there abandoned by her, went out of the shop.

She bought food for Jasper and went back to the squat. The street had a morning look, no one out, people had gone to work and to school; inside the women would be cleaning or with the kids. She did not expect anyone to be up yet in her house; in squats no one got up early.

But Pat was in the sitting room by herself, drinking coffee from the vacuum flask. She indicated with a gesture that Alice should help herself, but Alice was still full of her good breakfasts, and shook her head. She said, "I've got a bit of money, but not enough."

Pat said nothing. In this strong morning light she looked older, all loosened and used, not cherry-bright. Her hair had not been brushed yet, and she smelled of sex and sweat. Alice thought, Today we'll tackle the bathrooms. There were two.

Pat had still not said anything, but now she lit a cigarette, and smoked it as though she planned to drown in smoke.

Alice had seen that Pat was one of those who needed time to come to in the mornings, and was not going to say anything. She sat quietly and surveyed the state of the room: The curtains were rags, and could not be expected to stand up to dry cleaning. Well, perhaps her mother . . . The carpet—it would do. A vacuum cleaner?

She knew Pat was looking at her but did not meet the look. She felt Pat an ally, did not want to challenge this feeling.

Pat said, coughing a little from the smoke, "Twenty-four hours. You've been here twenty-four hours!" And laughed. Not unfriendly. But reserving judgement. Fair enough, thought Alice. In politics one had to. . . .

There was a sudden arrival of sound in the street, and the rubbish van stood outside. With an exclamation Alice ran out, and straight up to two men who were shouldering up rubbish bins from the next garden: "Please, please, please . . ." They stood there, side by side, looking down at her, big men, strong for this job, confronted by this girl who was both stubbornly not to be moved, and frantic. She stammered, "What will you take to clear this garden . . . ? Yes, I know. . . ." Their faces put on identical expressions of disgusted derision as they looked from the sordid mess to her, back to the mess, at her, and then steadily at the mess, assessing it.

"You should call in the Council," said one, at last.

"You *are* the Council," said Alice. "No, please, please . . . look, we've come to an arrangement. An agreed arrangement. We will pay the expenses. You know, an agreed squat."

"Here, Alan," shouted one of them towards the great shaking, throbbing lorry, which stood there ready to chew up any amount of plastic cartons, tins, papers—the rubbish that crammed the garden of her house to the level of the windows.

Out of the lorry came another large man in blue dungarees and wearing thick leather gloves. Alan, arbiter of her fate, yet another one, like Philip, like Mary Williams.

She said, "What will you take to clear it?" This was both calmly confident, as befitted her mother's daughter, and desperate; and they stared, taking their time, at that plump childlike formless face, the round anxious blue eyes, the well-washed but tidy jeans, the thick jacket, and the nice little collared blouse with flowers on it. And all, everything, impregnated with a greyish dust, which had been brushed and shaken and beaten off, but remained, obstinately, as a dimming of the colour.

They shrugged, as one. Three pairs of eyes conferred.

"Twenty quid," said Alan, the driver.

"Twenty pounds?" wailed Alice. "Twenty!"

A pause. They looked, as one, uncomfortable. A pause. "You get that lot into plastic bags, love, and we'll pick it up tomorrow. Fifteen."

She smiled. Then laughed. Then sobbed. "Oh, thanks, thanks," she snuffled.

"Be around tomorrow, love," said Alan, all fatherly, and the three moved off as one to the opposite house and its rubbish bins.

Alice checked for the safety of the money in her pocket, and went back into the house. Pat was where she had been, in a smoke trance. Jim had come down and was eating the food she had brought for Jasper. She said, "If we get the stuff into bags, they'll take it tomorrow."

"Money," said Pat.

"Money money money money," said Jim, stuffing in bananas.

"I've got the money. If I get the plastic bags . . ." She stood before them, all appeal.

"I'm on," said Jim.

"Right," said Pat, "but what about the house next door? We can clear this place up as much as you like, but that place is worse than this." As Alice stared and stared, her pink mouth slack and doleful, "Don't tell me you didn't notice? The house next door?"

Alice flew out, and looked first into the garden where the woman neighbour had spoken to her. Suburban order. But there was a tall hedge at the other side of this house, and beyond it . . . She ran into the main road, and along it a short way, and saw, as she had not done before because she had made her little excursions by another route, a house identical to the one she was reclaiming, with broken windows, slipped slates, a look of desertion, and a rubbish-filled garden. It stank.

She came thoughtfully and bitterly back to the sitting room, and asked, "Is it empty?"

Pat said, "The police cleared it three months ago, but it is full again now."

"That's not our problem," said Alice, suspecting it might turn out to be. "I'm going to get the plastic bags."

Enough cost her ten pounds.

Pat looked at the great heap of shining black on the steps and said, "A pretty penny," but did not offer. She said, "Are we going to do it with our hands?"

Alice, without a moment's hesitation, ran into the next garden, rang the bell, conferred with Joan Robbins, and came back with a spade, a shovel, a fork.

"How do you do it!" said Pat with tired irony, but picked up the fork and a sack and began work.

They laboured. Much worse than it looked, for the lower layers were pressed down and rotting and loathsome. Black glistening sack after sack received its horrible load and was stood next to another, until the garden was crammed with black sacks, their mouths showing decomposing refuse. The thin cat watched from the hedge, its eyes on Alice. Unable to bear it, she soon went in, filled a saucer with milk, another with scraps of cheese, bread, and cold chips, and brought them out to the cat, which crept on raggedy paws to the food and ate.

Pat stood resting, looking at Alice. Who was looking at the cat. Jim leaned on a shovel and said, "I had a little cat. It got run over."

Pat waited for more, but there was no more to come. She shrugged and said, "It's a cat's life." And went on working.

But Jim's eyes had tears in them, and Alice said, "I'm sorry, Jim."

"I wouldn't have another little cat," he said. "Not after that one," and went furiously back to work.

Soon both gardens, back and front, were cleared. Pallid grass was ready to take a new lease on life. A rose, long submerged, had thin whitish shoots.

"It was a nice garden," said Jim, pleased.

"I smell," said Alice bitterly. "What are we going to do? And I haven't even thought about hot water yet. If Philip comes, tell him I won't be a minute."

She flew inside; she stood buckets of cold water in the bathroom; she did what she could, inadequately. Hot water, she was thinking, hot water, that's next. *Money.*

Philip did not come.

Bert and Jasper descended together in responsible conversation about some political perspective. They told Alice and Pat they were going to get some breakfast, noticed the cleared garden and the ranks of sacks, said "Nice work," and departed to Fred's Caff.

Pat would have shared a laugh with Alice, but Alice was not going to meet her eyes. She would never betray Jasper, not to anyone!

But Pat persisted, "I left one squat because I did all the work. Not just men, either—six of us, three women, and I did it all."

At this, Alice faced Pat seriously, pausing in her labour of cleaning a window, and said, "It's always like that. There's always one or two who do the work." She waited for Pat to comment, disagree, take it up on principle.

"*You* don't mind," stated Pat.

She was looking neat and tight and right again, having washed and brushed up. Alice was thinking: Yes, all pretty and nice, her eyes done up, her lips red, and then he can just . . . She felt bitter.

She said, "That's how it always is."

"What a revolutionary," said Pat, in her way that was friendly but with a sting in it that referred, so it seemed, to some permanent and deeply internal judgement of hers, a way of looking at life that was ingrained.

"But I am a revolutionary," said Alice, seriously.

Pat said nothing, but drew in smoke to the very pit of her poor lungs, and held her mouth in a red pout to let out a stream of grey that floated in tendrils to the grimy ceiling. Her eyes followed the spiralling smoke. She said at last, "Yes, I think you are. But the others aren't so sure."

"You mean Roberta and Faye? Oh well, they are just—desperadoes!" said Alice.

"*What?*" and Pat laughed.

"*You* know." Foursquare in front of Pat, Alice challenged her to take a stand on what she, Alice, knew Pat to be, not a desperado, but a serious person, like herself, Alice. Pat did not flinch away from this confrontation. It was a moment, they knew, of importance.

A silence, and more smoke bathed lungs and was expelled, slowly, sybaritically, both women watching the luxuriant curls.

"All the same," said Pat, "they are prepared for anything. They take it on—you know. The worst, if they have to."

"Well?" said Alice, calm and confident. "So would I. I'm ready, too."

"Yes, I believe you are," said Pat.

Jim came in. "Philip's here." Out flew Alice, and saw him in

the light of day for the first time. A slight, rather stooping boy—
only he was a man—with his hollowed, pale cheeks, his wide blue
eyes full of light, his long elegant white hands, his sheaves of glistening pale hair. He had his tools with him.

She said, "The electricity?," and walked before him to the
ravaged kitchen, knowing that here was something else she must
confront and solve. He followed, shut the door after him, and said,
"Alice, if I finish the work here, can I move in?"

She now knew she had expected this. Yes, every time that
arrangement, he and his girlfriend, had come up, there had been
something not said.

He explained, "I've been wanting to be independent. On my
own." Knowing she was thinking of the others, their plans, he said,
"I'm CCU. I don't see why there should be any problem?"

But not IRA, thought Alice, but knew she would deal with all
that later. "If it's up to me, yes," she said. Would that be enough?
He had taken her as the boss here—as who would not?

He now turned his attention to the ripped wires that were
tugged right out of the plaster; the gas stove, which had been pulled
out to lie on its side on the floor.

Bitterness was on his face; the same incredulous rage she felt.
They stood together, feeling they could destroy with their bare
hands those men who had done this.

Men like the dustmen, thought Alice steadily, making herself
think it. Nice men. They did it. But when we have abolished fascist
imperialism, there won't be people like that.

At this thought appeared a mental picture of her mother, who,
when Alice said things of this kind, sighed, laughed, looked exhausted. Only last week she had said, in her new mode, bitter and
brief and flat, "Against stupidity the gods themselves."

"What's that?" Alice had asked.

"Against—stupidity—the gods—themselves—contend—in vain,"
her mother had said, isolating the words, presenting them to Alice,
not as if she had expected anything from Alice, but reminding
herself of the uselessness of it all.

The bitterness Alice felt against the Council, the workmen,

the Establishment now encompassed her mother, and she was assaulted by a black rage that made her giddy, and clenched her hands. Coming to herself, she saw Philip looking at her, curious. Because of this state of hers which he was judging as more violent than the vandalising workmen deserved?

She said, "I could kill them." She heard her voice, deadly. She was surprised by it. She felt her hands hurting, and unclenched them.

"I could, too," said Philip, but differently. He had set down grimy bags of tools, and was standing quietly there, waiting. He was looking at her with his by now familiar and heart-touching obstinacy. The murderess in Alice took herself off, and Alice said, giving him the promise he had to have before he did any more work, "It's only fair, if you do the work."

He nodded, believing her, and then transferred that obstinacy of his to the attention he gave the mangled wall. "It's not so bad," he said at last. "Looks as if they smashed the place up in a bit of a fit of temper: they didn't do much of a job of it."

"What?" she said, incredulous; for it seemed to her the kitchen, or at least two walls of it, was sprouting and dangling cables and wires; and the creamy plaster lay like dough in mounds along the bottom of these walls, which were discoloured and scurfy.

"Seen worse." Then, "I've got to have the floorboards up; can't work with that down there."

The fallen plaster had gone hard, and Alice had to smash it free. The kitchen was full of fine white dust. She worked at floor level, while Philip stood above her on the big table he had dragged to the wall. Then the plaster and rubbish were in sacks, and she swept up with the handbrush and pan, which were all she had. She was irritable and weepy, for she knew that every inch of the ceiling, the walls should be washed down, should be painted. And then the house, the whole house, was like that, and the roof—what would they find when at last they got that horrible upper floor free of its smelly pails? Who was going to replace slates, how to pay for it all? She was brushing and brushing, and each sweep scuffed up more filth into the air, and she was thinking, I've got to get to the Electricity Board; how can I, looking like this?

She stood up, a wraith in the white-dust-filled air, and said, "Your friend—is she at home, would she give me a bath?"

Philip did not reply; he was examining a cable with a strong torch.

She said, furious, "There were public baths till last year, nice ones, not far, they were in Auction Street. Friends of mine used them—they are in a squat in Belsize Road. Then the Council closed them. They closed them." She felt tears hot on her chalky cheeks, and stood, spent, looking imploringly at Philip's slight, almost girlish back.

He said, "We had a rare old row when I left."

She thought, She threw him out.

"Never mind," she said. "I'll manage. I'll get cleaned up and I'm going to the Electricity Board. So be careful, in case they switch it on."

"You think you can get them to do that?"

"I've managed it before, haven't I?" At the thought of this and other victories, her depression lifted and she was popping with energy again.

In the hall, the two desperadoes were just about to go out into the world of the streets, gardens, neighbours, cats, cars, and sparrows.

They looked just like everybody, thought Alice, seeing them turn round, the pretty fair Faye, delicate inside the almost tangible protective ambience of swarthy Roberta, as strong as a tank—as strong as I am, thought Alice, standing there, looking, she knew, like a clown who has just been showered with flour.

"Well," said Faye, humorous, and Roberta commented, "*Well*," and the two women laughed, and went out the door as though all this hard work had nothing to do with them.

"No good expecting anything," said Alice to herself, stoically, after so much experience of those who did and those who wouldn't. Again she went up to the bathroom and stood naked in desolation, while the bath filled with cold water to the level of the grime mark that showed where she had done all this earlier that day. And again she stood in cold water endeavouring to rid herself of the dirt, her mother's daughter, thinking viciously of the four years she had lived inside her mother's house, where hot water came obediently at a touch. They don't know what it costs, she was muttering, furiously. It all comes from the workers, from *us*. . . .

She did her best; she put on a nice neat skirt, which she had purloined from her mother with a joke that it suited her better: she needed a skirt sometimes for respectability, some types of people were reassured by it. She put on another of the little neat-collared shirts, in blue cotton this time, that made her feel herself. She did her best with her hair, which felt greasy and gritty, although she had stood with it held down in a bucket of the unyielding cold water. Then she went into the sitting room. Pat, relaxed in a big armchair, was asleep. Alice went over quietly and stared down at this unknown woman, who was her ally. She was thinking: She won't leave yet. She doesn't want to. She doesn't think much of Bert; she's going to stay because of all that *love*.

Pat lay sprawling all over the chair as if she had dropped down off the ceiling. Her head was back, her face lifted and exposed. Eyes, lips trembled on the verge of opening. Alice expected her to wake, and smile. But Pat stayed asleep, vulnerable under Alice's meticulous inspection of her. Alice continued to stand there, looking. She felt that she possessed Pat, in this look—her life, what she was and would be. Alice could never have allowed herself to sleep like that, open to anyone to come in and look at. It was careless, foolish, like walking about the streets with money held loose in a hand. Alice came closer and bent right down over Pat, to stare at that innocent face with its lightly shuttered eyes, behind which an inhabitant had gone off into that unknown country. Alice felt curious. What was she dreaming about, looking like a baby that has just napped off after a bottle? Alice began to feel protective, wanting Pat to wake up in case the others should come in and see her, defenceless. Then Alice thought, Well, it will probably be Bert, won't it? Sleeping Beauty! Now it was scorn that she felt, because of Pat's need. If she's got to have it, she's got to have it, said Alice judiciously to herself, making necessary allowances. And stepped lightly out of the sitting room, through the hall, and into the outside world. It was about three o'clock on a fresh and lively spring afternoon. She took the bus to Electricity, with confidence.

Electricity was a large modern building, set well back from the main road where seethed, in cars and on foot, the lively polyglot needy people whose lives it supported with light, boiling kettles, energetic vacuum cleaners . . . *power*. The building looked conscious of its role: nearly a million people depended on it. It stood solid and dependable. Its windows flashed. The cars of its functionaries stood in biddable lines, gleaming.

Alice ran lightly up the steps and, knowing her way from having been in so many similar buildings, went straight to the first floor, where she knew she was in the right place, because there was a room where ten or so people waited. Unpaid bills, new accounts, threats of disconnection: a patient little crowd of petitioners. From this room opened two doors, and Alice sat herself so as to be able to see into both rooms. As the doors opened to emit one customer and admit another, Alice examined the faces of these new arbiters, sitting behind their respective desks. Women. One she knew, after a single glance, she must avoid. The letter of the law, that woman, judged Alice, seeing a certain self-satisfaction in competence. A thin face and lips, neatly waved fair hair, a smile Alice had no intention of earning. But the other woman, yes, she would do, although at first glance . . . She was large, and her thick, tight dress held her solid and secure, performing the function of a corset, but from this fortress of a dress emerged a large, soft, rather girlish face and large, soft hands. Alice adjusted her seat, and in due course found herself sitting in front of this motherly lady, who, Alice knew, several times a day stretched things a little because she was sorry for people.

Alice told her story, and described—knowing exactly what she was doing—the large solid house that inexplicably was going to be pulled down so that yet another nasty block of flats could be built. Then she produced her official-looking Council envelope, with the letter inside.

This official, Mrs. Whitfield, only glanced at the letter, and said, "Yes, but the house is on the agenda, that's all, it hasn't been decided." She turned up a card in the cabinet beside her, and said, "Number forty-three? I know it. Forty-three and forty-five. I walk past them every day to the Underground. They make me feel sick." She looked, embarrassed, at Alice, and even blushed.

"We have already begun to clean forty-three up. And the dustmen are coming tomorrow to take it all away."

"You want me to get the power switched on now, before knowing what the Council decides?"

"I am sure it is going to be all right," said Alice, smiling. She was sure. Mrs. Whitfield saw this, felt it, and nodded.

"Who is going to guarantee payment? Are you? Are you in work?"

"No," said Alice, "not at the moment." She began to talk in a calm, serious way about the houses in Manchester, in Halifax, in Birmingham that had been rescued, where electricity had flowed obediently through wires, after long abstinence. Mrs. Whitfield listened, sitting solid in her chair, while her white large hand held a biro poised above a form: Yes. No.

She said, "If I order the power to be switched on, first I must have a guarantor."

"But do you know that it is only in this borough—well, one or two others. In Lampton, for instance, you'd have to supply electricity to us. If people demand it, then it must be supplied."

"Well," said Mrs. Whitfield mildly, "you seem to know the situation as well as I do! I do not make policy. I implement it. The policy in this borough is that there has to be a guarantor."

But her eyes, large, soft, and blue, were direct on Alice's face and not combative or hostile, far from it; she seemed to be appealing for Alice to come up with something.

"My father will guarantee payment," said Alice. "I am sure of that."

Mrs. Whitfield had already started to fill in the form. "Then that's all right," she said. "His name? His address? His telephone number? And we have to have a deposit."

Alice took out ten pounds and laid it on the desk. She knew it was not enough. Mrs. Whitfield looked at it cautiously, and signed. She did not look at Alice. A bad sign. She did not take the note.

Then she did raise her eyes to Alice's face, and seemed startled at what she saw there.

"How many of you are there?" she asked in a hurried, playing-for-time way, glancing at the note and then making herself confront Alice's face, that face which could not be denied. It was not fair! Mrs. Whitfield seemed to be feeling. They were inappropriate and wrong, these emotions that Alice had brought into this orderly and sensible office. Probably what Mrs. Whitfield should be doing was to tell Alice to go away and come back better supplied with evidence of her status as a citizen. Mrs. Whitfield could not do this. She could not. Alice saw from the way that large smooth confined bosom heaved, from the soft flushed shocked face, that she—Alice—was on the point of getting her way.

"Very well," said Mrs. Whitfield at last, and sat for a moment, not so much in doubt now that she had made a decision, but worried. For Alice. "Those are big houses," she remarked, meaning: they use a lot of electricity.

"It'll be all right," said Alice, sure that it would be. "Can you switch it on this afternoon? We have got an electrician at work. It would be a help. . . ."

Mrs. Whitfield nodded. Alice went out, knowing that the official was watching her go, disturbed, probably already wondering why she had given in.

Instead of going straight home, Alice went to the telephone box at the corner and dialled her mother. A voice she did not at first recognise; but it was her mother. That awful flat voice . . . Alice nearly said, "Hello, this is Alice," but could not. She gently replaced the receiver and dialled her father. But it was his partner who answered.

She bought a large Thermos (which would always be useful, for example on demos or at pickets), asked Fred's wife to fill it with strong tea, and went home.

The white dusty cloud in the kitchen had subsided. She said to Philip, now crouched on the floor with half the floorboards up, "Be careful, they might switch it on at any moment."

"It is on, I've just tested," said Philip, and gave her a smile that made it all worthwhile.

They sat on the great table, drank strong tea, and were companionable and happy. It was a large room. Once a family had had its centre here, warm and safe and unfailing. They had sat together around this table. But Alice knew that before all that could begin again, there must be money.

She left Philip and went to the sitting room, where Pat was awake and no longer lying abandoned and open to Alice's anxious curiosities. She was reading. It was a novel. By some Russian. Alice knew the author's name as she did know the names of authors—that is, as if they were objects on a shelf, round, hard, and glittering, with a life and a light of their own. Like marbles, which, though you could turn them between your fingers for as long as you liked, would not yield, give up their secrets, submit.

Alice never read anything but newspapers.

As a child she had been teased: Alice has a block against books. She was a late reader, not something to be overlooked in that bookish house. Her parents, particularly her mother, all the visitors, everyone she ever met had read everything. They never stopped reading. Books flowed in and out of the house in tides. "They breed on the shelves," her parents, and then her brother, happily joked. But Alice was cherishing her block. It was a world she could choose not to enter. One might politely refuse. She persisted, polite but firm, secretly tasting the power she possessed to disquiet her parents. "I do not see the point of all that reading," she had said; and continued to say, even at university, doing Politics and Economics, mainly because the books she would be expected to read did not have the inaccessible, mocking quality of those others. "I am only interested in facts," she would say during this period when there was no escaping it: a minimum number of books had to be read.

But later she had learned she could not say this. There had always been books of all kinds in the squats and communes. She used to wonder how it was that a comrade with a good, clear, and correct view of life could be prepared to endanger it by reading all that risky equivocal stuff that she might dip into, hastily, retreating as if scalded. She had even secretly read almost to the end of one novel recommended as a useful tool in the struggle, but felt as she had as a child: if she persevered, allowing one book to lead her on to another, she might find herself lost without maps.

But she knew the right things to say. Now she remarked about the book Pat was reading, "He's a very fine humanist writer."

Pat let *Laughter in the Dark* close and sat thoughtfully regarding Alice.

"Nabokov, a humanist?" she asked, and Alice saw that there was serious danger of what she dreaded more than anything, literary conversation.

"Well, I think so," Alice insisted, with a modest smile and the air of one who was prepared to defend an unpopular position reached after long thought. "He really cares about *people*."

Somebody—some comrade, at some time, in some squat or other—had said as a joke, "When in doubt, classify them as humanists."

Pat's steady, interested, thoughtful look was reminding Alice of something. Of someone. Yes, Zoë Devlin. Thus she would regard Alice when the subject of literature came up and Alice had had no alternative but to make a contribution.

Suddenly, Alice remembered something. Zoë Devlin. Yes.

A quarrel, or at least an argument between Dorothy Mellings and Zoë Devlin. Recently. Not long before Alice left.

Alice was concentrating so hard on what she remembered that she slowly sat down, hardly noticing what she did, and forgetting about Pat.

Her mother had wanted Zoë to read some book or other and Zoë said no, she thought its view of politics was reactionary.

"How do you know when you haven't read it?" Dorothy had asked, laughing.

"There are lots of books like that, aren't there," Zoë had said. "Probably written by the CIA."

"Zoë," had said Dorothy Mellings, no longer laughing, "is that you? Is that Zoë Devlin speaking? My good friend the fearless, the open-minded, the incorruptible Zoë Devlin?"

"I hope it is," said Zoë, laughing.

"I hope it is, too," said Dorothy, not laughing. "Do we still have anything in common, do you think?"

"Oh, go on, Dorothy, let up, do. I don't want to quarrel even if you do."

"You are not prepared to quarrel about anything so unimportant as a book? As a view of life?"

Zoë had made a joke of it all. Had soon left. Had she been back to the house again? Of course, she must have, she had been in and out of that house for . . . since before Alice was born.

Zoë was one of Alice's "aunties," like Theresa.

Why had Alice not thought of going to her for money? Wait, there was something there, at the back of her mind—what? Yes, there had been this flaming row, terrible, between Dorothy and Zoë. Yes, recently, good Christ, not more than a week or so ago. Only one row? No, more. A lot.

Dorothy had said Zoë was soft-centred, like a cream chocolate. *They had screamed at each other.* Zoë had gone running out. She—Alice—had screamed at her mother, "You aren't going to have any friends if you go on like this."

Alice was feeling sick. Very. She was going to vomit if she wasn't careful. She sat, very still, eyes squeezed tight, concentrating on not being sick.

She heard Pat's voice. "Alice. Alice. What's wrong?"

"Nothing," she said, in a hurried, low voice, still concentrating, "it's all right." In a minute or two she opened her eyes and said, normally, and as though nothing at all had happened, "I am afraid of the police crashing in suddenly." This was what she had come to say.

"The police? Why, what do you mean?"

"We've got to decide. We have to make a decision. Suppose they come crashing *in*."

"We've survived it before."

"No, I mean, those pails, all those pails. We daren't empty them into the system. Not all at once. We daren't. God knows what the pipes are like down there where we can't see them. If we empty them one at a time, one a day let's say, it'll take forever. But if we dug a pit . . ."

"The neighbours," said Pat at once.

"I'll talk to the woman next door."

"I can't see Joan Robbins being mad with joy."

"But it will be the end of it, won't it? And they would all be pleased about that."

"It would mean you, me, and Jim."

"Yes, I know. I'll go across to the Robbins woman. You ask Jim."

A pause. Pat yawned, wriggled around in her chair, lifted her book, let it drop again, and then said, "I suppose so."

In the next garden, which was wide, divided by a crunching gravel path, Joan Robbins worked on a border with a fork. Under a tree on the other side sat a very old woman, staring at the sky.

Joan Robbins stood up when Alice appeared, looking defensive and got at. But Alice did not give her time for grievance. She said, "Mrs. Robbins, can we keep the tools for a bit? We want to dig a pit. A big one. For rubbish."

Joan Robbins, who had withstood the annoyances of this dreadful number 43 for so long, looked as if she would say no, say she had had enough of it all. Her pleasant face was irritable, and flushed.

But now the old woman under the tree sat up in the chair, leaned forward, staring. Her face was gaunt and purplish, with white woolly hair sticking out around it. She said in a thick, old, unsteady voice, "You dirty people."

"No," said Alice steadily. "No, we're not. We're cleaning it all up."

"Nasty dirty people," said the old woman, less certain of herself, having taken in Alice, such a nice girl, standing on the green lawn with daffodils behind her.

Alice said, "Your mother?"

"Sitting tenant. Upstairs flat," said Mrs. Robbins, not moderating her voice, and Alice understood the situation in a flash. She went over to the old woman and said, "How do you do? I'm Alice Mellings. I've just moved into forty-three, and we're fixing the place up, and getting the rubbish out."

The old woman sank back, her eyes seeming to glaze with the effort of it all.

"Good-bye," said Alice. "See you again soon," and went back

to Mrs. Robbins, who asked sullenly, "What are you going to bury?," indicating the ranks and ranks of filled shiny black sacks.

She knew!

Alice said, "It'll get rid of all the smell all at once. We thought, get the pit dug this afternoon, and get rid of everything tonight . . . once and for all."

"It's terrible," said Mrs. Robbins, tearful. "This is such a nice street."

"By this time tomorrow the rubbish will be all gone. The smell will be gone."

"And what about the other house. What about forty-five? In summer, the flies! It shouldn't be allowed. The police got them out once but . . . they are back again."

She could have said *you*; and Alice persisted, "If we start digging now . . ."

Joan Robbins said, "Well, I suppose if you dig deep enough . . ."

Alice flew back home. In the room where she had first seen him, Jim was tapping his drums. He at first did not smile, then did, because it was his nature, but said, "Yes, and the next thing, they'll say Jim, you must leave," he accused.

"No, they won't," said Alice, making another promise.

He got up, followed her; they found Pat in the hall. In the part of the garden away from the main road, concealed from it by the house, was a place under a tree that had once been a compost heap. There they began digging, while over the hedge Mrs. Robbins was steadily working at her border, not looking at them. But she was their barrier against the rest of the busybody street, which of course was looking through its windows at them, gossiping, even thinking it was time to ring the police again.

The earth was soft. They came on the skeleton of a large dog; two old pennies; a broken knife; a rusting garden fork, which would be quite useful when cleaned up; and then a bottle . . . another bottle. Soon they were hauling out bottles, bottles, bottles. Whisky and brandy and gin, bottles of all sizes, hundreds, and they were standing to waist level in an earthy sweet-smelling pit with bottles rolling and standing around the rim for yards, years of hangovers, oblivion, for someone.

People were coming home from work, were standing and looking, were making comments. One man said unpleasantly: "Burying a corpse?"

"Old Bill'll be around," said Jim, bitter, experienced.

"Oh, God, these bottles," swore Pat, and Alice said, "The bottle bank. If we had a car . . . Who has a car?"

"They have one next door."

"Forty-five? Would they lend it? *We have to get rid of these bottles.*"

"Oh, God, *Alice*," said Pat, but she stood her spade against the house wall—beyond which was the sitting room where they knew Jasper and Bert were, talking—and went out into the side street and then the main street. She was back in a minute, in an old Toyota. They spread empty black plastic sacks on the seats, filled the car with bottles: to the roof at the back, the boot, the pit in front near the driver, leaving only that seat, into which Alice squatted, while Pat drove the car down to the big cement containers, where they worked for three-quarters of an hour, smashing in the bottles.

"That's it for today," said Pat, meaning it, as she parked the car outside 45, and they got out. Alice looked into its garden, appalled.

"You aren't going to take that one on, too!" said Pat in another statement.

She went into their house, not looking, and up to the first floor, to the bathroom.

She did not comment on the new electric bulb, shedding a little light in the hall.

Alice thought: How many rooms in the house? Let's see, an electric light bulb for each one? But that will be pounds and pounds, at least ten. I have to have money. . . .

It was dark outside. A damp, blowy night.

She went into the sitting room. Bert and Jasper were not there. She thought: Then I and Jim . . .

Jim was again with his drums. She went to him and said, "I

will carry down the pails. You stand by the pit and fill in the earth. Quickly. Before the whole street comes to complain."

Jim hesitated, seemed about to protest, but came.

She had never had to do anything as loathsome, not in all her history of squats, communes, derelict houses. The room that had only the few pails in it was bad enough, but the big room, crammed with bubbling pails, made her want to be sick before she even opened the door. She worked steadily, carrying down two pails at a time, controlling her heaving stomach, in a miasma that did not seem to lessen but, rather, spread from the house and the garden to the street. She emptied in the buckets, while Jim quickly spaded earth in. His face was set in misery. From the garden opposite came shouts of "Pigs!" Alice went out into the little street and stood against the hedge, which was a tall one, and said through it to someone who stood there watching, a man, "We're clearing it all up. There won't be any smell after tonight."

"You ought to be reported to the Council."

"The Council knows," said Alice. "They know all about it." Her voice was serene, confident; she spoke as one householder to another. She walked back under the street lights into her own dark garden in a calm, almost careless way. And went back to the work of carrying down buckets.

By eleven the pit was filled and covered, and the smell was already going.

Alice and Jim stood together in the dark, surrounded by consoling shrubs. He pulled out a cigarette and lit it, and though she never smoked she took one from him, and they stood smoking together, drawing in the sweet clouds and puffing them out deliberately, trying to fill the garden air with it.

Jim said, with a scared laugh, "That was all my shit. Well, most. Some was Faye's and Roberta's."

"Yes, I know. Well, never mind."

"Have you thought, Alice—have you ever thought?—how much shit we all make in our lives? I mean, I've only been here eight months, well, more or less. I mean, if the shit we made in our lives was put in a drum, or let's say a big tank, you'd need a tank like the Battersea power station for everyone." He was laughing, but he sounded frightened. "It all goes into the sewers, underneath here, but suppose the sewers just packed up?"

"They won't," said Alice, peering through the darkness at his dark face to find out what was really frightening him.

"Why shouldn't they? I mean, they say our sewers are all old and rotten. Suppose they just explode? With sewer gas?" He laughed again.

She did not know what to say.

"I mean, we just go on living in this city," he said, full of despair. "We just go on living. . . ."

Very far from his usual self was Jim now. Gone was that friendly sweet-cheeked face. It was bitter, and angry, and fearful.

She said, "Come in, Jim, let's have a cup of tea and forget it, it's done. "

"That's just what I mean," he said, sullen. "You say, Come and have a cup of tea. And that's the end of it. But it isn't the end of it, not on your life it isn't."

And he flung down the spade and went in to shut himself in his room.

Alice followed. For the third time that day she stood in the grimy bath, labouring with cold water to get herself clean.

Then she went upstairs. On the top floor all the windows were open, admitting a fresh smell. It was raining steadily. The sacks of refuse would have a lot of water in them, and the dustmen might be bad-tempered about it.

Midnight. Alice slumped down the stairs, yawning, holding the sense of the house in her mind, the pattern of the rooms, everything that needed to be done. Where was Jasper? She wanted Jasper. The need for Jasper overtook her sometimes, like this. Just to know he was there somewhere, or if not, soon would be. Her heart was pounding in distress, missing Jasper. But as she reached the bottom step, there was a pounding on the door as if a battering ram were at work. *The police*. Her mind raced: Jasper? If he was in the house, would he keep out of sight? Old Bill had only to take one look at Jasper and they were at him. He and she had joked often enough that if the police saw Jasper a hundred yards off and in the dark, they would close in on the kill: they felt something about him they could not bear. And Roberta and Faye? Please God they were still at the picket. The police would have only to take one look at them, too, to be set off. Philip? The wrong sort of policeman would find that childish appeal irresistible. But Pat would be all right, and Bert. . . . *Jim, where was he?*

As she thought this, Pat appeared at the sitting-room door, closing it behind her in a way that told Alice that the two men were in there; and Philip stood at the kitchen door, holding a large torch, switched on, and a pair of pliers.

Alice ran to the front door, and opened it quickly, so that the men who had been battering at it crashed in, almost on top of her.

"Come in," she said equably, having sized up their condition in a glance. They had their hunting look, which she knew so well, but it wasn't too bad, their blood wasn't really up, except perhaps for that one, whose face she knew. Not as an individual but as a type. It was a neat, cold, tidy face, with a fluffy little moustache: a baby face with hard cold grey eyes. He enjoys it, she thought; and, seeing his quick look around, straining to go, as if on the end of a leash, she felt sharp little thrills down her thighs. She was careful that he did not catch her glance, but went forward to stand in front of a big broad man, who must weigh fifteen stone. A sergeant. She knew his type, too. Not too bad. She had to look right up to him, and he looked down at her, in judgement.

"We told you lot to clear out," said this man, with the edge on his voice that the dustmen had, a hard contempt, but he was making a gesture to a couple of the men who were about to pull Pat aside and go into the sitting room. They desisted.

Alice held out the yellow paper, and said, "We are an agreed squat."

"Not yet you aren't," said the sergeant, taking in the main point at once.

"No, but it's only two days. I've done this before, you see," she said reasonably. "It's all right if you pay the bills and keep the place clean."

"Clean," said the sergeant, bending down over her, hands on hips like a stage sergeant, Mr. Plod the Policeman. "It's disgusting."

"You saw that rubbish outside," said Alice. "The Council are taking that tomorrow. I organised it with them."

"You did, did you? Then why were we having phone calls about you digging some pit in the garden and filling it with muck?"

"Muck is the word," said Alice. "The Council workmen filled the lavatories with cement, so there were buckets upstairs. We had to get rid of them. We dug a pit."

A pause. The big broad man stood there, leaning a little forward, allowing his broad red face to express measured incredulity.

"You dug a pit," he said.

"Yes, we did."

"In the middle of London. You dig a pit."

"That's right," said Alice, polite.

"And having dug a pit, you fill it with . . ." He hesitated.

"Shit," said Alice, calm.

The five other policemen laughed, sniggered, drew in their breath, according to their natures, but the young brute on whom Alice had been keeping half an eye suddenly kicked out at the door of the cupboard under the stairs, smashing it.

Philip let out an exclamation, and he was by him in a flash. "You said something?" he said, looming over Philip, who stood there in his little white overalls. A kick would smash him to pieces.

"Never mind," said the sergeant authoritatively. He wanted to pursue the main crime. The vicious one fell back a step and stood with clenched hands, his eyes at work now on Pat, who stood relaxed, watching Alice. Alice, seeing his look, knew that if Pat were to meet that one in a demo, she could expect the worst. Again the little cold thrill of sensation.

"You—stand—there—and tell—me—that you dig a pit in a garden, and just make a cesspit, without a by-your-leave, without any authority!"

"But what else could we do," said Alice in clear, reasonable tones. "We couldn't put dozens of buckets of shit into the sewage system all at once. Not in a house that's been empty. You'd really have cause to complain then, wouldn't you?"

A pause. "You can't do that kind of thing," said the sergeant, after a pause. In retreat. Please God, thought Alice, Pat or Philip won't say: But we've done it!

"It was a very large pit," she said. "We came by chance on some lush's bottle bin. It was a good five feet deep. We'd show you, but it's raining. If you came round tomorrow, we could show you then?"

A silence. It hung in the balance. Please, please God, thought Alice, nothing will happen, the two girls won't walk in—that really would finish it—or Jasper doesn't suddenly take it into his head . . . For Jasper, in a certain mood, might easily come out and enjoy provoking a confrontation.

But the thing held. The five policemen who had been scattered around the space of the hall came in closer to their leader, like a posse, and Alice said, "Excuse me, but could I have that?" For the sergeant still held the yellow paper. He read it through again, solemnly, and then gave it back.

"I'll have to report that pit to the Water Board," he said.

"There were no pipes where we dug," said Alice, "not one."

"Only a skeleton," said Pat, negligently. As one the six men turned, glaring. "A dog," said Pat. "It was a dog's grave."

The men relaxed. But they kept their eyes on Pat. She had got a rise out of them, but so smoothly. In the dim light from the single bulb, she lounged there, a dark handsome girl, politely smiling.

"We'll be back," said the sergeant, and hitched his head at the door. They all went out, the killer last, with a cold frustrated look at little Philip, at Pat, but not much at the ordinary, unchallenging Alice.

The door shut. No one moved. They all stood staring at that door; the police could come crashing back again. A trap? But the seconds went past. They heard a car start up. Alice shook her head at Philip, who seemed about to break into some effusion of feeling. And the door did open. It was the sergeant.

"I've been taking a look at those sacks," he said. "You said they were being taken tomorrow?" But his eyes were at work all around the hall, lingering with a slight frown on the smashed-in cupboard door under the stairs.

"Tomorrow," said Alice. Then, in a disappointed voice, "Not very nice, was it, smashing in that little door, for nothing."

"Put in a complaint," he said, briefly, almost good-naturedly, and disappeared.

"Fascist shits," said Pat, like an explosion, and did not move. They remained where they were. They might have been playing "statues."

They let a couple of minutes go past, then, as one, came to life, as Jim emerged from the shadows of his room, grinning, and the four went into the sitting room, where Jasper and Bert lounged, drinking beer. Alice knew from how they looked at her that Jasper had been telling Bert, again, how good she was at this—reflecting credit on himself; and that Pat had been impressed, and Jim was incredulous at the apparent ease of it all. She knew that this was a moment when she could get her own way about anything, and in her mind, at the head of her long agenda of difficulties to be overcome, stood the item: Philip and Jim.

She accepted a bottle of beer from Bert, who gave her, with it, the thumbs-up sign, and soon they were all sitting in a close group, in the centre of the tall room. Candle-lit: there had not been time to put a bulb in. But Philip had sat down a little apart, and tentatively.

"First," said Pat, "to Alice!"

They drank to her, and she sat silent, smiling, afraid she would cry.

Now, she thought, I'll bring up Philip. I'll bring up Jim. We'll get it *settled.*

But in the hall, suddenly, were voices, laughter, and in a moment the two girls came in, lit with the exaltation that comes from a day's satisfactory picketing and demonstrating and marching.

Roberta, laughing, came over to the carrier of bottles and put one to her mouth, and drank standing, swallowing the beer down, then handed the bottle to Faye, who did the same.

"What a day," said Roberta, and she let herself slide onto the arm of a chair, while Faye sat on the other. A couple apart, they surveyed the rest, as adventurers do stay-at-homes, and began their tale, Roberta leading, Faye filling in.

It was a question of the two or three hundred picketers—numbers had varied, as people came and went—preventing vans with newspapers from getting through the gates to distribute them. The police had been there to see the vans safely through.

"Two hundred police," said Roberta, scornfully. "Two hundred fucking police!"

"More police than picketers," said Faye, laughing, and Roberta watched her, fondly. Faye, animated and alive, was really very pretty. Her look of listlessness, even depression, had gone. She seemed to sparkle in the dim room.

"I had to stop Faye from getting carried away," said Roberta. "Otherwise she'd have been out there. Of course, with both of us having to keep a low profile . . ."

"Were there arrests?"

"Five," said Roberta. "They got Gerry. He didn't go quietly, though."

"I should say not," said Faye proudly.

"Who else?"

"Didn't know the others. They were the Militant lot, I think."

A pause. Alice knew she had lost her advantage, and felt discouraged. And, seeing Jasper's face as he watched the two campaigning girls, she was thinking: He'll be off down there tomorrow, if I know anything.

He said, "I'll go down tomorrow." And he looked at Bert, who said, "Right."

Bert looked at Pat, and she said, "I'm on."

A silence. Faye said excitedly, "I'd like to have a go at one of those vans. You know, when I saw that thing standing there, armoured, all lit up, it had wire over the windscreen, I just hated it so much—it it looked bloody *evil*."

"Yes," agreed Bert. "Epitomises everything we hate."

"I'd like to—I'd like to—" Here Faye, seeing how her lover looked at her, began playing up to it prettily, said with a mock shiver, "I'd like to sink my teeth into it!," and Roberta gave her a soft friendly clout across the shoulders, and then hugged her briefly.

"All the same," she said, "we two ought not to be there again. We mustn't be caught."

"Oh," pouted Faye, "why not, we just have to be careful."

"They'll have it all photographed, of course; they'll have your pictures," said Jim excitedly.

"Yes, but we weren't doing anything," said Faye, "worse luck, keeping our noses clean. . . ."

"I'll come down," said Jim. "I'd like to. Fucking pigs." And he spoke sorrowfully, genuinely, so that Faye and Roberta looked at him, curious, and Bert said, "The police were here tonight."

"Just as well we weren't, then," said Roberta.

"Alice handled them. A marvel, she is," said Pat, but not as friendlily as she would have if the two girls had not come in and split allegiances.

Ruined everything, Alice thought bitterly, surprising herself. A moment before she had been thinking: Here am I, fussing about a house, when they are doing something serious.

"Oh well," said Faye, dismissing the police's visit to the house as unimportant compared with the really big issues, "I'm off to sleep, if we are going to get up early tomorrow."

The two women stood up. Roberta was looking at Philip, who still sat there, apart, as if waiting. "You staying here tonight?" she asked, and Philip looked at Alice. She said, "I've told Philip he can live here." She heard the appeal in her voice, knew she had her look, knew she might simply break down and weep.

Roberta's body had subtly changed, hardened, looked affronted, though she made sure her face was impartial. Philip seemed as if he were sustaining invisible blows.

Roberta looked at Bert, eyebrows raised. Bert's gaze back was noncommittal: he was not going to take sides. Again Alice thought, He's not up to much! *He's no good.*

Alice looked at Pat, and saw something there that might save the position. Pat was waiting for Bert; yes, something had been said, discussed, when she was not there. A decision?

Pat said, since Bert did not, "Philip, Alice can't make decisions as an individual. Alice, you know that! We've got to have a real discussion." Here she glanced at Jim, who at once said, "I was here before any of you, this was my house." He sounded wild, was wild, dangerous, all his smiling amiability gone. "I said to you, come in, this is Liberty Hall, I said." Here was a point of principle. Alice recognised it. She thought: "It's Jim who will save Philip!" Jim was going on, "And then I hear, 'You've got to leave here, this is not your place!' How come? I don't get it."

Roberta and Faye stood up. Roberta said, "We should call a real meeting and discuss it, properly."

Philip stood up. He said, "I've been working here for two days. The fifty pounds wouldn't pay for the cable I've used."

Alice looked wildly at Jasper. Who was waiting on Bert. Who smiled calmly, white teeth and red lips glistening in the black beard.

Pat stood up. She said curtly, disappointed in Bert, "I see no reason at all why Philip shouldn't stay. Why shouldn't he? And Jim *was* here before any of us. Well, I'm going to bed. If we go to the picket tomorrow, then we should be up by eight at the latest."

"I'm coming to the picket," said Philip.

Alice drew in her breath, and stopped a wail. She said, "I'll have the money. I'll have it by tomorrow night."

Philip gave a little disappointed laugh. "Maybe," he said. "And that isn't the point. If I was going to take my stand on money, then I wouldn't be here at all."

"Of course not," said Pat. "Well, let's all go down tomorrow." She yawned and stretched energetically and sensually, with a look at Bert, who responded by getting up and putting his arm round her.

Oh no, thought Alice, not again.

Roberta and Faye went out, holding hands. Good night. Good night.

Bert and Pat went out, close.

Jasper went out after them; and Alice heard him run noisily up the stairs.

Alice said to Philip, and to Jim, "It'll be all right."

Philip said, "But you can't say it is, not as an individual."

"No," said Jim. He had lost his wild anger. Was his sane, smiling self. But Alice thought: If we throw him out, he's going to come back one night and wreck the place. Or something like that. She was surprised that the others hadn't seen this, felt it.

Philip said to Alice, taking a stand where, she knew, he had often made himself do it before, "I won't be working here to-morrow, I'm going with the others. After all, the fight against the capitalists is more important than our comfort." No pay, no work! He walked out and could be heard pounding up the stairs.

Jim went without saying good night and took refuge in his room. There began the sound of his drums, soft, emotional, like a threat.

Alice was alone. She went around the room putting out the candles, and then stood letting the dark settle so that she could see in the uneven darkness, where the shoulder of a chair, the hard edge of a table, took shape. She was thinking: The very next thing I do will be . . .

As she left the room, she was worrying—Has Jasper taken his things to another room?—and her heart seemed to give way. For if he was going to shut her out, then, with Bert here, she knew she would find it hard to keep the connection with him that was the meaning and purpose of her life. He would not leave her, she knew that; but he could seem to go very far away.

She went into the hall, now so empty and so large with no one in it, and put out the light. She went up the stairs in the dark, feeling the worn carpet slippery under her feet, and to the landing where the doors were behind which were disposed the others; Philip, too, in the little room beyond the large one Roberta and Faye had taken. Jim always slept downstairs, where his music was—and, for another thing, it was easy to jump out of a window there, and run for it, if necessary.

She opened the door into the room where, she saw with relief that made her knees go soft, Jasper lay curled against the wall, a grublike shape in the half-dark. Her sleeping bag lay on the same wall as his; he had been known, in the past, to move it. She slid straight in, fully dressed.

"Jasper?" she said.

"What is it?"

"Good night, then."

He said nothing. They both lay quiet, listening to hear whether Pat and Bert would start up again. They did. But Alice was worn out. She fell asleep, and when she woke it was light. Jasper had gone, and she knew that they had all gone, and she was alone in the house except perhaps for Philip. She went to see. No Philip; and his tools lay near the gap in the floorboards where he had been replacing cable.

She must get money. She must.

It was nine in the morning.

She was thinking: If I talk to Mum, if I explain . . . But the thought sank away into a pit of dismay. She did not remember what her mother had actually said, but her empty voice, as though all life had been sucked out of her—that Alice did remember. But what is the matter with her, Alice thought indignantly, what's she going on *about?*

Her father. But he must give it to me. He's got to! This thought, too, died in her; could not maintain itself. . . . She found she was thinking of her father's new house. Well, not so new; he had been there over five years, for she and Jasper had not moved in with her mother until her father had been gone for a good year or more. A new wife. Two new children. Alice stood, imagining the house, which she had been in several times. The garden: Jane. Jane *Mellings,* with her two pretty infants in the big green garden, full now of spring flowers and forsythia.

Alice came to life, ran downstairs, snatched up her jacket, and was out of the house and into the street, where people were starting up cars to go to work. As she ran she thought: The dustmen said they would come! But she would only be gone an hour: They won't come so early—but how do I know? If they come and find no one there . . . All the same she kept on running, thinking: But they won't come yet, I just *know* they won't.

She panted into the Underground, snatched a ticket from the machine, belted down the stairs, and there was a fortuitous train. Alice was not surprised, knowing that things were going her way this morning. She fidgeted as she stood on the crowded train, ran up the stairs at the other end, ran, ran along the leafy avenues, and then she came to a stop outside her father's house, which was no more than half a mile from her mother's.

In the garden she saw, not at all to her surprise, Jane, her father's new wife, sitting on the lawn, on a large red-and-green-striped blanket, with two little scraps of children, on whose fair heads the sun glistened.

Alice removed her eyes from the scene, as if her gaze might have the power to force Jane to look at her. Alice went straight up the path to the front door, found it locked, went round the house to the back. She was in full view of Jane if she had only turned her head. Alice walked into the kitchen, which made her heart ache, being large, and with that great wooden table set with bowls of fruit and flowers, which for Alice was the symbol of happiness.

Alice ran into the hall and up the stairs, thinking that if her father was late today going to work—only he never was—she would say: Oh, hello, Dad, there you are! She opened the door into their bedroom calmly, and saw, as she expected, the large marriage bed, which had on it thrown-back duvets, and Jane's nightdress (scarlet silk, Alice noted, severely), her father's pyjamas, a child's striped woolly ball, and a teddy bear.

She went straight to the sliding doors behind which her father's clothes were hanging. Neatly: her father was a methodical man. She went through his pockets, knowing she would find something, for it had been a joke, in *their* house, that Dorothy Mellings found money in his pockets, and made a point of using it on luxuries. He would say—Alice's father—"Right, come clean, what have you spent it on?" And Alice's mother would say, "Brandied peaches." Or *marrons glacés*, or Glenfiddich whisky.

Alice's hands darted in and out of the pockets and she was praying, Dear God, let there be some money, let there be, let there be a lot. Her fingers felt a soft thick wad and she brought it out, not believing in her luck. A thick soft pack of notes. Ten-pound notes. She slid them into her breast pocket, and was out of the room, down the stairs, and then through the kitchen into the back garden. She hardly paused to see whether Jane was safely looking the other way. Alice knew she would be.

Alice was out of the house and in the road and then out of sight of the house in a minute. There she stood, back to the road, facing into a tall hedge, and counted the notes. She could not believe it. It was true. Three hundred pounds.

Well, he would miss that sum: it wasn't just a jar of fucking bloody ginger, or peaches. Three hundred pounds: he would think *she* had stolen it—Jane had. Let him. A cold sour pleasure filled Alice, and she slid the notes back and began running. The dustmen!

Three-quarters of an hour after she had left, she was back at the house, and she saw the rubbish van turn in from the main road.

She knew, she *knew* that all would go well, and stood smiling, her pounding heart sending the blood hissing through her ears.

From the rubbish van jumped the same three men, who, having acknowledged her there, began to hump the black shining sacks. Not a word about the rain that squelched in the sacks with the rubbish.

It took them twenty minutes or so, by which time Joan Robbins had come out to stand at her door, arms folded, watching. And who else was watching? Alice did not look, but made a point of going to the hedge to speak to Joan Robbins and smile: neighbours and a little gossip, that's what observers would see; and then she stood at the gate from which the last black bag had been taken, and put into the hand of Alan the driver the sum of fifteen pounds, with the smile of a householder. And went indoors. It was just after ten in the morning. And the day lay ahead, and it would be filled every minute, with useful activity. It would, once she had started. For she had run out of steam. Now she was thinking of them, her friends, *her family*, who would by now be down at the Melstead works, would have blended with the others, would be standing taking the measure of the police, would be walking confidently about, exchanging remarks the police would have to hear and ignore—ignore until they got their own back later.

Bert and Jasper and Pat, Jim and Philip, Roberta and Faye— she hoped those two would be careful. Well, they were all politically mature; they would know how far they could go. Jasper? Jasper had not been in a confrontation for a long time; for one thing, he had only just finished being bound over. It was not that she wanted him safe, but that she wanted things done right. Jasper was wild, had been bound over once for two years, and not for anything useful—as she judged it—but because of carelessness.

Alice sat by herself, the large shabby sitting room comfortably about her, and thought that she was hungry. She did not have the energy to go out again. Against the wall was a crumpled carrier bag, and in it, a loaf of bread and some salami. God knew how long that had been there, but she didn't care. She sat eating, slowly, careful of crumbs. For this room, she would need help: it was so large and the ceilings so tall. But the kitchen . . . It took an hour or so to get herself going; she was really tired. Besides, she was enjoying mentally spending the money that she could feel in a large soft lump just under her heart. Then she did pull herself up, and went into the kitchen. Filling buckets with—unfortunately—cold water, she began to work. Swabbing down ceilings, walls, while she manoeuvred the stepladder around the cooker, which still lay on its side on the floor. At one point she knew that tears were running down her cheeks—she had been thinking of the others, all together, shouting in unison, "Thatcher out, out, *out!*," shouting "Blacklegs out, out, *out!*"

She could hear them chant, "The workers united shall never be defeated!"

She thought how one of them—Philip, yes, she thought, Philip —would go off to a pub and buy sandwiches and beer for all of them. There might even be a mobile canteen by now; there ought to be, the picket had been going on for some time.

She thought of how the atmosphere would get thick and electric, and how when the armoured vans—the symbol of everything they loathed—started to move, the crowd would struggle together and become like a wall against which the police . . .

Alice wept a little, aloud, snuffling and gulping, as she stood swabbing the floor. If *they* decided that Philip could not stay here, then . . . those tiles on the roof, those tiles . . .

Round about four in the afternoon the kitchen was scrubbed, not a smear of dust or grit anywhere. The big table stood where it ought, with its heavy wooden chairs around it, and on it a glass jam jar with some jonquils out of the garden. Only the poor cooker lay on its side, a reminder of disorder. Alice thought that she would get on a train and go down to the others—she had a right to it, she was the veteran of a hundred battles—but sat down for a rest in the sitting room and fell asleep, and woke to find the others noisily crowding in, laughing and talking, elated and full of accomplishment.

Alice, a sleepy creature in the big chair, was humble, even apologetic, as she struggled up to greet them. She felt she had no right to it when food and drink were spread about the floor and she was invited to join.

Then she remembered. She pulled out her thick roll of notes and, laughing, gave £150 to Philip. "On account," she said.

A silence. They stared. Then they laughed, and began hugging her and one another. Even Jasper put his arm around her briefly as he laughed, and seemed to show her off to the others.

"Better not ask where," said Roberta, "but congratulations."

"Honestly gained, I hope," said Faye primly, and they started again, embracing and laughing, but this was as much, Alice knew, out of the exuberant excesses of emotion from the day's energetic confrontations with Authority as because they were pleased with her.

"All the same," said Faye, "we have to come to a group decision," and Roberta said, "Oh, balls, Faye, come off it. It's all right. . . ."

The two women exchanged a look; and Alice knew: they had been discussing it down there, and had disagreed. Bert said briefly, as though it really didn't matter, and had not mattered: "Yes, as far as I am concerned it is all right." Jasper echoed, "Yes, I agree."

Pat said, "Of course it is all right."

Philip could not speak, for he would have wept; he was shining with relief, with happiness. And Jim: well, he was taking it, Alice could see, as a reprieve; she knew that nothing could ever seem, to Jim, more than a temporary good. But he was pleased enough. There was a warm, good feeling in the room. A family . . .

The good feeling lasted through the meal, and while Alice took them to the kitchen to show them its cleanliness.

"A wonder, she is," sang Faye. "Alice the Wonder, the wondrous Alice . . ." She was tipsy and exhilarated, and everyone enjoyed looking at her.

Without Alice's asking, Bert and Jasper lifted the cooker upright to stand in its place against the wall.

"I'll get it properly fixed tomorrow," said Philip, contentedly.

They went together up the stairs, reluctant to separate for the night, so much of a group did they feel.

Lying along the wall, in the dark, her feet a yard from Jasper's feet, Alice remarked dreamily, "What have you and Bert decided, then?"

A quick movement from Jasper, which she noted, thinking, I didn't know I was going to say that.

He was lying stiffly, found out; that was how he had experienced what she had said.

"Oh, I don't mind, Jasper," she said, impatient but conciliatory. "But you did discuss it, didn't you?"

After a pause, "Yes, we did."

"Well, it does affect us all."

A pause. Grudgingly, "We thought it mightn't be a bad thing, having other people here. But they have to be CCU. Jim will have to join."

"You mean, Philip and Jim will be a cover."

He said nothing. Silence means consent. She said, "Yes, and of course there'll be more people coming in, and . . ."

He said fussily, "You aren't to let just anyone come, we can't have just anybody."

"I didn't say, just anybody. But the others needn't ever know we are IRA."

"Precisely," said Jasper.

And then she remarked, in her dreamy voice and to her own surprise, "With the comrades in the other house, I wonder . . ." She stopped. Interested in what she had said. Respectful of it.

But he had shot up on his elbow and was staring at her in the half-dark, where headlamps from the road moved light across the ceiling, the walls, the floor, so they were both irregularly illuminated. He was silent. He did not ask, "How do you know about the other house?," or say, "How dare you spy on me?"—things that had been said often enough in the past, until he had learned that she could do this: know, without being told.

She was thinking fast, listening to what she had said. So, Bert and Jasper had been next door, had they? There are comrades there? Yes, that's it!

She said, "Did you just go there, on the off-chance, or—what happened?"

He replied stiffly, after a pause, "We were contacted. They sent a message."

"To you? To you and Bert?"

From his hesitation she knew that she had been included, but she did not intend to make an issue of it.

"A message came," he said, and lay down.

"And you and Bert and—the comrades there decided we should have more people in, as a cover."

Silence. But she knew he was not asleep. She let a few minutes go by, while she thought. Then she changed the subject, saying, "Quite soon people are going to have to start making a contribution. So far I've paid for everything."

"Where did you get that money?" he asked at once, reminded about it, as she had intended.

She had it ready for him; she leaned over in the dark and handed him some notes.

"How much?" he demanded.

"Fifty."

"How much did you get?"

"Ask no questions," she said, though she would have told him had he asked; but he only said, "That's right, squeeze the last blood out of them."

She said, "Tomorrow I've got to tackle the Council. Will you get my Social Security?"

"Right."

They were both waiting for the sounds of lovemaking from next door, but Bert and Pat must have dropped off. Jasper and Alice had been lying tense; now they relaxed and lay companionably silent, and Alice was thinking: We are together. . . . This is like a marriage: talking together before going to sleep. I hope he starts telling me what happened today.

She did not want to ask, but she knew that he knew she craved to hear it all. And soon he was kind; he began to talk. She loved him like this. He told her everything, right from the beginning: how the seven of them had been on the train, how they had bought sandwiches and coffee at the station, and had all crowded on the two seats facing each other and shared breakfast. Then how they went by taxi to the printworks. The taxi driver had been on their side: he had said "Good luck" as he drove off.

"That was nice," said Alice softly, smiling in the dark.

And so they talked, quietly, Jasper telling everything, for he was good at this, building up word pictures of an event, an occasion. He ought to be a journalist, thought Alice, he is so clever.

She could have talked all night, because of course she had slept a long time. But he fell asleep quite soon; and she was content to lie there, in the quiet, arranging her plans for the next day, which, she knew, would not be easy.

When she woke, Jasper was not there. She ran to the top of the house, and looked into the four rooms where she had left all the windows open. The two rooms where the horrible pails had been were already only rooms in which people would soon be living. But she had not come for that. On two of the ceilings were sodden brown patches, and, having located on the landing the trap door to the attic, she stood on a window sill to reach. She could, just, and felt the trap door lift under her fingers. No problem there!

Down she ran to the kitchen, where there were voices. What she saw made her eyes fill with tears. They were sitting round the table: Bert and Pat, these two close together; Jasper; Jim smiling and happy; and Philip, already working on the cooker, bending over behind it, a cup of coffee on its top. Bert had gone to his friend Philip's girlfriend, Felicity, the Thermos had been filled, he had bought croissants and butter and jam. It was a real meal. She slid into her place at the head of the table, opposite Bert, and said, "If this room had some curtains . . ." They all laughed.

"Before talking about curtains, you had better get things fixed with the Council," said Jasper, rather hectoring, but only because he was jealous of Pat, who said, "Oh, I'd back Alice. I'd back her in anything."

Coffee and croissants appeared before her, and Alice said, "Has anybody noticed the ceilings upstairs?"

"I have," said Pat.

Philip said, "I can't do everything at once." He sounded aggrieved, and Pat said, "Don't worry. It's not difficult to fix slates. I did it once in another squat."

"I'll do it with you when I've finished this," said Philip.

Pat said to Bert, "If someone could get the slipped-down tiles out of that guttering . . . ?"

"No head for heights," said Bert comfortably.

"I can do that," said Alice. Then she said to Jasper, not Bert, "If you could borrow the car from next door, you could go looking in the skips for some furniture? I saw four skips in my father's street with all sorts of good stuff." She added fiercely, "Waste. All this *waste*." She knew her look was about to overcome her, as she said, "This house, all these rooms . . . people throwing things out everywhere, when there's nothing wrong with them." She sat fighting with herself, knowing that Pat was examining her, diagnostic. Pat said to Bert, "There you are, Bert, job for the day. You and Jasper." As he sat laughing from some old joke about his laziness, she said, irritated, "Oh, for shit's sake, Alice has done all the work."

"And found all the money," said Philip, from the cooker.

"Put like that," said Bert.

"Put like that," agreed Jasper, pleased, already restlessly moving about because of wanting to be off with Bert, looting and finding, street-combing. . . .

Those two went off as Roberta and Faye came in, saw the remains of the croissants, and sat down to consume them.

Alice dragged Philip's heavy ladder to the front of the house, and went up it. Luckily the house was built squat, heavy on the earth, not tall and frightening. By the time she reached the top, Pat was already on the roof, sitting near the chimney with one arm round it: she had come up through the attic and a skylight. Around the chimney's base the roof looked eroded, pocked. A great many tiles had slipped and were now propped along the gutter. All that water pouring in, and going where? They had not properly examined the attics yet.

Alice was reaching out for the fallen tiles, and laying them on the roof in front of her. Pat seemed in no hurry to start; she was enjoying sitting there, looking at roofs and upper windows. And at neighbours, of course, watching them, two women at work on a roof. And where were the men? these people could positively be heard thinking—Joan Robbins, the old woman sitting there under her tree, the man staring grumpily out of a top window.

"Catch," called Alice, ready to throw, but Pat said, "Wait." She wriggled onto her stomach and squinted in through the roof.

"There's a nest on the rafter here," she said in a hushed voice, as though afraid of disturbing the birds.

"Oh *no*," said Alice, "oh, how awful!" She sounded suddenly hysterical, and Pat glanced at her, coldly, over her arm, which was stretched in under the roof. "Oh, for God's *sake*," said Alice, and began to cry.

"A *bird*," said Pat. "A *bird*, not a *person*." She pulled out handfuls of straw and stuff, and flung them out into the air, where they floated down. Then something crashed onto the tiles of the roof: an egg. The tiny embryo of a bird sprawled there. Moving.

Alice went on crying, little gusts of breathless sobs, her eyes fixed on the roof in front of her.

Another egg crashed on the roof.

Childlike frantic eyes implored Pat, who still was rooting about with her arm through the hole beneath her. But Pat was deliberately not looking at Alice snuffling and gulping below her.

A third egg flew in an arc and crashed splodgily in the garden.

"Now that's done," said Pat, and she looked at Alice. "*Stop it!*" Alice sniffed herself to silence and, at a nod from Pat, began to throw up the tiles. Pat caught them, carefully, one after another.

Roberta and Faye appeared below, and went off, waving to them.

"Have a good day," said Pat, brief, ironical, but with a smile saying that she, like Alice, did not expect anything else.

Soon Philip came up to join Pat, and Alice, having cleared all the gutters as far as she could reach, went down to move the heavy ladder along a few paces. She worked, in this way, all round the house, removing wads of sodden leaves, and fallen tiles. Above her, Philip and Pat replaced the tiles.

Alice felt low and betrayed. By somebody. The two minute half-born birds were lying there, their necks stretched out, filmy eyes closed, and no one looked at them. The parent birds fluttered about on the high branches nearby, complaining.

Alice tried to keep her mind on what had to be done next. The cleaning. The *cleaning!* Windows and floors and walls and ceilings, and then paint, so much paint, it would cost. . . .

In mid-afternoon she went off to ring the Council, as if this were not an important thing, as if things were settled.

She heard that Mary Williams was not there and her heart went dark.

Bob Hood, an official disturbed in his important work, said curtly that the matter of 43 and 45 had been put off till tomorrow.

Said Alice, "It's all right, then, is it?"

"No, it certainly is not," said Bob Hood. "It has not been agreed that you or anyone else can occupy those premises."

Alice said in a voice as peremptory, as dismissive as his, "You ought to come and see this place. It is a disgrace that it could ever be considered as suitable for demolition. Somebody's head should roll for it. I am sure heads will roll. These are two perfectly sound houses, in good condition."

A pause. Huffily he said—but he was retreating—"And there have been more complaints. Things cannot be allowed to continue."

"But we have cleaned up forty-three—the one we took over. The police would confirm that it has been cleaned up."

Alice waited, confident. Oh, she knew this type, knew how their cowardly little minds worked, knew she had him. She could hear him breathing, could positively note how mental machineries clicked into place.

"Very well," he said. "I will come round. I've been meaning to take a look at those two properties."

"Can you give me some indication as to time?" said Alice.

"There's no need for that, we have keys."

"Yes, but we can't have people just wandering around, can we? I'd like you to give us some approximate time."

This was such cheek that she wondered at herself. Yet she knew it was not over the top, because of her manner: every bit as authoritative as his. She was not surprised when he said, "I'll come round now."

"Right," said Alice. "We'll expect you." And put down the receiver on him.

She raced back. She called up to Philip and Pat that the Council was coming, and on no account should they stop, because it would be a good thing for them to be seen at work up there. She ran indoors to check on sitting room, kitchen. She went upstairs to the rooms where they slept, and marvelled that Roberta and Faye's room was a veritable bower of femininity, with dressing table, cushions, duvet on the double sleeping bag, photographs—all of it grubby, but it would make a good impression. She whisked on a skirt. Her hair, her nails. She heard a knock before she expected it and tripped down the stairs with a cool smile already adjusted on her face to open the door correctly on, "Bob Hood? I am Alice Mellings."

"I hope those two on the roof know what they are doing?"

"I expect so. He is a builder. She is assisting him. As an amateur, but she has done it before."

She had silenced him. Oh, you nasty little man, she was thinking behind her good-girl's smile. You nasty little bureaucrat.

"Shall I show you downstairs first? Of course, this will give you no idea of what it was like only three days ago. For one thing, the Council workmen had filled in the lavatory bowls with concrete and ripped the electric cables out—they left them anyhow, a fire hazard."

He said, "I have no doubt they were fulfilling their instructions."

"You mean, they were instructed to leave the cables dangerous, and to concrete over the main water tap? I wonder if the Water Board knows about that?"

He was red, and furious. Not looking at him, she flung open one door after another downstairs, lingering over the kitchen. "The electrician had made it safe in here, but you were lucky the place didn't go up in flames. Mary Williams said you had been over this house. How was it you didn't notice the cables?"

Upstairs, she said, knowing that to this man anything incorrect, even so much as a mattress on a floor rather than on a bed, must forever be an affront, "Of course, you will have to take my word for it—the state of these rooms was unspeakably awful when we came, but we have only just started."

"Unspeakably awful now," he said huffily, looking in at the room she and Jasper slept in, the two sleeping bags like the shed skins of snakes loose against the wall.

"It's relative. I think you will be surprised when you see it in a month's time."

He said, quick to take his advantage, "I told you, don't expect anything."

"If this house is left empty again, it will be filled to the brim with vandals and derelicts inside a week, you know that. You're lucky to have us. It's being put back into order, with no expense to the taxpayer."

He did not reply to that. In silence they went through the rooms on the top floor, now sweet-smelling, the air blowing through them. He instinctively closed the windows one after another, performing the task with a fussy, virtuous, irritated little air. Like a fucking housewife, thought the smiling Alice.

They went downstairs. "Well," he said, "I have to agree with you—there's no reason why these houses should come down, that I can see. I'll have to look into it."

"Unless," said Alice, sweet and cold, "someone was going to make a profit out of it. Did you see the article in the *Guardian?* 'The Scandal of Council Housing'?"

"As it happens, I did. But it is not relevant to this case."

"I see."

They were at the door.

She was waiting. She deserved a capitulation; and it came. The official said, unsmiling but with his whole body expressing unwilling complicity, "I'll put the case for you tomorrow. But I am not promising. And it is not just this house, it's the one next door. I'm going there now."

Again Alice had forgotten next door.

Bob Hood gone, she ran up to a little window that overlooked next door, and watched, in a rage of frustration, how the well-brushed, well-dressed, clean young man stood looking at the piles of rubbish in that garden, saw that the expression on his face was like that on the dustmen's faces: an exasperated, incredulous disgust.

Unable to bear the beating of her heart, her churning stomach, she went down, slowly, suddenly out of energy, and collapsed in the sitting room as Pat came in, with Philip.

"Well?" demanded Pat; and Philip's face was stunned with need, with longing, his eyes a prayer.

"It's dicey," said Alice, and began to weep, to her own fury. "Oh, God," she wept. "Oh, Christ. Oh, shit. Oh *no*."

Pat, close on the arm of the chair she was huddled in, put her arm around the dejected shoulders and said, "You're tired. Surprise! You are tired."

"It'll be all right," sobbed Alice. "I know it will be, it will, I feel it."

From the silence, she knew that above her head Philip and Pat shared glances that said she, Alice, had to be humoured, patted, caressed, given coffee from the flask, then brandy from a reserve bottle. But she knew that though Pat's interest was real, it was not like Philip's and like her own. Pat's heart would never pound, or her stomach churn. . . . For this reason, she did not accept Pat's encircling sisterliness, remained herself, alone, sad and isolated, drinking her coffee, her brandy. Philip was her charge, her responsibility: her *family*, so she felt, because he was as she was. She was pleased, though, to have Pat as an ally.

And at this point, Jasper and Bert arrived, with gleanings from London, that great lucky dip, and Alice flew into the hall, to welcome a load of stuff that had to be sorted out; and which switched her emotions back to another circuit. "Oh, the wicked waste of it all," she raged, seeing plastic bags full of curtains, which were there because someone had tired of them; a refrigerator, stools, tables, chairs—all of them serviceable, if some needed a few minutes' work to put right.

Bert and Jasper went out again; they were elated and enjoying it. A pair, a real pair, a team; united by this enterprise of theirs, furnishing this house. And they had the car for the whole day, and must make the most of it.

Philip and Pat let the roof go while they helped Alice allot furniture, flew out to buy curtain fittings for which Alice took the money from her hoard.

They ran around, and up and down, dragging furniture, hanging curtains, spreading on the hall floor a large carpet that needed only some cleaning to make it perfect.

Bert and Jasper came in the late afternoon, having scavenged around Mayfair and St. John's Wood, with another load, and said that was it, no more for today—and the householders sat in the kitchen drinking tea and eating bacon and eggs properly cooked on the stove, with the purr of the refrigerator for company.

And in the middle of this feast, which was such a delicate balancing of interests, the result of careful and calculated good will, there was a knock. It was, however, tentative, not a peremptory summons. They turned as one; from the kitchen they could see the front door, and it was opening. A young woman stood there, and as the others stared—*Whose friend is she?*—Alice's heart began to pound. She already knew it all, from the way this visitor was looking around the hall, which was carpeted, warm, properly if dimly lit, then up the solid stairs, and then in at them all. She was all hungry determination and purpose.

"The Council," reassured Alice. "It is Mary Williams. The colleague of that little fascist who was here today. But she's all right. . . ." This last she knew was really the beginning of an argument that would be taking place later, perhaps even that night. Perhaps not an argument, not bitterness, but only a friendly discussion—oh, prayed Alice, let it be all right, and she slipped away from the others, saying, "It's all right, I'll just . . ."

She shut the door on the kitchen, and on a laugh that said she was bossy, but not impossibly so. Oh, *please*, please, please, she was inwardly entreating—Fate, perhaps—as she went smiling towards Mary. Who was smiling in entreaty at Alice.

As Alice had absolutely expected, Mary began, "I dropped in at the office—I was at a course today, you know, they send you on courses, I am doing Social Relationships—and I saw Bob on his way out. He told me he had been here. . . ." Alice was opening the door into the sitting room, which was looking like anybody's warm living room, if a trifle shabby, and she saw Mary's anxious face go soft, and heard her sigh.

They sat down. Now Mary was petitioner, Alice the judge. Alice helped with, "It is a nice house, isn't it? Mad, to pull it down."

Mary burst out, "Well, they are mad." (Alice noted that "they" with a familiar dry, even resigned, amusement.) "When I opted for Housing, it was because I thought, Well, I'll be housing *people*, I'll be helping the homeless, but if I had known . . . Well, I'm disillusioned now, and if you knew what goes on . . ."

"But I do."

"Well, then . . ."

Mary was blushing, eyes beseeching. "I am going to come to the point. Do you think I could come and live here? I *need it*. It's not just me. We want to get married—I and my boyfriend. Reggie. He's an industrial chemist." This chemist bit was there to reassure her, thought Alice, with the beginnings of scorn that, however, she had to push down and out of sight. "We were just saving up to buy a flat and he lost his job. His firm closed down. So we had to let that flat go. We could live with my mother or with his parents, but . . . if we lived here we could save some money. . . ." She made herself bring it all out, hating her role as beggar; and the result of this effort was a bright determination, like a command.

But Alice was thinking, Oh, shit, no, it's worse than I thought. What will the others say?

She played for time with, "Do you want to see the house?"

"Oh, God," said Mary, bursting into tears. "Bob said there were rooms and rooms upstairs, all empty."

"*He's* not going to move in!" said Alice, not knowing she was going to, with such cold dislike for him that Mary stopped crying and stared.

"He's all right, really," she said. "It's just his manner."

"No," said Alice, "it's not just his manner."

"I suppose not. . . ."

This acknowledgement of Bob's awfulness made Alice feel friendlier, and she said gently, "Have you ever lived in a squat? No, of course you haven't! Well, I have, in lots. You see, it's tricky; people have to fit in."

Mary's bright hungry eyes—just like the poor cat's, thought Alice—were eating up Alice's face with the need to be what Alice wanted. "No one has ever said I am difficult to get on with," she said, trying to sound humorous, and sighing.

"Most of the people here," said Alice, sounding prim, "are interested in politics."

"Who isn't? It is everyone's duty to be political, these days."

"We're socialists."

"Well, of course."

"Communist Centre Union," murmured Alice.

"Communist?"

Alice thought, If she goes to that meeting tomorrow and says, They are communists . . . She's quite capable of it, and with a bright democratic smile! She said, "It's not communist, like the Communist Party of Great Britain." Keeping her eyes firmly on Mary's face, for she knew that what Mary saw was reassuring—unless she, Alice was wearing her look, and she was pretty sure she was not— she said firmly, "The comrades in Russia have lost their way. They lost their way a long time ago."

"There's no argument about *that*," said Mary, with a hard brisk little contempt, dabbing her eyes with a tissue. She sat restored, a pleasant ordinary girl, all brown shining curls and fresh skin. Like an advertisement for medium-quality toilet soap. But tomorrow she could decide the fate of all of them, thought Alice, curiously examining her. If she said to Bob, tomorrow morning, sharing cups of coffee before the meeting, "I dropped in last night at that house, you know, forty-three Old Mill Road, and my God, what a setup!," then he could change his mind, just like that, particularly with the house next door in such a mess.

She asked, "Did Bob Hood say anything about next door?"

"He said there's nothing structurally wrong."

"Then why, why, why, *why?*" burst out Alice, unable to stop herself.

"The plan was to build two blocks of flats, where these houses are. No, not awful flats, quite decent really, but they wouldn't fit, not with these houses around here." She added bitterly, forgetting her status, "But some contractor will make a packet out of it." And then, going a step worse, "Jobs for pals." Shocked by herself, she shot an embarrassed glance at Alice, and added a social smile.

"We can't let them," said Alice.

"I agree. Well, it's what Bob says that counts, and he is furious, he is really. He is really going to fight. He says it's a crime these houses should come down." She hesitated, and took the plunge into what she clearly felt was a descent into even worse indiscretion with, "I was in Militant Tendency for a bit, but I don't like their methods. So I left."

Alice sat silent with amazement. Mary, in Militant! Well, of course she wouldn't like Militant's methods. And she wouldn't like the methods of Alice, Jasper, Pat, Roberta, or Faye. Nor, for that matter, Jim's (so Alice suspected). But that Mary had gone any-where near Militant, that was the impossibility! She asked cau-tiously, "And Reggie?"

"He was trying out Militant for the same reason I was. I was shocked by what I saw going on at work, jobs for pals, as I said. . . ." Again the brief, social smile, like a frozen apology. "We decided at once Militant was not for us. We joined Greenpeace."

"Well, of course," said Alice, hopefully, "but if you are Trot-skyists . . ." With a bit of luck Mary would say yes, she counted herself with the Trots, and then of course this house would be impossible. . . . But Alice heard, "We're not anything at the mo-ment, only Greenpeace. We thought of joining the Labour Party, but we need something more . . ."

"Dynamic," said Alice, choosing a flatteringly forceful but not ideological word. "I think perhaps the CCU would suit you. Anyway, come and see the house." She got up, so did Mary—it was like the termination of an interview. Alice had decided that she really did like Mary. She would do. But what of Reggie? Thoughts of Reggie accompanied the two women as they went rapidly around the upper floors. Alice flung open doors on empty rooms, and heard how Mary sighed and longed, and was not at all surprised to hear her say, as they came down the stairs again, "Actually, Reggie is in the pub down the road."

Alice laughed, a robust girl's laugh, and Mary chimed in, after a pause, with a breathless little tinkle.

"The thing is," said Alice, "we have to discuss it. All of us. A group decision, you know."

"If we come back in half an hour?"

"Longer than that," said Alice, and added, because of Mary's beseeching eyes, "I'll do my best."

She went into the kitchen, where they sat in a fug of comfort (created by her), and sat down, and she put the situation to them.

Because of all that food and chat and good nature and togetherness, there was an explosion of laughter. Literally, they fell about. But there was a theatrical quality to it that Alice did not much like.

Silence at last, and Pat said, "Alice, are you saying that if we don't let them come here, we won't get this house?"

Alice did not reply at once. At last she said, "She wouldn't do anything spiteful on purpose, I am sure of that. But if she was coming here to live, she'd be careful about what she said. It's human nature," said Alice, feebly, using a phrase that of course was simply beyond the pale.

"What could she say that would make such a difference," Pat persisted.

"If she said, They are a bunch of reds, Bob Hood would soon find a reason to have us kicked out. She doesn't care, because she's one herself."

"That girl is a revolutionary?" asked Bert, laughing.

"She's a Trotskyist. Of a sort. Or she was one."

"Then how can they come and live here, Alice," said Bert, firm but kind.

"I don't think she's anything much, at the moment. Ideologically. And anyway," Alice persisted, courageously, knowing what this argument of hers had cost her in the past, earning her all kinds of accusations, "in a sense, aren't we? After all, we don't say that Trotsky never existed! We give him full credit for his achievements. We say that it was Lenin who was the real workers' leader, and then the comrades there took a wrong turning with Stalin. If saying that Trotsky was a good comrade and he took the wrong turning makes you a Trot, then I don't see why we aren't? Anyway, I don't seem to remember we actually defined our line on Trotsky. Not in the CCU, anyway."

"Oh, Alice," said Jasper, with the finality of superiority, "ideology is simply not your line."

"Well," said Pat, having exchanged efficient looks with Bert, "I for one don't think this is the moment to define our attitude towards Comrade Trotsky. There is something in what Alice says. That's not the point. My point is that this business of having a nice clean house and a roof over our heads is beginning to define us. It is what we *do*."

"It's taken four days," said Alice, "four days," and she was appealing for justice.

"Yes, but now it looks as if we are going to have two new people here just to keep the house."

Jim said, "Why don't we ask them to join the CCU. I'm going to join."

"Well, why not?" said Bert, after a considerable pause. Alice saw him and Jasper exchange a long thoughtful look. She knew they were thinking that perhaps they should go next door to ask someone —*who?*—for advice. Or instruction.

She said, "We must decide tonight. The meeting is tomorrow." And now she did have her look. Her voice told her so; and told the others, who turned to see how she sat swelling and suffering there.

Bert and Jasper still sat gazing at each other in an abstracted way. What they were doing, in fact, was playing back in their minds what had been said by someone next door, and wondering how to fit this situation into it.

Bert said, "I don't see why we shouldn't ask them to join. We keep saying we want to recruit. It sounds to me as if these two might be ripe. With a bit of political education . . ." And on these words he and Jasper got up, as one, and went out, Jasper remarking, "We'll be back in a minute."

Pat said, "And I'm off. I'm off to visit someone."

"But don't you want to meet Mary and Reggie?"

Pat shrugged, smiled, and left. Alice was reminded—as, she was sure, Pat had intended—that Pat did not really care, was going to leave anyway.

Remained Alice and Jim and Philip.

Soon in came Mary, with a man of whom Alice found herself thinking, at first glance, "Well, of course!"—meaning that he and Mary were a pair. Not in looks, for he was a tall, knobbly-looking man, with very white skin, small black eyes under strong black brows, and dense, very fine black hair. He would be bald early. Where he matched with Mary was in an air of measure, of common sense ordered by what was due. Due, that is, to their surroundings, their fellows, to society. Alice was looking, and she knew it, at respectability. It was not that she did not value this type of good sense; but it was not the kind of sense that would be appropriate here, in this household. It was with an infinite feeling of tolerance that she allowed that other people had need of these struts and supports. She was thinking, Good God, they were born to be two nice little bourgeois in a nice little house. They'll be worrying about their pensions next.

Seeing them together, she felt, simply, that a mistake was being made. They should not be here. Alone with Mary, she liked her. Seeing her with her mate, Reggie, Alice felt alienated, with the beginnings of a strong hostility.

"Sit down," she smiled. And she put the saucepan on the stove and switched on the electricity. A pity: a gas stove would be so much better. Well, they would find one on a skip, or even get a reconditioned one for ten pounds or so.

She turned to see Reggie examining Jim, and thought, With a bit of luck he's colour-prejudiced and won't want to be here. But no such luck: he seemed to like Jim. Or, if he didn't like blacks, his manner said nothing about that. Of course, thought Alice, this lot, the bloody middle classes, you'd find out nothing from their manner, politeness is all. But no, it was genuine, she was pretty sure of it; body language—something Alice was equipped by instinct to understand, long before there was a name for it—told her that Reggie was all right about colour, at least. She sat listening to them talk, everything easy, Reggie with Jim, Mary with Philip. She made mugs of coffee and set before them a plate of cake.

Chat. How she, Alice, had fixed things with Electricity, and would with the Gas Board. The Water Board, of course, would be told. Alice did not say that the Water Board would not catch up with them for months and that she had no intention of attracting their attention. These two were bill payers and keepers of accounts.

She said, to warn them, "I have lived in a lot of squats, and you'll have to accept it, some people don't pull their weight. They just don't."

At this Jim said, hurt, "Until you came there wasn't anything to pay, was there?" And she said, "No, I'm not talking about you, I'm talking about the situation. It's no good these two moving in and expecting everything to be regular."

Mary said, "But with so many people here, it will still be cheaper than anything else could possibly be, with no rent."

"Exactly," said Reggie. And came straight to his point, with, "Tell us about the CCU? You know, we've never heard of it. Mary and I were talking in the pub. It didn't ring a bell with either of us."

"Well, it's not a very big party, really," said Alice. "But it's growing. When we started it, we never meant it to be a mass party; we don't want it to be. These mass parties, they lose touch with the people."

"Well, that's true enough," said Reggie, but he said it carefully, as though he could have said other things; and Alice thought: He and Mary are going to exchange glances. . . . They didn't, but only with an effort so obvious she thought contemptuously: People are so amazing. They exchange glances as if no one can see them, and they don't know how they give themselves away. . . . Anyone can read what people are thinking.

Reggie: "The CCU—the Communist Centre Union?"

"Centre, because we wanted to show we were not left deviants or revisionists."

"Union—two parties joined, two groups?"

"No, a union of viewpoints, you see. No hairsplitting. We didn't want any of that."

"And you started the CCU?"

"I was one of them. And Jasper Willis. Have you heard of him?" As Reggie and Mary shook their heads, Alice thought, But you will. "Several of us. It was up in Birmingham. We have a branch there. And a comrade wrote last week to say he had started a branch in Liverpool. He has four new members. And there's the branch here in London."

Here Mary and Reggie were finally unable to prevent their eyes from meeting. Alice felt a flush of real contempt, like hatred. She said, "All political parties have to start, don't they? They start with only a few members. Well, we've only been going a year and we have thirty members here in London. Including the comrades in this house." She resisted the temptation to say: And of course there are some next door.

"And your policy?" asked Reggie, still in the same careful way that means a person is not going to allow a real discussion to start because his opinion has to be kept in reserve.

All right! thought Alice again, you just wait, you'll hear of the CCU. Anyway, you are going to join, because you want to live here. Opportunist! She was thinking at the same time, We'll educate you. Raw material is raw material. It's what you'll be like in a year that counts. If you haven't saved up enough to move out before then. Well, at least you two will be in no hurry to see this squat come to an end. She said, "We've got a policy statement. I'll give you one. But we are going to have a proper conference next month and thrash out all the details."

But they weren't listening, Alice could see. They were thinking about how soon they could move in.

They asked whether they could bring in some furniture, and offered pots and pans and an electric kettle.

"Gratefully accepted," said Alice, and so they chatted on until Jasper and Bert came back from next door, and Alice knew that there was no problem at all about these two staying. Not from that quarter, anyway, whatever it might turn out to be; though Roberta and Faye were another thing.

Reggie sat quietly, leaning back in the chair, summing up Jasper, summing up Bert. Alice knew that he warmed to Bert. Well, they were two of a kind. He did not much like Jasper. Oh, she knew that look when people first met Jasper. She remembered how she, too, when she had first seen Jasper all those years ago, had felt some instinctive warning, or shrinking. And look how mistaken she had been.

At eleven, Mary and Reggie went off; they were afraid to miss the last trains back to Muswell Hill and Fulham, where they respectively lived, so far apart.

Philip said he was tired and went to bed.

Jim went into his room, and they heard soft music from his record player, accompanied by his softer drums.

"What's happened to Faye and Roberta?" asked Alice, and Bert said, "There's a women's commune in Paddington, they go there a lot."

"Why don't they move in there?"

"They like it here," said Bert, with a grimace that said, Ask no questions and . . .

Bert went up to sleep. Jasper and Alice were alone in the kitchen.

"All *right*," said Jasper. "I'll tell you, give me a chance."

They went up to their room; Jasper had not said she must move out, or that he would; and Alice slid down into the sleeping bag the way a dog slinks, eyes averted, into a favourite place, hoping no one will notice.

They could hear Bert moving about next door. Jasper said, "Bert and Pat are going away for the weekend." His voice was painful to hear.

"Only for the weekend," Alice comforted him for the loss of Bert. As for her, her saddened heart told her how much she would miss Pat, even for the weekend. "Where are they going?"

"They didn't say, and I didn't ask."

They lay companionably by their wall, their feet not far from each other. They had not yet found curtains for this room, and the lights from the traffic still chased across the ceiling, and the whole house shook softly with the heavy lorries going north, giving Alice a comforting sense of familiarity, as if they had been living here for months, not days; she seemed to have lived all her life in houses that shook to heavy traffic.

"Would you like to come down to the picket tomorrow?"

"But I really have to be here," mourned Alice.

"Well, Saturday night we could go and paint up a few slogans."

She steadied her voice so that it would not betray her surge of delight, of gratitude. "That'd be nice, Jasper."

"Yes. Get some spray paint." He turned to the wall. She was not going to hear anything about next door tonight. But tomorrow, tomorrow night . . . she might. And on Saturday . . .

She woke when Jasper did, at seven, but lay still, watching him from nearly closed eyes. His wiry body was full of the energy of expectation. Everything from his gingery hair (which she thought of privately as cinnamon-coloured) to his small deft feet, which she adored because they were so white and slender, was alive. He seemed to dance his way into his clothes, and his pale face was innocent and sweet when he stood momentarily at the window, to see what the weather was like for the day's picketing. There was an exalted, dreamy look to him as he went past the apparently sleeping Alice to the door. He did not look at her.

She relaxed, lay on her back, and listened. He knocked next door, and she heard Bert's reluctant response, and Pat's prompt "Right, we're awake." Then the knock on Roberta and Faye's door. Philip? Oh, not Philip, she needed him here! But there was no other knock, and then she began worrying: I hope Philip won't feel left out, despised? A knock on the door of the room immediately below this one—the big room that was Jim's, though it was really a living room, and should perhaps be used as such . . . No, that was not fair. A startled shout from Jim; but she could not decide whether he was pleased to be aroused, or not.

The sounds of the house coming to life. She could go down if she wanted, could sit with the cheerful group and send them on their way with smiles, but her mouth was dry and her eyes pricked. For some reason—a dream, perhaps?—she wanted to weep, go back to sleep. To give up. She distrusted what she felt; for it had been with her since she could remember: being excluded, left out. Unwanted. And that was silly, because all she had to do was to say she was going, too. But how could she, when their fate, the fate of them all, would be decided that morning at the Council, and it was by no means certain the house was theirs. When Mary had gone off saying, "I'll do my best," it meant no more than that. Alice brought Bob Hood to life in her mind's eye and, staring at the correct, judicious young man, willed him to do what she wanted. "Put our case," she said to him. "Make them let us have it. It's *our* house." She kept this up for some minutes, while listening to how the others moved about the kitchen. Almost at once, though, they were out of the house. They were going to breakfast in a café. That was silly, raged Alice: wasting all that money! Eating at home was what they would have to learn to do. She would mention it, have it out with them.

Oh, she did feel low and sad.

For some reason she thought of her brother, Humphrey, and the familiar incredulous rage took hold of her. How could he be content to play their game? A nice safe little job—aircraft controller, who would have thought anyone would choose to spend his life like that! And her mother had said he had written to announce a child. The first, he had said. Suddenly Alice thought: That means I am an aunt. It had not occurred to her before. Her rage vanished, and she thought, Well, perhaps I'll go and see the baby. She lay smiling there for some time, in a silent house, though the din from the traffic encompassed it. Then, consciously pulling herself together, with a set look on her face, she rolled out of the sleeping bag, pulled on her jeans, and went downstairs. On the kitchen table were five unwashed coffee cups—they had taken time for coffee, so that meant they hadn't gone to the café; they would have a picnic on the train again; no, don't think about that. She washed up the cups, thinking, I've got to organise something for hot water—it used to come off the gas, but of course the Council workmen stole the boiler. We can't afford a new one. A second-hand one? Philip will know where and how. . . . Today he will fix the windows, if I get the glass. He said he needed another morning for the slates. Seven windows—what is that going to cost, for glass!

She took out the money that was left: less than a hundred pounds. And with everything to be bought, to be paid for . . . Jasper had said he would get her unemployment money, but of course she couldn't complain, he worked really hard yesterday, getting all that good stuff from the skips. At this moment she saw, on the window sill, an envelope with "Alice" scribbled on it, and under that "Have a nice day!" And under that "Love, Jasper." Her money was in it. She quickly checked: he had been known to keep half, saying, We must make sacrifices for the sake of the future. But there were four ten-pound notes there.

She sat at the table, soft with love and gratitude. He did love her. He did. And he did these wonderful, sweet things.

She sat relaxed, at the head of the great wooden table. If they wanted to sell it, they could get fifty for it, more. The kitchen was a long room, not very wide. The table stood near a window that had a broad sill. From the table she could see the tree, the place where she and Jim had buried the shit, now a healthy stretch of dark earth, and the fence beyond which was Joan Robbins's house. It was a tall wood fence, and shrubs showed above it, in bud. A yellow splodge of forsythia. Birds. The cat sneaked up the fence, and opened its mouth in a soundless miaow, looking at her. She opened the window, which sparkled in the sun, and the cat came in to the sill, drank some milk and ate scraps, and sat for a while, its experienced eyes on Alice. Then it began licking itself.

It was in poor condition, and should be taken to the vet.

All these things that must be done. Alice knew that she would do none of them until she heard from Mary. She would sit here, by herself, doing nothing. Funny, she was described as unemployed, she had never had a job, and she was always busy. To sit quietly, just thinking, a treat, that. To be by oneself—nice. Guilt threatened to invade with this thought: it was disloyalty to her friends. She didn't want to be like her mother—selfish. She used to nag and bitch to have an afternoon to herself: the children had to lump it. Privacy. That lot made such a thing about privacy; 99 percent of the world's population wouldn't know the word. If they had ever heard it. No, it was better like this, healthy, a group of comrades. Sharing. But at this, worry started to nibble and nag, and she was thinking: That's why I am so upset this morning. It's Mary, it's Reggie. They are simply not one of us. They will never really let go and meld with us, they'll stay a couple. They'll have private viewpoints about the rest of us. Well, then, that was true of Roberta and Faye, a couple: they made it clear they had their own attitudes and opinions; they did not like what was happening now, with the house. And Bert and Pat? No, they did not have a little opinion of their own, set against the others; but Pat was only here at all because she actually enjoyed being screwed (the right word for it!). Jim? Philip? She and Jasper?

When you got down to it, she and Jasper were the only genuine revolutionaries here. Appalled by this thought, she nevertheless examined it. What about Bert? Jasper approved of him. Jasper's attachments to men who were like elder brothers had nothing to do with their politics but with their natures; they had always been the same type. Easygoing. Kind. That was it. Bert was a good person. But was he a revolutionary? It was unfair to say Faye and Roberta are not real revolutionaries just because I don't like them, thought Alice. . . . Where were these thoughts getting her? What was the point? The group, her family, lay in its parts, diminished, criticised out of existence. Alice sat alone, even thinking, Well, if we don't get the house, we'll go down to the squat in Brixton.

A sound upstairs, immediately above. Faye and Roberta: they had not gone with the others. Alice listened to how they got themselves awake and up: stirrings, and the slithering sound the sleeping bags made on the bare boards; a laugh, a real giggle. Silence. Then footsteps and they were coming into the kitchen.

Alice got up to put the saucepan on the heat, and sat down. The two smelled ripe—sweaty and female. They were not going to wash in cold water, not these two!

The two women, smiling at Alice, sat together with their backs to the stove, where they could look out of the window and see the morning's sun.

Knowing that she was going to have to, Alice made herself tell about last night, about Mary and Reggie. She did not soften it at all. The other two sat side by side, waiting for their coffee, not looking at each other, for which Alice was greatful. She saw appear on their faces the irony that she heard in her own voice.

"So the CCU has two recruits?" said Roberta, and burst out laughing.

"They are good people," said Alice reprovingly. But she laughed, too.

Faye did not laugh; little white teeth held a pink lower lip, her shining brown brows frowned, and the whole of her person announced her disapproval. Roberta stopped laughing.

Hey, thought Alice, I've seen this before: you'd think it was Roberta who was the strong one—she comes on so butch-motherly, she's like a hen with one chick—but no, it's Faye who's the one, never mind about all her pretty bitchy little ways. And she looked carefully and with respect at Faye, who was about to pronounce. And Roberta waited, too.

"Listen, Alice, now you listen, you listen carefully, for I am about to say my piece. . . ." And Alice could see it was hard for her to assert herself, that this was why she had so many little tricks and turns, little poutings and hesitations and small wary glances and little smiles at Roberta and at herself, but underneath she was iron, she was formidable. "Once and for all, I do not care about all this domestic bliss, all the house and garden stuff. . . ." Here she waited, politely, while first Roberta and then Alice—seeing that Roberta did— laughed. "Well, for me it is all pretty classy stuff," said Faye. "This house would have seemed a palace to me once. I've lived in at least a thousand squats, dens, holes, corners, rooms, hovels, and resi-dences, and this is the best yet. And I don't care." Here she pet-tishly, humorously, wagged a finger at Alice. Roberta had her eyes on her love's face, exactly like an elder sister: *Is she going to go too far?* Too far, Alice knew, with all this presentation, the manner, the means that enabled Faye to say her piece. Roberta did not want Alice to think that this girl was frivolous or silly.

Well, she certainly did not.

"Any minute now we are going to have hot running water and double glazing, I wouldn't be surprised. For me this is all a lot of shit, do you hear? *Shit!*"

Alice got up, poured boiling water into the three mugs that already had coffee powder in them, set the mugs on the table, put the milk bottle and the sugar near Faye. She did this as something of a demonstration and saw that as Faye stretched out her hand for the coffee, which she was going to drink black and bitter, she knew it, and even appreciated it, judging from her quick shrewd little smile. But she was going on, with determination. She had also lost her cockney self, and the voice that went with it.

It was in all-purpose BBC English that she went on, "I don't care about that, Alice. Don't you see? If you want to wait on me, then do. If you don't, don't. I don't care, either way."

Roberta said quickly, protectively, "Faye has had such a terrible life, such an awful shitty terrible life. . . ." And her voice broke and she turned her face away.

"Yes, I did," said Faye, "but don't make a thing of it. I don't." Roberta shook her head, unable to speak, and put her hand, tentatively, ready to be rejected, on Faye's arm. Faye said, "If you are going to tell Alice about my ghastly childhood, then tell her, but not when I am here."

She drank gulps of the bitter coffee, grimaced, reached for a biscuit, took a neat sharp bite out of it, and crunched it up, as if it were a dose of medicine. Another gulp of caffeine. Roberta had her face averted. Alice knew that she was infinitely sorrowful about something; if not Faye's past, then Faye's present: her hand, ignored by Faye, had dropped off Faye's arm and crept back into her own lap, where it lay trembling and pitiful, and her lowered head with its crop of black silvered curls made Alice think of a humbly loving dog's. Roberta was radiating love and longing. At this moment, at least, Faye did not need Roberta, but Roberta was dying of need for Faye.

Faye probably has times when she wants to be free of Roberta, finds it all too much—yes, that's it. Well, I bet Roberta never wants to be free of Faye! Oh, God, all this personal stuff, getting in the way of everything all the time. Well, at least Jasper and I have got it all sorted out.

Faye was going on. Christ, listen to her, she could get a job with the BBC, thought Alice. I wonder when she learned to do it so well. And what for?

"I've met people like you before, Alice. In the course of my long career. You cannot let things be. You're always keeping things up and making things work. If there's a bit of dust in a corner you panic." Here Roberta let out a gruff laugh, and Alice primly smiled —she was thinking of all those pails. "Oh, laugh. Laugh away." It seemed she could have ended there, for she hesitated, and the pretty cockney almost reclaimed her, with a pert flirtatious smile. But Faye shook her off, and sat upright in a cold fierce solitude, self-sufficient, so that Roberta's again solicitous and seeking hand fell away. "I care about just one thing, Alice. And you listen to me, Roberta, you keep forgetting about me, what I am, what I really am *like*. I want to put an end to this shitty fucking filthy lying cruel hypocritical system. Do you understand? Well, do you, Roberta?"

She was not at all pretty, or appealing, then, but pale and angry, and her mouth was tight and her eyes hard, and this—how she looked—took sentimentality away from what she said next. "I want to put an end to it all so that children don't have a bad time, the way I did."

Roberta sat there isolated, repudiated, unable to speak.

Alice said, "But, Faye, do you think I'm not a revolutionary? I agree with every word you say."

"I don't know anything about you, Comrade Alice. Except that you are a wonder with the housekeeping. And with the police. I like that. But just before you came, we took a decision, a joint decision. We decided we were going to work with the IRA. Have you forgotten?"

Alice was silent. She was thinking, But Jasper and Bert have been discussing things next door, surely? She said, carefully, "I understood that a comrade next door had indicated that . . ."

"What comrade?" demanded Roberta, coming to life again. "We know nothing about that."

"Oh," said Alice. "I thought . . ."

"It's just amateurish rubbish," said Faye. "Suddenly some un-known authority next door says this and that."

"I didn't realise," said Alice. She had nothing to say. She was thinking: Was it Bert who led Jasper into . . . ? Was it Jasper who . . . ? I don't remember Jasper doing anything like this before. . . .

After some time, while no one said anything, but they all sat separate, thinking their own thoughts, Alice said, "Well, I agree. It is time we all got together and discussed it. Properly."

"Including the two new *comrades?*" enquired Faye, bitter.

"No, no, just us. Just you and Roberta and Bert and Jasper and Pat and me. "

"*Not* Philip and *not* Jim," said Roberta.

"Then the six of us might go to a café or somewhere for a dis-cussion," said Alice.

"Quite so," said Faye. "We can't have a meeting here, too many extraneous elements. Exactly."

"Well, perhaps we could borrow a room in forty-five," said Alice.

"We could go and have a lovely picnic in the park, why not?" said Faye, fiercely.

"Why not?" said Roberta, laughing. It could be seen that she was coming back into the ascendant, sat strong and confident, and sent glances towards Faye which would soon be returned.

Another silence, companionable, no hard feelings.

Alice said, "I have to ask this, it has to be raised. Are you two prepared to contribute anything to expenses?"

Faye, as expected, laughed. Roberta said quickly, reprovingly of Faye—which told Alice everything about the arguments that had gone on about this very subject—"We are going to pay for food and suchlike. You tell us how it works out."

"Very cheaply, with so many of us."

"Yes," said Faye. "That's fair. But you can leave me out of all the gracious living. I'm not interested. Roberta can do what she likes." And she got up, smiled nicely at them both, and went out. Roberta made an instinctive movement to go after her but stayed put. She said, "I'll make a contribution, Alice. I'm not like Faye—

I'm not indifferent to my surroundings. You know, she really is," she said urgently, smiling, pressing Alice with Faye's difference, her uniqueness, her preciousness.

"Yes, I know."

Roberta gave Alice two ten-pound notes, which she took, with no expression on her face, knowing that that would be it, and thanked Roberta, who fidgeted about, and then, unable to bear it, got up and went after Faye.

It was not yet ten. Mary had said to ring at one. Persuaded by the odours left on the air of the kitchen by Faye, by Roberta, she went up to the bathroom and forced herself into a cold bath, where she crouched, unable actually to lower her buttocks into it, scrubbing and lathering. In a glow she dressed in clean clothes, bundled what she had taken off with Jasper's clothes that needed a wash— determined by sniffing at them—and was on her way out to the laundrette when she saw the old woman sitting under the tree in the next garden, all sharp jutting limbs, like a heap of sticks inside a jumble of cardigan and skirt. She urgently gesticulated at Alice, who went out into the street and in again at the neat white gate, smiling. She hoped that neighbours were watching.

"She's gone out and left me," said the old woman, struggling to sit up from her collapsed position. "They don't care, none of them care." When she went on in a hoarse voice about the crimes of Joan Robbins, Alice deftly pulled up the old dear, thinking that she weighed no more than her bundle of laundry, and tidied her into a suitable position for taking the air. Alice listened, smiling, until she had had enough, then she bent down, to shout into possibly deaf ears, "But she's very nice to bring you out here to sit in the garden; she doesn't have to do that, does she?" Then, as the ancient face seemed to struggle and erupt into expostulation, she said, "Never mind, I'll bring you a nice cup of coffee."

"Tea, tea," urged the crone.

"You'll have to have coffee. We're short of a teapot. Now, you just sit there and wait."

Alice went back, made sweet coffee, and brought it to the old woman. "What's your name?"

"Mrs. Jackson, Jackson, that's what I am called."

"My name is Alice and I live at forty-three."

"You sent away all those dirty people, good for you," said Mrs. Jackson, who was already slipping down in her chair again, like a drunken old doll, the mug sliding sideways in her hand.

"I'll see you in a few minutes," said Alice, and ran off.

The laundrette used up three-quarters of an hour. She collected her cup from Mrs. Jackson, and then stood listening to Joan Robbins, who came out of her kitchen to tell Alice that she should not believe the old lady, who was wandering; there was not one reason in the world why she, Joan Robbins, should do a thing for her, let alone help her down the stairs to the garden and up again and make her cups of coffee and . . . The complaints went on, while Mrs. Jackson gesticulated to both of them that her tale was the right one. This little scene was being witnessed by several people in gardens and from windows, and Alice let them have the full benefit of it.

With a wave she went back into her own house.

It was eleven, and a frail apparition wavered on the stairs: Philip, who said, "Alice, I don't feel too good, I don't feel . . ."

He arrived precariously beside her, and his face, that of a doleful but embarrassed angel, was presented to her for diagnosis and judgement, in perfect confidence of justice. Which she gave him: "I am not surprised, all that work on the roof. Well, forget it today, I'd take it easy."

"I would have gone with the others, but . . ."

"Go into the sitting room. Relax. I'll bring you some coffee."

She knew this sickness needed only affection, and when Philip was settled in a big chair, she took him coffee and sat with him, thinking: I have nothing better to do.

She had known that at some time she would have to listen to a tale of wrongs: this was the time. Philip had been promised jobs and not given them; had been turned off work without warnings; had not been paid for work he had done; and this was told her in the hot aggrieved voice of one who had suffered inexplicable and indeed malevolent bad luck, whereas the reason for it all—that he was as fragile as a puppet—was not mentioned; could never, Alice was sure, be mentioned. "And do you know, Alice, he said to me, Yes, you be here next Monday and I'll have a job for you—do you know what that job was? He wanted me to load great cases of paint and stuff into vans! I'm a builder and decorator, Alice! Well, I did it, I did it for four days, and my back went out. I was in hospital for two weeks, and then in physio for a month. When I went to him and said he owed me for the four days, he said I was the one in the wrong and . . ." Alice listened and smiled, and her heart hurt for him. It seemed to her that a great deal had been asked of her heart that morning, one poor victim after another. Well, never mind, one day life would not be like this; it was capitalism that was so hard and hurtful and did not care about the pain of its victims.

At half past twelve, when she was just thinking that she could go to the telephone booth, she heard someone coming in, and flew to intercept the police, the Council—who this time?

It was Reggie, who, smiling, was depositing cases in the hall. He said that Mary had slipped out from the meeting to telephone him the good news. And she would be over with another load in the lunch hour. The relief of it made Alice dizzy; then she wept. Standing against the wall by the door into the sitting room, she had both hands up to her mouth as if in an extreme of grief, and her tight-shut eyes poured tears.

"Why, Alice," said Reggie, coming to peer into her tragic face, and she had to repel friendly pats, pushes, and an arm around her shoulders.

"Reaction," she muttered, diving off to the lavatory to be sick. When she came out, Philip and Reggie stood side by side, staring at her, ready to smile, and hoping she would allow them to.

And, at last, she smiled, then laughed, and could not stop.

Philip looked after her; and Reggie, embarrassed, sat by.

And she was embarrassed: What's wrong with me? I must be sick too.

But Philip was no longer sick. He went off to measure up the broken windows for new glass, and Reggie climbed the stairs to look over the rooms. Alice stayed in the kitchen.

There Mary came to her with a carton of saucepans, crockery, and an electric kettle. She sat herself down at the other end of the table. She was flushed and elated. Alice had heard her laughing with Reggie in the same way Faye and Roberta laughed; and, sometimes, Bert and Pat. Two against the world. Intimacy.

Alice asked at once, "What are the conditions?"

"It's only for a year."

Alice smiled, and, on Mary's look, explained, "It's a lifetime."

"But of course they could extend. If they don't decide to knock it down after all."

"They won't knock it down," said Alice confidently.

"Oh, don't be so sure." Now Mary was being huffy on behalf of her other self, the Council.

Alice shrugged. She waited, eyes on Mary, who, however, really did not seem to know why. At last Alice said, "But what has been decided about paying?"

"Oh," said Mary, airily, "peanuts. They haven't fixed the exact sum, but it's nothing, really. A nominal amount."

"Yes," said Alice, patient. "But how. A lump sum for the whole house?"

"Oh no," said Mary, as though this were some unimaginably extortionate suggestion—such is the power of an official decision on the official mind—"Oh no. Benefit will be adjusted individually for everyone in the house. No one's in work here, you said?"

"That isn't the point, Mary," said Alice, hoping that Mary would get the point. But she didn't. Of course not; what in her experience could have prepared her for it?

"Well, I suppose it would be easier if it was a lump sum, and people chipped in. Particularly as it is so small. Enough to cover the rates, not more than ten or fifteen pounds a week. But that is not how it is done with us." Again spoke the official, in the decisive manner of one who knows that what is done must be the best possible way of doing it.

"Are you sure," enquired Alice carefully, after a pause, "that there really is no possibility of changing the decision?"

"Absolutely none," said Mary. What she was in fact saying was: This is such a petty matter that there is no point in wasting a minute over it.

And so unimportant was it to Mary that she began to stroll around the kitchen, examining it, with a happy little smile, as if unwrapping a present.

Meanwhile Alice sat adjusting. Faye and Roberta would not agree, would leave at once. Jim, too. Jasper wouldn't like it—he would demand that both he and Alice should leave. Well, all right, then they would all go. Why not? She had done it often enough! There was that empty house down in Stockwell. . . . Jasper and she had been talking for months of squatting there. It would suit Faye and Roberta, because their women's commune was somewhere down there. God only knew what other places, refuges, hideouts they used. Alice had the impression there were several.

A pity about this house. And as Alice thought of leaving, sorrow crammed her throat, and she closed her eyes, suffering.

She said, sounding cold and final, because of the stiffness of her throat, "Well, that's it. I'm sorry, but that's it."

"*What do you mean?*" Mary had whirled round, and stood, a tragedienne, hand at her throat. "I don't know what you mean!" she exclaimed, sounding fussy and hectoring.

"Well, it doesn't matter to you, does it? You and Reggie can stay here by yourselves. You can easily get friends in, I am sure."

Mary collapsed into a chair. From being the happiest girl in the world, she had become a poor small creature, pale and fragile, a suppliant. "I don't understand! What difference does it make? And of course Reggie and I wouldn't stay here by ourselves."

"Why not?"

Mary coloured up, and stammered, "Well, *of course* . . . it goes without saying . . . *they* can't know I am living here. Bob Hood and the others can't know I am in a *squat*."

"Oh well, that's it, then," said Alice, vague because she was already thinking of the problems of moving again.

"I don't understand," Mary was demanding. "Tell me, what is the problem."

Alice sighed and said perfunctorily that there were reasons why some of them did not want their presence signposted.

"Why," demanded Mary, "are they criminals?" She had gone bright pink, and she sounded indignant.

Alice could see that this moment had been reached before, with Militant. Methods!

Alice said, sounding sarcastic because of the effort she was making to be patient, "Politics, Mary. Politics, don't you see?" She thought that with Jim it was probably something criminal, but let it pass. Probably something criminal with Faye and Roberta, for that matter. "Don't you see? People collect their Social Security in one borough, but live somewhere else. Sometimes in several other places."

"Oh. Oh, I see."

Mary sat contemplating this perspective: skilled and dangerous revolutionaries on the run, in concealment. But seemed unable to take it in. She said, huffily, "Well, I suppose the decision could be adjusted. I must say, I think it is just as well the Council don't know about this!"

"Oh, you mean you can get the decision changed?" Alice, reprieved, the house restored to her, sat smiling, her eyes full of tears. "Oh, good, that's all right, then."

Mary stared at Alice. Alice, bashful, because of the depth of her emotion, smiled at Mary. This was the moment when Mary, from her repugnance for anything that did not measure up against that invisible yardstick of what was right, suitable, and proper that she shared with Reggie, could have got up, stammered a few stiff, resentful apologies, and left. To tell Bob Hood that the Council had made a mistake, those people in number 43 . . .

But she smiled, and said, "I'll have a word with Bob. I expect it will be all right. So everyone will chip in? I'll get them to send the bills monthly, not quarterly. It will be easier to keep up with the payments." She chattered on for a bit, to restore herself and the authority of the Council, and then remarked that something would have to be done about number 45. There were complaints all the time.

"I'll go next door and see them," said Alice.

Again the official reacted with, "It's not your affair, is it? Why should you?" Seeing that Alice shrugged, apparently indifferent, Mary said quickly, "Yes, perhaps you should. . . ."

She went upstairs, with a look as irritated as Alice's. Both women were thinking that it would not be easy, this combination of people, in the house.

Soon Mary went off with Reggie. He would drop her back at work, and they both would return later with another load. They were bringing in some furniture, too, if no one minded. A bed, for instance.

Alice sat on, alone. Then Philip came to be given the money for the glass, and went off to buy it.

Alice was looking at herself during the last four days, and thinking: Have I been a bit crazy? After all, it *is* only a house . . . and what have I done? These two, Reggie and Mary—revolutionaries? *They* were with Militant? Crazy!

Slowly she recovered. Energy came seeping back. She thought of the others, on the battlefront down at Melstead. They were at work for the cause; and she must be, too! Soon she slipped out of the house, careful not to see whether the old lady was waving at her, and went into the main road, walked along the hedge that separated first their house from the road, and then number 45. She turned into the little street that was the twin of theirs, and then stood where yesterday she had seen Bob Hood stand, looking in that refuse-filled garden.

She walked firmly up the path, prepared to be examined by whoever was there and was interested. She knocked. She waited a goodish time for the door to open. She caught a glimpse of the hall, the twin of theirs, but it was stacked with cartons and cases. There was a single electric bulb. So they did have electricity.

In front of her was a man who impressed her at once as being foreign. It was not anything specific in his looks; it was just something about him. He was a Russian, she knew. This gave her a little *frisson* of satisfaction. It was power, the idea of it, that was exciting her. The man himself was in no way out of the ordinary, being broad—not fat, though he could easily be—and not tall; in fact not much taller than herself. He had a broad, blunt sort of face, and little shrewd grey eyes. He wore grey twill trousers that looked expensive and new, and a grey bush shirt that was buttoned and neat.

He could have been a soldier.

"I am Alice Mellings. From next door."

He nodded, unsmiling, and said, "Of course. Come in." He led the way through the stacks of cartons into the room that in their house was the sitting room. Here it had the look of an office or a study. A table was set in the bay window; his chair had its back to the window, and that was because, Alice knew, he wanted to know who came in and out of the door; he did not want his back to it.

He sat down in this chair, and nodded to another, opposite it. Alice sat.

She was thinking, impressed: This one, he's the real thing.

He was waiting for her to say something.

The one thing she now knew she could not say was, "Have you been telling Jasper and Bert what to do?," which was what she wanted to know.

She said, "We have just got permission from the Council; we are short-term housing, you know." He nodded. "Well, we thought you should do the same. It makes life much easier, you see. And it means the police leave you alone."

He seemed to relax, sat back, pushed a packet of cigarettes towards her, lit one himself as she shook her head, sat holding a lungful of smoke, which he expelled in a single swift breath, and said, "It's up to the others. I don't live here."

Was that all he was going to say? It seemed so. Well, he had in fact said everything necessary. Alice, confused, hurried on, "There's the rubbish. You'll have to pay the dustmen. . . ." She faltered.

He had his eyes intent on her. She knew that he was seeing everything. It was a detached, cold scrutiny. Not hostile, not un-friendly, surely? She cried, "We've been given a year. That means, once the place is straight, we can give all our attention to"—she censored "the revolution"—"politics."

He seemed not to have heard. To be waiting for more? For her to go? Floundering on, she said, "Of course not everyone in our squat . . . For instance, Roberta and Faye don't think that . . . But why should you know about them? I'll explain. . . ."

He cut in, "I know about Roberta and Faye. Tell me, what are those two new ones like?"

She said, giving Reggie and Mary the credit due, "They were once members of Militant, but they didn't like their methods." Here she dared to offer him a smile, hoping he would return it, but he said, "She works for the Council? On what sort of level?"

"She doesn't take decisions."

He nodded. "And what about him? A chemist, I believe?"

"Industrial chemist. He lost his job."

"Where?"

"I didn't ask." She added, "I'll let you know."

He nodded. Sat smoking. Sat straight to the table, both forearms on it, in front of him a sheet of paper on which his eyes seemed to make notes. He was like Lenin!

She thought: His voice. American. Yes, but something funny for an American voice. No, it was not the voice, the accent, but something else, in *him*.

He didn't say anything. The question, the anxiety that were building up in her surfaced. "Jasper and Bert have gone down to Melstead. They went early."

He nodded. Reached for a neatly folded newspaper and opened it in front of him, turning the pages. "Have you seen today's *Times?*"

"I don't read the capitalist press."

"I think perhaps that is a pity," he commented after a pause. And pushed across the paper, indicating a paragraph.

Asked whether they welcomed these reinforcements to the picket line, Crabit, the strikers' representative, said he wished the Trotskyists and the rent-a-picket crowd would keep away. They weren't wanted. The workers could deal with things themselves.

Alice felt she could easily start crying again.

She said, "But this is a capitalist newspaper. They're just trying to split the democratic forces, they want to disunite us." She was going to add, "Can't you see that?," but could not bring it out.

He took back the paper and laid it where it had been. Now he was not looking at her.

"Comrade Alice," he said, "there are more efficient ways of doing things, you know."

He stood up. "I've got work to do." She was dismissed. He came out from behind the table and walked with her to the door and back through the hall to the front door.

"Thank you for coming to see me," he said.

She stammered, "Would there be a room in this house we could use for a . . . discussion. You see, some of us are not sure about . . . some of the others."

He said, "I'll ask." He hadn't reacted as she had feared he would. Bringing it out had sounded so feeble. . . .

He nodded and, at last, gave her a smile. She went off in a daze. She was telling herself, But he's the real thing, he *is*.

He had not told her his name.

She walked along the short stretch of main road slowly, because in front of her, in the middle of the pavement, was a girl with a small child in a pushchair. The child looked like a fat plastic parcel with a pale podgy spotty face coming out of the top. He was whining on a high persistent note that set Alice's teeth on edge. The girl looked tired and desperate. She had lank unwashed-looking pale hair. Alice could see from the set angry shoulders that she wanted to hit the child. Alice was waiting to walk faster when she could turn off into her own road, but the girl turned, still in the middle of the pavement. There she stopped, looking at the houses and, in particular, at number 43. Alice went past her and in at her gate. She heard the girl say, "Do you live here? In this house?"

"Yes, I do," said Alice, without turning, in a curt voice. She knew what was coming. She walked on up the path. She heard the wheels of the pushchair crunch after her.

"Excuse me," she heard, and knew from the stubborn little voice that she could not get out of it. She turned sharply, blocking the way to the front door. Now she faced the girl squarely, with a *no* written all over her. This was not the first time, of course, that she had been in this position. She was feeling: It is unfair that I have to deal with this.

She was a poor thing, this girl. Probably about twenty. Already worn down with everything, and the only energy in her the irritation she was containing because of her grizzling child.

"I heard this house is short-term housing now," she said, and she kept her eyes on Alice's face. They were large, grey, rather beautiful eyes, and Alice did not want the pressure of them. She turned to the door, and opened it.

"Where did you hear that?"

The girl did not answer this. She said, "*I'm going mad.* I've got to have a place. I've got to find somewhere. I've got to."

Alice went into the hall, ready to shut the door, but found that the girl's foot stopped her. Alice was surprised, for she had not expected such enterprise. But her own determination was made stronger by her feeling that if the girl had that much spirit, then she wasn't in such a bad way after all.

The door stood open. The child was now weeping noisily and wholeheartedly inside his transparent shroud, his wide-open blue eyes splashing tears onto the plastic. The girl confronted Alice, who could see she was trembling with anger.

"I've got as much right here as you have," she said. "If there's room I'm coming here. And you have got room, haven't you? Look at the size of this place, just look at it!" She stared around the large hall, with its glowing carpet that gave an air of discreet luxury to the place, and to the various doors that opened off it to rooms, rooms, a treasury of rooms. And then she gazed at the wide stairs that went up to another floor. More doors, more space. Alice, in an agony, looked with her.

"I'm in one of those hotels, do you know about them? Well, why don't you, everyone ought to. The Council shoved us there, my husband and me and Bobby. One room. We've been there seven months." Alice could hear in her tone, which was incredulous at the awfulness of it, what those seven months had been like. "It's owned by some filthy foreigners. Disgusting, why should they have a hotel and tell us what to do? We are not allowed to cook. Can you imagine, with a baby? One room. The floor is so filthy I can't put him to crawl." This information was handed out to Alice in a flat, trembling voice, and the child steadily and noisily wept.

"You can't come here," said Alice. "It's not suitable. For one thing there's no heating. There isn't even hot water."

"Hot water," said the girl, shaking with rage. "Hot water! We haven't had hot water for three days, and the heating's been off. You ring up the Council and complain, and they say they are looking into it. I want some space. Some room. I can heat water in a pan to wash him. You've got a stove, haven't you? I can't even give him proper food. Only rubbish out of packets."

Alice did not answer. She was thinking, Well, why not? What right have I got to say no? And as she thought this, she heard a sound from upstairs, and turned to see Faye, standing on the landing, looking down. There was something about her that held Alice's attention; some deadliness of purpose, or of mood. The pretty, wispy, frail creature, Faye, had again disappeared; in her place was a white-faced, malevolent woman, with punishing, cold eyes, who came in a swift rush down the stairs as though she would charge straight into the girl, who stood her ground at first and then, in amazement, took a step back, with Faye right up against her, leaning forward, hissing, "Get out. Get out. Get out. Get out."

The girl stammered, "Who are you, what . . ." while Faye pushed her, by the force of her presence, her hate, step by step back towards the door. The child was screaming now.

"How dare you," Faye was saying. "How dare you crash in here? No one said you could. I know what you're like. Once you were in, you'd take everything you could get, you're like that."

This insanity kept Alice silent, and had the girl staring open-eyed and open-mouthed at her cruel pursuer as she retreated to the door. There Faye actually gave her a hard shove, which made her step back onto the pushchair and nearly knock it over.

Faye crashed the door shut. Then, opening it, she crashed it shut again. It seemed she would continue this process, but Roberta had arrived on the scene. Even she did not dare touch Faye at that moment, but she was talking steadily in a low, urgent, persuasive voice:

"Faye, Faye darling, darling Faye, do stop it, no, you must stop it. Are you listening to me? Stop it, Faye. . . ."

Faye heard her, as could be seen from the way she held the door open, hesitating before slamming it again. Beyond could be seen the girl, retreating slowly down the path, with her shrieking child. She glanced round in time to see Faye taken into Roberta's arms and held there, a prisoner. Now Faye was shouting in a hoarse, breathless voice, "Let me go." The girl stopped, mouth falling open, and her eyes frantic. *Oh no*, those eyes seemed to say, as she turned and ran clumsily away from this horrible house.

Alice shut the door, and the sounds of the child's screams ceased.

Roberta was crooning, "Faye, Faye, there, darling, don't, my love, it's all right." And Faye was sobbing, just like a child, with great gasps for breath, collapsed against Roberta.

Roberta gently led Faye upstairs, step by step, crooning all the way, "There, don't, please don't, Faye, it's all right."

The door of their room shut on them, and the hall was empty. Alice stood there, stunned, for a while; then went into the kitchen and sat down, trembling.

In her mind she was with the girl on the pavement. She was feeling, not guilt, but an identification with her. She imagined herself going with the heavy awkward child to the bus stop, waiting and waiting for it to come, her face stony and telling the other people in the queue that she did not care what they thought of her screaming child. Then getting the difficult chair on the bus, and sitting there with the child, who if it wasn't screaming would be a lump of exhausted misery. Then getting off the bus, strapping the child into the chair again, and walking to the hotel. Yes, Alice did know about these hotels, did know what went on.

After a while she made herself strong tea, and sat drinking it as if it were brandy. Silence above. Presumably Roberta had got Faye off to sleep?

Some time later Roberta came in, and sat down. Alice knew how she must look, from Roberta's examination of her. She thought: What she really is, is just one of these big maternal lezzies, all sympathy and big boobs; she wants to seem butch and tough, but bad luck for her, she's a mum.

She did not want to be bothered with what was going to come.

When Roberta said, "Look, Alice, I know how this must look, but . . ." she cut in, "I don't care. It's all right."

Roberta hesitated, then made herself go on: "Faye does sometimes get like this, but she is much better, and she hasn't for a long time. Over a year."

"All right."

"And of course we can't have children here."

Alice did not say anything.

Roberta, needing some kind of response she was not getting, got up to fuss around with teabags and a mug, and said in a low, quick, vibrant voice, "If you knew about her childhood, if you knew what had happened to her . . ."

"I don't care about her fucking childhood," remarked Alice.

"No, I've got to tell you, for her sake, for Faye's. . . . She was a battered baby, you see. . . ."

"I don't care," Alice shouted suddenly. "*You* don't understand. I've had all the bloody unhappy childhoods I am going to listen to. People go on and on. . . . As far as I am concerned, unhappy childhoods are the great con, the great alibi."

Shocked, Roberta said, "A battered *baby*—and battered babies grow up to become adults." She was back in her place, sitting, leaning forward, her eyes on Alice's, determined to make Alice respond.

"I know one thing," Alice said. "Communes. Squats. If you don't take care, that's what they become—people sitting around discussing their shitty childhoods. Never again. We're not here for that. Or is that what you want? A sort of permanent encounter group. Everything turns into that, if you let it."

Roberta, convinced that Alice was not going to listen, sat silent. She drank tea noisily, and Alice felt herself wince.

There was something coarse and common about Roberta, Alice was thinking, too disturbed and riled up to censor her thoughts. She hadn't washed yet, even though water was running in the taps. There was the sharp metallic tang of blood about her. Either she or Faye, or both, were menstruating.

Alice shut her eyes, retreated inside herself to a place she had discovered long years ago—she did not know when, but she had been a small child. Inside here she was safe, and the world could crash and roar and scream as much as it liked. She heard herself say, and it was in her dreamy, abstracted voice:

"Well, I suppose Faye will die of it one of these days. She has tried to commit suicide, hasn't she?"

Silence. She opened her eyes to see Roberta in tears.

"Yes, but not since I . . ."

"All those bracelets," murmured Alice. "Scars under bracelets."

"She's got one tiny scar," pleaded Roberta. "On her left wrist."

Alice had shut her eyes again, and was sipping tea, feeling that her nerves would soon begin to stand up to life once more. She said, "One of these days I'll tell you about my mother's unhappy childhood. She had a mad mum, and a peculiar dad. 'Peculiar' is the word. If I told you!" She had not meant to mention her mother. "Oh, never mind about her," she said. She began to laugh. It was a healthy, even jolly laugh, appreciative of the vagaries and richnesses of life. "On the other hand, my father—now, that was a different kettle of fish. When he was a child he was happy the whole day long, so he says, the happiest time in his life. But do we believe him? Well, I am inclined to, yes. He is so bloody *thick* and *stupid* and *awful* that he wouldn't have noticed it if he was unhappy. They could have battered him as much as they liked, and he wouldn't even have noticed."

She opened her eyes. Roberta was examining her with a small shrewd smile. Against her will, Alice smiled in response.

"Well," said Alice, "that's that, as far as I am concerned. Have you got any brandy? Anything like that?"

"How about a joint?"

"No, doesn't do anything for me. I don't like it."

Roberta went off and came back with a bottle of whisky. The two sat drinking in the kitchen, at either end of the big wooden table. When Philip came staggering in under the heavy panes of glass, ready to start work, he refused a drink, saying he felt sick. He went upstairs, back to his sleeping bag. What he was really saying was that Alice should be working along with him, not sitting there wasting time.

Roberta, having drunk a lot, went up to Faye, and there was silence overhead.

Alice decided to have a nap. In the hall was lying an envelope she thought was junk mail. She picked it up to throw it away, saw it was from the Electricity Board, felt herself go cold and sick; decided to give herself time to recover before opening it. She went to the kitchen. *By hand.* Mrs. Whitfield had said she came past on her way to and from work. She had dropped this in herself, on her way home. That was kind of her. . . . Alice briskly opened the letter, which said:

Dear Miss Mellings,

I communicated with your father about guaranteeing payment of accounts for No. 43 Old Mill Road, in terms of our discussion. His reply was negative, I am sorry to say. Perhaps you would care to drop in and discuss this matter in the course of the next few days?

Yours sincerely, D. *Whitfield.*

This pleasant, human little letter made Alice feel supported at first; then rage took over. Luckily, there was no one to see her as she exploded inwardly, teeth grinding, eyes bulging, fists held as if knives were in them. She stormed around the kitchen, like a big fly shut in a room on a hot afternoon, banging herself against walls, corners of table and stove, not knowing what she did, and making grunting, whining, snarling noises—which soon she heard. She knew that she was making them and, frightened, sat down at the table, perfectly still, containing what she felt. Absolute quiet after such violence, for some minutes. Then she whirled into movement, out of the kitchen and up the stairs, to knock sharply on Philip's door. Stirrings, movements, but no reply, and she called, "Philip, it's me, Alice."

She went in as he said, "Come in," and saw him scrambling up out of his sleeping bag and into his overalls. "Oh, sorry," said she, dismissing his unimportant embarrassment and starting in at once.

"Philip, will you guarantee our electricity bill?" As he stared, and did not understand: "You know, the bill for this house? My mother won't, my father won't, bloody bloody Theresa and bloody bloody Anthony won't. . . ."

He was standing in front of her, the late-afternoon light strong and yellow behind him, a little dark figure in a stiff awkward posture. She could not see his face and went to the side of the room, so that he turned toward her, and she saw him confronting her, small, pale, but obstinate. She knew she would fail, seeing that look, but said sharply, "You have a business, you have a letterhead, you could guarantee the account."

"Alice, how can I? I can't pay that money, you know I can't." Talking as though he would have to pay, thought Alice, enraged again. But had he heard her joke that the first payment would be the last?

She said, bossy, "Oh, Philip, don't be silly. You wouldn't have to, would you? It's just to keep the electricity on."

He said, trying to sound humorous, "Well, Alice, but perhaps I would have to?"

"No, of *course* not!"

He was—she saw—ready to laugh with her, but she could not.

"What can I do?" she was demanding. "I don't know what to do!"

"I don't think I believe that, Alice," he said, really laughing now, but nicely.

In a normal voice, she said, "Philip, we have to have a guarantor. You are the only one, don't you see?"

He held his own, this Petrouchka, this elf, with, "Alice, no. For one thing, that address on the letterhead is the place I was in before Felicity—it's been pulled down, demolished. It isn't even there."

Now they stared at each other with identical appalled expressions, as if the floorboards were giving way; for both had been possessed, at the same moment, by a vision of impermanence: houses, buildings, streets, whole areas of streets, blown away, going, gone, an illusion. They sighed together, and, on an impulse, embraced gently, comforting each other.

"The thing is," said Alice, "she doesn't want to disconnect. She wants to help; she just needs an excuse, that's all. . . . Wait—wait a minute, I think I've got it. . . ."

"I thought you would," he said, and she nodded and said excitedly, "Yes. It's my brother. I'll tell Electricity he will guarantee, but that he's away on a business trip in . . . Bahrein, it doesn't matter where. She'll hold it over, I know she will. . . ."

And, making the thumbs-up sign, she ran out, laughing and exultant.

Too late to ring Mrs. Whitfield now, but she would tomorrow, and it would be all right.

No need to tell Mary and Reggie anything about it. Of course, if Mary was any good, she would be prepared to guarantee the account; she was the only one among them in work. But she wouldn't, Alice knew that.

She needed sleep. She was shaky and trembling inside, where her anger lived.

It was getting dark when Alice woke. She heard Bert's laugh, a deep "ho ho ho" from the kitchen. That's not his own laugh, Alice thought. I wonder what that would be like? "Tee hee hee," more likely. No, he made that laugh up for himself. Reliable and comfortable. Manly. Voices and laughs, we make them up. . . . Roberta's made-up voice, comfortable. And that was Pat's quick light voice and her laugh. Her own laugh? Perhaps. So they were both back, and that meant that Jasper was, too. Alice was out of her sleeping bag and tugging on a sweater, a smile on her face that went with her feelings for Jasper: admiration and wistful love.

But Jasper was not in the kitchen with the other two, who were glowing, happy, fulfilled, and eating fish and chips.

"It's all right, Alice," said Pat, pulling out a chair for her. "They arrested him, but it's not serious. He'll be in court tomorrow morning at Enfield. Back here by lunchtime."

"Unless he's bound over?" asked Bert.

"He was bound over for two years in Leeds, but that ended last month."

"Last month?" said Pat. Her eyes met Bert's, found no reflection there of what she was thinking—probably against her will, Alice believed—and, so as not to meet Alice's, lowered themselves to the business of eating one golden crisp fatty chip after another. This was not the first time Alice had caught suggestions that Jasper liked being bound over—needed the edge it put on life. She said apologetically, "Well, he has had to be careful so long, watching every tiny little thing he does, I suppose. . . ." She was examining Bert, who, she knew, could tell her what she needed to know about the arrest. Jasper was arrested, but Bert not; that in itself . . .

Pat pushed over some chips, and Alice primly ate one or two, thinking about cholesterol.

"How many did they arrest?"

"Seven. Three we didn't know. But the others were John, Clarissa, and Charlie. And Jasper."

"None of the trade-union comrades?"

"No."

A silence.

Then Bert: "They have been fining people twenty-five pounds."

Alice said automatically, "Then probably Jasper will get fifty pounds."

"He thought twenty-five. I gave him twenty pounds so he'd have enough."

Alice, who had been about to get up, ready to leave, said quickly, "He doesn't want me down there? Why not? What did he say?"

Pat said, carefully, "He asked me to tell you not to come down."

"But I've always been there when he's been arrested. Always. I've been in court every time."

"That's what he said," said Bert. " 'Tell Alice not to bother.' "

Alice sat thinking so intently that the kitchen, Bert and Pat, even the house around her vanished. She was down at the scene of the pickets. The van loaded with newspapers appeared at the gates, its sinister shining look telling everyone to hate it; the pickets surged forward, shouting; and there was Jasper, as she had seen him so often, his pale face distorted with a look of abstracted and dedicated hate, his reddish crop of gleaming hair. He was always the first to be arrested, she thought proudly, he was so dedicated, so obviously—even to the police—self-sacrificing. Pure.

But there was something that didn't fit.

She said, "Did you decide not to get arrested for any reason, Bert?"

Because, if that had been so, one could have expected Jasper, too, to return home.

Bert said, "Jasper found someone down there, someone who might be very useful to us."

At once the scene fell into shape in Alice's mind. "Was he one of the three you didn't know?"

"That's it," said Bert. "That's it exactly." He yawned. He said, "I hate to have to ask, but could you let me have the twenty pounds? Jasper said I should ask you."

Alice counted out the money. She did not let her gaze rise from this task.

Pat said nicely, "That little bundle won't last long at this rate."

"No."

Alice was praying: Let Bert go. Let him go upstairs. I want to talk to Pat. She was thinking this so hard that she was not surprised when he stood up and said, "I'm going to drop around to Felicity and get myself a real bath."

"I'll come in a minute," said Pat.

Bert went, and the two women sat on.

Alice asked, "What is the name of that man next door?"

"Lenin?" said Pat. Alice gratefully laughed with her, feeling privileged and special in this intimacy with Pat that admitted her into important conspiracy. Pat went on, "He says his name is Andrew."

"Where would you say he was from?"

"Good question."

"Ever such an American accent," said Alice.

"The New World language."

"Yes."

They exchanged looks.

Having said all they needed to on this subject, they left it, and Alice said after a pause, "I went round this afternoon. To ask them to do something about that mess."

"Good idea."

"What's in all those packages?"

"Leaflets. Books. So it is said."

"But with the police around all the time?"

"The packages weren't there the day before yesterday. And I bet they'll be gone by tomorrow. Or are gone already."

"Did you actually see the leaflets?"

"No, but I asked. That's what he said—Andrew. Propaganda material."

Again a subject was left behind, by unspoken consent.

Pat said, "I gather Bert thinks this comrade—the one Jasper was talking to at Melstead—may have some useful leads."

"You mean, for the IRA?"

"Yes, I think so."

"Did you hear anything of what they said?"

"No. But Bert was there part of the time."

At this Alice could have asked, What does Bert think of him? But she did not care what Bert thought. Pat's assessment, yes.

"What did he look like? Perhaps I know him," she asked. "He wasn't one of the usual crowd?"

"I've never seen him before, I am sure. Nothing special to report."

"Did . . . Comrade Andrew tell you to go down to the pickets? Did he say anything about Melstead to you? How many times have you been next door?"

Pat smiled and replied, though she indicated by her manner that there was no reason why she should, "I have been next door twice. Bert and Jasper have been over much more often. As for Melstead, I get the impression that Comrade Andrew"—and she slightly emphasised the "Comrade," as if Alice would do well to think about it—"that Comrade Andrew is not all that keen on cadres from outside joining the pickets."

Alice said hotly, "Yes, but it is our struggle, too. It is a struggle for all the progressive forces in the country. Melstead is a focal point for imperialist fascism, and it is not just the business of the Melstead trade unionists."

"You asked," said Pat. And then, "In my view, Comrade Andrew has bigger fish to fry." A thrill went through Alice, as when someone who has been talking for a lifetime about unicorns suddenly glimpses one. She looked with tentative excitement at Pat, who, it seemed, did not know what she had said. If she had not been implying that they, the comrades at number 43 Old Mill Road, had unwittingly come closer to great events, then what had she meant? But Pat was getting up. Terminating the discussion. Alice wanted her to stay. She could not believe that Pat was ready to go off now, at this thrilling moment when fabulous events seemed imminent. But Pat was stretching her arms about and yawning. Her smile was luxurious, and as her eyes did briefly meet Alice's, she seemed actually to be tantalising and teasing. She's so sensual, Alice thought indignantly.

But she said, "I asked . . . Comrade Andrew if we can use a room in that house for meetings. I mean, meetings of the inner group."

"So did we. He said yes."

Pat smiled, lowered her arms, and then stood looking at Alice, without smiling, saying with her body that she had had enough of Alice and wanted to go. "Where are our new comrades?" She was on her way to the door.

"They are upstairs."

"I doubt whether we shall see much of them. Still, they are all right." She yawned, elaborately, and said, "Too much effort to go chasing out for a bath. Bert can put up with me as I am."

She went, and Alice sat still until she had heard her go up the stairs and close her door.

Then Alice swiftly went out of the house. It was too early for what she was going to do. The street, though dark, had the feeling of the end of the day, with cars turning in to park, others leaving for the evening's entertainments, a restlessness of lights. But the traffic was pounding up the main road with the intensity of day-time. She dawdled along to look into the garden of 45. It seemed to her that a start had been made on the rubbish; yes, it had, and some filled sacks stood by the hedge, the plastic gleaming blackly. She saw two figures bending over a patch towards the back; not far from the pit she and Pat and Jim had dug, though a big hedge stood between. Were they digging a pit, too? It was very dark back there. Lights from Joan Robbins's top windows illuminated the higher levels of number 45, but did not reach the thicket of the overgrown garden. Alice loitered around for a while, and no one came in or out; she could not see Comrade Andrew through the downstairs windows, for the curtains were drawn.

She went to the Underground, sat on the train planning what she was going to do, and walked up the big rich tree-lined road where Theresa and Anthony had their home. She stood on the pavement looking up at the windows of their kitchen on the third floor. She imagined that they were sitting there on opposite sides of the little table they used when they were alone. Delicious food. Her mouth was actually watering as she thought of Theresa's cooking. If she rang the bell, she would hear Theresa's voice: Darling Alice, is that you? Do come in. She would go up, join them in their long comfortable evening, their food. Her mother might even drop in. But at this thought rage grasped her and shook her with red-hot hands, so that her eyes went dark and she found herself walking fast up the road, and then along another, and another, walking as though she would explode if she stopped. She walked for a long time, while the feeling of the streets changed to night. She directed herself to her father's street. She walked along it casually. The lights were on downstairs; every window spilled out light. Upstairs was a low glow from the room where the babies slept. Too early. She walked some more, around and back, past Theresa and Anthony, where kitchen windows were now dark, up to the top of the hill, down and around and into her father's street. Now the lights were dark downstairs, but on in the bedroom. An hour or so ago, she had seen a stone of the right size and shape lying on the edge of a garden, and had put it into her pocket. She looked up and down the quiet street, where the lights made golden leafy spaces in the trees. A couple, arm in arm, came slowly up from the direction of the Underground. Old. An old couple. They were absorbed in the effort of walking, did not see Alice. Who went to the end of the street, nevertheless, and came back briskly on the impetus of her need, her decision. There was now not a soul in the street. As she reached her father's house, she walked straight in at the gate, which she hardly bothered to open quietly, and flung the stone as hard as she could at the glass of the bedroom window. This movement, the single hard clear line of the throw, with her whole body behind it; and then the complete turn in the swing of the throw, and her bound out to the pavement—the speed and force of it, the skill, could never have been deduced from how Alice was, at any other time of the day or night, good girl Alice, her mother's daughter. . . . She heard the shattering glass, a scream, her father's shout. But she was gone; she had run down in the thick tree shadows to a side street, was down that and in the busy main street within sixty seconds after she had thrown the stone. She was breathing too hard, too noisily. . . . She stood looking into a window to slow her breath. She realised it was crammed full of television sets, and sedately moved to the next, to examine dresses, until she could walk into the supermarket without anyone's remarking her breathing. There she stayed a good twenty minutes, choosing and rejecting. She took the loaded wire basket to the outlet, paid, filled her carrier bags, and went homewards by Underground. Since the stone had left her hand, she had scarcely thought about what might be happening in her father's house.

Now, seeing the sober blue gleam from the police station, she went in. At the reception desk, no one, but she could hear voices from a part of the room that was out of sight. She rang. No one came. She rang again, peremptorily. A young policewoman came out, took a good look at her, decided to be annoyed, and went back. Alice rang again. Now the young woman, as tidy and trim in her dark uniform as Alice in hers—jeans and bomber jacket—came slowly towards her, an annoyed, decided little face showing that words were being chosen to put Alice in her place.

Alice said, "It might have been an emergency, how were you to know? As it happens, it isn't. So you are lucky."

The policewoman's face suddenly suffused with scarlet, she gasped, her eyes widened.

Alice said, "I have come to report on an agreed squat—you know, short-term housing—surely you know . . ."

"At this time of night?" the policewoman said smartly, in an attempt to regain mastery.

"It can't be much more than eleven?" said Alice. "I didn't know you had a set time for dealing with housing."

The policewoman said, "Since you're here, let's do it. What do you want to report?"

Alice spelled it out: "You people were around—a raid, three nights ago. You had not understood that it was an agreed tenancy—with the Council. I explained the situation. Now I've come to confirm it. It was agreed at the regular meeting of the Council, today."

"What's the address."

"Number forty-three Old Mill Road."

A little flicker of something showed on the policewoman's face. "Wait a minute," she said and disappeared. Alice listened to voices, male and female.

The policewoman came back, with a man; Alice recognised him as one of those from the other night. She was disappointed it was not the one who had kicked in the door.

"Ah, good evening," she addressed him kindly. "You remember, you were in forty-three Old Mill Road, the other night."

"Yes, I remember," he said. Over his face quivered shades of the sniggers he had just been enjoying with his kind. "You were the people who had buried . . . who dug a pit. . . ."

"Yes. We buried the faeces that the previous people had left upstairs. In buckets."

She studied the disgusted, prim, angry faces opposite her. Male and female. Two of a kind.

She said, "I really cannot imagine why you should react like this. People have been burying their excrement in pits for thousands of years. They do now, over most of the world. . . ." As this did not seem adequately to reach them, "In this country, we have only generally had waterborne sewage for a hundred years or so. Much less in some areas."

"Yes, well, we have it *now*," said the policewoman smartly.

"That's right," said the policeman.

"It seems to me we did the responsible and the hygienic thing. Nature will take care of it soon enough."

"Well, don't do it again," said the policeman.

"We won't have any need to, will we?" said Alice sweetly. "What I came to say was, if you check with the Council, you will have confirmation: number forty-three is now an agreed squat. An agreed short-term tenancy."

The policewoman reached for a form. Her colleague went back to join his mates. Soon there was a burst of loud scandalised laughter. Then another. The policewoman, diligently filling in her form, tightened her lips; Alice could not make out whether in criticism or not.

"Small things amuse small minds," said Alice.

The policewoman shot her a look that said it was not for her to say so, even if she, herself, had been thinking it.

Alice smiled at her, woman to woman. "And so," she said, "that's it. Number forty-three is now legal, and in order. Any more raids and you'll be stepping well over the line."

"That's for us to say, I think," said the policewoman, with a tight little smile.

"No," said Alice. "As it happens, no. I think not. There will certainly be no further complaints from the neighbours."

"Well, we'll have to hope not," and the policewoman retreated to join her own in the back room.

Alice, satisfied, went out, and home, directing herself to pass 45. No one in the garden now. But in the deep shade in the angle of the two hedges she could just make out that a pit had been dug. She could not resist. For the second time that night, she slid silently in at a garden gate. Forty-five looked deserted; all the windows were dark. The pit was about four feet deep. There was a strong sweet earthy smell from the slopes of soil around its edges. The bottom looked very flat—water? She bent to make sure. A case, or carton, something like that, had been placed at the bottom. She swiftly straightened, looked around. Consciously enjoying her condition, the sense of danger, of threat, she thought: They will be watching from those curtains or upstairs—I would be, in their position. What a risky thing to do, though; she turned to examine the strategy of the operation. No, perhaps it was all right. Whereas the digging of their own pit on the other side of the fence could have been observed by the occupants of three houses and by anyone about in Joan Robbins's house, here two sides were tall fence and hedge, the third the house. Between here and the gate were shrubs and bushes. Joan Robbins's upper windows were dark. Over the road, set back in its own garden, a house; and certainly anyone could see what they liked from the upstairs windows. Which were still dark; the people had not yet gone upstairs to bed. She had seen what she needed to see. She would have liked to stay, the sweet earthy smells and the impetus of risk firing her blood, but she moved, swift as a shadow, to the front door and knocked, gently. It was opened at once. By Andrew.

"I knew you must be watching," she said. "But I've come to say that I told the police station forty-three is an agreed squat. So they will be quite prepared to accept it when you say you are."

Her pulse was beating, her heart racing, every cell dancing and alert. She was smiling, she knew; oh, this was the opposite of "her look," when she felt like this, as if she'd drunk an extra-fine distilled essence of danger, and could have stepped out among the stars or run thirty miles.

She saw the short, powerful figure come out of the dark of the hall, to where she could see his face in the light from the street lamps. It was serious, set in purpose, and the sight of it gave her an agreeable feeling of submission to higher powers.

"I've buried something—an emergency," he said. "It will be gone in a day or two. You understand."

"Perfectly," smiled Alice.

He hesitated. Came out farther. She felt powerful hands on her upper arms. Did she smell spirits? Vodka? Whisky.

"I am asking you to keep it to yourself."

She nodded. "Of course."

"I mean, no one else." She nodded, thinking that if only one person was to know in 43, nevertheless in this house surely several must?

He said, "I am going to trust you completely, Alice." He allowed her his brief tight smile. "Because I have to. No one in this house knows but myself. They have all gone out. I took the opportunity to . . . make use of a very convenient cache. A temporary cache. I was going to fill in another layer of earth, and then put in some rubbish."

Alice stood smiling, disappointed in him, if not in her own state; she was still floating. She thought that what he had said was likely to be either partly or totally untrue, but it was not her concern. He still gripped her by her upper arms, which, however, were on the point of rejecting this persistent, warning, masculine pressure. He seemed to sense this, for his hands dropped.

"I have to say that I have a different opinion of you than of some of the others from your house. I trust you."

Alice did not say anything. She simply nodded.

He went indoors, nodding at her, but did not smile.

She was going to have to think it out. Better, sleep on it.

Her elation was going, fast. She thought, "But tomorrow Jasper and I are going out together, and then . . ." It would be a whole evening of this fine racing thrilling excitement.

But poor Jasper, no, he would not feel like it, probably, if he had spent the night in the cells. What was Enfield Police Station like? She could not remember any reports of it.

From the main road, she saw outside number 43's gate a slight drooping figure. An odd posture, bent over—it was the girl of this afternoon, and she was going to throw something at the windows of the living room. A stone! Alice thought: Throwing underhand, pathetic; and this scorn refuelled her. Alive and sparkling, she arrived by the girl, who turned pathetically to face her, with an "Oh."

"Better drop that," advised Alice, and the girl did so.

In this light she had a washed-out look: colourless hair and face, even lips and eyes. Whose pupils were enormous, Alice could see.

"Where's your baby?" hectored Alice.

"My husband is there. He's *drunk*," she said, and wailed, then stopped herself. She was trembling.

Alice said, "Why don't you go to the short-term-housing people? You know, there are people who advise on squats."

"I did." She began weeping, a helpless, fast, hiccupping weeping, like a child who has already wept for hours.

"Look," said Alice, feeling in herself the beginnings of an all-too-familiar weight and drag. "You have to do something for yourself, you know. It's no good just waiting for people to do something for you. You must find a squat for yourself. Move in. Take it over. Then go to the Council. . . . Stop it," she raged, as the girl sobbed on.

The girl subdued her weeping and stood, head bent, before Alice, waiting for her verdict, or sentence.

Oh, God, thought Alice. What's the use? I know this one inside out! She's just like Sarah, in Liverpool, and that poor soul Mabel. An official has just to take one look, and know she'll give in at once.

An official . . . Why, there was an official here, in this house; there was Mary Williams. Alice stood marvelling at this thought: that only a couple of days ago Mary Williams had seemed to hold her own fate—Alice's—in her hands; and now Alice had difficulty in even remembering her status. She felt for Mary, in fact, the fine contempt due to someone or to an institution that has given way too easily. But Mary could be appealed to on behalf of this . . . child. Alice again took in the collapsed look of her, the passivity, and thought: What is the use, she's one of those who . . .

It was exasperation that was fuelling her now.

"What is your name?"

The drooping head came up, the drowned eyes presented themselves, shocked, to Alice. "What do you think I'm going to do?" demanded Alice. "Go to the police and tell them you were going to throw a stone through our window?" And suddenly she began to laugh, while the girl watched her, amazed; and took an involuntary step back from this lunatic. "I've just thought of something. I know someone in the Council who might perhaps—it is only a perhaps . . ." The girl had come to life, was leaning forward, her trembling hand tight on Alice's forearm.

"My name is Monica," she breathed.

"Monica isn't enough," said Alice, stopping herself from simply walking away out of impatience. "I have to know your full name, and your address, don't I?"

The girl dropped her hand and began a dreary groping in her skirts. From a pocket she produced a purse, into which she peered.

"Oh, never mind," said Alice. "Tell me, I'll remember."

The girl said she was Monica Winters, and the hotel—which Alice knew about, all right—was the such-and-such, and her number, 556. This figure brought with it an image of concentrated misery, hundreds of couples with small children, each family in one room, no proper amenities, the squalor of it all. All elation, excitement gone, Alice soberly stood there, appalled.

"I'll ask this person to write to you," said Alice. "Meanwhile, if I were you, I'd walk around and have a look at what empty houses you can see. Take a look at them. You know. Nip inside, have a look at the amenities—plumbing and . . ." She trailed off dismally, knowing that Monica was not capable of flinging up a window in an empty house and climbing in to have a look, and that, very likely, her husband was the same.

"See you," said Alice, and turned away from the girl and went in, feeling that the 556—at least—young couples with their spotty, frustrated infants had been presented to her by Fate, as her responsibility.

"Oh, God," she was muttering, as she made herself tea in the empty kitchen. "Oh, God, what shall I do?" She could easily have wept as messily and uselessly as Monica. Jasper was not here!

She toiled up the stairs and saw that a light showed on the landing above. She went up. Under the door of the room taken by Mary and Reggie a light showed. She forgot it was midnight and this was a respectable couple. She knocked. After stirrings and voices came "Come in."

Alice looked in at a scene of comfort. Furniture, pretty curtains, and a large double bed in which Mary and Reggie lay side by side, reading. They looked at her over their books with identical wary expressions that said, "Thus far and no further!" A wave of incredulous laughter threatened Alice. She beat it down, while she thought, These two, we'll see nothing of them, they'll be off. . . .

She said, "Mary, a girl has just turned up here, she's desperate; she's in Shaftwood Hotel, you know. . . ."

"Not in our borough," said Mary instantly.

"No, but she's . . ."

"I know about Shaftwood," said Mary.

Reggie was examining his hand, back and front, apparently with interest. Alice knew that it was the situation he was examining; he was not used to this informality, to group living, but he was giving it his consideration.

"Don't we all? But this girl—her name is Monica—she looks to me as if she's suicidal, she could do anything."

Mary said, after a pause, "Alice, I'll see what there is tomorrow, but you know that there are hundreds, thousands of them."

"Oh yes, I know," said Alice, added, "Good night," and went downstairs thinking, I am being silly. It isn't as if I don't know the type. If you did find her a place, she'd muck it all up somehow. Remember Sarah? I had to find her a flat, move her in, go to the Electricity Board, and then her husband. . . . Monica's one of those who need a mother, someone who takes her on. . . . An idea came into Alice's head of such beauty and apt simplicity that she began laughing quietly to herself.

Now she was in their bedroom, Jasper's and hers. Alone. His sleeping bag was a dull blue tangle, and she straightened it. She thought: It has been lovely, sharing a room with Jasper. Then she thought: But he's only here because Bert is just through that wall there. She listened: silence. Pat and Bert were asleep. This thought, of why Jasper consented to let her sleep here, instead of going up to another room or asking her to go, made her mind swirl, as if it— her mind—were nauseated. She sat down on her sleeping bag, stripped off her sweater, her jeans, pulled on an old-fashioned nightdress in scarlet Viyella that had been her mother's. She felt comfortable and comforted in it.

Again she began to laugh: her mother liked looking after people!

She was inside the sleeping bag. Lights from the traffic fled across the ceiling. She thought with envy of Jasper in his cell. He would be with this mysterious new contact of his. . . . Well, she would hear about it all tomorrow. He would be here by lunchtime.

Alice slept late. When she went down to the kitchen, eight mugs on the draining board said that someone had washed up; she was the last. On the table a note addressed to her: "We're off for the weekend. Back Sunday night. Jasper knows." Pat had signed, "Pat and Bert."

Philip was working on the electrical wiring of the top floor with the easy-paced, contemplative manner of a workman. Alice, helpfully squatting by him, thought: This one would never make a boss; he's an employee; he can't work without somebody holding his hand. Philip was being obliging, feeling that yesterday he had not been. He talked of all that remained to be done, of how he would do it all, bit by bit; said that first of all the attic should be examined, for so much rain soaking in must have affected the beams. Alice said she would go up there with him, but first of all she must quickly ring Electricity. And where was Jim? He could help in the attics. Alice was thinking: Jim's so big and strong, Philip isn't; together they'd need half the time. But Philip said he had asked Jim, only that morning. Jim was a moody sort of individual, wasn't he? He hadn't liked being asked. In Philip's opinion there was more to Jim than met the eye. Here Alice and Philip exchanged, with their eyes, feelings about Jim; exactly as people looked, but did not speak, apprehensions over Faye—as if something there was too dangerous for words, or at least volatile, to be set off like a risky electronic device by an injudicious combination of sounds.

"Perhaps I'll have a chat with him," said Alice vaguely, and went downstairs to survey her territory before going to the telephone.

Mary, of course, was at work. Reggie? As she wondered, in he came with more cartons of gear. He looked exultant, as befits a man who has conquered territory, but abashed, too, because of all these evidences of concern for the material. He would have preferred, in short, not to have run into Alice. But now said that although he and Mary were already filling a second room with their bits of furniture and stuff, of course they would move it all out at once if that room were needed by anyone to live in.

"There's the attic," said Alice. "Or there will be. It has to be cleared out." She waited for him to offer to help clear it, but that did not occur to him. He went off at once to fetch another load.

Alice thought she would get the business of ringing Electricity over with. She resented having to run out to the telephone, in the middle of this useful busyness, wasting time over something that was just a routine.

But as soon as she heard Mrs. Whitfield's voice she knew she must pay out more of her time and attention to the situation than she thought. Mrs. Whitfield was, if not hostile, stiff with reproach. She said that in her opinion it would be desirable if Alice came in, as soon as possible. Alice said she would come now, it was only just down the road, in a bright chatty voice that insisted there was no real problem, nothing wrong. And put down the receiver gently, in a way that went with the voice. But she was being attacked by one of her rages. Her father! What had he said? It must have been pretty bad for Mrs. Whitfield to change like this.

She was too angry to run down at once to Electricity, had to calm herself by walking briskly around the streets, postponing thoughts about her father till later. But she would show him, he needn't think she wouldn't.

In the anteroom at Electricity she smiled and waved to Mrs. Whitfield: Here I am, a good girl! But Mrs. Whitfield looked away. Four people went in before Alice. What a waste of time.

She sat in front of the official, in the large light office, and knew that Mrs. Whitfield would not cut off the electricity. At least, she did not want to. It was up to Alice. Who began talking about her father. He was rich, he owned a printing firm. Of course he could easily pay the bills if there was need. But he was, Alice admitted, in a bad phase at the moment.

"He's had a lot of trouble," breathed Alice, on her face the look of one who compassionately contemplates human misery, absolving it from blame. And at that moment, it was what she felt. "The breakup with my mother . . . then all kinds of problems . . . his new wife, she's nice, she's a good friend of mine, but she's not a coper, you know what I mean? He's got a lot on his back." She burbled on like this, feeling dismally she was not helping herself, while Mrs. Whitfield sat, eyes lowered, pricking out a pattern with the tip of her ballpoint on the top left-hand corner of Alice's form.

"Your father," she remarked at last, "was quite definite about not being prepared to guarantee payment."

She did not want to look at Alice. Alice was trying to make her raise her eyes, *take her in*. What could Cedric Mellings have said?

She said, "There are ten of us in the house now. That's a lot of money coming in every week."

"Yes, but is some of it going to come this way?" Mrs. Whit-field was too dry to relent, yet. "Aren't any of you in work?"

"One is." She added, on an inspiration, "But she is a Council employee. She works in Belstrode Road, and she doesn't want to give her address as a squat. She couldn't find a place; she was desperate."

Mrs. Whitfield sighed, said, "Yes, I know how bad things can be." But now she raised her eyes and did look differently at Alice, the housemate of a Council official who worked at the main office for this area. She said, "Well, what are we going to do?"

That was it, she had won! Alice could hardly prevent herself from openly exulting.

She said humbly, "I have a brother. He works for Ace Airways. I'll ask him." Mrs. Whitfield nodded, accepting the brother. "But he's in Bahrein at the moment."

Mrs. Whitfield sighed. Not from irritation, but because she

knew it was a lie, and felt sorrowful because of Alice. She had lowered her eyes again. A second tricky little pattern was appearing beside the first on Alice's form.

She enquired mildly, "And your brother would be prepared to guarantee the electricity bills for ten people?"

Alice said, "But he would know he wouldn't have to pay them, wouldn't he?" She hurried on, in case Mrs. Whitfield felt obliged actually to answer the question: "But I am sure he'll say yes."

"When is he coming back from Bahrein?"

"In about a month. But I'll go up and see him about it, talk to him and explain. That's where I went wrong with my father. I should have gone over and explained, instead of just assuming . . ." Her voice trembled. It sounded pathetic, but hot red waves of murder beat inside her. I'll blow that house of theirs up, she was thinking, I'll kill them.

"Yes, I do think that would be a good idea," said Mrs. Whitfield.

A long pause. Not because she was undecided: the decision had been made. She wanted Alice to say something more that would make the situation better, or seem better. But Alice only sat and waited.

"Well," said Mrs. Whitfield at last, sitting upright inside the corset of her strong, short-sleeved brown dress, with her fat arms and fat brown forearms, fat hands with the little rings twinkling on them, all disposed regularly about her, her feet—no doubt, though Alice could not see them—placed side by side. "Well, I'll give you five weeks. That should be plenty of time to see your brother." She was not looking at Alice. "And I'll need more in the way of a deposit."

Alice took out a ten-pound note—not enough, she knew—and placed it in front of Mrs. Whitfield, who took it up, smoothed it flat, placed it in an old-fashioned cashbox in a drawer, wrote out a receipt. Then she said, "I'll see you in five weeks," and sighed again. "Good-bye," said the kindly, decent woman, her distress at the ways of this wicked world written all over her. Almost certainly in her eyes, too, but she was not looking, would not look, at Alice; only said, "Ask the next one to come in."

Alice said, nonchalantly, so as not to make too much of it, though she was soft with gratitude and relief, "Thanks. 'Bye, then," and went out. Five weeks was a lifetime, anything could have—would have—happened. But she was on a winning streak, a lucky wave; she would nip down to the Gas Board and fix things up.

There, she said number 43 Old Mill Road was an agreed tenancy, Mary Williams of Belstrode Road would confirm; electricity was being supplied, Mrs. Whitfield of the Electricity Board would confirm; and her brother, now in Bahrein, would guarantee payments. She had waited until this sympathetic-looking man, elderly, fatherly, was free, and now she pleaded, "Can we have the gas on now, please, it is so cold . . . no hot water . . . it's awful. . . ." His concerned, shocked face! This man could not easily imagine life without hot water, at least not for people like himself and Alice.

A deposit?

She laid down twenty pounds and fixed on him girlish, friendly eyes.

He took up the money. Accepted. But he was unhappy about the situation. Like Mrs. Whitfield at the first interview, he was not sure why he was being compelled by Alice.

"We do have to have a guarantor," he remarked, as much to himself, and said, "Very well, you said your brother would be back in a month? Good."

It was done. Alice went off, demurely grateful.

She was going to have to get some money. Had to. *Where?*

Sobered, she went back home, told Philip that the gas would be on. If they could lay hands on a second-hand boiler, did he know enough to fix it?

They squatted opposite each other on the top floor, on the landing, in the bright April light, which came, slightly dimmed by dirt, through the window on the stairs. He was smiling, pleased with her, with this house, with his place in it; ready to go on working. But, she knew, sorrow and resentment were there, only just subdued; and soon she must find more money for him. For the boiler. For new floorboards in the hall, in a corner where water had dripped from a leaky pipe. For . . . for . . . for . . .

She said, "Philip, I know that if you had taken on this job on a business basis you would have had to charge hundreds. Well, don't worry . . . but wait a bit. I'll have it."

He nodded, he smiled, he went on with his work, sitting in a tangle of new black cable like some kind of leprechaun among urban roots. Frail—you could blow him away, thought Alice, her heart aching for him.

And where was Jasper? He had not been in court that morning after all? Or he had been, had been silly, was bound over again?

Worry, worry, worry; she felt bruised with it.

She sat in a heap at the kitchen table. She thought, looking at the pleasant room: I'm taking it for granted already!

Forcing herself, she worked for an hour or two on the great heap of stuff purloined from the skips that lay in a corner of the hall; fitting a curtain here, laying a rug there. Everything needed a good scrub! Well, she would take down all these curtains when there was time and get them to the laundrette, but meanwhile . . . She found a nice solid little stool, thrown away only because a leg was loose. She glued it back in, put the stool in the corner of the kitchen, went out into the garden to the forsythia bush, cut some branches. The old woman was asleep in her chair under the tree. Joan Robbins was only a yard away through the fence. She was glad to see Alice, began talking in a heavy tired voice about how the old woman had her running up and down the stairs, even got her up in the middle of the night. What was she to do? She was sick and tired of it.

Alice, familiar with this situation from somewhere in her well-stocked past, knew there was little that could be done; in fact, it would get worse. She asked whether Mrs. Robbins knew about the services available for the old. Yes, but she didn't like the idea of all these people in and out all day; who were they? She'd have no check on them.

She went on and on, digging viciously into the soil of her border. For years the house had been civilised and orderly; she and her husband downstairs, with the garden; Mrs. Jackson, a widow, keeping herself to herself in the flat above. But now she might just as well be living with Mrs. Jackson! You'd think she was her daughter! The old woman certainly seemed to think so.

Alice, with all the time in the world and nothing better to do, stood with the branches of forsythia blazing yellow in her arms, listening and advising. Surely it would be better to have Home Helps, Meals on Wheels, all that, and a social worker to advise and take on responsibility, than have to do it all yourself?

Joan Robbins agreed that perhaps it might, she would think. . . . With a smile at Alice of real gratitude, neighbourliness, she said that she was glad Alice was there, glad that decent people were in poor Number 43 at last.

Alice went in, stacked the forsythia in a jug on the stool in the corner of the kitchen, sat down.

Where was Jasper?

This was the night they were going spray-painting. She had the paint—two cans, in scarlet and black—ready in the corner of the hall.

At the kitchen table, she pencilled slogans on an envelope.

What was the message they wanted to convey? The full message, exact—that was where she must start.

The Use of Supergrasses Unmasks the True Nature of British Democracy. One Law for England, Another for Northern Ireland, England's Colony.

That was it. Possibly they'd find a good space, like a bridge, or a long low wall, to get all that in.

She must work out something shorter.

Supergrasses Threaten Democracy!

No, too abstract.

Supergrasses—Unfair!

Supergrasses a Shameful Blot on Britain!

Supergrasses—Shame on Us!

She sat still, with the blaze of the forsythia in her eyes. She shut her eyes, and the yellow blurred and danced on black. She was smiling, remembering the last time she and Jasper had gone out together. Only two weeks ago. In scarlet and black they had written "Support the Women of Greenham Common" on the dull grey-green paint of a bridge two hundred yards from a police station. She had sprayed; Jasper kept watch, from the other side of the station. She had finished when she heard his signal, a yell he had perfected to sound like a car hooting. She had thrust the spray paint in her carrier bag. Not looking back, she strolled along the pavement, thinking that Jasper was sauntering past the police station. Between him and her, probably two policemen. But the footsteps that came up beside her were Jasper's—light and urgent. That meant the police had gone up the other way—but could see them by turning. Jasper and she stood looking into each other's faces, alive and tingling and delighted, knowing that anyone looking at them could guess, simply from the waves of energy that danced from them. Jasper's eyes said, Let's . . .

She raced back to the smooth green paint that was evenly lit by a street lamp ten yards away. The policeman and a woman sedately progressed away from them. Jasper waited where he was. She took out the red spray and, in letters a foot high, began "Greenham Common Women . . ."

She kept her attention half on what she did, half on Jasper, who suddenly raised his arms. Without looking round she sped toward him, hearing the heavy feet running behind her. Now she was spitting: Filthy beasts, fascists, pigs, pigs, pigs. . . . She had come up to Jasper, who caught her wrist in his bony grip, and they ran together up towards the Underground. But before they reached it, they turned into a side street and then, they hoped before the police reached that street, into another. They knew someone living in a house there. But their blood was racing, they were inspired, and she was not surprised that Jasper panted, "Let's chance it. . . ." They tore down that street and into a main road that was crowded with people—fish-and-chip shops, take-aways, a disco, a supermarket, still open. Again, they could have gone into the supermarket, but they thought the police had had a good look at them, so they sprinted through the crowds, who took as little notice as they expected, and across the street just after the lights had changed, so that the traffic, beginning to move, hooted.

Down they went into the Underground. They had not looked to see whether the police had come into the main road in time to see. Again, Jasper's eyes demanded they chance it; they walked smartly up out of the Underground on the other side, and saw two policemen—different ones—coming towards them. Cool and in-different, Alice and Jasper walked past. Then down again into the Underground. They went two stops, to where Alice had seen a long low bridge along a main road over railway lines. By then it was ten, and raining a little. Here the police station was a good way off. On the other hand, cars were passing regularly. On the bridge was already written, in white letters that had run and streaked, "Women Are Angry."

They stood arm in arm, backs to the traffic, as though looking over the railway lines, and Alice, holding the spray low down, wrote, "We Are All . . . ," which is as far as she could go without having to move. They moved on a few steps, again stood together, and wrote, "Angry. Angry About . . ." Another move. "Ireland. About Sexism. About . . ." They moved. Then they heard—their ears alert for the slightest changes in the grind of the traffic—a car slowing down just behind them. They both shot looks over their shoulders: not a police car. But two men sat side by side in the front seat, staring.

". . . Trident"—Alice finished. And they walked on, slowly, very close, knowing the car crawled behind. The intoxication of it, the elation: *pleasure*. There was nothing like it!

Now, remembering, Alice craved and longed. Oh, she did so hope that Jasper would not be late, would not be tired, would want to go out. He had *promised. . . .*

. . . They had walked, perhaps 150 yards. Luck! A one-way street! The car, of course, did not follow. At the end of that street, they went back to the bus stop and to Kilburn, where they had worked before.

"No to Cruise! No to Trident!"

No one had so much as noticed them there.

Let down, their elation leaking away, they had decided to give up, and taken a taxi back to Alice's mother's house, where Alice made them both coffee and scrambled eggs.

Now it was six-thirty.

Mary came in, sat briefly with Alice, said she and Reggie were going to the pictures. She had had a word about this girl, Monica;

there was really nothing, nothing at all. She had done her best, Alice must understand.

"Never mind," said Alice, "I've thought of something."

Mary saw the scribbled-over envelope, smiled, and said, "Reggie and I are going to the Greenpeace demo tomorrow."

"Good for you," said Alice.

"But it's shocking, it's terrible, the despoliation of our country-side. . . ."

"I know," said Alice. "I've been on some of their demos."

"You have!" Mary was relieved, Alice could see, that they shared this; but Reggie "hallo"ed from the hall, and, with a smile, Mary went.

Where were Roberta and Faye? Probably at their women's-commune place. Where Philip? He might have been thrown out by his girlfriend, but he was going round there still for meals and baths, so Bert had said. Jim? Now, that was a serious question, where was he? The smiling face, the jokey mellow voice—but what was going on, really?

Apart from having *his* home, *his* place taken over like this.

Worry, worry, Alice sat worrying.

In came Jasper, smiling, jaunty, stepping like a dancer, and at once he said, "Oh, lovely," at the forsythia. There: people said this and that about him, but no one knew how sensitive he was, how kind. Now he bent and kissed her cheek; it was a thin papery kiss, but she understood that; understood when—rarely—she simply had to put her arms around him out of an exuberance of love, the instinctive shrinking, as though she held a wraith, something cold and wailing, a lost child. And he would try to stand up to it, the sudden blast of her love; she could feel a brave little determination to withstand it, and even an intention to return it. Which, of course, he could not—not the physical thing; she knew that what she felt as a warmth of affection was experienced by him as a demand for *that*.

He stood near her, beaming, positively dancing, with the excess of his pride and pleasure.

"So it was all right."

"Thirty pounds."

"A lot, surely?"

"They knew me," he said with pride.

"How was the cell?"

"Oh, not bad. They fed us—not bad. But I was with Jack—though it's an alias, you understand!"

"Yes, of course," she beamed back. "What I don't know . . ."

". . . won't hurt you." He rubbed his hands, and began a light, smart quick-stepping about the kitchen: to the forsythia, which he touched delicately; to the window; and back to her. She put on the kettle, put coffee into a mug, and stood by the stove, so as to be standing, not sitting, while he moved so electrically and finely about.

"Bert doesn't know, either. Where is he? Bert?"

"But he told you, he's gone for the weekend with Pat."

"Oh yes . . . for the weekend—how long?" He was now standing still, threatened, frowning.

"Sunday night."

"Because we're going for a trip," he said. "He knew we were going, but not so soon. Jack says . . ."

"A fine Irish name," said Alice.

He chuckled, enjoying her teasing him. "Well, there are Jacks in Ireland." He went on, "And how did you know . . . But you always do, don't you," he said, with a flash of acid.

"But where else?" she wailed, humorously, as she always did when he was surprised by what to her was obvious. "You and Bert and Jack are going to Ireland, because Jack is IRA?"

"In touch. In contact. He can arrange a meeting."

"Well, then!" said Alice, handing him a mug of black coffee, and sat down again.

He stood silent, stilled a moment. Then he said, "Alice, I've got to have some money."

Alice thought: "Well, that's that"—meaning, the end of this delightful friendliness. She strengthened herself for a fight.

She said, "I gave Bert the money he gave you for your fine."

"I've got to have my fare to Dublin."

"But you can't have spent your dole money!"

He hesitated. He had? How? She could never understand what

he did with it, where it went—he had not had time for . . . that other life of his, he had been with Bert, with Jack!

"I said I'd pay Jack's fare—the fine cleaned him out."

"Was he fined thirty pounds, too?"

"No, fifteen."

"I have been spending and spending," said Alice. "No one chips in—only a bit here and there." She thought: At least Mary and Reggie will pull their weight, at least one can say that of their kind. . . . To the *exact* amount, no more, no less.

"You can't have spent all that," said Jasper. He looked as though she were deliberately punishing him. "I saw it. Hundreds."

"What do you suppose all this is costing."

Now—as she had expected—his hand closed around her wrist, tight and hurtful. He said, "While you play house and gardens, pouring money away on rubbish, the Cause has to suffer, do without."

His little blue eyes in the shallow depressions of very white, glistening flesh stared into hers, unblinking, as his grasp tightened. But long ago she had gained immunity from this particular accusation. Without resisting, leaving her wrist limp in his circle of bone, she looked hard back at him and said, "I see no reason why you should pay Comrade Jack's fare. Or expenses. If he hadn't met you, what would he have done for the fare?"

"But he's only going over for our sakes—so we can make contact."

She forced herself to fight him: "You picked up three weeks' money this week. You had a hundred and twenty pounds plus. *And* I paid your fine. You can't have spent more than at the most twenty pounds on train fares and snacks."

When she did this, let him know that she made this silent, skilled reckoning of what he spent, what he must be doing, he hated her totally, and showed it. He was white with his hatred. His thin pink lips, which normally she loved for their delicacy and sensitivity, were stretched in a colourless line, and between them showed sharp discoloured teeth. He looked like a rat, she thought steadily, knowing that her love for him was not by an atom diminished.

"Why don't you go and get some more from your fucking bloody mother, from *her*? Or from your father?"

She had not told him exactly where she had got all the money that had been spent so freely around this house, but of course he had guessed.

She said steadily, "I shall. When I feel I can. But I can't now."

He let go her wrist and stood up.

Now he is going to punish me, he's going to take his things into another room to sleep.

A long silence, while he fidgeted disconsolately about.

"Let's go out for a meal," he suggested, dolefully.

"Yes, let's." Her spirits swooped up again, although there had been no mention of spray-painting, and he had seen the scribbled slogans on the envelope on the table.

He said, nicely, "I am sorry about not going out painting tonight, Alice. But what's the sense? I don't want to draw attention to myself just before something important."

"Quite right, of course," she said. Thinking that in years of spray-painting, of darting about near the police and taunting them with their nearness, they had been caught only when they wanted to be. That was the truth of it.

Jasper wanted to talk about the two days down at Melstead, about the pickets, the excitement of it all, the arrest, the night in the cells—and about Jack. They went to an Indian restaurant, where he talked and talked, and she listened very carefully, matching what he said with her imaginings of it all. She paid for the meal. They went into a pub and he drank his usual white wine, and she, tomato juice.

Back at the house, she waited, tense, to see whether he would take his things up to another room, but he said nothing about it, only slid into his bag with a sigh that assuaged her; it was the sigh of a child finding a safe place.

He had not said anything more about money, but now he started again. That was why he had not taken his things out.

They argued, steadily, in the dark room, while the lights whirled over the ceiling. In the end she agreed to give him the money for "Jack's" fare. She knew that for some reason it was important for Jasper to have it from her. Essential. There always had been these moments between them when she had to give way, against reason, against sense: he simply had to win. She knew that he had a hundred pounds, probably more. Perhaps even very much more. Once he had told her, in a mood of taunting cruelty that sometimes overtook him, that he had been saving up quietly all these years, enough money "to be rid of you forever."

This did not make any sense that she could see when she *thought:* but she *felt* the power of it.

His mother—well, Alice wasn't going to get involved even with the thought of all that dreary psychology, but no wonder he had problems with women.

In the morning, after their breakfast coffee, he stood silently and balefully near her until she gave him the fare to Dublin. Then he said that he was going to meet Jack and talk things over. If he was not back tonight, he would be tomorrow, and she must tell Bert that they were going to Ireland on Tuesday, early.

He left. She thought: Is he going on one of his *things*, then— cottaging, cruising . . . ? She believed not. He wouldn't risk it, not with his whole soul set on the trip to Ireland. Was "Jack," then, like him? No, she was sure not. Talking about Jack, it was how he talked about Bert, how he talked about the men with whom he had this particular relationship: admiring, dependent, you could say passive . . . but who was it now who set the pace, making Bert go to Ireland, making Jack take them? No, not simple at all, this younger-brother thing.

She had the whole day. Alone, you could say.

Philip had climbed up into the attic—she must go up and help him, stand by him, or he would start feeling ill again. Jim— where was Jim, what was wrong? He had not been in since yesterday.

Faye and Roberta? She had heard them come in very late. Pat said they went to late-night movies, and then on to parties. Their other life—women. The close, sweet, bitchy—as far as Alice was concerned—cloying, claustrophobic world of women. Not for her! But they were welcome to it. Let a thousand flowers bloom, and all that. . . . Ten in the morning, and Mary and Reggie were still in bed. Mary had come down, made mugs of coffee, taken them up, and they lay, no doubt, side by side, in that amazing double bed, which had a proper headboard and little built-in side tables. Even the thought of that bed, the life that the bed implied, made Alice feel threatened. Stuck together for a lifetime in that bed, drinking cups of coffee, looking at people who were not like themselves in that cautious keep-off way.

Where was she going to get money. Where. She had to have it. Had to have money. Had to.

Sunday.

Good grief, it was only Sunday, six days after she and Jasper had left her mother's—had left home. She had achieved all that, in such a short time. Full of energy, she went up to the attic and to Philip, in his white overalls, a brave manikin moving about under the rafters of the attic. There was a horrible smell of rot.

"Two of these beams ought to be replaced," he said. "Dry rot. We'll have the whole house down."

Money. She had to have money.

Too early to ask Mary and Reggie. At some point a negotiation would take place. Already she could see their faces, the faces of the fucking bloody middle class, when the subject of money was on the agenda. God, how she hated them, the middle classes, penny-pinching, doling out their little bits, in their minds always the thought of saving and accumulating, *saving*—thought Alice, her mouth full of bile, as she stood gazing up at a beam a foot across that looked grey and flaky, with whitey-yellow fibres in it. The dry rot itself, which would lay its creeping arms over all the wood, if it were allowed, then creep down the walls, into the floor below, spread like a disease . . .

She thought: I've been living like this for years. How many? Is it twelve, now? No, fourteen—no, more . . . The work I've done for other people, getting things together, making things happen, sheltering the homeless, getting them fed—and as often as not paying for it. Suppose I had put aside a little, even a little, of that money, for myself, what would I have now? Even if it were only a few hundred pounds, five hundred, six, I wouldn't be standing here sick with worry. . . .

"How much will it cost to replace those two beams?"

"The wood, about fifty—second-hand. Though I could probably find what I need on a skip if we could borrow the car again.

"As for the labour . . ." he said with a defiant little laugh.

"Don't worry," said Alice. She was thinking: And he'll need help. He can't possibly shoulder great beams into place, stand about propping up beams; he'll need scaffolding or something. That means money.

She would go down and ask Mary and Reggie.

On the table a note, "We've gone to the Greenpeace demo. Love. Reggie and Mary." His writing. "Love"! She sat at the table and counted what she had left. She had thirty-five pounds.

She went up again and worked on with Philip, clearing rubbish out of the attics. Where did it all come from, always rubbish and rubbish, sacks of it again, old clothes, rags most of them, and an old carpet, quite fit for use, more old clothes. Junk. Junk? At the bottom of an old black tin trunk, under cracking and broken shoes, were layers of fine soft material, dresses wrapped in black tissue paper. Evening dresses. She threw them down through the trap door and jumped after them to look. Well, look at that! Three really beautiful evening dresses, each individually wrapped in the black tissue paper. The early thirties. One was of black and orange and yellow lace, with gold thread in it. It had a plain smooth bodice to the hips, then flared out in a lot of little points, like petals. The metallic smell of the gold lace made her want to sneeze.

Alice stood back away from the trap door up into the attic so that she was out of Philip's sight, and took off her sweat shirt. She slipped the bright dress on over her head. It would not go down past her hips, and stuck in a thick roll around her waist. There being no mirror in the house, she could not see what her arms and shoulders looked like, but she saw her sturdy freckled hands fidgeting at the roll of material, and felt that the dress was laying a claim on her, like an impostor demanding to be recognised. She stripped it off again angrily, and put back the sweat shirt, and with it a feeling of appropriateness and even virtue, as if she had been tempted briefly by the forbidden. She did not try on the apricot chiffon, with panels of silver beads back and front, some of them loosened, some vanished away as though a bead-eating insect had been at it. She held the sage-green lace with its swirling skirt up against her. It was tight above, with a pale-pink vee for modesty in the front, and the back cut down to the coccyx, with another little vee there. And afternoon dresses, the "New Look," quite glossy and good. Who had put them up there, unable to throw them away? Who had forgotten about them and gone off, leaving all those trunks up there? She showed the dresses to Philip, who laughed at them, but when she said she would get something for them, quite a lot, shrugged, unwillingly respectful.

She put them in a suitcase and took the bus to Bell Street, to a shop where her mother, being hard up, had sold some dresses. She had got over a hundred pounds.

Saturday. The markets were crammed. The woman in the shop that sold antique clothes was already busy with a customer who was after a white crêpe-de-chine 1920s dress that had gold sequins in thick crusty-looking roses all round the hips. She paid ninety pounds for it. And it had a stain on the shoulder, which she said she would hide with a gold rose.

Alice went forward with her suitcase, saw the woman's eyes narrow in greed as she took in what was there. Alice was determined to get every penny she could. She bargained closely over each garment, watching the woman's eyes, which gave her away. They were clever, narrow eyes, used to poring over small stitches, a tiny rent, the set of a panel of embroidery. When Alice took out the apricot chiffon with the silver beads, she even sighed, and her tongue, which was large and pale, slid over her lips.

For that Alice got sixty pounds, though the woman kept saying a skilled sempstress would have to replace the missing beads, and it would cost—Alice had no idea what it would cost. Alice smiled politely, nodded, and stood her ground.

She went home with £250, knowing that the woman would sell those clothes for four times as much. But she was satisfied.

She was not going to tell Jasper. This meant that loyalty forbade her to tell Philip—who wouldn't have believed her in any case. She told him she had got £150, gave him a hundred, and heard him sigh a little; such a different sigh from that sharp escape of breath of the woman in the shop. Like a child—like Jasper getting into his sleeping bag last night, coming home, to safety.

Well, that would keep things going, but not for long. Philip and she spent sixty pounds of it that afternoon on a second-hand gas boiler. And five pounds for its delivery. By the end of the week there would be hot water. Even heat, if those radiators that had not been stolen had not suffered by their neglect.

Not that Alice cared about warmth, not even after four years in her mother's warm house. She had become used to adapting to different temperatures. Before her mother's house she had gone through a winter in a squat that had no heating at all. She had simply worn a lot of clothes, and kept moving. Jasper had complained, had got chilblains, but even he had put up with it; yet that was one of the reasons he had been pleased to move in to live with her mother's warmth, after a cold winter.

She spent a long evening working with Philip, as his assistant, handing him tools, holding steady the beam of a powerful torch. She watched his deft slender hands bleached by the light, and knew that this one could have been, should be, some kind of fine and meticulous craftsman, should never have to be wrestling with pipes and floorboards that seemed heavier than he was. This, the waste of it, fuelled in her the indignation that kept her going, filled her mind with the thoughts that justified everything she did: one day, it would be impossible that fine people like Philip would be misused, kept down, insulted by circumstances; one day—and because of her, Alice, and her comrades—things would be different.

At midnight, she knew that Jasper would not be coming. Her heart began a small private wailing, which made her ashamed and which she suppressed. She cooked bacon and eggs for Philip, and when he had gone up to sleep, waited, not only for Jasper but for Jim, too. Trouble! She could feel it coming.

Mary and Reggie came in, smiling, and glowing with that special look of the successful demonstrator. Sitting with Alice, drinking coffee, they told her how hundreds had marched against the polluting of a certain stretch of shore. They left Alice with a little pile of pamphlets and leaflets, and, hearing that hot water would soon be among the amenities of this house, Reggie remarked that they must have a talk about finance. But tonight they were ready to drop, must sleep. They went up, very close. They were going to have sex, Alice knew. Well, she would stay down here a bit longer, then.

Mary and Reggie came back down, full of smiles, asking about the clothes, the junk that littered the landings of the top floor. Alice had forgotten she had meant to tidy up, said she would, tomorrow. More smiles, and again the two went upstairs.

And if I don't clear up? thought Alice. Of course they wouldn't! It didn't occur to them! *I* made the mess, and so *I* clear up. Oh yes, I know them, I know those two, I know the middle classes. . . . Fuck them all.

But as she sat on there, thinking of all that rubbish, which would have to be parcelled up, and carried down, and put in the garden, and then taken away by the dustmen, who would have to be paid, a new thought startled her mind. She had, on seeing those exquisite evening dresses, thrown them down through the hatch and scrambled after them. But she hadn't finished examining what was in the attics. There were other cases, trunks, roped bundles up there still. Why, there might be a lot more antique clothes, a lot more money.

She raced upstairs, forgetting all about Mary and Reggie in their room under part of the attic, and shot up the ladder, which was still in position, for Philip had not finished. She turned on his heavy-duty torch. In fact, most of the cases had been opened. But along the edge of the attic, under the low eaves, stood three old-fashioned trunks, of the kind people once took on cruises, "for use on the voyage." They were of some kind of fibre, painted glossy chestnut, now dimmed and dulled, with bands of wood to give them strength. She flung them open, one, two, three, her heart hammering. Inside the first, newspapers. Newspapers? She knelt by the trunk, flinging aside papers, reaching down and down, scrabbling in the corners. Yellow piles of papers, and that was all. Why? What for? What *lunatic* . . . The second had newspapers covering books. No special books, no treasures here, only the random collection of some family. Old, faded books. *The Talisman,* with its brown board cover eaten away. *Little Gems from the Bible.* Henty. *She Loved, and Lost . . . The Treasure of the Sierra Madre . . . Crocheting Made Simple.* A set of Dickens.

She might get a pound or two for that lot. But there was another case. She opened it prayerfully, saw it was empty except for half a dozen old jam jars rolling around.

A storm of rage shook her. She was on her feet, kicking the trunks, then flinging books, papers, jars, all around the attic, shouting abuse at the people who had left this garbage up here. "Filthy shits," she was yelling. "Fascist shits. I'll kill you, I'll pound . . . you . . . to pulp. . . ."

The storm went on, and she heard her name being called from below: "Alice, Alice, what's wrong?"

"Bloody filthy *accumulating* middle-class creeps"—and papers, jars, boots, rags went hurtling through the trap around Mary and Reggie.

"What is wrong, can we help?"

She saw the two agitated, concerned faces, responsible citizens, turned upwards, side by side, illuminated by her jerking, wavering torch, and suddenly she laughed. She stood above them and staggered about, laughing.

"Oh, Alice," cried Mary, "Oh, Alice," squealed Reggie, and they sounded admonishing, petulant, reproachful, and Alice fell, rolled to the trap-door edge, caught its edges with her strong hands, swung herself down, to land on her feet by Mary, by Reggie, laughing and pointing at them, "If you could see yourselves, if you could just see . . ."

And she staggered and hooted among the sordid piles, and kicked shoes and clothes around. Broken glass scattered.

Mary and Reggie looked at each other, at her, and went hastily into their bedroom. The sound of that door closing, polite and restrained despite everything, made Alice laugh again. She collapsed on the floor, among all the rubbish, laughed herself out to silence, and looked up into the trap, to see the torchlight shining there. It showed the slanting beams of the roof, it showed the two rotten beams, which even down here and in this light looked cheesy.

She climbed up again and, refusing to look at the dangerous beams, began soberly to close the trunks, tidy up a little. Was she really going to clear everything out of here? For what? For whom?

She put out the light, leaving it exactly where it had been, for Philip. She left the attic, by the ladder this time, and then kicked all the junk into a great heap along the banisters. She was making a frightful noise, but what of it. Do them good, she was thinking. One day Mary and Reggie will say, Yes, we did try living in a commune, we gave it a fair trial, but we are afraid . . .

She was shaking with laughter again. She went downstairs, yelling, sobbing with mirth. If mirth it was: she heard these sad wails and thought, I'm laughing out of the wrong side of my mouth. . . .

At three in the morning, she went forlornly to bed, promising herself to get at least one room painted tomorrow. This one, perhaps. She knew Jasper would be pleased, even if he did seem to jeer. With her mind on Jasper, what he was doing, with whom, she slept fitfully, rose many hours before anyone else was likely to, cleared the room of the little that was in it, fetched up Philip's trestles and the paints and rollers, rubbed over ceilings and walls with a duster tied around the head of a broom, swept off the floor the resulting films of dust. It was still only seven o'clock.

Sitting by herself in the kitchen with coffee, looking at the golden forsythia, she was aglow with health, energy, accomplishment. If Jasper had been here, she could not have done this, she would have had to adapt her pace to his. . . . Sometimes, very seldom, the thought came into her head: If I were alone, if I did not have Jasper to worry about . . . Rarely, and this was one of the times, she knew she was tied to him by what seemed like a tight cord of anxiety that vibrated to his needs, never hers; she knew how she was afflicted by him, how he weighed her down. Supposing she left him? (For he would never leave her!) If she found a place of her own, with other comrades, of course—why, she had moved so often, it was nothing, she could do it easily. Without Jasper. She sat quietly, her freckled girl's hand just encompassing the big brown mug, as though it had alighted there, her eyes held by the blessed, blissful forsythia that filled the whole kitchen with energy, with pleasure. Without Jasper. She began to make uneasy, restless little movements, and her breathing became faster, then slowed to a sigh. How could she live without Jasper? It was true, what people said: they were like brother and sister. But supposing . . . The thought of another man made her give an incredulous little shake of the head. Not that plenty hadn't come near, to ask, Why Jasper, why not me? Had said, But he doesn't give you anything.

But he did; he did! How could she leave him?

She got up slowly from the table, washed up the mug, and stood for some time absolutely still, staring. She thought: I keep forgetting that time is going on. She was over thirty. Well over thirty, in her mid-thirties . . . Thirty-six, actually. If she was going to have a child, ever . . . No, no; real responsible revolutionaries should not have children. (But they did!)

She flung the whole tangle of thought away from her and ran fast up the stairs, as though in the room some delight or pleasure awaited her, not the hard task of painting.

She worked steadily on, until she had finished the first coat. Ceilings and walls were all fresh white where dirt and dinginess had been. Some people would leave it at that, but not Alice: there would be a second coat. She strode through the newspapers all over the floor, some of them with dates from the thirties, even the war. "Second Front!" in big black print slid away under another sheet, and "Attlee Promises . . ." She was not interested in what Attlee or anyone else had promised. Again in the kitchen, she rested herself, and thought: I'll have finished our room by midday, I could do another. Well, I'd need help for the sitting room. The worst is the girls' room, Faye and Roberta's. I'll just have a quick look now. . . .

She was sure they had not come in, but knocked to make sure.

Silence. She went in and, because her eyes were on ceilings and walls, did not realise at once that they were, after all, there, two low huddling mounds under blankets, shawls, and all kinds of bits and pieces of stuffs, mostly flowered. Roberta, disturbed but not knowing why, had stretched up arms to yawn, then sat up, womanly breasts lolling, and she stared with displeasure at Alice. Who said, "Sorry, I thought you were out."

"Well, we are not!" But the look of dislike, which Alice was afraid might be what Roberta did feel for her, was replaced with Roberta's more amiable look, and she sat up, feeling for cigarettes. From the tense look of the bundle that was Faye, Alice knew she was awake. She explained reasonably, "I am painting our room. I'll have finished in a couple of hours. I thought I could do yours today, if you like."

At this Faye sat up, flinging aside covers, in one movement, like a swimmer surfacing, and she glared at Alice as she had at poor Mónica.

"No," she said, in a deadly, cold voice. "You will *not* paint this room, Alice. You will not. You will leave us alone."

"Faye," said Roberta quietly. "It's all right."

"No, it's not all right," shrilled Faye. "You paint your own fucking room, Alice. Just keep your shitty little hands off us, do you hear?"

Alice, well used to such situations, was standing her ground, was not hurt, or offended, or any of the things she knew Faye wanted her to be. She was thinking: Full marks to Roberta. Just imagine, having to cope with Faye all the time.

"It's all right, Faye," said Alice. "Well, of course, I won't if you don't want. But the room is pretty far gone, isn't it?" And she looked with interest at the walls, which, in the strong morning light —the sun was only just leaving one of them—seemed that they might start sprouting mushrooms.

They sat there side by side, Faye and Roberta, staring at Alice, so unlike Mary and Reggie that Alice was even amused—inside, of course, not letting it show. And her heart hurt for the girls. Mary and Reggie—those *householders*, as Alice contemptuously thought of them—sitting upright in their marriage bed, examining Alice, knew that nothing could ever really threaten them. But Roberta, for all her handsome, dark solidity, her motherliness, and Faye, like a flimsy chick or little bird huddling there behind Roberta's large shoulder, were vulnerable. They knew that anything, even Alice, could advance over them like bulldozers, crush them to bits.

"It's all right," said Alice gently, infinitely pitying. "Don't worry. I'm sorry." And she went out, hearing how Faye's voice shrilled as the door shut, and how Roberta's voice consoled and gentled.

Alice returned to the second coat and her work of balancing on the trestles, and thought for the first time: I'm silly. They like it. Roberta, certainly Faye, like living in filth. She contemplated this idea for some time, steadily laying on a fresh film of white to strengthen the white already there, over her head, one knuckle just touching the ceiling to steady her. They like it. They need it. If they didn't like it, they would have done something about it long ago. It's easy to get things straight and clean, so if they didn't, they wanted it.

She allowed this thought plenty of time and scope. But Jim, no, he didn't like it: Look how pleased he was when I started clearing up. He didn't like all those horrible buckets up there, he just doesn't know how to . . . Jim, he hasn't got the expertise of the middle class (how often had she heard this at her mother's house); he is helpless, he doesn't know how things work. But Faye and Roberta—well, they aren't middle-class, to put it mildly, but surely they . . . yes, they would have picked up the know-how, the expertise, so if they didn't get things straight, it's because they didn't want to.

Imagine wanting to live in that room, that awful room, with walls like dung heaps, *what* has happened in there, what has been done in the room? Well, probably it wasn't Roberta. Faye: anything wrong, anything pitiful and awful, would have to be Faye, never Roberta. Probably when Faye had one of those turns of hers . . . all kinds of awful things happening, and then Roberta, coping: Darling Faye, it's all right; don't, Faye; please, Faye; relax, darling. . . .

Alice finished the second coat at midday, washed the roller, put lids on the paint tins, took them to a room upstairs. While Philip slept, while Mary and Reggie slept, while Roberta and Faye slept (they had not come out of their room), she had painted a whole room. And done it well, no smears or skimped corners, and the papers were all bundled up ready for the dustbins, which would soon be full again.

Alice cooked herself eggs, drank tea, and washed herself in cold water, standing in the bath. Alice then, all clean and brushed, and in a nice blouse with the small pink flowers and the neat round collar, walked out of the house and went next door, to number 45, as though she had been planning to do this all day.

She was sure that Comrade Andrew would not still be in bed, whoever else was.

About two-thirds of the sacks of refuse had gone, and the pit she had seen was as if it had never been, under a litter of dead leaves where a couple of blackbirds foraged.

The door opened to show a young woman who was both tall and slender, and baggy and voluminous, for she wore battle dress in khaki and green, similar to an outfit that Alice had seen in an army-surplus shop not long ago.

"I am Alice," she said, as the girl said, "You are Alice," and then, "I am Muriel." Smiling nicely, Muriel stood aside for Alice to enter a hall where not a trace remained of the stacks of pamphlets, or whatever they were. Number 45 had no carpet on the floor; otherwise the two halls were the same. There was even a broom leaning in a corner.

"Can I see Comrade Andrew?" Alice said, and Muriel replied, disappointingly, "I think he is asleep." Seeing Alice's commenting face, Muriel said swiftly, "But he only got back at three this morning, and those Channel boats . . ." Then, having given this information to which Alice felt she was not entitled, Muriel said, with a look of irritated guilt because of Alice's critical face, that she would go and see. She went to the door of the room Alice had been in, and lifted her hand as if to knock. She scratched delicately, not to say intimately, with her forefinger. The cold and dreadful pain that she never told herself was jealousy went through Alice. She could have fainted with it. Certainly she was dizzy, and when her head cleared Muriel still stood there, complacently smiling, and scratching with that raised forefinger, like a bird's beak. Yes, she did look like a goose, or, better still, a gosling, lumpy and unformed; like a German Royal, with a smooth, tight bosomy droop in front, and a face with protruding nose and gobbly lips. Which face was now turning a pleased smile towards Alice. "I can hear him now, he's moving." Speaking as though Comrade Andrew's moving was in itself evidence of his superiority, which she was prepared generously to share with Alice. The door opened and Comrade Andrew stood there, blinking and red-eyed. He wore creased trousers and a white tee shirt that needed washing. Again Alice smelled spirits, and repressed disapproval: he must have been tired, coming in so late. He smiled at Muriel in a way Alice did not feel inclined to analyse, then saw Alice and nodded familiarly at her, indicating she should enter.

She went into the room, while the man shut the door, smiling at Muriel, to exclude her.

This room had been cleared of all but two of the great packages. A low folding bed stood against a wall, with a single red blanket on it. It was untidy, but, then, he had got straight out of the bed to answer the scratching. There was a pillow without a pillow slip, and the old-fashioned striped ticking looked greasy. This little scene of the bed was different from the impersonality of the rest of the room, and suggested a rank and even brutal masculinity.

Yawning, not hiding it, the man sat down on an ancient easy chair on one side of the dead fireplace. She sat opposite in another.

"I was in France," he said easily. "Just a quick trip."

She found herself looking covertly at the bed, which had so much the air of being from a foreign country. Or perhaps from some different moral climate, like a war, or a revolution. He saw her examining the bed. He was still waking himself up. Suddenly he rose, went to the bed, tugged up the red blanket to lie straight, hiding the ugly pillow. He sat down again.

He remarked, "I got rid of what you saw in that hole out there. It's gone to where it can be of use."

"Oh, good," said Alice indifferently. The point was, he might or might not have sent, or taken, "it"; but so what? She didn't want to know.

"You must be wondering what it was. Well, all I can say is, it is something of which a very small amount goes a very long way."

A fine contempt was rising in Alice, because of his clumsiness. She said sternly, "In my view, the less people know about such things, the better." Meaning, the less she knew.

His eyes narrowed and grew hard; then he stiffly smiled. "You're right, comrade. I suppose I am off guard. I am a man who needs his sleep. Seven hours in the twenty-four, or I function less than my best."

Alice nodded, but she was examining him critically. She was finding him unimpressive. A stocky, stubby man. His hair, cut short, was flattened here and there, like an animal's fur when it is out of sorts. A stale breath came from him, sour, which was not only because he might have drunk too much. He should be watching his weight.

"I am glad you dropped in, Comrade Alice. I have been wanting to talk things over with you." Here he got up and went to the desk, to look for cigarettes, and stood with his back to her, going through the business of putting one in his mouth and lighting it. This procedure, during which he seemed to be returning to himself, a quick, efficient, considered series of movements, subdued Alice's criticism. She thought: Well, for all that, he's the real thing; and she allowed herself to feel confidence in him.

Then began a remarkable conversation, which went on for some time; it was getting on for five when she left. She knew that he was finding out from her what he needed to know—testing her—and that he must know, surely, that she allowed this, understood that it was happening. It was a dreamy, thoughtful sort of state that she was in, passive yet alert, storing up all kinds of impressions and ideas that she would examine later.

He wanted her to sever herself from "all that lot there; you are made of much better stuff than they are"; and to embark on a career of—respectability. She was to apply for a job in a certain firm with national importance. She would get the job because he, Andrew, would see that she did, through contacts that were already established there. He referred several times to "our network." Alice was to work in computers—he, Andrew, would arrange for her to have a quick course of training, which would be a sufficient basis on which an intelligent woman like her could build. Meanwhile, she would live in a flat, not a squat, lead an ordinary life, and wait.

Alice listened modestly to all this, her lids kept down.

She was thinking: And *who* is he? For *whom* would I be working? She had a good idea—but did it matter? The main point was, did she or did she not think that the whole ghastly superstructure should be brought down and got rid of, root and branch, once and for all? A clean sweep, that was what was needed. And Alice saw a landscape that had been flattened, was bare and bleak, with perhaps a little wan ash blowing over it. Yes. Get rid of the rotten superstructure to make way for better. For the new. Did it matter all that much who did the cleansing, the pulling down? Russia, Cuba, China, Uncle Tom Cobbley and all, they were welcome as far as she was concerned.

But she said, after a while, in a pause that was there for her to fill, "I can't, Andrew." And suddenly, arising from her depths, "A bourgeois life? You want me to live a middle-class life?" And she sat there laughing at him—sneering, in fact—all alive with the energy of scorn, of contempt.

He sat facing her, no longer tired now, or stale with sleep, watching her closely. He smiled gently.

"Comrade Alice, there is nothing wrong with a comfortable life—it depends on what the aim is. You wouldn't be living like that because of comfort, because of security"—he seemed to be making an effort to despise these words as much as she did—"but because of your aim. Our aim."

They stared at each other. Across a gulf. Not of ideology, but of temperament, of experience. She knew, from how he had said, "there is nothing wrong with a comfortable life," that he felt none of the revulsion she did. On the contrary, he would like such a life. She knew this about him; how? She did not know how she knew what she did about people. She just did. This man would blow up a city without five seconds' compunction—and she did not criticise him for that—but he would insist on good whisky, eat in good restaurants, like to travel first-class. He was working-class by origin, she thought; it had come hard to him. That was why. It was not for her to criticise him.

She said, definitely, "It's no good, Comrade Andrew. I couldn't do it. I don't mean the waiting—for orders—no matter how long it was."

"I believe you," he said, nodding.

"I wouldn't mind how dangerous. But I couldn't live like that. I would go mad."

He nodded, sat silent a little. Then, sounding for the first time humorous, even whimsical, "But, Comrade Alice, I have been getting daily, sometimes hourly, reports of your transformation of that *pigsty* there." The dislike he put into that word was every bit as strong as her parents' could ever have been. Leaning forward, he took her hand, smiling humorously, and turned it so that it lay, the back upwards, in his strong square hand. Alice's hand shrank a little, but she made it lie steady. She did not like being touched, not ever! Yet it was not so bad, his touch. The firmness of it—that made it possible. Along her knuckles, a crust of white paint.

He gently replaced her hand on her knee and said, "You'll have the place like a palace in no time."

"But you don't understand. We aren't going to live in that house as *they* do. We aren't going to *consume*, and *spend*, and go soft and lie awake worrying about our pensions. We're not like *them*. They're *disgusting*." Her voice was almost choked with loathing. Her face twisted with hatred.

There was a long silence, during which he decided to leave this unpromising subject. (But, thought Alice, he would not be abandoning it for long!) He offered her some coffee. There was an electric kettle, and mugs and sugar and milk on a tray on the floor. He quickly, efficiently, made coffee.

Then he began to talk about all the people in Number 43. His assessment of them, Alice noted, was the same as hers. That pleased and flattered her, confirmed her in her belief in herself. He spoke nicely about Jim, about Philip; but did not linger on questions. Bert he seemed to dismiss. Pat he wanted to know more about, where she had worked, her training. Alice said that she did not know, had not asked. "But, Comrade Alice," he reproved her in the gentlest way, "it is important. Very important."

"Why is it? I haven't had a job since I left university. I've done all right."

This caused a check or hitch in the flow of their talk; he was suppressing a need to expostulate. There's a lot bourgeois about him, she was thinking, but only mildly critical because of her now established respect for him.

Jasper—but he simply would not talk about Jasper. Because, she thought, of her link with him. She didn't have to ask, though: Comrade Andrew did not have much time for Jasper. Well, he'd see!

Roberta and Faye. He asked many questions about them, but what interested him was their lesbianism. Not out of prurience, or anything Alice could dislike: there was a total noncomprehension there. He simply had no idea of it. No experience, ever, Alice guessed. He wanted to know what the women's commune was like that Roberta and Faye frequented. What the connection was between lesbians and the revolutionary formulations of the political women. Alice offered pamphlets and books, which she would procure for him. He nodded, but pressed on: how did women like Faye and Roberta see the relations between men and women after the revolution? Alice suppressed an impulse to say: Liquidate all men. She was remembering long and hot arguments with Molly and Helen in Liverpool, during which she, Alice, had said that their attitude amounted to a contempt for men so total that in effect they suppressed all serious thought about them.

What Alice said was, "There are many different formulations in the Women's Movement. I would say that Faye and Roberta represent an extreme."

Then there were Mary and Reggie; and, as she expected, Comrade Andrew refused to dismiss them as she wanted to. Precisely what she disliked most about them was what interested him: she knew that he wondered whether they could be persuaded to become sleeping partners in the revolution, a phrase that she used and he approved with a dry smile and a nod.

Alice didn't know. She doubted it. They were naturally conservers. (Not that she had anything against Greenpeace. On the contrary.) They were, in short, bourgeois. In her view, Andrew should discuss it with them. She could not answer for them.

This, she knew, cut across the underlying premise of the conversation: that she was willingly acting as his aide in assessing possible recruits. For something or other. Not stated. Understood.

Did they plan—number 43—to take in more members of their squat or commune?

"Why not? There's plenty of room."

"I agree, the more the better."

And so the talk went on, reaching back, for some rather tense minutes, to her childhood. Alice's mother did not really interest Comrade Andrew, but Cedric Mellings, that was a different matter. How big was his business? How many employees? What were they like?

Alice's brother: Alice decided not to say Humphrey worked in a top airline firm. "Oh, don't waste your time on him," she said.

More cups of coffee, and some rather satisfying talk about the state of Britain. Rotten as a bad apple, and ready for the bulldozers of history.

When Alice said she had to go, she was expecting Jasper, and stood up, Andrew did, too, and seemed to hesitate. Then he said quickly, for the first time sounding awkward, "You have been with Jasper a long time, haven't you?"

"Fifteen years." Knowing what was coming, recognising it from many such moments in the past, she turned to go. He was beside her, and she felt his arm lightly about her shoulders.

"Comrade Alice," he said. "It's not easy to understand . . . why you choose such a . . . relationship."

The usual ration of affront, resentment, even anger was in her. But this was Comrade Andrew, and she had decided that what came from him was, had to be, different. She said, "You don't understand. No, you don't understand Jasper."

His arm still lay there, so gently that she could not find it a pressure. He said, gently, "But, Alice, surely you could . . ." *Do better* was what he wanted to say.

She turned to face him, with a bright, steady smile.

"It's all right," she said, like a schoolgirl. "I love him, you see."

Incredulity made his smile ironic, patient.

"Well, Comrade Alice . . ." He allowed it to trail away, in humour. "Come in any time," he said.

"Why don't you come in and see our palace?"

"Thanks, I will."

And so she went home, her mind a dazzle of questions.

She had been going up to admire her newly painted room, but something took her to Jim's door. She knocked, heard nothing, went in. Jim lay on the top of his sleeping bag, facing her, his eyes open.

"Are you all right, Jim?"

No reply. He looked so dreadful. . . . She went to him, knelt, put her hand on his. It was dry, very hot.

"Jim! What's wrong?"

"Ah, hell, what's the point?" came out of him in a choking sob, and he put his arm over his face.

Under the loose sleeve was a red wound that went from elbow to wrist. Wide. Nasty. It seemed filled with red jelly.

"Jim, what happened?"

"I got in a fight." The words came out of a sobbing smother of frustration and rage. "No, leave it, it'll heal, it'll be all right, it is clean."

He seemed to be fighting with himself as he lay there, banging his fist to his head, clenching up his legs, then shooting them out straight.

"But the police didn't get you."

"No. But they will know I was there by now. There's someone who'll make sure of that! What's the use? There's no way you can get *out* of trouble, you can't get *out*, what's the use of trying."

"Did you try for a job?"

"Yes, what's the use?" And he turned over and lay on his back, arms loose by his side.

She had known it. There was a certain struggling fury that went with being jobless, and persevering, and being turned down, that was different from simply being jobless.

"What were you trying for?"

"A printing firm in Southwark. But I don't know all this new technology—I learned the old printing. I did a year's course, I thought it would get me somewhere."

"Printing! You didn't say. But there must be hundreds of little firms all over the country who still use it for special jobs."

"Then I must have applied to half of them in the last four years."

"My father has a printing firm. A small one. They do all kinds of things. Pamphlets and brochures and catalogues."

"He won't be using the old way for long."

"I'll write to him. Why not? He's supposed to be a fucking socialist."

"What's the use, I'm black."

"Wait, I'm thinking."

He was still tense and hot and miserable, but, she thought, better. Like a nun, or his sister, she sat holding his hand, smiling gently down at him.

"Yes," she said at last. "I'll write to my father. I'll do that. Make him practise what he preaches. He's had blacks before, anyway."

She could see he was, in spite of himself, beginning to hope again.

"I'll write it now," she said.

In the backpack in which she seemed to keep half her life she burrowed and came up with a biro and writing pad.

Dear Dad,
    This is Jim

"What's your name, Jim?"

"Mackenzie."

"I have a cousin who married a Mackenzie."

"My grandfather was Mackenzie. Trinidad."

"Then perhaps we are related."

A small gust of laughter blew through him, and left him smiling. He sighed, relaxed, turned towards her, put his hand under his cheek. He would be asleep soon.

She wrote:

> This is Jim Mackenzie. He can't get a job. He is a printer. Why don't you give him a job? You are supposed to be a fucking progressive? He has been out of work for four years. In the name of the Revolution.
>
> *Alice.*

She neatly folded the letter, put it in a nice blue envelope (choosing the blue in preference to cream, for some reason), and addressed it.

Jim's lids were drowsing.

"Why don't you take this round tomorrow. Your cut won't show."

She pulled back the sleeve gently. He did not resist her. It was a really bad cut, which would leave a thick scar. It needed stitching. Never mind.

"I like you, Alice," he stated. "You are a really sincere person, you know what I mean?" He did not add "unlike the others."

She could have wept, knowing that what he said was true, feeling confirmed and supported. She stayed near him till he slept, went out into the dark hall, switched on the light with pride and with the knowledge of what that little act meant, what it had cost, would cost: she pressed a tiny switch on the wall, and electrons obediently flowed through cables, because the woman in Electricity had so ordered it.

Money. Where from?

Standing there, surveying the hall, so pleasant now (though she knew that really she ought to get carpet foam and do over the carpet, which after all had been folded up in the dust of the skip), she saw that Philip had mended the little cupboard under the stairs that the policeman had kicked in.

At this moment, a knock, and with a premonition she went to open the door, a look of authority already on her face.

It was the policewoman she had seen in the police station. At the gate stood her partner, a young man Alice had not seen before.

"Good evening," said Alice, "can I help you?"

She stood with the door open behind her, so that the order of the hall could be properly seen; she saw the policewoman taking it in. The young policeman was, as Alice was not surprised to see, trying to locate with his eyes the place in the garden where these crazies had buried . . .

"Does a James Mackenzie live here?"

"Yes, he does," said Alice at once.

"Can I speak to him?"

"You could, but he's not here."

"When will he be back?"

"He might not be back tonight. He's gone to visit friends in Highgate."

"He wasn't here this weekend, then?"

"He was here last night."

"He was here all last night?"

Alice said, "Yes. Why?"

"He was here all through the evening?"

"Yes, he had supper here, and then we spent the evening playing cards."

There had been the slightest tremor in Alice's voice; she had been going to say, "We all spent the evening," but remembered in time that "all" might not be prepared to stick their necks out for Jim, if "all" could be reached and warned in time.

"You and he were here?"

"And a friend of his. A white boy. William something-or-other."

Alice knew that the little hitch in the smoothness had reached the policewoman, even if only subliminally. But it was all right, she thought; she could tell that from the indecision of the woman's manner.

Alice yawned, put her hand over her mouth, said, "Sorry, we

were up late . . . ," and yawned again, offering the right sort of smile to the policewoman. Who smiled briefly in return, as she again looked carefully into the reassuring hall.

"Thanks," she said, and went off to the gate, where she and her companion resumed their sharp-eyed stroll around the guilty streets.

Alice glanced quietly into Jim's room. He was asleep.

She then went into the kitchen and wrote a letter to her mother, which she would have ready for Monica Winters, who would certainly be turning up here in the next day or two.

While she was doing this, within a few minutes of one another came Jasper, then Pat and Bert, then Roberta and Faye. The six sat round the table in the kitchen, with an assortment of take-away, which they had brought in separately and would now consume together: pizzas, and fish and chips, and pies. Alice made coffee, set the mugs around, and sat at the head of the table. Her happiness because of this scene was so strong she closed her eyes so that it would not beam out in great mellow streams and betray her to the sternness of the others.

Bert wanted to know about Jack. Jasper reported. The glances exchanged by Faye and Roberta told Alice that trouble would ensue.

It did. Faye demanded, in her pert, pretty way that did nothing to hide her seriousness, why all these plans had been made without a meeting to get everyone's approval? Pat said she agreed: Jasper had no right to take it on himself. . . .

This, Alice knew, was partly directed at Bert, who had been Jasper's accomplice.

Jasper, and then Bert, said that no one was being committed to anything. All that was planned was a quick, exploratory trip to Ireland, to meet a representative of the IRA, and to offer cooperation with a group here.

"A group of what?" demanded Faye, showing her pretty little teeth.

"Yes," said Pat, though with a little edge of humour that told Alice it would be all right, "are we still committing all the vast resources of the CCU, or only ourselves?"

Alice saw that Roberta would have laughed at this, had Faye's mood permitted it.

Bert, because he wanted to reinstate himself with Pat, took command and, his white teeth showing in the thickets of his beard while he offered a steady, responsible, forceful smile, said, "I can appreciate the comrades' reservations. But in the nature of things"—and here he twisted his red lips to signal and to share with them the perspectives of this operation—"certain approaches have to be tentative and even, apparently, *ad hoc*. After all, the meeting with Jack was fortuitous. It was chance, and became productive, thanks to Comrade Jasper. It was he who made the first approaches. . . ." Alice could see that it was not going to be easy for any of them to admit obligation to Jasper, even though he was being correctly impersonal, sitting somewhat to one side of the scene, waiting for their approval, the image of a responsible cadre.

But just then there was a sound in the hall, the door to outside shut, and Jasper, jumping up to look, reported it was Philip going down the street. The fact that he had not come into the kitchen meant he felt unwanted, and this brought Faye in with, "And there is no place we can talk in this house now. Alice has seen to that."

Pat said quickly, "Well, we can go next door. But surely it is all right for a few minutes here."

"And then Jim will come in. Why not?" demanded Faye sweetly. " 'Oh Jim,' we can say, 'we are just having a little chat about the IRA.' "

"Or Mary and Reggie," said Roberta, allying herself with Faye out of love. Actually, as the others knew, she agreed with them, did not need the furious condemnation that Faye had to use as a fuel to keep going.

"Why don't we just agree, quickly, now, to one or two basics," said Pat. "There isn't very much to discuss, is there?"

"No," said Faye. "I'm serious about it, if no one else is." And with petulant little movements of her lips and eyes, she challenged them; then reached for a cigarette, and lit it, and blew out thick smoke in irritation.

And, to support her, came sounds from the hall: Mary and

Reggie, who, full of talk and laughter, opened the door of the kitchen and were silent. With no reason not to come in—since it was the spirit of the house that people should sit around the kitchen table talking—they seemed to sense a unity, to know they were not wanted. Smiling politely, they said, "Oh, we were just . . ." And, in spite of cries of invitation that they should stay—from Alice, from Pat—went off up the stairs.

"Brilliant," said Faye.

"I agree," said Pat. "That wasn't good. Well, I suggest some-one nips over next door to see if we can borrow a room—that is, if it is felt that we need actually to discuss anything more."

"I need to discuss a good deal," said Faye.

Jasper went, was gone it seemed only for a minute, came back to say that they would be welcome.

He returned next door at once. Then Alice went, and Bert and Pat. Then Faye and Roberta.

The goose-girl admitted them, indicating a room at the top of the stairs—the same as that which in their house was inhabited by Jasper and Alice. It had been a nursery, and had lambs, ducks, Mickey Mouses, humorous dinosaurs, coy robots, witches on broom-sticks, and the other necessities of the middle-class child's bedroom.

"Christ," said Faye violently, "what utter bloody *shit*," and she even held out her pretty hands, clawed to show slender nails painted bright red, as if she would scratch the pictures off the walls. She smiled, however, if you could call it a smile.

It turned out that, after all, there was nothing much more to be said.

What was evident was that they had all expected Comrade Andrew to join them, even Alice, who knew he disapproved. Of what, exactly, she wondered now? Of the IRA? No, of course not. Of working with the IRA? How could he? Then, it must be, of *them*, this group, approaching the Irish comrades in this way. Or this group. Period.

But not of her, Alice. He approved of her. Secretly warmed, supported by this thought, which she could share with no one at all, Alice sat reticent, watching the "meeting" develop, seeing on

Jasper's and Bert's faces how they longed to hear steps, hear a knock, hear, "May I join you, comrades?"

But nothing.

It was reiterated that Bert and Jasper would make the trip purely as a reconnaissance. They could find out what kind of support the Irish comrades would accept. This being found somewhat lukewarm, somewhat unsatisfying and unsatisfactory, the formulation was amended and became: that Bert and Jasper were empowered by those present to offer support to the Irish revolutionaries, and ask to be given concrete tasks.

They did not linger. No one was comfortable in this former nursery, which had the ghosts of privileged children—of loved children?—so strongly in it.

Quickly they finished, and left, severally going back to number 43. Roberta and Faye went away to the pictures. They liked violent, even pornographic films, and there was one at the local cinema. The other four found Mary and Reggie in the kitchen, eating properly off plates. The mess of pizza fragments, uneaten chips, beer cans, papers had been swept into the litter bin.

Mary and Reggie said, "Do sit down and join us," but just as the six had repelled Mary and Reggie, so now did Mary and Reggie seem surrounded by an invisible current: Keep off. Well, thought Alice, they are probably still sulky about last night. I did go too far, I suppose. Well, let them.

With many smiles and good-nights, the four went upstairs, and another meeting took place in the newly painted room, where they sat on the floor and discussed the new problem posed by Faye and Roberta, who did not like Comrade Andrew's role in their affairs. That was why they had hoped he would drop in on the meeting next door. "Who *was* Comrade Andrew?" they had wanted to know. By the time the four had finished critically discussing the two women, they were a warm, close unit, comrades to the death. And yet Alice kept thinking that Pat, no matter how committed she sounded now, did not really stand by Bert. The attractive, lively girl, affectionate and easy with Bert after their weekend away together, presumably alone, did not convince Alice. Glossy cherry lips and shining cheeks would be pressed to Bert's sensual red lips, and then doubtless all those white teeth would clash and nip, all that bushy black hair of Bert's . . . But nevertheless, thought Alice, nevertheless . . . And Pat very much did not like Bert's going with Jasper to Ireland. She did not like Jasper. This wasn't a unit at all, only seemed like one, and Alice sat inwardly separated, thinking that Pat probably felt the same.

The smell of paint was very strong. Soon Jasper said he couldn't sleep in it and went upstairs. His tone was such that Alice did not dare to go with him. She went down into the sitting room for the night.

She slept badly, often waking to listen so that she would not miss his going in the morning. She heard the two men come down the stairs and go into the kitchen. She followed them; felt herself already excluded, not wanted. It was only six, a fresh sunny chilly late-spring morning.

It seemed to Alice that Jasper hardly saw her as he went off. He waved to her from the gate, where she stood like any housewife seeing off her man.

She went back to her sleeping bag, with the feeling that a lot of time had to be got through before Jasper came home to her.

But the days went by pleasantly. Pat was infinitely available to Alice, helping with painting and cleaning; between them the two women accomplished miracles, dingy caves being transformed one after another to fresh and lively rooms. Pat was funny and sweet, agreeable, entertaining. Alice opened and expanded in this normality, this ease, and thought again how much of her time was spent with a tightened heart and grim expectation of another put-down from Jasper. Yet, while she enjoyed it all, liked Pat, felt she had never been so happy, she was thinking, Yes, but this is how people behave when they have decided to go away: in a sense she has already left.

Philip, affectionately supported by the two women, got the hot-water system working. They all had celebratory baths. Even

Faye did, when encouraged by Roberta. Philip went back onto the roof and finished the tiling. He replaced floors and fallen plaster, mended the machineries of lavatory cisterns, and, borrowing the car from next door, got new piping to replace old. He found a thrown-away central-heating panel or two, and there was real heating. He located two great beams of good timber lying on a waste lot half a mile away, but could not lift them; they would have to wait for Bert and Jasper to help him.

Between Alice and Mary and Reggie took place the accounting session that would bring in a regular contribution to the household. Mary, who of course knew exactly what would have to be paid, had already worked out her and Reggie's shares. It was very little. Electricity, gas? With ten in the house, what could that come to? An assessment was made. Water? The Water Board had not yet caught up with them. It seemed this was as far as the couple had thought; as though that would be it. Alice said dryly that this and this and this had been brought in.

"Yes, but from the skips," said Mary sharply, betraying that she had not omitted to notice what was being brought in.

This was taking place at the kitchen table. Reggie and Mary opposite each other, so amiable and self-assured; Alice sitting at the head of that table, waiting for what would come her way. She knew already. She could see in Mary's eyes a gleam that meant she was calculating, not what she might owe to Alice, but what she was accumulating, of course at the moment only in imagination, for the purchase of their flat, or house.

Alice said, "We've paid for the gas boiler, for a lot of cable, for tools, for wood, for glass."

She did not expect very much. Rightly. Glances flew back and forth between Reggie and Mary, and a sum of twenty pounds was offered and accepted.

No mention was made of Philip's work. Alice could positively hear the thought: But of course he wouldn't do it if he weren't going to live here.

Smiling, even demure, Alice accepted the tea that Mary offered to prepare—out of guilt, of course—and looked at the other two and thought: God, how I hate you people. How I hate your mean, scrimping, grabbing, greedy guts. Because she knew she swelled and paled, in the grip of her look, she smiled even more and then invited them to start talking about their plans for their future home, which they did at once, and ceased to notice her.

Jim took the letter to Cedric Mellings, and came back limp and weepy with happiness. He could start tomorrow. By chance someone was leaving. By chance, Jim would suit Cedric Mellings very well. Jim could look forward, too, to training in the new technical mysteries.

Alice said sharply, "Guilty conscience. That lot—it's all guilt with them."

Jim said, "He's very nice, Alice. He was very nice to me." They were in the kitchen. Jim, seated, or perched, on his chair, could not settle, but got up and stumbled about, laughing helplessly, or sat and laid his head on the table and laughed, sounding as if he wept, then, in an excess of happiness and gratitude, banged his two fists on either side of his head, which banging turned into a little sharp jubilant rhythm. Next he sat up and flung wide his arms in the same movement, his eyes rolling, his black face smiling wide, white teeth showing.

Alice, with a thousand terrible things to say about her father, kept them back, because she loved Jim, loved his helplessness, his vulnerability, and her own part in alleviating these wounds; because she knew this man, or boy—he was twenty-two—was really sweet, had a sweet gentle warmth in him; and she knew that a spell of happiness, of success, would transform him. She could imagine how he would be, earning money, taking command of his life. She could see him clearly: Jim as he was now, but filled out with confidence and new skills. Therefore, she said not one more word about her shitty father, but only listened, sharing in what she knew was a moment in his life he could never forget.

Then she took him out to supper to celebrate, Philip and Pat joining in, and the evening became one of those when the participants have to pause, to say to themselves: Yes, this *is* me, it really *is* me. . . . Happiness sat with them at the table in the Seashell Fish-and-Chips; they could not stop smiling, or Jim from laughing and sighing. When he said, "I can't believe this is *me*, man," they looked at one another, unable to bear that they could not express what they felt for him, but they could laugh, and—it was Pat who sat next to him—stroke or pat him, or embrace him. The other people in the restaurant, who might at other times have had stringent thoughts about race, or about white women publicly embracing black men (or at least not with such total lack of self-consciousness), were, it could be seen from faces that also showed tendencies to laugh without reason, subdued to the demand of the occasion, which was for a total and uncritical abandon to happiness.

The four went back to number 43, in a close, tender group, Jim as king, as victor, and, unwilling that the evening should be lost, they sat on around the kitchen table, sentinelled by the yellow forsythia, and could not bear to part.

Alice was already thinking: Yes, tonight you'd think we'll all be friends for life, we could never harm each other, but it could all change, just like that! Oh, *she* knew, she had seen it all. Her heart could have ached, could have dragged her down, but she did not let it, was keeping that lump of a heart on a short, cruel chain like a dangerous dog.

A postcard showing the Wicklow Mountains arrived from Jasper, with the message "Wish you were here!" She knew exactly the freakish mood he had been in, and her face assumed that smile the thought of Jasper so often evoked: modest, wistful, and admiring, as if his vagaries of genius would forever be beyond her. She kept the card to herself because she knew the others would not understand. Coming downstairs early, long before the others, she had seen it lying on the floor inside the door.

Jim went off for his first day at work in a mood of tender incredulity, still unable to stop smiling.

Pat, instead of joining Alice in their scrubbing and painting, went off to "a friend," came back saying that Bert had telephoned a message. All was well, and they would be back soon.

What are they doing for money? was Alice's thought, kept to herself. She also thought: When Bert comes back, Pat will not be here. She could read this from Pat's face. But she kept that to herself, too.

That evening a knock—furtive and hasty, telling Alice who it was—brought her out to find Monica on the path near the gate—not outside the door, for the girl had been afraid that Faye might open it.

But, seeing Alice, she approached swiftly, her hungry eyes on Alice's face.

Faye was in the kitchen with Roberta, so Alice shut the door quietly behind her and went with Monica out to the road, and along it to where they were hidden by the healthy bushes of Joan Robbins's garden.

"Did you hear of anything?" Monica asked, already sullen and hopeless, apparently seeing from Alice's face that there was no news. She looked puffy and pale. Her hair straggled greasily. From her came such a whiff of defeat that Alice had to force herself to stand up to it.

"There's nothing to hope for from the Council," said Alice, and, seeing a sneer or snarl of *Well, of course not!*, persisted, "but I've thought of something else." She asked Monica to stay where she was, sneaked back into the house as though she were guilty of something, came out again with the letter she had written to her mother. Monica had drifted halfway back to the main road, apparently expecting Alice not to reappear.

"Did you think I was not coming back?" she scolded. "Really, if you are going to expect the worst, then that is what you'll get."

A weak, conscious smile.

"Take this to this address. And take your baby with you."

"But it's so late. God knows it's hard enough to get him off to sleep in that place, and he's asleep now."

"Go tomorrow. It's my mother. She likes babies. She likes looking after people."

The doubt on Monica's face did not in any way diminish the total confidence Alice felt. Look what she had achieved with Jim! No, she was on a crest of ability and luck, and she could make no mistakes. She felt that her mother would be good to poor Monica. She said briskly, "It's all right, Monica. Well, it's worth trying, isn't it?"

Peering down dubiously at the envelope, Monica departed to the bus stop in the main road, and Alice went in to join the others around the table. She had prepared a large stew, or thick soup, her speciality, brought to perfection in years of communal living. How many people had joked that Alice could feed crowds out of it! Like the Bible's loaves and two fishes.

How many had come into this squat or that asking, "Any of your soup left, Alice?" and then sat breaking bread into it, handing back their plates for more. No dietary deficiencies in people who lived on her soup! And in times when there had been very little money, it had kept them going, Jasper and her, for months.

Alice slid back into her place, saying, to their querying, ready-for-any-emergency looks, "It's all right, it was nothing."

Roberta and Faye, Mary and Reggie, Philip and Jim, Pat and Alice sat around all evening, compelled into being a family by the magic of that soup, and the red wine that Reggie had contributed, and the good bread, healthy wholemeal, and the frivolous white that Faye insisted on.

This was another evening of pleasure, and Jim was full of tales about Alice's father and the others working with him, twelve or more, and how lucky Alice was to have such a father—while Alice smiled and kept a lock on her tongue.

Next morning Alice was alone in the house when there was a tumult of thudding knocks on the door, and a voice screamed, "Come out, you, come out of there, come out."

Alice went out to Monica, who was transformed by fury, ready to kill, as Alice could see. The child in the pushchair, poor ugly little thing, grizzled steadily.

"Why did you do that? Why did you send me there? What have I done to you?" And Monica began kicking out at Alice's legs, and beating about with her arms.

"What is the matter? What happened? Didn't she take you in?"

"There's no one there," screeched Monica. "Why did you send me there?"

"Well, she's only out shopping, isn't she? She'll be back."

Monica stopped screeching, her limbs stopped flailing, and she stared, appalled, at Alice. "It's an empty house," she said. "No one there. There's a 'For Sale' notice up."

"You went to the wrong house," said Alice, vaguely. She was, indeed, struck by something, a thought, or a memory: cases on a kitchen table, filled with crockery wrapped in newspaper. She stared at Monica, who stared at her.

"There's a mistake," said Alice, who was as pale as Monica, and as breathless by now. "Something's wrong."

"It's you who's wrong," said Monica, with a sudden ugly laugh. She still stared at Alice, as if unable to believe what she saw. "Why did you do this to me? What for? You get some kind of a kick out of it, I suppose. You're evil," she pronounced. "You are all evil and mad in this house." And, bursting into wails, she went running off, pushing and jolting the pushchair so that the child wailed, too. The two went noisily to the bus stop, leaving Alice on the doorstep, stunned, and staring without seeing at the letter she had written to her mother, thrust into her hand by Monica.

Dear Mum,

This is Monica. She is living with her baby in one of those ghastly hotels, you know. Well, if you don't you fucking well ought to know. Why don't you take her in? It's the least you can do. You've got three empty rooms now. Monica and her baby are living in one shitty room, with no place she can cook or anything.

Your daughter, *Alice*.

P.S. And there is a husband, too.

She went in and sat on the bottom step of the staircase. Sat there for a long time, her mind blank. Then she began a curious movement, rubbing her hand over her face, as though feeling for something or wanting something. It was quite a hard movement, dragging the flesh this way and that, and it went on for some time, perhaps ten minutes. A task she had to perform, a necessity; an observer could have thought she had been ordered to do this, to sit on that step with her fingers pushing her flesh about over her face.

Then she methodically collected her bag, and went off to the Underground, walked up the streets to her mother's house, and stood outside it looking at the "For Sale" sign. She could not take it in. Using her key, she briskly admitted herself. But inside it was as if something had sucked out furniture, leaving the spirit of the house intact. The cooker was in the kitchen, though the refrigerator was gone. Curtains hung pleasantly in the windows, and it seemed that if she turned her head away and back, then the table where she had sat, where she had served her soup to her mother, sometimes to her mother's guests, might reappear. The rest of the house was the same. In the bedrooms were the curtains she had known all her life, and the fitted carpets remained, but beds and cupboards had been spirited away. Alice went up to her room, and squatted down in the corner where her bed had been, the narrow white bed she had slept in since she was ten years old. On the window was a blue-and-red peacock she had stencilled there on a wet afternoon when the garden was blanked out with grey rain. A 1980 calendar hung on a wall; she had kept it because she liked the picture: Manet's *Bar at the Folies-Bergère*. She identified with that girl who stared out, trapped by bottles, tangerines, mirrors, the counter, a wall of people with ugly faces.

In the garden there was sunlight, and cats on a lawn that needed cutting.

She went downstairs, like a sleepwalker. Then, in a frenzy, having come awake, furious, betrayed, deadly, she tore down curtains from room after room, bundled them, and staggered out of the house, forgetting to lock the door, hardly able to walk under the load. She saw a woman looking from a window and thought: So what, they are mine, aren't they? She managed to reach the corner, staggering. She stopped a taxi, returned in it to the house, made it wait while she ran in to drag down any other curtains that remained. Then she was driven back to the squat, where she spent all afternoon putting up her curtains where none had been, or replacing curtains for which she had no feeling. Anyway, these curtains were a thousand times better than the ones off the skips: lovely, real linen or silk or thick velvet, lined and interlined, fringed and tasselled.

How dare her mother give these away without even asking her, Alice?

When she went into the kitchen, Philip was there, and she knew from his manner that he had something to say.

It was that he had had printed a leaflet, which he was taking to hotels, restaurants, shops, advertising his firm, Philip Fowler, Builder and Decorator; that he had to get real work, soon; that he thought he had contributed more than his share to this house, which was now in working order. If "they" wanted him to do any more, then he insisted on being paid; no, of course not at the proper rates, but enough to make it worth it.

The things that still needed to be done here were: Guttering to be replaced. Also a section of exterior drainpipe (he advised that this should be done soon, because the wall was badly soaked, and they were asking for dry rot). The cold-water tank in the attic was almost rusted through. In his opinion it might burst, flooding the house at any moment. The window sills were rotten on the top floor, and were letting in rain. And of course there was the question of the two rotten beams in the attic.

He laid before Alice a list of these necessities in order of urgency, the water tank being first.

Money. She would have to get some.

She sat a long time by herself, looking at the forsythia. It was wilting. Brilliant yellow petals lay on the floor. She went out, cut more branches, threw the dying ones away, and sat on through the afternoon, thinking.

Where was her mother, for a start? Did she imagine she could run away from Alice, just like that? Was she mad? Well, she must be, not telling Alice and Jasper . . . Here somewhere deep in her mind a thought began tugging and nagging, that her mother had told her. Well, if so, not in such a way that Alice could take it in.

Could she get some money from her mother? Not if she had

just moved. With all that expense. Besides, she probably hadn't got over being angry; she needed time to cool down.

How about Theresa and Anthony?

Over this, Alice thought long and intently. Theresa would slip her another fifty pounds, but it wasn't enough. What was the good of fifty pounds? She had got the forty-odd due to her that week from Social Security, and it had melted away on things Philip needed. She thought that if she went there while the maid was cleaning, Theresa and Anthony out at work, she could nick the netsukes if she was quick and clever, and the maid would not notice. But the thought did not stay with her; affection drove it off. Theresa had been so good to her always, she could not do that to Theresa. Anthony was another matter. If it was only Anthony: she would take anything she could get from him!

Zoë Devlin? But for some reason Alice would not go on with that thought. She felt sick, as if Zoë had quarrelled so horribly with her, as well as with her mother.

Perhaps she could actually pick out a suitable house and rob it? Clearly, she was not without talents in that direction. She felt confident that she could succeed.

But to become a thief, a real thief—that was a step away from herself. How could she describe herself as a revolutionary, a serious person, if she was a thief? Besides, if she was caught, it would be bad for the Cause. No. Besides, she had always been honest, had never stolen anything, not even as a child. She had not gone through that period of nicking things out of her mother's handbag, her father's pockets, the way some small children did. Never.

She could imagine herself choosing a likely house, watching for its inhabitants to be out, gliding into it, getting her hands around valuables—after all, she did know what was valuable and what wasn't. She wasn't one of those poor deprived kids who slipped in through an open window or an inadequately locked door and then did not know better than to steal a television or a video. But she could not really see herself with whatever it was: vase or rug or necklace, trying to sell it.

No, that was out.

She had to have money. Look at all these people, taking and taking . . . though Jim had said proudly last night that now he would contribute properly; he would pay his way, Alice needn't think that he wouldn't.

The only place she could think of was her father's. Not his house: it was too early to try that again. The firm. She sat, eyes shut, visualising the inside of the building that housed C. Mellings, Printers and Stationers. The safe in her father's office downstairs had cheques in it, but she did not want cheques. Downstairs, in the little stationery shop in the back, which her father had started in a small way as a trial and which had become so successful that sometimes he joked it financed everything else, was a safe full of cash. But only in the daytime, when the shop was full of people. Every night the cash was carried upstairs to the other safe. Next morning it was taken to the bank. How was she to get that money? She did not know the combination of the safe, and did not propose to turn professional with explosives, or whatever they used.

No, she needed something else; she needed cheek. It was Friday. They did better business downstairs on Friday than on any other day. The shop closed at five, and then the money was taken straight upstairs to be counted. It stayed in the safe until Monday morning. On Friday evening her father often went home early, because he and Jane and the infants liked to drive into Kent, where they had friends. A real, typical, bourgeois arrangement: Cedric and Jane stayed weekends with the Boults; the Boults would use Cedric and Jane's house for trips into London. Nothing like this had ever happened while Cedric still lived with Dorothy! Of course not. Her mother was too full of mine and thine: you couldn't see *her* sharing her house with another family. For some reason, this business of the weekends, the visiting Boults, always made Alice weak with anger.

But, with luck, her father would have left at three.

To reach her father's business, she had to go two stops further on the Underground than for her father's house, or her mother's— well, where her mother had been. She walked, deliberately not thinking too much, into the stationer's, where she was greeted, the boss's daughter. She walked through the shop, saying she wanted to see her father, then upstairs to the office floor. People were tidying their desks for the weekend. She said Hello, and How are you, and went into her father's office, where the secretary, Jill, sat in her father's chair, counting money from the till downstairs.

"Oh, he's gone then," said Alice, and sat down. Jill, counting, leafed through ten-pound notes, smiled, nodded, her mouth moving to indicate that she could not stop. Alice smiled and nodded, and got up to stand at the window, looking out. Indolent and privileged, daughter of the establishment, she leaned on the sill, watching the goings-on in the street, and listened to the sounds of paper sliding on paper.

Should she say her father had agreed she should have some money? If she did, Jill could not say no; and then, on Monday, her father, on being told, would not give her away, would not say: My daughter is a thief. She was about to say: He said I could have five hundred pounds. But then it happened, the incredible, miraculous luck that she now expected, since it happened so easily and often: in the next office the telephone rang. Jill counted on. The telephone rang and rang. "Oh, flick it," muttered Jill daintily, for she was the kind of good girl favoured by her father as secretary, and she ran next door to the telephone. Alice saw on the desk that there was a white canvas bag in which stacks of notes had already been put. She slid her hand in, took out a thick wad, then another, put them inside her jacket, and again leaned, her back to the room, at the window. Jill returned, saying that it was Mrs. Mellings, for her father, and it took Alice some moments to realise that this must be her mother, not the new Mrs. Mellings, who at this moment would be already on her way to the pleasures of a weekend in Kent.

She did not want to ask, Do you know her address?, thus betraying herself; but she asked, idly, "Where was she ringing from?" Jill again did not reply, since she was counting, but at last said, "From home. Well, I suppose so."

She was not noticing anything. Alice waited until Jill stood up, with three white canvas bags, notes and cheques and coins separately, and put them into the safe.

"Oh well, I'll be off," Alice said.

"I'll tell your father you were here," said Jill.

When Alice arrived home, she counted what she had. It was a thousand pounds. At once she thought: I could have taken two thousand, three—it would come to the same thing. In any case, when they know the money has gone, when they remember I was there, they'll know it was me. Why not be hung for a sheep as for a lamb?

Well, it would have to do.

Alice thought for some time about where to put it. She was not going to tell Jasper. At last she zipped open her sleeping bag, slid the two packets of notes into it, and thought that only the nastiest luck would bring anyone to touch it, to find what she had.

Friday night. Jasper and Bert had been gone for ten days. They had said they would come at the weekend.

Thinking Pat, where's Pat?, she went down to the kitchen, and found Pat, with her jacket on, a scarf, and her bright scarlet canvas holdall. She was scribbling a note, but stopped when she saw Alice, with a smile that was both severe and weak, telling Alice that Pat had not wanted to face the business of good-byes, and would now hurry through them.

"I'm off, Alice," she said, quickly, hardly allowing her eyes to meet Alice's.

"You're through with Bert?"

Tears filled Pat's eyes. She turned away. "Some time I've got to break it. I've got to."

"Well, it's not for any outsider to say," remarked Alice. Her heart was sick with loss, surprising her. It seemed she had become fond of Pat.

"I've got to, Alice. Please understand. It's not Bert. I mean, I love him. But it's the politics."

"You mean, you don't agree with our line about the IRA?"

"No, no, not that. I don't have any confidence in Bert."

At least, she did not say, as well, "in Jasper."

She said, "Here is my address. I'm not fading out. I mean, I don't want to make any dramatic breaks, that kind of thing. I'll be working in my own way—the same sort of thing, but what I see as rather more . . . serious."

"Serious," said Alice.

"Yes," she insisted. "Serious, Alice. I don't *see* this tripping over to Ireland, on the word of somebody called Jack." She sounded disgusted and fed up, and the word "Jack" was blown away like fluff. "It's all so damned amateur. I don't go along with it."

"I thought you'd be off."

Pat swiftly turned away. It was because she was crying.

"We've been together a long time. . . ." Her voice went thick and inarticulate.

"Never mind," said Alice dolefully.

"I do mind. And I mind about leaving you, Alice."

The two women embraced, weeping.

"I'll be back," said Pat. "You were talking about a CCU Congress. I'll be back for that. And for all I know, I won't be able to stand breaking with Bert. I did try once before."

She went out, running, to leave her emotion behind.

The two men came back on Sunday night. Alice knew at once they had failed. Jasper had a limp look, and Bert was morose even before he read the letter Pat had left for him.

She made supper for Jasper, who at once went up to his sleeping bag on the top floor. Bert said he was tired, but she followed him, and found him standing alone in the room he had shared with Pat. She went in and, though he was not thinking of Ireland, said, "I want to ask some questions. Jasper's sometimes funny when he has had a disappointment."

"So am I," said Bert, but softened and, standing where he was, hands dangling down, said, "We didn't get anywhere."

"Yes, but why?"

She was thinking that rejection brought out the best in Bert. Without his easy affability, the constant gleam of his white teeth amid red lips and dark beard, he seemed sober and responsible.

He shook his head, said, "How do I know? We were simply told no."

She was not going to leave until he told her everything, and at last he did go on, while she listened carefully, to make a picture for herself that she could trust.

"Jack," in Dublin, had been to bars and meeting places, had made enquiries, had met this man and then that, reporting back to Bert and Jasper that things were going on as they should. Then Bert and Jasper—but not Jack, a fact that had to give her food for thought—met a certain comrade in a certain private house in a suburb. There they had been questioned for a long time, in a way that—Alice could see, watching Bert's face as he recited the tale—had not just impressed but sobered the two. Frightened them, judged Alice, pleased this had been so, for she did feel that Jasper was sometimes a bit too casual about things.

Towards the end of this encounter, or interview, a second man had come in, and sat without saying a word, listening. Bert said with a short laugh and a shake of the head, "He was a bit of a character, that one. Wouldn't like to get across *him*."

At last, the man who had done all the talking said that while he, speaking for the IRA, was grateful for the support offered, they —Bert and Jasper—must realise that the IRA did not operate like an ordinary political organisation, and recruitment was done very carefully, and to specific requirements.

Jasper had cut in to say that of course he understood this: "Everyone did."

Then the comrade had repeated, word for word, what he had just said. He went on to say that it was helpful to the Republican cause to have allies and supporters in the oppressing country itself, and that Jasper, Bert, "and your friends" could play a useful part, changing public opinion, providing information. They could be supplied, for instance, with pamphlets and leaflets.

Jasper had apparently become excited and expostulatory, and made a long speech about fascist imperialism. To this speech both men, the talking man and the silent one, listened without comment, and without expression.

Then the silent man simply walked out of the room, with a nod and a smile. The smile apparently had impressed Bert and Jasper. "He did smile, in the end," Bert repeated, with the ruefulness that was the note, or tone, of his account. You could even say that Bert was embarrassed. For him and for Jasper? For Jasper? Alice hoped it was not on account of Jasper, though, clearly, to make that emotional speech had not been too clever.

Alice would have liked to go on, but Bert said, "Look, I've had enough for today. This business with Pat . . ."

"I'm sorry," said Alice. "And I know she is."

"Thanks," he said, dryly, "oh, *thanks!*," and began stripping off his jersey, as though she were already gone.

Alice decided to sleep in the sitting room again, because to choose herself a room would be a final separation. Just as she was settling in, Jim appeared. He had spent the weekend jubilantly with friends. These were friends not seen for a long time, visited now because there was something to celebrate. She saw that already, after only three days, there was an alertness and competence coming into Jim; he had been dulled and slowed by unemployment. Well— of course!—everyone knew that, but to see the results so soon . . .

Delighted about Jim, apprehensive for Jasper, Alice lay for a long time awake in the silent room. On this side of the house the traffic from the main road could not be heard.

She knew that neither Jasper nor Bert would be up early, but made herself get up in time to join Jim for tea and cornflakes. She thought she was rather like a mother, making sure a child had eaten before going off to school, and did not scruple to say, "Are you sure you've had enough? There's no canteen there, you know. You'd better take some sandwiches." And he, like a son with an indulged mother, "Don't worry, Alice. I'm all right." Then in came Philip, and the question of the new water tank was discussed. Rather, a good second-hand one. Did Alice have any idea what a new one would cost? No, but she could guess! Philip would go this morning to his source for such things, talk it over; if one was available, did she want him to buy it, and if so, did she have the money? She empowered him to get the tank, the section of drainpipe, the guttering. Quickly in and out of the sitting room, she slid three hundred pounds from out of her sleeping bag, not wanting Philip to know how much was there—but only because she did not want anyone

to know. A disconcerting, even shameful thought had taken posses-
sion. It was that when this final list of necessities had been bought,
she should put some money into the post office. For herself. Money
no one should know about. She should have, surely, a little put
away? Yes, she would open a new post-office account, and not tell
Jasper.

Philip and Jim were out. Roberta and Faye were asleep or at
their women's place. Mary and Reggie had gone away for a long
weekend, and would not be back until evening. Bert and Jasper
slept, or were very silent, in their respective rooms. Alice sat on at
the end of the table, in the quiet kitchen. The cat, absent for days,
reappeared on the window sill, was let in, accepted cornflakes and
milk, carefully licked up every little smear from the dish, miaowed,
and went away again.

Alice was full of woe. This business of the IRA had been
Jasper's impetus for months. Long before the dramatic exit from
her mother's, it had been the IRA . . . the IRA . . . every day.
She had not at first taken it seriously. But then had had to. Now all
that had collapsed. Distributing pamphlets and leaflets was not
going to satisfy Jasper. Nor, she was sure, Bert, whom she had seen
yesterday for the first time as a potentially responsible comrade.
Never once had it crossed Jasper's or Bert's mind that they might be
refused. Would not be found good enough. The IRA had not taken
Jasper and Bert seriously? Making herself examine this thought,
slowly and properly turning it around in her mind, re-creating the
scene she could see so vividly of Jasper and Bert with the two IRA,
she had to admit that Jasper and Bert had made a bad impression.
Well, it could happen! It did happen, with Jasper, all the time.

Another possibility was that they, Jasper and Bert and the
others—herself included—would be tested. Yes, that could be it.
An eye would be kept on them, without their knowing. (Comrade
Andrew here appeared powerfully before Alice, and she smiled at
the image.) But certainly Jasper and Bert had not thought this; and
the Irish comrades had not given them anything specific to do.

This meant—Alice faced it—a bad few days with Jasper. She
would not be seeing much of him. He would be gone from here,

perhaps returning briefly at night for some food, then off again. Once, in a very bad patch, Jasper had been *like that* for weeks, over a month, and she had lived in terror for the knock of the police at the door, and news about Jasper she had been dreading since she had first met him. When he was *like that*, he was not careful about much.

The only hope was his link with Bert. Steadying. Bert might save the situation without ever knowing that one existed.

A couple of hours passed, her spirits sinking lower, and then Philip came in, pleased, to say that his chum at the yard, with contacts where demolition work was going on, had all that 43 needed, and it was in a van outside. But Philip had spent the three hundred pounds and needed money to pay for delivery. Just as he was saying all this, while he and she crossed the hall, Jasper appeared, running lightly down the stairs. Alice stood still to watch him, her heart lifting. She always forgot, when she had not seen him for some time, how he affected her. That lightness of his—each step as though he might take off altogether!—and then how he stood there, at the foot of the stairs, straight and slender; you'd think he was from another world, he was so pale and fine, with his glistening cropped hair. . . . But he was scowling most horribly. Under his gaze she had to go to the sitting room where she had slept, while he knew why she went and knelt by the sleeping bag, which was only just out of his line of sight. She was risking that he might come in; and she had the disconnected, breathless, out-of-control feeling that was fatal with Jasper. He would realise she had come here for money. What was she to do? She quickly thrust what remained of the one package, together with the fat whole package, down her shirt, where it was visible. She put on a jacket, though he would know why she had the jacket on, and went out under his cold, furious, dissecting gaze. Bert had appeared on the stairs, looking tired and demoralised. What a contrast, Jasper and Bert: one like an avenging angel—the thought came compulsively into her mind—the other so brought down and weakened.

Philip said cheerfully to the two men, "Could you give me a hand?" Jasper did not move. Bert did not move.

Ashamed for them, Alice said, "I'll come," and ran out with Philip. The driver, Philip, and she wrestled with the tank. It was heavy, and large—"The size of a small skip!" she joked—but they got it out of the van and up the path and into the house. There the driver said his responsibility ended. Philip ran out to fetch the guttering and the pipe and came in again. Bert and Jasper were in the kitchen, and the door was shut against her. She went straight in and said to them, "For shit's sake, can't you help us take the things up the stairs?"

They had been communicating disapproval, anger behind that closed door. Now Jasper said, "Alice, you've gone crazy, do you know that? What do you think you are doing? What is all that junk?" She made herself stand up to him: "The water tank up there is rotten, it's rusting. Do you want God knows how many gallons of water cascading down all over us?"

"I don't care," said Jasper. "If it does we'll just move on, as we always do."

This cold cruel treachery reached her guts, made her eyes go dark. When she recovered, she was holding on to the edge of the table for balance. She looked at him, ignoring Bert, who was putting on the kettle, cutting bread. "You know you like a decent place, somewhere nice. Of course you do. . . ."

"Oh, bullshit," he said, melodramatic because she was destroying the image he liked to present to Bert. "Well, I'm not having anything to do with it. And what is it costing? What have we spent this time?" His little blue bright eyes, hard and round, which seemed this morning to be protruding out of the shallow creamy lakes around them, were full of hate for her. She knew what she had to expect the moment they were alone.

She appealed to Bert: "Please help. Philip and I can't manage. I mean, look at Philip!"

Slowly, with no change of expression, Bert buttered bread, then sat down. Then, glancing up and seeing her face, unexpectedly got up, as quick and full of energy as he had just been lethargic (but it was the energy of anger) and came out with her into the hall, where Philip, frail as a leaf, was standing by the great dark-grey water tank. Without a word, Bert bent and lifted, leaving Alice and

Philip to fit themselves in, and, with him banging and bumping because he was so angry, the white teeth now showing between red lips stretched in a grimace of effort, the tank was raced upstairs, with much damage to the banisters. On the top floor, Bert simply dumped the tank, and ran down again. She and Philip heard the kitchen door slam again, excluding both of them. She looked apologetically at Philip. He was not looking at her. The tank had to go at the end of the little landing. The existing tank was in the attic. There was no way this tank could get through the trap door into the attic. Mystery! How did the first builders think a new tank would get itself up there, when the original tank, presumably put in before the roof went on, reached its natural end? They could only have believed that tanks had eternal lives.

But the distance from where the tank now sat, blocking the way at the head of the stairs, and where it had to be was too great for them to shift it.

Alice saw Philip distressed, ashamed, vulnerable.

"You wait," she said. She marched down the stairs, and saw Jasper coming out of the sitting room, where, of course, he had been searching for her money. Standing on the bottom step, she said, not knowing she was going to, "I've had enough, Jasper. If you can't help with a little thing like this, when I do so much, then I'm quitting."

Just as though he had not been going to walk past into the kitchen, he wheeled, and pounded up the stairs in front of her. When she got there, he was moving the tank with Philip to where it had to go. Here was the other Jasper, quick, intelligent, resourceful. For Philip said that board, thick papers, something, should be put under the tank to raise it, because of some tricky protruding pipes, and Jasper, seeing the stacks of newspaper that had come down from the attic, swiftly gathered them up and built them, while he knelt there beside it, into an eighteen-inch-high platform. Alice could see that though he slid the papers into place so swiftly, he was dealing to one side, as in a card game, newspapers with headlines of interest: "The Jarrow Marchers ..." "Hitler Invades ..." "The Battle of El Alamein ..."

If the Irish comrades could see him now! thought Alice, watching this deft, swift, accomplished work; and then how he, with Philip and herself, lifted the great tank, as if it weighed nothing, onto the top of the papers. . . .

He had not looked at her. She was half fainting with the power of her beating heart. Oh, it was a dangerous thing, to threaten Jasper. Suppose he left her? Oh no, he would not, she knew that absolutely. He could not.

He ran off down the stairs, without a smile or a look, and she was left again with Philip. Who was distressed. By the atmosphere he had been in, which, she knew, was pure poison.

She knew he was thinking: If I had not put so much of myself into this house, perhaps I'd leave. Besides, he was upset about Pat's going.

She left Philip to his work, thinking that this time she had given him the money for the materials but none for his labour. Almost, she went back up the stairs to give him what she had. . . . She took a few steps down . . . *almost* went back up, hesitated, then —luck being on her side—she did it. She gave him what was left of the already denuded packet—not quite two hundred pounds, it was true, and nothing like what it should be—and went down into the kitchen, whose door she boldly opened, not caring that it had been shut to bar her out.

Bert had gone.

Jasper was waiting for her.

"Where did you get that money?"

"It's not your money, so shut up," she said.

"You are making us all sick," he said. "We all think you've gone rotten. All you care about is your comfort."

"Too bad," said she, sitting down. In the bright mid-morning light he looked, standing there, rather commonplace and even ugly —so thought Alice, who a few moments before had been melting in a familiar ecstasy of admiration for him.

He was staring at her midriff. The jacket, hastily put on, was open. At the front, inside the thick cotton shirt, was the flat protuberance of the packet.

For a moment she feared he would simply step over, grab her

wrist, pull out the money. He did not, but went to stand at the window, looking out.

He said, "You needn't think I'm just going to give up, that I'm just going to take their word for it!"

It took a moment for it to penetrate: he was talking about his rejection by the Irish comrades.

She said companionably, "No, of course not."

She believed, and with what a lightening and easing of her poor heart, that now could begin the real, the responsible, discussion she loved so much to have with Jasper. But the door opened and she looked up to see Jim. Who at first she thought was not Jim. The brown glossy skin was ashy and rough, and his eyes stared.

"What's wrong, what *is* wrong?" And she went to him.

He shook her off. "They gave me the sack."

"Oh no," she said at once, decisively. "Oh no, he couldn't have."

He stood, breathing in, breathing out in a big gasp, breathing in. A loud, painful sound. "They said I stole money."

"Oh no," said Alice. And then again, but differently, "Oh *no*."

Meanwhile Jasper stood taking all this in.

"What's the point?" demanded Jim, of the heavens, not of her, and it sounded histrionic, but was not; for the question had behind it his whole life. Then he did look properly at Alice, seeing her, and said, "Well, thanks, Alice, I know you tried. But there's no point." And he went stumbling out, crying.

She went after him. "Wait. You wait. I'm going right over there. I'll fix it, you'll see."

He shook his head, went into his room, shut the door.

Alice remained outside, thinking. Jasper appeared from the kitchen. He was grinning complicity, even congratulation. The whole truth of course he had not sussed out, for who could possibly imagine that luck of hers, which had caused the telephone to ring at precisely the right moment. But he had grasped, being so quick, the bones of it.

She said, "I'm going over to my father."

"You'd better not go over with that on you," he said, looking at her middle. He spoke nicely, like a comrade at a tricky moment. Without thinking, as though there were nothing else she could do, she slipped her hand in under her thick shirt. The package of notes had got caught in her jacket waistband and she stood fumbling. Her fingers were sliding over the satiny warmth of her skin, and in a sweet intimate flash of reminder, or of warning, her body (her secret breathing body, which she ignored for nearly all of her time, trying to forget it) came to life and spoke to her. Her fingers were tingling with the warm smoothness, and she stood there looking puzzled or undecided, the packet of notes loose in her hand. She looked as if she were trying to remember something. Jasper neatly took the packet from her, and it disappeared into the heart pocket of his bomber jacket.

"I'm going to my father's," she said again, slowly, still puzzling over that message from her buried self, which sang in her fingertips and up her arm.

She went slowly down the path to the gate, turned into the main road for the Underground, still dreamwalking, still caught in a web of intimations, reminders, promptings. She even put her seduced fingers to her nose and sniffed them, seeming even more puzzled and dismayed. She understood she was standing on the pavement with people walking past, the traffic rushing up and down —had been standing there, stock-still, for how long? She could not help glancing back at number 43, in case Jasper was spying on her. He was. She caught a glimpse of his paleness at the window of the bathroom on the first floor. But he at once disappeared.

Her energies came back at her in a rush, with the thought that now, having all that money, Jasper would be off somewhere, and if she wanted to catch him, she must hurry.

At C. Mellings, Printers and Stationers, she went straight through the shop and upstairs, and into her father's room. He sat behind his big desk, and Jill the secretary sat at her table opposite him across the room. Alice stood in front of her father and said, "Why did you sack Jim? Why did you? That was a shitty bloody fascist thing to do. It was only because he was black, that's all."

Cedric Mellings, on seeing his daughter, had gone red, had

gone pale. Now he sat forward, weight on his forearms, hands clenched.

"What are you doing here?" he asked.

"What? Because you sacked Jim, how dare you do it? It was unfair!" And Alice kicked the front of the desk, hard, several times.

"I gave Jim Mackenzie a job, because it has always been our policy to employ blacks, Indians, anyone. We have always operated a nonracial policy here. As you know very well. But I should have known better than to accept anyone recommended by you."

His voice was now low and bitter, and he looked ill. "Just go away, Alice. Just get out, will you, I've had all I can take of you."

"Will you listen," she shrieked. "Jim didn't take that money. I took it. How can you be so stupid?" This last she addressed to Jill. "I was in this office, wasn't I? Are you blind or stupid or something?"

Jill stood up, and papers, biros, went flying. She stared, as pale as her employer, and dumb.

"Don't speak to Jill like that," said Cedric Mellings. "How dare you just come in here and . . . What do you mean, you took the money, how could you . . ." Here he put his head into his hands and groaned.

Jill made a sick sort of noise and went out to the lavatory.

Alice sat down in the chair opposite her father's and waited for him to recover.

"You took that money?" he asked at last.

"Well, of course I took it. I was here, wasn't I? Didn't Jill tell you?"

"It didn't cross my mind. And it didn't hers. Why should it?"

Now he sat back, eyes closed, trying to pull himself together. His hands trembled, lying on the desk.

Seeing this, Alice felt a little spurt of triumph, then pity. She was glad of this opportunity to look at him unobserved.

She had always thought of her father as attractive, even handsome, though she knew not everyone did. Her mother, for instance, had been wont to call him "Sandman" in critical moods.

Cedric was a solid, tending-to-fat man, pale of skin, lightly freckled, with short fair hair that looked reddish in some lights. His eyes were blue. Alice was really rather proud of his story, his career.

Cedric Mellings was the youngest of several children. The family came from near Newcastle. There were Scottish connections. Cedric's grandfather was a clergyman. His father was a journalist and far from rich. All the children had had to work hard to become educated, and launched. Cedric had been just too young for the war, and for this he had never forgiven Fate.

Unlike his brothers, he did not seem able to get himself together; wasted his time at university, married very young, came to London, did this job and that; wrote a book that was noticed but made no money, then another, a jaunty and irreverent account of a journalist's career in the provinces. This was based on his father's life, and it did well enough to bring in five thousand pounds, a lot of money in the mid-fifties. He saw—Dorothy advising and supporting him—that this was a chance that might not recur. He bought a small printing firm that had gone bankrupt, and because of contacts in the Labour Party and all kinds of left-wing political groups, soon had a bread-and-butter basis of pamphlets, brochures, tracts, leaflets, and then a couple of small newspapers. The firm flourished with the good times of the sixties, and Cedric started the stationer's as a speculation, but it at once did well. The family thankfully left the small shabby flat in Stockwell, and bought a comfortable house in Hampstead. Good times! That was what they all remembered of the sixties, the golden age when everything came so easily. Times of easy friendships, jobs, opportunities, money; people dropping in and out, long family meals around an enormous table in the big kitchen, achievements at school, parties, holidays all over the Continent.

Cedric Mellings had an affair or two, and then so did Dorothy Mellings. Shocks, storms, rages, accusations; long family discussions, the children much involved, things patched up and smoothed over, the family united. But by then the children were growing, growing up, grown, going, going, gone—Alice up north, back to her father's territory, though at first she did not see this.

Cedric Mellings and Dorothy Mellings were alone in the too-large house. Which did not cease to be full of visitors coming and going, eating and drinking. Cedric fell in love with Jane. He went off to live with her. Dorothy remained in the large house.

All gone. Blown away, and gone, the good times, the easy jobs, even, it seemed, the accomplishment, the friends, affection, money.

Cedric and Dorothy had seemed a centre, even an essential one; so many well-known people had been in and out with their politics, books, causes, marches for this and that, demonstrations. There had seemed to be a shine or gloss on Cedric and Dorothy, an aura or atmosphere about them, of success, of confidence. But then . . . what had happened to all that? Cedric with Jane was a very different matter! For one thing, a much smaller house, because, after all, C. Mellings, Printers and Stationers, had to support two establishments; Cedric and Jane's house did not have that elusive but unmistakable atmosphere of ease, of success. Dorothy, left in the bigger house, alone for a time and later with Alice and Jasper, seemed to have fewer friends. Certainly those who came for a meal with Dorothy Mellings—while Alice was there, with Jasper —tended to come in ones or twos, mostly women, perhaps needing Dorothy's advice, or even to borrow money; divorced friends—so many of the couples that had been to the Mellingses' in the good days, had split up. Or a couple, who talked a lot about how things had been, and how they weren't the same now. If Dorothy gave a party, and it was only a small party, it was an effort, and she appeared to be tired of it all, to have forgotten how, in the sixties and early seventies, parties just happened. They took the house over and sucked in people from everywhere and telephones rang with careless invitations and orders to wine merchants and grocers.

Whereas, for a time, Cedric Mellings had been the ugly duckling of the family turned swan—for who else of his siblings lived this glittering glamorous life?—now there was a shabby-duckling quality again. Anyway, what had it all amounted to? scorned Alice, triumphantly examining that too-pale, anxious, strained face, with beads of sweat on the forehead: printing fucking garbage for this or that bloody faction in the fascist bloody Labour Party, printing dishwater newspapers for bloody liberals and revisionists, sucking up to shitty politicians on the make and bourgeois trash anyway doomed to be swept into the dustbins of history?

It had all been rubbish, all of it. What Alice could not forgive herself for was that she had been taken in by it all. . . . Well, she had had the sense to get out in time, and meet people who could lead her on the right path. . . .

At last Cedric Mellings sighed, opened his eyes, and, having thought out his position, leaned forward and, without looking at Alice but keeping his eyes down, said, "Very well, you took the money, if you say so. I am sorry about that young man. Tell him to come back and . . . I am sure we can make it all right. Now, as for you, Alice. I suppose it will be a surprise to you, you live in such a dreamworld, but that thousand pounds is not a sum that the firm can afford to lose. We are suffering from the recession, too, you know. It is touch and go—we might have to fold. The printing firm, not the stationer's." He let out the incredulous, admiring little snort of laughter he usually did when mentioning the stationer's: "Greeting cards! That's the thing. And, of course, the sweets and chocolates and all that sort of rubbish."

Now he did look at Alice, and was able to sustain the look, though it was evident it was a strain, keeping his eyes on his daughter's eyes; he simply did not understand what he was seeing.

"I suppose it is no good asking you to return the money?" he almost pleaded.

At this Alice laughed. The laugh acknowledged, even admiringly, some sort of necessity that Cedric, poor fool, could not begin to understand. He, however, nodded, having understood. He said, "I suppose that Jasper of yours has already got it. Well, I know it is no use saying anything to you about him. You have a blind spot of some kind. But you must understand this: you are not having any more money from me. I see no reason why I should support that—well, let that go. I am very pushed for money, Alice— do you understand that? And it's not just this thousand. A few days ago, some hooligan or other walked into our bedroom, mine and Jane's—and lifted . . ." Suddenly, as the thought struck him, he jerked back in his chair as if he had been given a minor electric shock and stared at Alice, his jaw literally dropping. Until this moment, that theft had not been connected with Alice. She merely smiled, admitting nothing, but knowing that she need not bother with denials.

Again he had been shocked to the heart, could not speak, sat struggling to order his thoughts. He was breathing shallowly, in quick gasps. Then he fumbled for a cigarette, lit it clumsily, and sat drawing in smoke as if it were a narcotic.

At last he said, "Alice, I don't know. . . . Now you are a thief? Is that it? Is that how you live? I don't understand." Putting out the cigarette again, as though stubbing Alice out of existence, he said, "I thought it was some hooligan, these kids who come into a house on an impulse. . . ." It was at this point that the next thought hit him, and again he sat staring. "Was that you?" he asked blankly; "did you throw that stone?" He knew it was; this was not a question.

He said, "That stone missed little Deborah by six inches. There was glass everywhere—Jane got a splinter in her leg. . . ."

He shook his head, like a dog with pain in its ears. He was shaking Alice off—forever.

"You are, of course, quite right in your calculations," he said. "You worked it all out. You decided I would not go to the police, because you are my daughter. I won't this time. But next time I shall. As far as I am concerned, you've become some sort of wild animal. You are beyond ordinary judgement."

Alice stood up. She did not feel pain at this casting off; she felt that she had been cast off, abandoned, long ago.

She said, "What is my mother's address?"

This query took some time to reach Cedric. He had to give himself time to let the thought reach him. He said, "Have you lost her address, then?"

"I never had it. She just left, didn't she? Just left our house, just abandoned it." Alice's voice was all furious accusation.

"What are you talking about? She's been going to move for months."

"Because you won't support her," she shrieked.

"Because I won't support bums like you and Jasper."

"Well, what is her address?"

"Find it out yourself. The next thing, I suppose, you'll be stealing from poor Dorothy and throwing stones through *her* windows."

But this came out in a stumbling, heavy voice; he still could hardly believe it all.

Alice went out of his office and along a passage to the general office at the end. To the girl there in charge of the files, she said: "What is my mother's address? Dorothy Mellings, what is her address?" This girl had, of course, not been told of the scandal of the boss's daughter, and she willingly went to the tall cabinet, found the card, read it to Alice, who memorised it and ran out. She passed Jill, who stared at her, almost pleadingly, as if Alice were a murderer, or thug, who could attack her.

Alice ran through the stationer's, where idiots bought magazines about gracious living, romantic or adventure novels, and pretty cards saying "For a Special Friend," "Love on Your Birthday," or "I'm Thinking of *You*." Or boxes of letter paper with daffodils or roses on them. Or . . . just shit and rubbish.

Alice went to a café in Finchley Road, and sat for a long time quietly by herself over strong coffee. She needed to think.

She decided that the link with Bert was unlikely to hold Jasper back from one of his binges; that she would have to sit it out; that Bert was almost certainly going after Pat; that the best thing she could do was to organise a Congress of the CCU for as soon as possible. The work for this would foment in the house the right kind of feeling, atmosphere, to do away with the nastiness of the last day or so. She had just saved the situation with Jim. But Philip, a gentle and even timid soul, would leave if something were not done.

When she got home, the door into Jim's room was open, and all his things gone.

This really did hit her, hard. She wailed, standing there, looking in at the room that had nothing left of him. Not his musical instruments—drums, guitar, accordion; not his sleeping bag, or his clothes, or his record player . . . nothing. Jim had been blown out of this room as though he had never been.

She did not have any addresses of friends, or family.

She stood at the open door, fists up on either side of her head, banging it, banging it hard, and wailing, "No, no, no, oh no . . ."

Feet running down the stairs; Faye stood there, indignant, outraged: "Whatever is the matter?" she called.

"Jim—he's gone, he's gone."

"Good riddance," said Faye, smartly, laughing. "We didn't want him anyway."

Looking up, Alice could see, above Faye, Philip, whose face said that he heard this, as—no doubt—Faye wanted him to. But she saw, too, Roberta, who came swiftly to Faye, and seized her two arms, and pulled her back out of sight. Roberta's face was grave and shocked—hurt because of Faye.

Roberta's low urgent voice; Faye's tittering, high laugh. A door slammed. Roberta came running down, grasped Alice, stood rocking the sobbing girl: "There, there, there . . ."

"It's my fault," sobbed Alice. "Mine. I did it. It's because of me."

"There, there, there. Never mind."

She took Alice to the sitting room and made her get inside the sleeping bag. She fetched her a tumbler of whisky, bade her drink, sleep, forget it.

Hysterical Alice, like the so-often hysterical Faye, was being doped into harmlessness.

She slept until evening. Then she found, in the kitchen, Roberta and Faye, Mary and Reggie. Jasper was not there. Bert had gone to see whether he could persuade Pat to return to him.

Alice, sitting down, said, "I think we should organise a CCU Congress."

"Another democratic decision?" said Faye, laughing.

"I'm suggesting it," said Alice. "I'm putting it forward."

"And I'm in favour," said Roberta. "There are all kinds of members we have never met. A new branch, new groups—we should meet."

"It sounds a good idea," said Reggie in a judicial way, one who would always welcome congresses, discussions, any manifestations of the democratic process.

"Yes, I agree," said Mary. "I've been thinking, it might be just the kind of political party I've been looking for. I've no time for the big bureaucratic parties, anyway."

"When?" said Faye.

"Soon," said Alice. "The sooner the better. The party has grown quite fast. We need to consolidate and formulate policies now."

General agreement, though Faye came in only because Roberta did.

Five days, five nights followed, without Jasper. Bert returned, unfulfilled, and with a gaunt bitter look to him that Alice continued to feel as an improvement. Bert asked where Jasper was; Alice, as usual covering up, said that Jasper had decided to visit a brother. Bert, who had after all spent a fair bit of time with Jasper, was surprised that a brother had never been mentioned. Alice said that Jasper did visit his brother, who was his only "viable relative." This phrase caused Bert to look at her oddly, but she said he had a shitty family, and the brother was the only decent person in it. (Jasper's visits to his brother did in fact happen, if rarely.)

Bert, Alice was pleased to see, missed Jasper, tended to be at a loose end. But they were in a phase of intense activity, for the Congress was to be the weekend after next, in this house, number 43. Message sending and letter writing went on, and they were always running up to the telephone booths at the station.

Alice undertook most of this; but Bert visited the branch in South London to make sure everyone would be inspired to come. Number 45 was asked whether people wished to attend, if not as members or potential members, as delegates or observers. Observers, Alice knew, there would certainly be; and was not surprised when goose-girl Muriel said she would attend. Comrade Andrew said he would have liked to be present, only he would be away.

Both houses could be used as dormitories, if number 43 proved inadequate.

Alice undertook to provide filling but cheap food. For once some contributions to her funds were assured, since delegates would be charged a small fee for their food and lodging. After discussion, this was set at two pounds a head for the weekend.

Alice also said it would be a good thing if all the rubbish remaining in number 45 were to be disposed of, for it gave such a bad impression. As nothing was done, she borrowed the car and made several trips, Philip assisting, to the rubbish dumps.

Philip's misgivings, his hurt over Jim, were being assuaged by the Congress, and the happy atmosphere that was leading up to it.

Bert repeatedly visited number 45 during those five days. He was seeing Comrade Andrew, as Alice knew, for she, too, visited Comrade Andrew, who seemed to want to talk about Bert, making no secret of his plan for him, which was that he should follow the path of job, flat, security, and respectability. And "special training," unspecified but understood. Alice rather wondered at the choice of Bert; why had Andrew changed his mind about him? She herself would not rely much on him. Too easily led, for instance! Was there anything else that Bert discussed with Andrew? Alice was anxious to know, for if the IRA wouldn't have Bert and Jasper (and, by extension, the rest of them, Alice included), then something else of the kind would certainly make its appearance. They all wanted to be of use, to serve! Alice probed Andrew, but he was either not giving anything away, or was ignorant of Bert and Jasper's alternative ideas. Alice probed Bert, but it seemed he was waiting for Jasper to "formulate a commitment appropriate to our resources." Again Alice was thinking, "So much for easy impressions!" —the impression in this case, and she knew that many people thought this way, being that Jasper was Bert's hanger-on, his disciple.

Jasper had several times mentioned Muriel, and this could have given Alice a clue, if her dislike of Muriel did not always rise promptly in her, preventing her from hearing what she might have done. Muriel, Jasper had said, was leaving 45. She was going to begin work. "Real work," he had emphasised, with a proud, but discreet smile, inviting Alice with his eyes and his manner to understand him. But what she had needed to hear from him was that he found Muriel as off-putting as she did: he certainly didn't like her, Alice knew that. "Comrade Andrew has fixed it all up, you know, the training and everything." His respect for Andrew clearly made what he felt about Muriel unimportant.

Alice even tried to find out from Muriel what Jasper's plans might be, but as soon as Muriel heard Jasper's name, she said briskly that in her opinion Andrew was "basically" a sound and useful cadre. This seemed to Alice thoroughly off the point. Was it said, she wondered, because of her—Alice's—occasional doubts over Andrew?

These doubts, hard to pin down, because reason easily disposed of them all, crystallised around the fact that Comrade Andrew too often smelled of drink; she could not bring herself to criticise him for his partiality to the goose-girl, because she had learned so long ago and so thoroughly simply to switch off in this area. People had to have all this sex, she knew that; they had to have it with surprising people and in sometimes surprising ways. Just because Comrade Andrew was . . . what he was, did that mean he had taken a vow of celibacy? No! All the same . . . Bottles of whisky and vodka stood on the mantelpiece of his room, often replaced.

There was another girl, Caroline, who, it appeared, lived at 45, though she was not much seen. Alice would have liked to talk to her, for she felt drawn to her in some kind of kinship; but Caroline did not feel this, it seemed. At any rate, she remained aloof. She was a short, rather plump woman—or girl, for she was in her early twenties—dark, not unattractive, who gave the impression of smiling a lot. Perhaps it was this easy smile that drew Alice, although her eyes, never off guard, were like hard little brown buttons. Yet the general impression was of good nature, wanting to please. Caroline, said the goose-girl crisply, was not prepared to follow Comrade Andrew's prescriptions for becoming a really useful cadre, but had (Muriel thought, and therefore Andrew must think) tendencies towards liberal idealism.

Caroline had a friend called Jocelin who visited number 45, and who it seemed might even decide to live there. She, unlike Caroline, was off-putting. A stocky, even heavy woman, with straight blond hair that was parted in the middle and otherwise unregulated, she padded about with firm, deliberate steps, not looking much at anyone, not smiling easily as Caroline did, only nodding indifferently when Alice caught a glimpse of her through a door or coming efficiently through the hall.

There were also a couple of young men who lived in 45, who had not actually been seen by Alice. The goose-girl said that Andrew was "working on them"—apparently with success. They were from the North of England, working-class, unemployed—but, it was thought, only temporarily. These four—Caroline, Jocelin, Paul, and Edward—refused to attend the CCU Congress, but would come to the party afterwards, on Saturday night. There would be, in short, a good many observers around that weekend; and, as far as Alice was concerned, why not?

Jasper came home on the Sunday night. As always after these excursions, he looked ill. He had lost weight, and was more than usually thin. There was a dull spotty look to his creamy skin, his eyes were bloodshot, he had a shredded, weak appearance as though his essential self had been attacked or depleted. He found Alice at once, and she fed him her soup, good bread, and glass after glass of cold milk: milk that she had made certain to have in the refrigerator for him. Nothing was said about the money.

Told about the Congress, he was at first indifferent, and soon asked for Bert, who joked about his appearance, and said his brother could not have given him anything to eat. Jasper joked that his brother wasn't, like Alice, a cook. Although it was evident he should be in bed, he insisted on going with Bert up to the top of the house to talk. Some plan or decision had been maturing in him, even while he pursued the excitements of the homosexual scene. He had to talk about it at once.

When he did decide to go to bed, he went back to the room on the top floor, as Alice had expected.

As for her, she was again sleeping in the room she had shared with Jasper, next to Bert's. For one thing, she knew that if Pat came back, then Jasper would be back, too.

On that Monday, Philip said he had had one serious answer to all his advertising. But he wanted help. The trouble was that time after time he went along to offer his services, and people took one look at him and made excuses. Yet he could do the job perfectly well—as everyone in number 43 could verify. He wanted Bert to go with him as his mate. He could remain silent if he wanted; it was just for the first interview. Once the thing had been agreed, it would not be easy for the clients to turn him, Philip, down, even though he would arrive for work without Bert. This plan caused a lot of good humour around the supper table. Bert agreed, and the plan succeeded. The work in number 43 was deemed finished, even though in the attic were two rotten beams that were spreading their infection through the house. Philip said he would attend to them when he had done this job, for which he would be properly paid. He had refused to start without a good sum down in advance, and would not complete the work unless paid step by step. It was at a new take-away restaurant half a mile away.

The first delegates arrived in midweek, Molly and Helen from the Liverpool branch. They were militants in the Women's Movement, and had written to say they would be prepared to organise a crèche. If there were no crèche, mothers with small children would not be able to come; it was a question of principle. It must be understood, though, that they would cater only for girl children; that, too, was their principle, successfully applied, apparently, in all the crèches they undertook.

Alice had vaguely supposed that there would be children coming with parents; but now, reminded of the thorns and snags of the thickets of principle and, too, of Faye's probable reactions, sent off a second batch of messages and letters in all directions to say that children could not come. Molly and Helen had a good deal to say about this when they arrived; and Alice was relieved when they decided to make the most of their stay in the capital, with its amenities, and went off at once for a day with the pickets in Melstead. They spent another day visiting Faye and Roberta's women's commune, followed by a late-night porno movie with

Faye and Roberta, from which they returned laughing, restless with vitality—*much* better not ask what kind—and very hungry. Offering their two pounds each, they said they would not go shopping with Alice tomorrow, for they needed to buy clothes, but they would help her cook later.

Meanwhile, four comrades had arrived from Birmingham: two men, two women who, as a matter of course, spent a day with the pickets, and a night in jail. Because every penny brought with them had gone on fines, they were unable to contribute to the weekend's expenses. Two more comrades would come on Friday night from Liverpool—they had jobs and could not arrive earlier. There would be six more from Birmingham, also on Friday, also in work. Four people from Halifax thinking of starting a branch would come on Friday.

All the thirty-odd London members would arrive on Saturday morning, and would sleep where they could, in either 43 or 45, on Saturday night.

Alice was evolving her soup. But she needed, and did not want to buy, an extra-large saucepan. Her mother had such a saucepan. Leaving her assistants chopping vegetables and soaking lentils, she took the Underground, and then walked until she found herself standing in front of the "For Sale" sign. She had forgotten her mother had moved. This made her impatient and angry; she was again angry with her mother. The new address was competently filed away in her mind. It brought with it a feeling of shame, of regret. Not a very nice area; it could just—Alice supposed—be called Hampstead, by someone charitable. Soon she was standing outside a four-storey block of flats, with a small dirty garden in front. Surely her mother was not living here? Yes, her name was on a scrap of paper inserted in a slot opposite number 8: Mellings. An entry phone. Alice was in the grip of an inexplicable panic, could not make herself ring it. But an old woman was standing next to her, putting a key in the door. "Excuse me," Alice improvised, "I'm looking for a Mrs. Forrester. Number two."

"You wouldn't find a Mrs. Forrester in number two, love. I'm number two. And I am Mrs. Wood."

"That's funny," said Alice, all bright and chatty, every granny's dream. "Do you know if there's a Mrs. Forrester in this building at all?"

"No, I am sure not, no Forresters here," and the old girl laughed at her joke. Alice laughed. Then, as Alice had prayed she would, she said, "I'm going to put the kettle on. Would you like a cup of tea?" Oh yes, wouldn't she; and in went Alice, pushing the shopping trolley, opening the door into number 2, and going into the little kitchen to help with the disposal of the shopping. Part of her mind was sternly chiding: What do you think you are doing, letting just anybody in? Why, I might be a mugger. Another screamed: My mother can't be living here, she can't. Still another was saying: I'm going to blow this place down, I am, it shouldn't be allowed.

Mrs. Wood's flat, and presumably Dorothy Mellings's flat, contained two not very large rooms, with a kitchen just big enough to take a little table, at which Mrs. Wood and Alice sat close to each other, side by side, staring at a dingy yellow wall, drinking tea and eating two biscuits each. Mrs. Wood was on the pension. Working-class. She had a son in Barnet who visited on Sundays. She did not like her daughter-in-law, God forgive her. She had a grandson, aged five.

Dorothy Mellings had no family to visit her at weekends; this thought brushed the surface of Alice's mind, but was rejected with a gust of emotion: if her mother had decided to live in a place like this, then she must have gone mad!

By the time Alice left, she knew to the last inch of cupboard space what her mother, three floors up, would have; and there certainly would not be room for an enormous aluminium saucepan.

Alice stayed a good hour or more, and left with promises to return. She went to the hardware shop and bought the necessary saucepan, thinking that after all there would be many more congresses and meetings at number 43, and if she had to move, the saucepan would go with her.

But she had received a blow; her heart whimpered and hurt her; she had no real home now. There was no place that knew her, could recognise her and take her in.

Suddenly a whole army of recollections invaded her.

Alice was standing in the middle of the pavement, in the rush hour, embracing an aluminium saucepan large enough to cook a small shrub, staring and apparently in a state of shock.

She was remembering her mother's parties. They had gone on all through her childhood and adolescence. After Alice had departed to university, seldom to return home, they had gone on still; she would hear about them from someone, probably Theresa. "One of your mother's parties, you know—it was marvellous." They always happened the same way. Her mother would remark, with a restless, harassed look, "It's time we had a party; oh *no*, I can't face it." Then she would start, asking this person and that, for a date a month ahead. Her reluctance towards the party vanished, and she began to shine with energy. She asked Cedric's political colleagues, all the people working in C. Mellings, Printers and Stationers, the innumerable people she knew, who always seemed to be floating in and out of the house anyway. She knew everyone in the street, and they were all invited. She asked a woman met at the grocer's with whom she got into conversation, the man who came to mend the roof, a new *au pair* from Finland (met on a bus) who must be lonely. By the day of the party, which started at midday, as many as a hundred people were jostling one another all over the house, and half of them were probably still there at midnight, being fed out of Dorothy's saucepan, the size of a hip bath. They were wonderful parties. Everyone said so. Alice said so. "Oh, good," she would cry, "are we going to have another party," and at once began fretting to help. When she was older, after ten or so, she could tell she was being useful, but as a small child she was tolerated (only just, she knew) by this whirlwind of efficiency that was her mother organising a party. Still, she insisted on arranging fruit on a dish, or disposing ashtrays around the house, while her mother reduced her pace to Alice's. At least while "helping," Alice did not feel quite so much as if she were a tiny creature on top of a great wave, frantically and hopelessly signalling to her mother, who stood indifferently on the shore, not noticing her.

When there were parties, when there were people in the house, it seemed Alice became invisible to her mother, and had no place in her own home.

People always stayed the night after the parties: drunks, or those who didn't want to drink and drive, or some who had come from other towns. And then Dorothy would say to Alice, casually, in the full ringing confident voice that went with being so successfully in control of this great gathering of people which had made the whole house—not to mention the street—explode with noise and music for hours and hours, "Alice, you'll just have to give up your room. Can you go down the road and sleep with Anne?" (Alice's best friend during most of her childhood). "No, why not? Oh, go on, Alice, don't be difficult. Then you'd better bring your sleeping bag into our room."

Alice always protested, complained, sulked, made a scene—manifestations that of course scarcely got noticed, so many other things were going on by that stage of the party: women guests in the kitchen washing up, intimate conversations between couples up and down the stairs, the last tipsy dancers circling around the hall. Who could possibly have time to care that Alice was sulking *again*? Sleeping in her parent's bedroom made her violently emotional, and she could not cope with it.

Four in the morning, and she was in her sleeping bag on a foam-rubber pad along the wall under the window. Cedric Mellings, in his dashing pyjamas, dark red, dark blue, was drunk or tight; at any rate expansive. He loved his wife's parties and was proud of her. He always did the drinks, hired the glasses—coped with all that. Dorothy Mellings wore one of the beautiful things she used for sleeping in, a "Mother Hubbard" perhaps, or a kimono, or a kanga from Kenya wrapped around her in one of innumerable ways. She was tight, not much, but did not need to be, for she was high, she was exalted, she was floating, she could not stop smiling as she slid into bed by Cedric and lay there groaning theatrically, "My God, my feet."

He would put his arm round her, she snuggled up—a glance, a quick reminder from one or the other that Alice was in the room—some sleepy kisses, and they would be off, asleep. But Alice was not asleep. She lay there tense, in the—at last—silent house, in that room which was far from silent because . . . how much noise two sleeping people did make! It was not just their breathing, deep and unpredictable, coming regularly, then changing on a gulp, or a snort. Cedric tended to snore, but, apparently becoming aware of this himself, would turn over on his side, and thereafter sleep more becomingly. Not silently, though.

That breathing of theirs going on up there in the dark, she could not stop listening, for it seemed that something was being said that she ought to be understanding—but she could not quite reach it, grasp it. The two different breathings, in and out, in and out, went *on* and went *on*, had to go on—yet could stop unpredictably for what seemed like minutes; though of course Alice knew that was nonsense, it was only because she was straining her ears with such fury of concentration that time slowed down. While one of them, Dorothy or Cedric, was in lull of breath, the other went on breathing, in and out, keeping life going, and the silent one took a breath and came back into the dialogue that seemed to be going on between them. A conversation, that was what it seemed like to the child listening there, as if her parents talked to each other still, not in words now, but in a language Alice did not know. In and out, in and out, with many little halts and hesitations and changes of pitch, they might have been questioning each other— and then (and Alice waited for it) the stage where the breathing became regular, deep and far off, further away every minute.

Those two people there, the two great powerful people in that large bed which was the other focus of the house (the great table in the kitchen being the first)—why, it was like sleeping in the same room as two creatures that were hardly human, so alien and secretly dangerous did they seem to Alice as a child, and then growing older, at eleven or twelve, and then older still, at fifteen or so. She changed, grew up, or at least grew older, but it seemed that they did not. Nothing changed. It was always the same, that scene after the party, with the two of them, her parents, sliding into that bed of theirs, arms around each other, and then willingly sliding into the sleep which took them so far from Alice that she was always lifting herself up on her elbow to strain her eyes through the dark of the room towards the two mounds, long, heavy, that were her parents. But were not now her parents, had become impersonal, had gone away from her. Could not be reached. Not unless she crept out of her sleeping bag and went to touch one of them awake. At which Cedric, or Dorothy, would indeed come awake, return to being himself, herself; as if impostors, dark and frightening and mysterious, had inhabited those sleeping bodies but had been chased away by Alice's touch. But then Dorothy, or Cedric, would say, sleepy and startled, "What is the matter, Alice? Go to sleep." And they would have already turned away from her, have gone swiftly off into that other country—and the impostors were back, not Dorothy, not Cedric. And then Alice would lie awake, listening to the breathings, the snufflings, thick inarticulate mutterings coming out of that sleep that was going on above her, on the plateau of the bed; and listening to her own blood pumping and swishing through her body, and thinking how gallons of blood were swirling around up there in those two bodies. . . . She could not sleep; or slept, coming awake with anxiety, and, the moment there was any light behind the silent, listening curtains, which hung there all night, witnesses with her of the absence of Dorothy and Cedric from their bed, their room, their home, their children, she crept out of the room. The house, of course, was in chaos. Everywhere in it people still slept, so that she could hardly dare open a door for fear of what she would see. But in the kitchen it was safe, and there she worked away. She would have liked some help— her brother, Humphrey, for instance. But he was only too happy to accept his parents' invitation to find some other roof to sleep under, and he was seldom there.

After the age of about twelve, Humphrey was less and less at home, staying not just down the street for a night, but with friends all over the country, sometimes for weeks at a time. To Alice it seemed that it was the parties that began this process. Feeling the way she had done (not that they had ever talked about it, but she just knew), like some small sea creature clinging for dear life to a rock but then being battered and bashed by great waves and washed off, he had drifted away. As she had done, later. But separately; they scarcely saw each other. Asked whether she had brothers and sisters, Alice had to remind herself she had a brother.

Alice had not thought of this for years; it was her arms stretched round the great silvery saucepan that brought it all back. And she could have gone on standing there, but someone touched her on the shoulder: a man, a workman, for he was in white overalls and carried a bag of tools—yes, the shop she stood outside was being done over—and he said, "Are you all right, love?"

"Yes," said Alice, "yes." As if to say, "Why ever should you think I wasn't?"

"We were beginning to wonder about you," said he. "You'd taken root, from the look of it!" He laughed, hoping she would; his kindly face—almost certainly a father's, not to mention a husband's—was concerned for her. And she laughed, and went on to number 43, where she carried in her saucepan to applause because of its magnificence and scope and potential, and she smiled as she stood in the kitchen working at her soup while comrades came in and out to sample it, or to make sandwiches, or sit down to eat take-away. She was, quite simply, dissolved in grief because of the loss of her real, her own home, and because of what she had been remembering as she stood there on the pavement. Good Christ, she was thinking as she stood in the kitchen smiling away (everyone's Alice, dependable, helpful, a treat), how could they have done that to me? They took my room away from me, just like that, as if it wasn't my room at all, as if they had only lent it to me—"Alice, you'll just have to give up your room again." It went on for years. What the fucking hell did they think they were doing? Why, every time she had felt that it was not really her home at all, she had no right to a place in it, and at any moment her parents would simply throw her out altogether. . . .

But this is all *silly*, Alice was thinking, chopping, slicing, mixing, smiling. Most of the people in the world don't have half what I had, and as for their own rooms . . .

Never mind, the Congress would be such hard work, she would have to stop thinking about it all, thank goodness.

On the Friday night, when everyone had arrived, and there were twenty-four people crowding in, the amazing soup pot fed them all, and was stocked again, at one in the morning, when everyone went to bed, to be ready for next day.

By half past nine next morning, all the London comrades had arrived. They went over the house, exclaiming, as well they might, at its size, its comfort, its amenities. More than one, from less well endowed squats, took baths at once. The stacks of bread in the kitchen were immediately depleted, and Alice quickly ran out for some more. This weekend was going to cost . . . she did not want to think about it.

Everyone praised, too, the decoration of the sitting room.

Over the mantelpiece was an enormous red flag, with the emblem of the CCU in one corner, embroidered last night by two of the girls from Birmingham. In one corner of the soft living red was a hammer and sickle in gold, and in another a rooster and a rose, in green.

A picture of Lenin was on the wall opposite the flag. Next to Lenin, and several times the size, was a poster of a whale: "Save the Whales!" On other walls were posters saying "Save Britain from Pollution!," "Save Our Countryside!," "Remember the Women of Greenham Common!," and an IRA poster with a picture of a British soldier hitting a young boy whose arms were tied. On a table in the hall were pamphlets: *The Case for the IRA*, all the Greenpeace pamphlets, several books about Lenin, a long poem in free verse about Greenham Common, a large variety of pamphlets from the Women's Movement, and on antivivisection, vegetarianism, the use of chemicals in foodstuffs, Cruise, Trident, the dumping of radioactive waste in the sea, the ill-treatment of calves and chickens, and the conditions inside Britain's prisons.

In the familiar, heady, but comforting atmosphere that attends the opening of such events, forty-odd people crowded into the sitting room, seating themselves as they found places, on the floor, or on the window sills. Outside was a fitfully sunny day. Inside, the new heating was too much for some, and windows had to be opened.

Nearly all were under thirty. Alice, she believed, was by far the oldest. Except, that is, for Roberta, who only laughed when asked her age.

It was to Bert and Jasper that everyone looked, though it had been agreed that if Pat did in fact come, she would give the opening address.

Bert had been listening and watching for her for days, as all the residents in number 43 knew.

Now Bert stood at ease by the fireplace, in which was a great jar of daffodils and narcissus, leaning his elbow on the mantelpiece to show informality, and said, "This is the first National Congress of the Communist Centre Union. From small seeds grow great trees." Energetic applause. Smiles, pleased laughter. Mary Williams and Reggie were clapping, sober but emphatic. Muriel was in a corner, on the floor. She was here as a spy, Alice reminded herself.

Bert did not laugh. Or smile. His problem with Pat had fined him down, giving him a look of suffering restrained by thought. His easy affability had gone. He nodded briefly at the applause, and went on to say that the CCU proposed to be a nonsectarian party, taking the best from the existing socialist parties, learning from their mistakes and failures. It was determined to base itself on the great traditions of the British working class, working for radical social change towards a revolution "if needs be—and every day teaches us that the class that controls this country of ours is not going to let itself be dislodged without force. . . ." Applause and laughter and jeers. A revolution that would learn from the experience of the Russian Revolution, the Chinese Revolution, and, if necessary, the French Revolution, for it was not too much to say that the lessons of the French Revolution had by no means been exhausted. The Congress this weekend had not been called with the aim of formulating a detailed policy, for much more work would have to be done; but to lay down broad principles. And now he, Bert Barnes, would stand down and let a much more accomplished and developed revolutionary, Comrade Willis, take the floor.

Jasper took Bert's place. He did not lean on the mantelpiece, but stood like an arrow, arms down by his sides, his reddish-gold crest of hair glistening, and his eyes fixed on the portrait of Lenin. He began his speech in a voice higher than his usual one, which made it sound to Alice rather strained. But, then, she was used to his platform style, and judged him by other criteria: for instance, she knew he had hardly slept last night, for he had been engaged in passionate and voluble discussion, and going without sleep did not suit him.

His style was to use the familiar phrases of the socialist lexicon, but as though he had only just that moment discovered them, so that when he began, there was often a moment when people showed a tendency to laugh. This stopped at once, because of his desperate, even ecstatic seriousness.

"Comrades! Welcome to you all, comrades. This is for all of us a historic moment. There are very few of us in this room today, but we are a chosen few—chosen by the time we live in, chosen by history itself!—and there is nothing we cannot achieve if we set ourselves to do it." Here, if Bert or anyone else had been speaking, there would have been applause. There was a tense silence. The truth was, the comrades had not expected this note of high seriousness; or, at least, not so early in the proceedings.

"We all know the criminal, the terrible condition of Britain. We all know the fascist-imperialistic government must be forcibly overthrown! There is no other way forward! The forces that will liberate us all are already being forged. We are in the vanguard of these forces, and the responsibility for a glorious future is with us, in our hands."

He went on like this for about twenty minutes. Alice listened to every word, with a sweet, trustful, even beautiful smile; this was the Jasper she loved best, and it was wonderful for her to see how other people responded to him. Even people whom she knew to be critical of him, at such moments admired him. Or, at any rate, recognised that here was something extraordinary and much more than that after all not exactly rare phenomenon, the natural speaker, the orator. No, here was a leader. The real thing.

Alice stood by the door, ready to nip out quickly when it was time to get the tea making started. She was listening, and she was watching the faces: how they responded, how the levels of their attention were being raised by him, by Jasper. This thing that often happened when Jasper began to speak—a nervousness, even a tendency to titter, or perhaps to interject the odd deflating sardonic remark—was because his style was not the common-or-garden British style, a bit homespun, humorous by preference, down to earth. And, of course, Alice in the usual way would be the first to admire this Britishness. It was ours! National characteristics were precious. But Jasper was a special case. He had to impose his own exaltation on them from the start; and today there were no titterers instantly suppressed by others who were on a worthier, higher level. The strained expressions she saw were not because of criticism, far from it; rather, they did not trust themselves to believe some beautiful message or gift that was being offered to them by Jasper, did not feel themselves to be worthy. She had learned long ago that when Jasper spoke people did not clap or shout approval. They remained absolutely silent—after the tricky first few moments, that is; and when he had finished speaking, there would be a silence lasting perhaps as long as fifteen seconds, more. Then there would be applause, sudden, fervent, even violent; people would stand up and shout and cheer. The applause would go on like this, and then suddenly stop.

And this is what happened today. The final applause was as though something had been liberated in them. Some of the women were in tears. Everyone seemed deeply moved. (Not everyone; Alice noted that the goose-girl sat as if part of another audience, not this one, and she didn't applaud at all. Her eyes encountered Alice's but moved on, as if she had not seen Alice, did not want to be called to account for this lapse in real feeling, let alone ordinary good manners.) Then everyone stood up, those not already on their feet, in the need to applaud more passionately, so inspired and fired by Jasper had they been, this emissary from what he had been apostrophising as "the future, our glorious future." They could not, in fact, bear to sit down again, and although the tea break had not been envisaged for another hour, tea was set in motion then and there.

The tea break took a long time, because so many people were busy with conversations. These were not, in fact, about the CCU, or, indeed, about anything Jasper had said; his opening speech was hardly mentioned. When the tea break was ending—Comrades Alice, Roberta, and Bert having to shout above the din with all kinds of dire threats and warnings, all humorous, of course, to get people back to the sitting room—Pat appeared. Quite frankly, she looked terrible. Just like Bert, in fact. She was pale and thin and had lost her glossy-cherry look. Bert and she embraced quickly, in a convulsive and even guilty way; but she would not look at him, and from this Alice saw that Pat would not stay long.

Scheduling Pat, not Jasper, to make the opening speech had been a sensible decision. Her style was very different from Jasper's, being low-key, humorous, informative. She did not know about Jasper's inspirational speech, of course. She told how the CCU had come into being—not in a way that appealed to emotion, but saying it was because of dissatisfactions with the existing socialist parties, which she then analysed. In fact, she was giving a short but rather competent analysis of the existing economic situation in Britain. People were listening attentively, though not at all as they had to Jasper. They were chipping in with facts and figures, they laughed sarcastically at particularly telling points, and there were little ripples of applause. It was a tragedy, Alice knew, that Pat had not arrived in time to make the opening speech, so that Jasper could have made his, as had been planned, at the end of the day. As things were, it was almost as though Jasper's speech had not been made at all; it was all wasted; nothing seemed to have flowed from it.

When Congress broke up early for soup and sandwiches and whatever food the London comrades had brought with them, the talk during the long break, when it was about politics, was prompted by Pat's remarks. But in fact most of the discussion was not about politics at all. People were meeting who had not been together for some time, years perhaps. Like-minded people were encountering one another for the first time in the beginning of friendships or love affairs. News was being demanded of the comrades still in Birmingham, Liverpool, Halifax who had not been able to come.

And former lovers were meeting, too: Pat and Bert's interrupted relationship was not the only one. It was nearly three when they reassembled; and, again, Bert, Roberta, and this time Pat had to go shouting up and down the house to break up the many conversations in progress, so that the Congress could go on.

The goose-girl did not come in for the afternoon session—in fact, had disappeared before lunch. It was clear that she had approved of Pat's speech as much as she had disapproved of Jasper's, and Alice mourned secretly over this. Muriel would have felt quite different, Alice was sure, if she could only have heard Jasper speak in his proper place at the end, when he could have exemplified, have summed up, everybody's emotions.

After lunch (though it was nearly teatime), point one of the agenda was discussed: what trends in the current British scene showed the way to the future? The chosen trends were: one, dissatisfaction over unemployment, "which has to be exploited"; two, "the mass disgust of the British people for the government's policy over nuclear armaments"; and, three, "the budding and still-unexpressed rejection of the British people for the Tory policy in Northern Ireland."

After tea, which did not take place until five, ways were discussed in which these three trends could be emphasised and exploited. But they had hardly settled before more people came from various parts of London, who had heard of the Congress and were interested—and had heard, too, of the party afterwards. Comrades arrived from Liverpool and Birmingham who for one reason or another could not come earlier. And a group arrived from number 45 (not, however, Comrade Andrew). There were suddenly sixty people in the room, and it was uncomfortable. Some retreated to the hall, where they sat talking, with much laughter and noise. The Congress was ended early, before seven, and with point two on the agenda not reached. Point two was: "The future of Britain: full socialism."

The evening's party started. Like an explosion. The din was amazing, even before daylight had gone. Gate crashers arrived, making serious political talk impossible. Alice and Jasper and Pat and Bert kept running out to get more supplies of food and drink. Reggie and Mary contributed a gallon of Devon cider. The police arrived at eleven o'clock, found no evidence of wrongdoing, and were dealt with efficiently and calmly by Alice; among them was the police-woman who by now seemed almost like an old friend. Some neigh-bours banged on the door at one in the morning and complained they could not sleep. Alice said that they were sorry, but there were seventy people in the house, and with so many there had to be a noise. Perhaps they would like to come in and join the party?

Not until four in the morning did the exhausted comrades crawl into sleeping bags all over the two houses, and no one got up until midday, when it was time for some, at least, to leave for towns in the North. No one got up, that is, except Alice, who was clearing up.

Alice was busy serving soup and sandwiches and tea and coffee all afternoon and evening. A few revellers stayed over Sunday night and left early on Monday.

Pat left then, too. She was weeping. So was Bert.

Alice said irritably, "Oh, for shit's sake, why don't you just give in to it," and then felt she had to apologise. But she did not kiss Pat when she left; said, "Oh, God, I'm so fed up with every-thing!" and burst into tears. She left the washing up for others to do and went to bed, not caring whether Jasper was near or not.

But he was there when she woke, squatting lightly beside her, a cup of coffee in his hand. He was beaming, like a boy conscious of behaving well.

"Oh, what is it, Jasper?"

"Clever Alice," he said gently. "It was wonderful, what you did."

But she lay straight in her sleeping bag, arms by her side, feet stretched out. She was not thinking of Jasper, or of the Congress, or of the weekend's fun and games. There was an empty place in her, a pit, a grave; she had been dreaming, she knew, of the house, now boarded up, with the "For Sale" notice outside. And she knew that she must be glistening all over with pale, unshed tears.

"Alice," said Jasper, "I want to tell you something."

"I'm listening," she said, severe and remote, and saw him hesitate, wince. He felt snubbed. She should have cared, but could not.

"Bert and I—we are going to the Soviet Union."

Having taken this in, she said, "The Irish comrades won't have you, but the Soviet comrades will?" This was not derisive in the least—only a statement of the position—but she earned a look of hatred. He was on his feet, hovering above her, a furious angel, ready to throw revengeful bolts.

"Look, I don't want any negative and destructive attitudes from you, Alice."

Pause. She neither moved nor spoke.

Indecisive, he squatted down again, ready to win her.

"How are you going so quickly? You can't go just like that to the Soviet Union."

"On Saturday night one of the comrades from Manchester said that he knew of a tourist group going to Moscow, this week. There are some empty places, because some people fell out, with flu. But we can get visas through the tour organiser. We have sent in our passports, and we'll get them by the time we leave."

"Good."

A pause.

"Alice," he began tentatively, and stopped. He had been going to ask her for money, but now felt its uselessness.

She said, "You have taken every fucking penny off me already. I've spent last week's dole money on the party. It's no good trying to get any out of me." Seeing his face beginning to gather into an avid, cruel look, she said, indifferently, "And it is impossible for me to get money out of Dorothy, or out of my father."

He remained there, lightly squatting, one hand on the floorboards, studying her face. Then, as lightly, he got up and went to the door. As he left she said, "If Pat comes back before you two leave, Bert won't go with you." He slammed the door; she did not turn her head to watch him go, but remained still, like a stone or a corpse, no life in her, looking at the window, now framed by the beautiful brocade curtains, green and gold, that had hung in the sitting room of her mother's house.

She slept. In the late afternoon she woke in an empty house, bathed, put on a skirt that had been her mother's, of soft wool that had great pink roses on a soft brown background, and a pink sweater Pat had given her.

She walked straight out of the house and over to 45, where she went in without knocking: the weekend had made the two houses one. Out of the kitchen—a dreary hole, not nice and bright and decorated with flowers, like 43's—came goose-Muriel, who offered strictly rationed postparty smiles.

"If Andrew is here, I want to see him."

To prevent any more coy scratchings at the door, Alice went to it with Muriel, and knocked.

"Come in," she heard, and Alice went in, shutting the door on Muriel.

Comrade Andrew lay, stretched out like a soldier, as Alice had just been doing, on his low bed, but with his arms crossed on his chest.

He swung his legs over and down, sat, made a place for Alice to sit by him.

She did so, at a proper distance. "I have to know some things," she announced.

"Very well."

But she sat on there, in a droop, listless, and did not continue.

He studied her for a while, openly, not hiding it, then lay down again, but farther over on the narrow bed, near the wall. He pulled her by her arm; and, without resisting, she lay down next to him, stretched out. There were a good six inches between them. He did not touch her.

"Did you know Bert and Jasper are going to Moscow?"

"Yes."

A pause. She was thinking. As she always did: a slow, careful working out of the possibilities latent in everything.

"But you didn't suggest it."

"No, I certainly did not."

"No."

The silence prolonged itself. He even wondered whether she had dropped off to sleep—she had seemed so pale and exhausted. He studied her, turning his head a little, then took her right wrist gently with his left hand. She tensed up, then relaxed: this was very different from the killing grip Jasper used.

"Alice, you should really get free of this riffraff."

"Riffraff!" she expostulated, with as much energy as she had left. "These are *people*."

He said deliberately, "Riffraff."

She drew in her breath; but let it out quietly.

"What did Muriel tell you, then?"

"What do you suppose she told me? You aren't stupid, Alice."

She could feel herself swelling and oozing. Tears ran down her cheeks, she supposed.

"And what about the party," she almost sobbed. "You weren't there."

He remained silent.

Then, gently, he put his arm under her neck, and his left hand on her left upper arm, on the side away from him. He seemed, at the same time, to be lightly supporting her and holding her so as to make sure she would not slide away from him.

"Alice, you must separate yourself from them."

"From Jasper, you mean."

"From Jasper, Bert, and the rest. They are just playing little games."

"They don't think so."

"No, but you do, I believe."

A silence again. She had now at last almost relaxed in his hold, and he reached over with his right hand to lay it on her waist under her breasts. But she wouldn't, couldn't have this, and irritably shook him off.

"They are playing, Alice, like little children with explosives. They are very dangerous people. Dangerous to themselves and to others."

"And you aren't dangerous."

"No."

She gave a little laugh, derisive but admiring.

"No, Alice. If you do things properly and carefully, then only the people get hurt who should get hurt."

She thought about this for a long time, and he did not interrupt her. She said, "Who do you take orders from?"

"I take orders. And I give them."

She thought.

"You were trained in the Soviet Union?"

"Yes."

"You are Russian," she stated.

"Half Russian: I had an Irish father. And, no, I am not going to bore you with my interesting history."

Now a long time went by, about ten minutes. She could easily have been asleep, for she breathed slowly and deeply, but her eyes were open.

He turned slightly towards her, and she instantly clenched up and moved away from him, though still inside his arm.

"You are a very pure, good woman," said Comrade Andrew softly. "I like that in you."

This, it seemed, she could have contemplated for even longer than his previous remarks. What he could see on her face was an abstracted, bemused look due to exhaustion, but there was a demureness, too, which almost incited him to further efforts. Almost: something stopped him, perhaps the fact that the demureness was masking a surprisingly violent reaction to the word "pure." Was she, Alice, pure? Was that what she had been all this time without knowing it? Well, perhaps she would have to think about it; if pure was what she was, then she would have to live with it! *It was the word!* You couldn't use the word "pure" like that in Britain now, it simply wasn't on, it was just silly. If he didn't know that, then . . . How were they trained, people like Andrew? Perhaps it didn't matter that he was so alien, so different; after all, Britain was full of foreigners. Had it mattered here, in 43 and 45? Well, that depended on what he wanted to achieve. Carrying on like Lenin hadn't upset anyone (except Faye and Roberta), but then, she, Alice, knew only part of the picture. What else was he up to?

At last he broke the silence with, "Alice, I think you should take a holiday."

This so amazed her that she tried to sit up, and he pulled her down.

Now she lay close beside him, and his hot strong body began to send waves of sensation right through her. She was fascinated and disgusted. She kept her eyes straight up at the ceiling, for she knew what she would see if she looked down along his body. She wasn't going to get involved with *that*, "pure" or not!

She said, "I don't understand why you are always wanting me to do such middle-class things."

"What's middle-class about a holiday? Everyone has to have holidays. Modern life is very bad for everyone." She thought he was teasing her, but a glance showed him to be serious.

"Anyway, where could I go? You despise all the people I know."

"I didn't say all of them. Of course not."

"You don't mind Pat, I seem to remember. Did you know she's left Bert because she doesn't think he is serious, either?"

"Yes, I did know. *She* is a serious person. Like you, Alice."

"Well, you yourself were wanting Bert to do something or other."

"I have changed my mind about him," he said severely. "That was an error of judgement on my part."

"Well, I don't know," she said drearily at last. She began a small childish snuffling.

"I do. You are tired, Comrade Alice. You work and you work, and most of these people aren't worth it."

At this she let out a real wail, like a child, turned to him, and was held, like a child, against him, while he made consoling, soothing noises. She cried herself out.

"Poor Alice," he said at last. "But it is no good crying. You are going to have to make a decision. Look, these two Errol Flynns are going to Moscow. Why don't you leave before they come back?"

"Errol Flynn!"

"Don't you like Errol Flynn? I have always enjoyed his films."

"There is a great difference in our two cultures," she said, dreamily, speaking into his chest. They were lying in such a way that his hard protrusion was kept away from her, so she didn't mind it.

"That is very true. But surely people like Errol Flynn? Why, otherwise, is he a famous star?"

"Well," she said, "I'm going to think about all this."

"Yes, you must."

"And when are you coming back?"

"How did you know I was going away?"

"Oh, I just thought you might be."

He hesitated. "You are right, as it happens. I shall be away, probably, for some weeks—" He felt her seem to shrink, and he said, "Or perhaps only for a week or two." Another pause. "And, Alice," he said, "you must, you *must* separate yourself. Believe me, Alice, I'm not without experience of . . . this type of person. Where they are, there is always trouble."

After some minutes, she sat up, putting aside his hands in a tidy, housewifely way.

She said, "Thank you, Comrade Andrew. I shall think carefully about everything you have said."

"And thank you, Comrade Alice. I am sure you will."

From the door, she turned to give him an awkward smile, and went out, hurrying so as not to have to talk to Muriel, who, though a serious person, was not one Alice was prepared to like, even at the behest of Comrade Andrew.

The few days that followed were the happiest she had known.

Usually, when Jasper was in tow—a phrase other people had used, not she—to a brother figure, like Bert, she saw little of him. But they were asking her to accompany them in everything they did. The cinema, more than once. The National Theatre—Bert said that Shakespeare had many lessons for the struggle, and they must learn to use every weapon life offered them if they were not to be primitive Marxists. They spent an evening in a pub that Alice knew was chosen carefully by Jasper so as not to show her even a whisker of that other life of his. And not to show Bert, either . . .

But best of all, though they did not go slogan-painting, which

was Alice's favourite, Jasper suggested a day's demonstrating. This
he did, she knew, to please her, and to make up for his being away.

The discussions about where, and against whom, they would
demonstrate were as agreeable as the expedition itself. Of course, in
this fascistic stage of Britain's history, there could not be any lack
of something to protest about; but it happened that the coming
weekend would be rich in choice. The Defence Secretary was to
speak in Liverpool, the Prime Minister in Milchester, and a certain
fascistic American professor in London. His "line"—that the differences between human beings were genetically, not culturally determined—incensed, as was to be expected, the Women's Movement,
and Faye became hysterical at the mention of his name. On the
Friday evening, they sat around, after a good supper of Alice's soup
and pizza, and talked about the next day.

The kitchen was mellow, alive. The jug on the little stool held
tulips and lilacs. Reggie and Mary had contributed two bottles of
red wine, about which Reggie—*naturally*—talked knowledgeably.

Although tomorrow it would be May, they seemed enclosed by
a steady cold rain, and that made this scene, this company, even
pleasanter. So Alice thought, smiling and grateful, although her
heart ached. Her poor heart seemed to live a life of its own these
days, refusing to be brought to heel by what she thought. But to
linger there all evening, with good friends, was agreeable. For,
since the party which had made them one, many of the stresses
seemed to have gone.

Even Philip, who would be working all weekend and could not
demonstrate with them, contributed useful thoughts. For instance,
that the Greenpeace demo would have been his choice: it was only
because of the efforts of Greenpeace that the government had had to
admit the extent of the radioactive pollution; otherwise it would
certainly have gone on lying about it. Reggie and Mary, bound
tomorrow for Cumberland, liked this: what they felt had been said.
For they—they could not prevent it from showing that they felt
this—believed that demonstrating on specific issues, such as the
spoiling of a coastline, was more effective than a general protest,
like "shouting and screaming at Maggie Thatcher."

Thus showing what he felt about much of their politics, or at least their methods, Reggie did slightly chill the good humour, which was strong enough to let them tease the Greenpeace couple in a robust chorus of "ohhh"s and groans.

"That's right," said Mary, putting her hand into Reggie's for support; "you aren't going to change *her* ideas with a few boos. But facts will unlodge them."

"I agree," said Philip. It was an effort for him to do this—challenge the real power holders of the commune (as they were now calling it, not a squat). But he did it. He looked even frailer and smaller than he had before he started this new job. There was a peaky, sharp-edged look to him. His eyes were red. But there was a tough, angry little look, too; he was being given a bad time at his work, which, said the Greek, his employer, went too slowly.

Oh yes, all this love and harmony was precarious enough, Alice was thinking as she sat and smiled; just one little thing—puff!—and it would be gone. Meanwhile, she put both hands around her mug of coffee, feeling how its warmth stole through her, and thought: It is like a family, it *is*.

Faye was saying, her teeth showing as she bared them, in her characteristic cold excitement, "Boos! Screams! I'm going to *kill* him! What right has he got to come here with all the filthy poison of his about women. We have enough reactionaries of our own!"

Roberta said, "All creeping out of their little holes and showing their true colours. Are you coming with us, Jasper? Bert? Show solidarity with the women?"

A pause. It was to Milchester that Alice longed to go. To Mrs. Thatcher. But here was a lift to Liverpool, and that would cost nothing. Jasper knew she wanted Milchester. So did Bert. She had said she had no money. Which was true; only her Social Security. She was ready to go to Liverpool. She hated the Defence Secretary, and not only because of his policies—there was something about that sly, malevolent Tory face of his. . . .

As for the fascist American professor, she could not see what Roberta and Faye and all the others were on about. She had never been able to see why the word "genetic" should provoke such rage.

She thought they were silly, and even frivolous. If that's how things were, then—they were. One had to build around that.

Once, long ago, during her student days, she had said—earnestly, enquiringly (in a genuine attempt at harmony based on shared views)—that women had breasts "and all that kind of thing," whereas men "were differently equipped," and surely that must be genetic? And if so, then the glands and hormones must be different? Genetically? This had caused such a storm of resentment that the commune had taken days to recover. All this sex business, she thought, was like that! Anything to do with sex! It simply made people unbalanced. Not themselves. One simply had to learn to keep quiet and let them all get on with it! Provided they left her out of it. . . .

Twenty years ago, more, her mother, in her slapdash, friendly, loud, earth-motherish way, had informed Alice that she would shortly menstruate, but she was sure she knew all about that anyway. Of course Alice had known about it from school, but her mother's saying it put it on her agenda, so to speak, made it all real. She was angry, not with Nature, but with her mother. Thereafter, her attitude towards "the curse"—her mother insisted on using this jolly word for it, saying it was accurate—was one of detached efficiency. She was not going to let anything so tedious get in the way of living.

When people probed her about her attitudes towards feminism, sexual politics, it was always this beginning (as she saw it) that she went back to in her mind. "Of course people *ought* to be equal," she would say, starting already to sound slightly irritated. "That goes without saying." In short, she was always finding herself in a false position.

Now she sat silent, cuddling her rapidly cooling coffee, smiling away, and waiting for the subject of the fascist professor to pass.

It did, and Bert remarked, "I've always liked Milchester."

This seemed to various people thoroughly off the point. Was he drunk, perhaps? He certainly was drinking more than his share. Everyone was humouring him these days, because of Pat. Unconsciously, probably. His appearance, his condition claimed this from them. He was gaunt, morose, even absent-minded; it was as though other thoughts ran parallel to the ones he expressed.

He went on, "It's always been a garrison town."

Incredulous exclamations. Faye said, "God, you're mad, you like that? War, soldiers?"

Bert said, "But it's interesting. Why should towns go on being the same, century after century. Milchester was a garrison town under the Romans."

A silence. Thrown off balance by this note so different from their usual one, they remembered that he had done History at university.

"Countries, for that matter," said Bert. "Britain goes on being the same. Russia goes on being the same. Germany—"

"Any minute now we are going to have national characters, like genetic doom," said Faye, furious.

Bert, recalled to himself by her tone, shrugged, and sat silent.

"We'll go to Milchester," said Jasper, and, catching Alice's glance, smiled, then winked. Proudly: he was proud of being nice to her. This meant he would pay for her, the train fare. Weekend return. *Eleven pounds.* For the three of them, thirty-three pounds. With that they could buy . . . But that was silly; people had to have a break. Holidays. Comrade Andrew had said so.

She smiled intimately at Jasper, tears of gratitude imminent, but his eyes shifted away from the pressure of her emotion.

Faye said violently to Roberta, "It looks as if you and I will be on our own!"

"Hardly alone, darling. There'll be a good turnout, I'm sure."

Faye tittered, looking accusingly at her comrades, and then said, "Well, I'm for bed." She went out without saying good night. Roberta smiled at them all, asking toleration for Faye, and went after her. They could hear how Faye said on the stairs that they were all fascists and sexists. They smiled at one another.

Then Reggie and Mary said they were to be picked up tomorrow at five, so as to get to Cumberland in time for the demo, and they wanted an early night.

Philip went, too; he was starting work at eight in the morning.

Jasper, Bert, and Alice sat on discussing tomorrow. Alice saw that Jasper did not want her to throw eggs or fruit at Mrs. Thatcher. He did not say so, but it was obvious. That meant he wanted her here with him, not in prison. This made her wildly happy and grateful. Affectionate impulses kept attacking her arms; they yearned to embrace him. Sisterly kisses inhabited her smiles. He felt this, and, though he was explaining plans to her, addressed himself to Bert. He was not going to let himself be arrested, because he and Bert were so soon off to the Soviet Union. The visas might come any day, but if not in time for this trip, then there was another with vacancies in a week.

Alice was disappointed that she must stay in an orderly part of the crowd, but never mind, another time.

Bert said he was going to bed. At once Jasper got up and said he was, too. Alice understood he did not want to be alone with her, though she knew he was happy enough to have her there when Bert was. She went up into the room she had shared with him, next to Bert's. Bert was of course less noisy without Pat; but he was sleeping badly, as she could hear. And tonight, even with the door tight shut, she could hear that Faye was having one of her turns.

"Faye had one of her turns last night," Roberta might say, having forgotten that the old-fashioned phrase—Victorian?—once used humorously by Faye ("I was 'aving one of me turns, me dear") —was meant to be humorous, so that it had become ordinary speech. At the moments when Roberta used it, she acquired a workaday, bygone look, was like a servant or a lower-class person from a play on the box. Theatrical. When were Faye and Roberta themselves? Only when they had been beaten back, down, by some person or situation, into being the people who used those clumsy blurting labouring heavy voices, which made them seem as if they had been taken over by pitiful strangers who could not be expected to know Faye, know Roberta.

Alice slept badly. She woke to hear Reggie and Mary go downstairs; their cheerful voices were loud, as if they were alone in the house and it belonged to them. She heard Roberta and Faye go down, quiet, not talking. It was nine before Bert woke next door; he was lighting cigarettes one after another. She thought, Perhaps we're not going to get to Queen Bitch Thatcher today. And descended to the empty kitchen, determined not to show disappointment. Then Bert did come. At once he went to wake Jasper, who, she could see, would easily call the whole thing off. It was raining steadily.

But they did get out of the house and to the train; and watched London give way to the country through the dirty train windows and grey shrouds of rain. Bert was silent, thinking his thoughts, which—Alice suspected—he would be sharing with Jasper were she not there. Jasper was being polite with her.

At the station they took a bus to the university. The great cold lunatic buildings looked at them through the downpour, and Alice felt murder fill her heart. She knew most of the new universities; had visited them, demonstrated outside them. When she saw one she felt she confronted the visible embodiment of evil, something that wished to crush and diminish her. The enemy. If I could put a bomb under that lot, she was thinking, if I could . . . Well, one of these days . . .

They were late. Outside the main entrance about sixty demonstrators huddled under plastic hoods and umbrellas, herded by eighty-odd policemen. At the sight of this, Jasper came to life, and ran forward, jeering, "Fascist pigs, pigs, pigs. Cowards! How many of you do you need for one demonstrator?" Alice ran to catch up with him, so as to be beside him, ready to calm him down. Bert came on slowly behind, walking, not running.

The official cars came sweeping up, and before Alice, Jasper, and Bert could reach the crowd, Mrs. Thatcher had got out, and was being led quickly in. Fruit and—as Alice had hoped—eggs sailed through the air, exploding with a dull squelch. Mrs. Thatcher had gone inside.

The demonstrators began a steady chant of "Nuclear missiles out. Out, out, out. Nuclear missiles out, out, out."

They kept it up bravely. Mrs. Thatcher would be inside for two hours, at least.

The policemen were bored and resentful, forced to stand there in the rain; they were only too ready to be provoked. A girl near Alice picked up a large orange from the ground and flung it at a policeman. His helmet was dislodged. Delighted, two policemen came to her. She dodged about in the crowd for a bit, then they caught her, and she went limp and was dragged to a van, her long brown hair trailing wetly. The two policemen came back to a chorus of boos and jeers. Alice could feel Jasper beside her, pulsating with frustrated excitement. He was longing for a real tussle. So was she. So were the police, who grinned challengingly at the demonstrators. Alice, remembering her role, said to Jasper, "Careful, that one over there, he's a brute, he's just waiting to get you." And, since Jasper seemed to be about to explode into action, "Remember, it's Saturday. We don't want to spend the weekend inside. And, anyway, there's your trip, don't forget."

Others, less burdened by circumstance, were throwing fruit and eggs at the police, and were promptly being taken to the vans.

"Fucking police state," shouted Jasper, almost out of control with excitement. He was dodging about in the crowd, as if he were being pursued.

The crowd took it up: "Police state, police state," they yelled.

Alice saw an eye signal pass among the policemen; she knew that they would all be arrested at the slightest provocation. She yearned for it, longed for the moment when she would feel the rough violence of the policemen's hands on her shoulders, would let herself go limp, would be dragged to the van. . . . But she said to Jasper, "Come on, run," and she grabbed him by the hand and they ran. Bert, standing rather by himself at the edge of the crowd, stepped back as the arrests started. He stood watching. But he, too, would be arrested in a moment. Alice, her blood on fire, her face distorted with excitement, rushed in, darted among the policemen, admiring her own skill in it, grabbed Bert, and said, "Come *on*." Bert, roused, said, "Oh yes. Yes, Alice, you're right." And followed her.

"Get them," shouted a policeman, as the three sprinted away.

Five or six policemen set off after them, but one slipped in a puddle, rolled over, and slid along in the mud, and when he tried to get up, he fell again. It seemed that he had hurt himself. The others crowded around him. Meanwhile, disappointed that the chase had been so short, the three found their way to the bus stop. It was pouring steadily, a cold hard rain.

Their spirits sank, now that the challenge of the police was taken off them. It had not been very satisfactory. They were all thinking that they had spent a lot of money for very little.

They went into a café. The men ate sausages and chips; Alice, a salubrious vegetable soup.

They debated about whether to go back to the university for Mrs. Thatcher's exit to the cars. Alice was for it, though she was afraid of the effect of that pink-and-white, assured, complacent Tory face on Jasper. If he were kept in for the weekend, the weekend ticket return would be invalid, and the fares back on Monday would be double.

But she did feel she hadn't had her money's worth.

They agreed they would go back, to show solidarity with the others—if any demonstrators still remained. But it began to rain even harder. A real tropical deluge, if such cold rain deserved the name "tropical."

They returned to the station and, dispirited, to London. There they went to the pictures, and then, finding Faye and Roberta in the kitchen, they all swapped notes. Clearly, they—Jasper and Alice and Bert—would have done much better to have gone to the anti-professor demo, which had been a great success. About a thousand people, Faye said—Alice automatically corrected this to "six hundred." Mostly women, but quite a lot of men. They had jostled the professor badly, had nearly brought him down, had got him really rattled. "Well, that ought to give him pause for thought, at least," said Roberta happily, thinking of how she had shrieked he was a scummy sexist and in the pay of the fascists.

Even the Thatcher demonstration sounded effective, in retrospect. After all, quite a few had been arrested. Reggie and Mary had—of course!—a television in their room. They all went up, and crowded in, making jokes about the large bed, the tidy furniture, the carpets. They sat on the bed and watched the news. There was no mention of the fascist professor, but there was a brief scene of the demonstrators struggling with the police at the university. The three were disappointed that they did not appear on the screen. The newscaster said that at one point the police were afraid a bomb had been thrown. "It was an orange," screamed Alice, and they all laughed and jeered, and went down for more talk in the kitchen, taking with them four bottles of wine from a case of it that Reggie and Mary had under the dressing table.

"They won't mind," said Faye, laughing, but in a way that said they all knew they would mind very much.

Philip came in, but he was tired and went to bed.

The five sat up drinking and talking till late.

The demonstrations sounded better and better as the night wore on. They drank to the comrades in the police cells. Alice was sad she was not there—as it happened she had not been arrested for some time; she was beginning to feel she was not pulling her weight in the Struggle. But it was just as well, for on Monday Jasper and Bert were told the visas had gone through and the trip was on. They went off that afternoon.

Alice said, as they left, "See you in ten days."

She saw them glance at each other—yet again the ridiculous, insulting, perfectly obvious "secret" shared look that people used all the time. It came to her, stunningly, that they did not expect to be back in ten days.

She thought this all over carefully, slept on it, and then wrote to the address she had for Pat.

Bert and Jasper have gone off, she wrote. Why don't you come down for a day or two? Or, if you can't come, please write. Do you know anything about this trip? Did Bert say anything about not coming back in ten days?

This letter brought a card, "Ring me at nine o'clock Thursday or Friday. Much love, Pat." This "Much love" hurt Alice, and she wept a little.

When she heard Pat's bright, firm, likable voice, Alice pleaded, "Do come down, do, Pat."

"But I am short of money."

"I'll pay for your ticket. Do come."

Pat said she would, and Alice understood, from the rise in her own spirits, how little she felt at home with Faye and Roberta, how little she had in common with the respectable Reggie and Mary.

Pat came next day, and the two young women commandeered the sitting room and stayed there, gossiping, exchanging news. Pat had met people Alice knew, in the commune she now lived in. Alice had to tell about the anti-Thatcher demo. She also delicately mentioned the fascist professor, hoping for some kind of support from Pat in her own private thoughts. But on Pat's face came the helpless resentful look Alice half expected, and Pat reached for a cigarette and began to smoke furiously.

"You don't imagine it's any accident," she said, "that all this stuff about genetic differences is being peddled now!"

"Why?" asked Alice, timid but dogged. "You mean he's being paid to do it? Who? The CIA?"

Pat tossed her head angrily, blew out bitter clouds, and said vaguely, "Well, why not?"

Alice decided to leave it; no point in going on. Instead she asked Pat why she, Alice, had this impression that Bert and Jasper were not planning to come home at once. Pat sighed, and looked with unmistakable pity at her friend.

"They will be home, Alice," she said gently. "On the day appointed. But *they* think they won't be, do you see?"

Alice saw. In fact she had seen the moment Jasper had first mentioned it. But then she had blocked it off, for it was all so painfully ridiculous.

"Look, it's Ireland, all over again. They had it all worked out. They will say to the Intourist guide: 'Comrades, we want to speak to someone in authority.'"

"Oh, God," muttered Alice, ashamed. "Oh, no!"

"Oh, yes! Yes, yes! The Intourist guide will of course say at once, 'Whom would you like to see, comrades? Comrade Andropov?' 'Oh no, not really,' Jasper and Bert will say modestly. 'Someone less important will do for us.'"

Pat was laughing, but not happily, since she was mocking Bert; and Alice was suffering for Jasper.

"At once some very important comrade will appear, and say,

'Comrade Willis, Comrade Barnes? At your service!' Jasper and Bert will explain that they have decided to train as spies, preferably in Czechoslovakia or in Lithuania, where all the best spy schools are. The Russian will say, 'Of course, what a good idea! But it will take an hour or two to fix up. Just wait for my return, comrades.' "

Alice dubiously laughed, stopped laughing, and remarked, "Well, all right. But what about Comrade Andrew?"

"What about Comrade Andrew?"

"It's pretty casual with him, don't you think? I mean, he says to just anybody he fancies, how about a spot of training."

"He's not done too badly, who he's chosen."

"Bert?"

"Bert said no. But just imagine Bert actually under discipline somewhere. In some kind of structured situation. He has a lot of qualities, Bert has."

"Me?" enquired Alice, dubiously. "Are you going to say I need a structured situation?"

"No! I am certainly not. What you need is . . ."

"Oh, all right, I know. To be free of Jasper."

"Poor Alice," said Pat gently.

"Then poor Pat!"

"That, too!"

Alice put her head down on the arm of her chair, all energy gone out of her, as happened at those times when she was seeing Jasper clearly.

The two women stayed where they were for a few minutes, silent. Alice did not move; Pat smoked restlessly.

Alice said, "There's another thing, so many people knowing. What's to stop people from informing?"

"You mean, the police?"

"Yes."

"Well, who of us would?"

Alice allowed the faces of those in the know to pass before her. Sat straight up, eyes shut, looking at these mental portraits. Faye. Roberta. Bert. Jasper. Pat. Herself. Muriel. Caroline? Jocelin?

"I suppose not," she said. But she remained where she was, upright, looking. Now it was at the scene of her with Andrew after she had seen the . . . whatever it was at the bottom of the pit in the garden at 45. Pat did not know about that. Only she, Alice, knew. . . . Only she, Alice, knew because she had not told, would never tell, anyone else. She was reliable, she was. Because this was true, and because she had confidence in her absolute discretion, she felt confidence in Comrade Andrew.

"Yes, I think I agree with you," she said. She spoke modestly, with a little air of discretion, of judgement. Pat smiled, and with affection, because this was very much Alice; and she said, deliberately changing the subject and their mood, "And now we are going to have a good time. That's what I've come for!"

Then Pat suggested all kinds of little treats that Alice would never have thought of for herself.

They went to tea at the Savoy, for a start. Pat treated Alice. Pat wore a very smart black wool dress embroidered with bright wools she had bought at a jumble sale, and looked more striking, more fashionable than any other woman in the great pillared, gilded, romantic Savoy. Alice wore a skirt, but otherwise was as usual. They ate a lot, and Pat was fussy about her tea. They came out like successful buccaneers.

Then they spent a morning in Harrods, buying with their eyes. Rather, Pat did: Alice did not care about luxury, but she enjoyed Pat's enjoyment. Again Pat wore this best dress of hers, the dramatic black wool, which made her, with her vivid glossy colouring, seem exotic, un-English. Then, next day, with the rain easing off, they went to Regent's Park and walked about among puddles and lilacs and flowering cherries.

Then Pat said she must go back home. She said "home," Alice noted.

She said to Pat, "Will you come down again? Soon?"

Pat looked self-conscious, laughed, and said, "Alice, I don't think we will be seeing each other again. Well, perhaps. And yet again, perhaps not . . ." She was making a joke of it, in her way, but her eyes sent messages of regret.

"Why?" demanded Alice. "But why, why, why?"

Pat sobered, and said, "Alice, I keep telling you, I am serious, unlike those two bloody lunatics of ours."

And with this she kissed Alice, tears in her eyes, and went off, running, to the tube. Out—Alice could see—of her life.

Alice slept on this, too, but did not feel enlightened when she woke in the morning. Perhaps she did not want to be.

She seemed to have lost impetus, did not feel like doing anything. Joan Robbins was in her garden. Alice stood talking with her for a time. Among other things, she learned that the two houses had been empty for six years. "Well, not exactly empty," said Joan Robbins, embarrassed; and went on to talk of the people who had been there before the Council had commandeered the homes, families with children, grandparents, many visitors. They had been keen gardeners; the two gardens had been wonderful.

Soon some kind of social worker arrived and brought the old lady down to sit in the garden. Alice talked to her, too. As always when she stepped out of her own life, into the world of ordinary people, she felt divided, confused. Thus had she felt all the time she lived with Jasper in her mother's house; it was why she had not wanted to stay there, was always pressing Jasper to leave. Now, after weeks with her own kind, comrades of one sort or another, her belief that her kind of life was the only one (for her now, for everybody later) was strengthened. Joan Robbins seemed to her pathetic, fussing over her clematis with fungicides and sprays; the old woman was half demented, and driving Joan Robbins crazy with continual demands. Alice, thinking firmly, "Life simply oughtn't to be like this!," went back to number 43, and there on the doorstep was Caroline from next door. She had a packet for Alice. She handed it over, said no, she wouldn't come in, and went off to the bus stop. Alice looked into the packet. It was money. Inside the hall she quickly counted it. Five hundred. With a note from Muriel, saying, "Comrade Andrew said this was for you."

Alice slid the packet into her sleeping bag, and went to number 45. As she arrived, Muriel was coming out, with a suitcase. But at first Alice did not recognise her.

She saw then that Muriel was not happy to see her, that she had probably counted on going off before Alice got there.

Alice said, "I must talk to you."

Muriel said, "I don't think I have got anything to say."

They went quickly into the room used by Comrade Andrew, which had become a bedroom, for there were four sleeping bags arranged along the wall.

Muriel stood in the centre of the room, waiting for Alice to get on with it. Her suitcase stood beside her.

Muriel was not wearing battle dress today, or anything like it, but a very well cut linen suit in blue. From Harrods. Alice had seen it there the day before yesterday.

Muriel had her hair in the Princess Diana sheepdog cut.

Alice knew that Muriel was an upper-class girl and this was why she disliked her so much. She, like all her kind, had this decisive putting-down manner, implicit in every word and glance. Alice, at her democratic progressive school, which was full of such girls, had decided in the first week that she loathed them and always would.

Another thought well to the forefront of her mind was that Comrade Andrew had had an affair with Muriel because of the attraction of such girls for working-class people who professed to despise them.

"Why did Comrade Andrew leave this money for me?"

"It is nothing to do with me. Nothing at all," said Muriel, as cuttingly and definitively as Alice expected.

"He must have said something."

The two young women were standing facing each other in the large room, full of light, and also of traffic noise from the main road.

"Damn this bloody traffic," said Muriel, and went to the windows, one, two, three, shutting each with a slam.

She returned to stand opposite Alice, having in the interval (which was why she had gone to the windows) made up her mind what to say.

Alice forestalled her with, "What am I supposed to do in return?"

At this Comrade Muriel showed a nicely controlled irritation.

"That you would have to discuss with Comrade Andrew, wouldn't you?"

"But he's not here. When is he coming back?"

"I don't know. If he doesn't come, there will be someone else." And, since Alice remained obstinately confronting her, she defined the situation as she saw it: "Alice, you are either with us or against us."

"I'd be with you—with Comrade Andrew—without the money, wouldn't I?"

"Or do you simply want to go on being one of the useful idiots?"

Alice did not react to this, remained in her stance of infinitely patient, dogged enquiry.

"Lenin," said Muriel. "A useful idiot: vague and untutored enthusiasm for communism. For the Soviet Union. Fellow travellers. You know."

Alice had in fact hardly read Lenin. She felt for him a kind of bowing down of her whole person, like a genuflexion, as to the Perfect Man. That such a giant can have lived! was her feeling, and it was enough. If it came to that, she had read not much more of Marx than the *Communist Manifesto*. She had always said of herself, "Well, I am not an intellectual!"—with a feeling of superiority.

Now she felt that the goose-girl was being irrelevant, as well as offensive.

"I do not believe that Comrade Lenin despised people who sincerely admired the achievements of the working class in the communist countries," said Alice, every bit as decisively, as authoritatively, as Comrade Muriel. Who was silent, gazing at Alice with slightly protuberant, light-blue eyes.

She then remarked, "Comrade Andrew thinks highly of your potential."

The flash of delight that went through Alice made her impervious to anything Muriel might be thinking. She said humbly, "I'm glad."

"Well, that's it, I think," said Muriel, and picked up her case.

"You're off to start your career of crime, then?" said Alice, and laughed heartily at what she'd said. Muriel politely smiled, but she was furious.

"I expect it is the BBC," said Alice thoughtfully. "Or something like that," she added hastily.

At this, Muriel stood for a moment, with her case in her hand, then she set it down, came a step nearer to Alice, and said deliberately, "Alice, you do not ask such questions. You—do—not—ask—such—questions. Do you understand?"

Alice felt herself in the grip of the dreamy knowing state that she had trusted in all her life. "But first I suppose you are off to one of those spy schools in Czechoslovakia or Lithuania," she remarked.

Muriel gasped, and went red. "Who told you?"

"No one told me. If you are off somewhere, looking like that, then I suppose . . . I suppose that's it," she ended lamely, wondering at herself.

Muriel was looking at her very carefully, her eyes like guns.

"If you have such brilliant inspirations, you should keep them to yourself."

"I don't see what you are making such a fuss about; everyone knows that's where the Soviet spy schools are."

"Yes, but . . ." The goose-girl seemed quite wild with exasperation. She was looking at Alice as Alice often found herself being looked at. As though she were, quite simply, not to be credited, not possible! As with Jasper, in such moments, she said stubbornly, "I don't see it. There's something perfectly obvious going on, I say something, and then people get upset. I think it is childish," insisted Alice.

"Then I suppose Andrew told you," concluded Muriel. "He shouldn't have." She stood reflecting for a moment, and then said, "I am quite relieved to be moving out of his sphere. I'll be happier with someone on a higher level."

"Isn't he on a high level?"

"If he were, he wouldn't be dealing with people like us," said Muriel, with a sudden, unexpected, intense sentimentality.

Alice laughed in astonishment that Muriel could admit, even in a maudlin moment, she was on a lower level than anyone at all.

"No," said Muriel, "he's off for more training, too. And in my view he could do with it. There's something a good deal wrong with his judgement, sometimes."

With this, she again grasped her case, lifted it, and went to the door, saying, "Well, good-bye. I don't suppose we shall see each other again. Unless you decide to go for training, too. Comrade Andrew is going to suggest it." Her tone made it quite clear what she thought of Comrade Andrew's plan.

But Alice had suddenly understood something else. She said wildly, "Good God, I've just seen— Pat is going, too, she is, isn't she?"

"If she told you, she shouldn't have," said Muriel.

"She didn't, no, she didn't. I've just . . ."

"I'm late," said Muriel, and walked firmly away from Alice, showing a degree of relief that made Alice think, Well, she's going to need a lot of training, not to show every little thing that's going through her mind.

She went slowly back to number 43 and sat by herself in the kitchen, at the table, thinking.

The strongest thought, which was more a feeling, or an ache, was that Jasper had not told her he had believed he would be away for months. Yes, he had been "nice" to make up for it. But he had not told her! He had never before betrayed her. Yes, of course, there had always been a part of his life she was not told about; she accepted that. But politics—there everything had been discussed.

He had become capable of going off for six months, a year, and not saying a word. Bert? It was Bert's influence?

Yes, of course, there was the question of security, she could see that. But that did not change how she felt.

Something had been cut between him and her; he had severed himself from her.

She was going to do something about it—leave, go to another commune, give him up (but at this she went cold and sad all over), tell him that . . . tell him something or other, but she wouldn't go on like this. People were right, he made use of her.

With this, she took the packet of Comrade Andrew's money from its place in the sleeping bag and went to the post office.

Then she returned to the kitchen table, and sat on in the late afternoon, watching the light go out of the sky, feeling the house go dark about her. She did not want to have to talk to anyone, so when she heard Reggie and Mary, she went walking around and about the streets by herself. For some time she stood outside the flats where her mother lived. The lights she could see up the front of the building were none of them her mother's, for the flat was at the back. She went to peer at the little glow that showed *Mellings*, scribbled on a card. Then she walked home, hoping the kitchen would be empty. It was eleven.

No one was about. She would have a good sleep, and decide what to do in the morning. Probably visit one or other of the communes or squats where she had friends. Or perhaps she would go to the Marxist Summer Festival in Holland. She would be bound to meet people she knew there; and if not, she would soon make new friends.

One thing she was already determined on: she would not be here when Jasper and Bert returned in ten days' time—no, less than a week now.

She would have liked to sink at once into a deep sleep and get away from thinking, but no one slept much in number 43 that night, for Faye was shouting and screaming and hammering on the walls.

Alice thought, for the first time, that the reason Faye was here, and not in the women's commune where the two spent so many of their days, was that she was not welcome there—had been thrown out, in fact. They would not put up with this madwoman. They had had enough. Obvious, when you thought of it: she could spend the day there, but not the night, disturbing people's sleep. But poor Roberta! Her low, urgent, kind voice was at work nearly all night, soothing and admonishing.

Lying awake, listening to Faye's distress, her misery, Alice thought as usual that one day soon there would be no people like Faye. Because of people like Alice. Even Muriel. No more people damaged by life.

She thought, too—steadily, letting her mind open out into one perspective after another—of the implications of what she had learned since she had come here. She simply hadn't had any idea before! All over the country were these people—networks, to use Comrade Andrew's word. Kindly, skilled people watched, and waited, judging when people (like herself, like Pat) were ripe, could be really useful. Unsuspected by the petits bourgeois who were in the thrall of the mental superstructure of fascist-imperialistic Britain, the poor slaves of propaganda, were these watchers, the observers, the people who held all the strings in their hands. In factories, in big industries (where Comrade Andrew wanted her, Alice, to work); in the Civil Service (that was just the place for Comrade Muriel!); in the BBC, in the big newspapers—everywhere, in fact, was this network, and even in little unimportant places like these two houses, numbers 43 and 45, just ordinary squats and communes. Nothing was too small to be overlooked, everyone with any sort of potential was noticed, observed, treasured. . . . It gave her a safe, comfortable feeling.

Alice slept at last, when Faye became silent, and would have slept on through the morning, but Roberta knocked on her door, then called through it that there was something important she had to say.

Alice sat up at once, ready for bad news.

Roberta looked awful, naturally enough. Her eyes were red, her face dragged with exhaustion. More, she had been broken down, or back, into the other Roberta. There was a sluttish look about her, like a slum woman from a 1930s film, particularly when she put a cigarette into her mouth and let it hang on her lip as she talked, crouching beside Alice's sleeping bag. She was in a soiled dressing gown.

"Alice, I've had bad news. My mother is in hospital in Bradford. I've got to go. Do you see? I've got to."

Alice saw that Roberta was still reasoning with Faye in her mind, and asked, "What's wrong with her?"

Roberta said, sullen, "Cancer. She's been ill for a long time. Should have gone before."

Her voice, too, was regressing: North Country intonations strengthened there. Did she come from some awful slum in a Northern industrial town?

Alice was already seeing it all. She was going to be asked to "keep an eye" on Faye, who could not be left in the women's commune; without Roberta they would not have Faye even in the day. She, Alice, for an unspecified period of days, would have to . . .

She said, "As a matter of fact, I had just decided to take off." Her voice sounded hard and sullen, like Roberta's.

But at this Roberta began a noisy weeping. She grabbed Alice's hand and held it hard, looking into Alice's eyes, with, "Oh, Alice, please, please, please, I can't leave Faye with no one, how can I?"

Roberta was trembling. Alice could feel her exhaustion coming into her, through her tightly grasping hand.

"And you have no idea how long you will be gone, or anything," said Alice.

Roberta let go Alice's hand, and sat staring over her hunched-up knees, the cigarette lolling on her lip, eyes empty. The last ditch.

"Oh, God," said Alice. "I suppose I've got to. But I'm not you, Roberta. I'm not going to baby Faye along, the way you do. . . ."

Roberta suddenly went limp. She put her head on her knees, knocking the cigarette onto the sleeping bag. Alice tidily retrieved it, and sat watching Roberta crouched in a womb position, arms around her knees.

"Alice," she heard, "you don't know what this means to me. You can't . . ."

"Of course I do," said Alice. "Without you, Faye couldn't manage at all. She would be in a loony bin. You spend all your time making sure she doesn't fall into *their* hands."

Roberta straightened, sat up, tears spilling everywhere, said in appeal, "*Alice* . . ."

"But there's another side to it, too. She behaves worse with you than with anyone. You let her."

As Roberta protested, Alice went on reasonably, "Oh no, I'm not saying she isn't a nut—she is—but I've noticed before that sometimes someone like that behaves quite ordinarily with everybody, manages everything, you'd never think she was a nut, but there's just one person, with that person, she's out of control. It makes you wonder," said Alice.

Roberta was watching her closely. A new cigarette was being lit, but while this operation went on, Roberta's eyes did not leave Alice's face. Alice saw that the Roberta of number 43 was there again, and the poor Roberta of some dreadful past, once more buried and gone.

Roberta said, not at all annoyed, "Yes, I've thought that myself. It is strange, isn't it? Faye is normal with everyone else— well, nearly always. . . ." Here she invited Alice, with a small rueful smile, to remember the incident when Faye ran shrieking downstairs to expel Monica. And other things. "She'll probably be all right with you."

"If she doesn't try to commit suicide."

A sharp look, repudiating. A quick shake of the head, which meant, Alice knew: I am not prepared even to think about that.

"Well, we have to think about it."

"Look, Alice, I must get dressed and go. I've got an hour to catch the train."

Roberta ran out, and came back, as Alice knew she would, with bottles of pills.

"If you make sure she takes these in the morning, and these before she goes to bed . . ."

Alice took the bottles with a look that said: You know very well I can't make her do anything.

Roberta said, "It's no good saying thank you, what's the good of thank you. But if I can help you some time . . ."

She went, and five minutes later Alice heard her go downstairs, running, and out of the house.

Faye would not wake till midday, or later.

Alice took her time with bathing and dressing, and was in the kitchen drinking coffee when Caroline came in.

She had been wanting to be friends with Caroline, but now she felt that this was bound to be some last straw.

Caroline said, moving to the kettle and the coffee jar, as if she already lived there, "Alice, I've come to ask if it would be all right if I moved in."

Alice only shrugged; but held out her mug to Caroline, for a refill.

Caroline, after a quick inspection of Alice from those sharp eyes of hers, filled the two cups and sat down with hers, at the other end of the table.

"What's wrong?"

Alice told her.

"Only a short-term problem," pronounced Caroline, dismissing it.

Alice laughed. "Very well, then," she said, "so what's wrong next door?"

Caroline sat briskly stirring sugar into her cup, in itself a gesture that announced self-determination in these days when people confess to sugar as once they might have done to a drink problem. One, two, three large teaspoons went in, and Caroline took up the mug to drink, with a frank and greedy enjoyment.

Alice laughed again, differently. She had been right: she and Caroline were already at the start of that mysterious process known as "getting on."

"The police raided us again last night."

"Haven't you arranged with the Council yet?"

"We were always going to do it, but we didn't get around to it. Anyway, that wouldn't make any difference."

"So what were they looking for?"

"They were certainly looking for something. They took the place apart."

"But nothing there?"

"Nothing."

Caroline was waiting for the questions that Alice was framing in her mind.

"So somebody did inform?"

"We think not. Actually, I think they were looking for smack."

"But nobody uses it, do they?"

"Pot, of course. Not heroin. No, I think they thought forty-five was a cache. You know, a bale or two of best-quality heroin lurking beneath the floor."

Alice was thinking, intently. Her face was puckered up, like an anxious dog's.

"Hey, relax," said Caroline, "no harm done."

"How long were . . . *things* coming in and out, next door?"

"Not long. A few weeks. And usually only for a day or so. Sometimes an hour or two."

"Always for Comrade Andrew?"

"Well, he organised it all."

"How did Comrade Andrew get to next door in the first place?"

"He met Muriel somewhere. He really goes for Muriel."

"You're saying that he chose forty-five to live in because Muriel was there?"

"He hasn't been living there. He's in and out. I don't suppose he's ever been there longer than two or three days at a time."

"And Comrade Muriel goes for Andrew."

"Actually, I think it is she who turns the cheek."

"Oh well, I don't care about all that," said Alice, as usual saddened and disgusted. "Anyway, it all seems very hit and miss."

"Why? The proof's in the pudding. The police have actually been in three times while I've been here. They never found anything. Once half the rubbish sacks had just enough rubbish to cover what was really in them."

"Which was?"

"Oh," said Caroline airily, spooning up thick wet yellow sugar from the bottom of her mug, and licking it slowly with a fat pink tongue, "things, you know."

Alice was silent. She was taking in everything she could of this plump, healthy creature who sat there exuding physical enjoyment. She was trying to understand the secret of it. But, noted Alice, though she might look like a sleek seal, smiling away and talking—presumably—about explosives, her pupils remained tight and unrelenting. They gave her a shrewd, even cold, look, and Alice was relieved to see it. She felt Caroline could be relied on.

"Well, I suppose explosives," she remarked indifferently. "That's what I thought from the start, really."

"Well, that kind of thing. But I said to Comrade Andrew, I said, 'Have any of us actually been asked about what comes in and out? I don't seem to remember a vote being taken?' "

"You were there before he was?"

"Long before. I moved in a year ago. I was there alone for weeks. Then Muriel came. Then, suddenly, Andrew came. We never knew how Muriel had heard of it—Comrade Muriel is not, I would say, one of the world's natural squatters."

"No."

"But she took the place over. The next thing was Paul and Edward—now, I think that she asked them in because Andrew told her to. Then I asked some friends of mine, three girls, who were in a bad squat in Camberwell. But Muriel soon got rid of them."

"How?"

"Not so much"—said Caroline judiciously, smiling with the pleasure she was getting from talking and being understood—"not so much by what she did, but by what she *is* . . ." She waited for Alice to laugh. Alice laughed. Caroline went on, "They simply did not like the way Muriel assumed command, and then when Andrew moved in, they left."

Alice sat thinking. She knew, from how Caroline was eyeing her, that thinking was what she was supposed to be doing.

"Very well," said Alice at last. "So you don't like Comrade Andrew."

"Who *is* Comrade Andrew?" asked Caroline. "Who is he to give orders and say what is and what is not to happen?"

"We don't have to do what he says. It is up to us to say no or yes."

"But difficult to say no when a car simply arrives with five cases of pamphlets. Or something."

More coffee. More sugar. Alice could not prevent herself from thinking: But your *teeth* . . .

"And," pronounced Caroline, smiling, amenable, sociable, but her little brown eyes hard and controlled, "do you know something? I do not give a damn about the fucking bloody Soviet Union. Or about the fucking KGB. Or any of that."

"KGB" used like that did give Alice a bit of a shock; she had not actually said to herself, I am involved with the KGB. Besides, the words had a ruthless quality which was hard to associate with Comrade Andrew. She was silent, then said, "But it is a useful way to get trained. I mean, for some people."

"For some people. And if they want that kind of training."

"There is something about it all that doesn't fit," Alice said at last, with difficulty. It was hard to criticise Comrade Andrew. Aloud, at least; in her thoughts she could not prevent herself.

"Exactly. And do you know what it is? I have—strangely enough—been giving the matter my most earnest consideration."

Alice laughed, as she was expected to.

"Yes. In my experience, which is not vast, but enough, everything turns out to be some kind of a muddle. You are imagining amazing fantastic brilliant plots, organised down to the last fantastically efficient detail, but no, when you discover the truth about anything, let alone KGB plots, it is always some stupid silly mess."

Now Alice was really disturbed. It was because this was something her mother said. Had been saying recently—part of this new, upsetting phase she was in. Over and over again in the last four years, how many times had Alice not heard Dorothy Mellings exclaim, and with a relish in the scandal of it all that made Alice furious, "Just another bloody balls-up, that's all. They've blown it! They've fucked it up. Oh, don't waste your time sitting there trying to work it all out! It's just another little *mess*." Usually to

Zoë Devlin. Who would try to reason with her—with Dorothy. In the way that she had recently been doing—reasoning with her mother, patiently, perseveringly, when she said this kind of thing. "Dorothy, *everything* can't be a muddle, it's just not *on* to slide out of it all like that! What's got into you, Dorothy? It's as if you can't be bothered to think anything out any more?" And Dorothy Mellings to Zoë Devlin: "Who's sliding out? I think you are. You are living in some kind of rose-pink dreamworld, you think everything goes along, all sensible and as the result of mature decisions! Well, it doesn't! It's just a great big bleeding *mess.*"

To hear her mother's words coming so complacently out of Caroline's plump smiling face was so much of a blow to Alice, her two worlds becoming confused in this way, that she missed a good bit of what Caroline was saying. When she listened again she heard, "I think our Comrade Andrew was not up to his job. I think the West went to his head. The fleshpots, you know."

"Then God help him," said Alice, disgusted.

"Quite so. And Muriel was just too much for him, girl from the shires, Roedean and all that."

"Roedean, is she?"

"Roedean and finishing school and gourmet-cooking school. Isn't it amazing how the upper classes go for communism? Do you think Comrade Marx foresaw that in his crystal ball?"

"Who's talking," said Alice, knowing it was not right to talk about Marx like this.

"I? I'm not upper-class. Just boring old middle-class, like you."

"I am one generation away from working-class. On my mother's side."

"Congratulations," said Comrade Caroline, laughing.

"For all that," said Alice, "I am sure Comrade Muriel will be very good."

"Who said she wouldn't? Born for it. I can see the headlines now: 'Red Mole Caught Red-Handed in the . . .' where, do you think?"

"BBC," said Alice, unable to prevent herself.

"Right on. Or the *Times.* The *Guardian,* do you think?"

"No, the *Times*, wrong style for the *Guardian*. But probably by the time she's been trained . . . She's very clever, I am sure she is."

"So am I, but Comrade Andrew didn't fall for Comrade Muriel because of her espionage potential. They were hardly ever out of bed. Or, to be accurate, off the floor."

Alice turned the switch. She said vaguely, "Oh well, I don't care about all that. And so. Muriel's gone. Andrew's gone. You want to come here. That leaves . . ."

"And Jocelin wants to come here, too."

"So there will only be Paul and Edward next door?"

"They are moving into a flat this week. They've found work. Rather, Andrew found them work. In a very strategic place. 'Nuff said."

"So, soon there'll be a different set of squatters next door."

"Provided I'm not there. No hot water. Cold as Siberia. Not like this house."

There was an empty room on the top floor, and another next to Roberta and Faye's room.

"I don't see why not," said Alice.

"I can't wait to come. Apart from anything else, the police dug up that pit in the garden, and all the rubbish we buried is blowing everywhere."

For some reason this seemed to Alice the last straw she had been expecting. "Oh no," she wailed. "Oh, God, no."

"Oh yes. Back to square one. We said to them, when they had dug up everything, Aren't you going to put all that rubbish back? 'Piss off,' they said. Charming, Old Bill is. Well, I'll get my things."

Alice went next door with her and stood at the gate looking in. Rubbish everywhere, and a brisk spring wind was blowing it about. The pit where she had seen—but what?—was an ugly trench, with pale earth in untidy heaps.

But she could not leave Faye alone like this, and so she went back.

. . .

Faye did not come down until evening, wan and sad, and ready to weep. But she was in command of herself and willing to take part in the communal evening meal, with Caroline and Jocelin, Mary and Reggie, Philip and Alice.

It was all going on very nicely when, about nine, there was a violent knocking at the door.

"Oh no, not again," said Caroline. Alice was already off and at the front door, opening it with a smile.

Two policemen, one of them the youth with the vicious face. They were in a bad mood, sent out to do something they didn't want to do.

"We've been informed you have something buried in your garden," said the ugly youth. "We are going to dig."

"You know what's there. We've told you," said Alice. She was far from laughing. She knew that very little would make these two start breaking the place up.

"We know what you have told us," said the other policeman, whom Alice had not seen before.

"I'll get you our spade," said Alice.

"We've got our own, thank you."

Alice took them round to where the pit had been dug. The light from the kitchen fell out here.

"This is where the earth has been disturbed," said the vicious youth to the other.

Alice retreated indoors swiftly. She said to the others, who were ready to explode into laughter, "Don't, don't, don't laugh, or they'll get us for it." To Faye, who was tittering and swaying, on the verge of hysteria, "Faye, don't." Alice knew if that little psychopath outside was provoked by Faye at her worst, he could do anything. "We can laugh afterwards, not now."

"She's right," said Caroline, and they sat, their faces wooden, containing an anguish of laughter.

Outside, in the streaming light from the window, the two men dug. Not for more than a couple of minutes. They straightened, stood on their spades, then disappeared.

Alice had been careful to leave the front door open, so that they would be visible sitting round their meal: the comfortable kitchen, the flowers, the food.

She went to the front door, looking polite and helpful.

The vicious one was ready to explode with temper.

"You people should be prosecuted," he shouted, looking past Alice into the scene in the kitchen.

"We told you everything as we did it," said Alice. "I came myself, to file a report." She knew that phrase, "file a report," was the right one.

He stood there literally grinding his teeth at Alice, ready to charge in and smash and destroy. But she was careful to keep her eyes away from him, and to look passive and even indifferent.

The other man was already in the police car.

In a minute they had gone. Alice fetched their own spade and swiftly filled in what they had taken out. Not too bad; Nature, as expected, was doing her job nicely.

She went back into the kitchen, and her appearance was the signal for a celebration of laughter and jeers. It seemed they could not stop laughing, particularly Caroline and Jocelin, for whom the whole story was new. Alice did not feel much like laughing. She knew that it was not the end; their visitors would be back.

She knew, too, looking at Faye, that she was unlikely to have much sleep that night. Indeed, it was past three when Faye went back upstairs. She accepted two Mogadons from Alice, and said good night prettily enough.

Very soon, however, she started weeping. Not the noisy angry weeping that she used when Roberta was there, but the heart-breaking helpless sobs of a child. Alice went in, and sat with her, holding her hand. Faye did not sleep until seven in the morning, and Alice slept sitting there beside her.

Several days passed. Faye was trying hard, and they all knew it, and supported her. When she heard people in the kitchen, she would come down and sit with them, chatting about everything quite amusingly, as she could, doing her little cockney act, but she tended to fall silent suddenly, staring; and then someone would gently try to rouse her and bring her back in with them again.

She offered to show Alice an economical vegetable stew, and it was very nice, and they all enjoyed it. Alice wondered how she could stand—if she was conscious of it—the way everyone was on tenterhooks for her to break out, break down. But she did not break down, or cry. She seemed to be quite normal, even ordinary; and Caroline and Jocelin even said they couldn't see why people went on and on about Faye. She was very pleasant, she was very clever, and what a lot she knew about politics. It turned out that Faye had read a great deal, more than any of them, and was particularly well up on Althusser. She had written part of a thesis on Althusser at university, where, however, she had stayed only two terms before cracking up.

Faye did not go to bed until very late and, when she did, said to Alice that she would be all right by herself.

Alice got up in the night quite often, to listen outside Faye's door. She thought that Faye hardly slept; often she wept, quietly, not wanting to disturb the others. Sometimes Alice could hear her moving about the room, lighting cigarettes, even singing a little to herself.

Roberta had written; they had the address of the hospital. Her mother was slowly dying; Roberta would come back as soon as she could.

A week had gone by. Jasper and Bert should be there. Then arrived a postcard written by Jasper, signed by them both, from Amsterdam, saying, "Wish you were here. Back soon."

Caroline and Alice spent a lot of time together. Alice, drained and tired, needed Caroline's natural vitality, her good spirits. Caroline admired Alice, could not stop talking about how Alice had transformed this house.

Most of the time Jocelin was in her room. She was at the top of the house. She seemed to have little to say to them or, indeed, much to say to anybody. She was a silent, observant—and, thought Alice, frightening—girl. What did she do in her room? Caroline said she was studying handbooks on how to be a good terrorist. She said this laughing, as was her way.

A weekend approached.

On the Friday, Reggie and Mary left for Cumberland after Mary finished work, for another Saturday of demonstrations. Jocelin departed, saying only, "See you Monday."

Caroline said she was off to spend the weekend with a former boyfriend, who had married someone else, was now separated, and wished still to marry Caroline. Sometimes she thought that she would; more often, that she wouldn't. Still, she liked being with him; they had a good time together, she said. She had invited Alice to come as well. Alice would have gone, but there was Faye. She felt bitter, sitting alone at the kitchen table, Faye having gone up to bed, and Philip upstairs, too.

All things being equal—this meant, without Faye—she would have gone off without leaving an address for Jasper; it didn't matter where. She really must put her foot down, say she'd had enough. She might even leave him.

Repeating to herself how much better off she would be by herself, she felt how her heart chilled and saddened; and she stopped, saying again, "I'm just going to show him, that's all."

But how could she show him anything, if she was obediently waiting here when he got back? Which would almost certainly be in a day or two.

No, this business of Roberta's mother was a disaster, for her as much as for Roberta and for Faye.

So she brooded, drinking coffee, and more coffee, sitting alone.

It was not yet twelve when she went up. Outside Faye's door she stood listening: not a sound. This was unusual. Faye did not sleep, ever, until two or three.

Alice saw herself, standing there, her ear to a door panel on the dark landing, and was angry with herself, with everyone—self-pity raged. She went into her room and decided to go to sleep at once. But she did not. When she was safely in her scarlet Victorian nightdress, she went to the window and stood watching the traffic rushing past. She was remarkably uneasy and restless. Again outside Faye's door, she said to herself: Now, this is enough, go to bed and stop it! But she did nothing of the kind. Gently she opened the door and stood there like a ghost, ready to hear Faye

shout at her to go away, to leave her alone, to stop prying. . . .
The light was out, and the room was dark. Faye could just be seen,
a bundle in the corner. There was a strong smell. As Alice realised
this smell was blood, she switched on the light and screamed.
Faye lay on her back, propped slightly up on embroidered and
frilled cushions, ghastly pale, her mouth slightly open, and her cut
wrists resting on her thighs. Blood soaked everything.

Alice stood screaming.

She had foreseen this, dreaded it, half knew it was bound to
happen. She had always known she could not bear blood, would
go to pieces if she found herself in this situation. She simply had
to stand and scream.

Philip arrived beside her. His shout, hushed and wary, reached
her, "Alice, Alice, what is it?"

She stopped screaming. In her scarlet voluminous nightdress
she was like a female in a Victorian melodrama. She pointed a
finger at the horrid sight, and shuddered.

Philip said, "She has cut her wrists."

He then put his arm round Alice, who, being so much taller
and heavier than he was, made him stagger. Together, they lost
balance, and found it by clinging to the doorframe.

Alice had got back her common sense, her control.

She was by Faye's side. The blood was still pulsing out in
red waves.

"We have to stop it," she said. She looked around for anything that would tie, found a scarf lying on a chair, and tied it
round Faye's wrists, like handcuffs. The bleeding stopped.

Philip, also back in control, said, "I'll ring for an ambulance."

"No, no, no," screamed Alice, "you mustn't."

"Why not, she's going to die."

"No, no, no, she won't. Don't you see? She mustn't go to
hospital."

"Why not?"

"Roberta would never forgive us, she wouldn't want that. The
police, don't you see? The *police* . . ."

Philip was staring at Alice as at a madwoman.

"Have we got any elastic bandage in the place?"

"Why should we have any?" he said, distressed.

"I know. Your masking tape. The tape you use for your electrics."

He had already gone to get it. Alice knelt by Faye, who seemed to have become as light and empty as a dead leaf. How can you take the pulse of a woman whose wrists are butchered? Where else is there a pulse, wildly wondered Alice, peering here and there. She held her cheek to Faye's nostrils and felt a slight breath. She wasn't dead. But so much blood lost, so much . . . Everything was soaked with it. Faye was lying in a thick red pool.

Philip ran in, with a roll of black tape. Alice fitted her hand, like a bracelet, around one wrist, to stop the blood from bubbling and spurting, while Philip strapped up the wound. Then she held the other wrist, and they cut the scarf away.

"She's lost so much blood," said Alice.

"She ought to have a transfusion," said Philip, obstinately. His face was full of criticism of Alice.

"We've got to get liquid into her. No, wait. . . ."

Down ran Alice to the kitchen. She made a mixture of warm water and salt and sugar, glucose not being available. Up she ran with it.

"She's unconscious, Alice," said Philip, still with that look of dislike, hostility. "How can she drink if she's unconscious?"

Alice knelt down, slid her arm under Faye's lolling head, so that she was well propped up, and began trying to pour the liquid into Faye.

"It'll go into her lungs, you are drowning her," said Philip.

And then, miraculously, Faye swallowed.

"Faye," commanded Alice, "Faye, drink, you've got to drink."

Faye seemed to want to shake her head, but swallowed. It was because she was in the habit of taking orders, commands from Roberta. Alice knew that, so she made her voice soft and full and loving like Roberta's and said, "Drink, you must drink."

Slowly, over twenty minutes, Alice got a pint or so of the mixture into Faye.

Then she rested. She was running with sweat. The sweat was from terror, she knew that.

Philip knelt at Faye's feet, watching. His look of disapproval, even of horror, had not abated. It was Alice who horrified him, and she knew and could not care.

"She's not going to die," she said, loudly, for Faye's benefit as well as Philip's.

She said, "You stay here. Make her drink some more, if you can. She must have done it only a minute before we came in. I'm going to telephone Roberta."

Philip took her place, his arm under Faye's head. He reached for the jug full of liquid.

Alice thought, seeing them like that—frail white Faye, frail pale Philip—that they were two of a kind, victims, born to be trampled over and cut down. There was a flash of vindictiveness in this thought, as far as Philip was concerned, for she knew that he still hated her.

She ran next door to Joan Robbins. The house was in darkness, and Alice put her finger on the bell and kept it there. She could hear it shrilling. A window went up above her head, and she heard Joan Robbins's voice, sharp, "What is it? Who is it?"

"Let me in, let me in," cried Alice, her voice like a child's, or like Faye's. "It is Alice," she wept, since Joan Robbins did not at once leave the window. "Alice from next door."

The lights went on in the hall, and Joan Robbins stood there in a flowered dressing gown and bright-red mules, looking angry, puzzled, and afraid.

"I must ring someone—I must—someone's ill," she stammered, and Joan Robbins stood aside.

At the telephone, she fumbled for the books, which Joan took out from a plastic cover and gave to her.

She found "Directory Enquiries," got the number, rang the hospital in Bradford, left a message for Roberta. "Tell her her friend is ill, she must come at once."

Then she started turning the pages over, looking for another number, and it was not until she saw "Samaritans" that she knew what she wanted.

"Don't you want nine-nine-nine?" asked Joan Robbins curiously. Alice shook her head and stood, eyes shut, breathing irregularly, as if she might faint, and Joan padded off to her kitchen to make her a nice cup of tea.

Alice rang the Samaritans. A pleasant, steady voice spoke. Alice did not hear the words, only the tone. She stood silent, listening. She was going to have to say something, or this voice would stop, go away.

She said, "I want your advice, that's all, your advice."

"What's the trouble?"

She said nothing, but stood listening to the sensible, helpful voice. Which went on, saying that Alice should not ring off, that no one would put any pressure on Alice or on anyone else, no one would report Alice, no matter what she or anyone else had done.

Alice did not speak until she heard Joan Robbins coming back. She said quickly, "Someone has cut her wrists."

There was no time for more. Joan arrived with two mugs of hot tea.

Alice picked up hers at once, knowing how badly she needed it. She stood trying to drink the boiling liquid, listening, listening. "You must get your friend to hospital. As quickly as you can. Call the ambulance. Call nine-nine-nine. It's a matter of life and death. You really must."

"Suppose I don't?" said Alice at last, choosing her words because of Joan, who stood helplessly by, urging her with smiles and looks to drink up.

"Then, if you don't—but you really should—the main thing is to keep your friend awake and get as much liquid into her as possible. Can she drink?"

"Yes," said Alice, and went on listening as if she heard some impossible, far-off music that beguiled and comforted, soothed and offered infinite, unfailing support.

After some minutes, she simply put down the receiver, letting that gentle, sensible voice disappear into the realm of the unreachable. She adjusted her face to her usual bright, good-girl's smile, and said to Joan Robbins, "Thank you. Thanks a lot. That was the Samaritans. Do you know about them?"

"I have heard of them, yes."

"They are very good, really," said Alice, vaguely. "Well, I had better get back. I've left someone coping and I don't think he's much used to people being ill."

Joan followed Alice to the door, with the look of someone who feels that everything has not been said, and who hopes that it might be said even now.

"Thank you," said Alice politely. Then, wildly and gratefully, "Thank you, thank you." And she ran away into the dark. Joan Robbins waited to see her go in at the door of number 43. Then she went back into her kitchen, where she examined the smears of blood on the telephone directories and on the table. She wiped the table and stood thinking for some minutes. Then she decided not to call the police, and went quietly to her bed.

Alice found Philip and Faye exactly as she had left them. But Faye's eyes were open, and she stared, expressionless, at the ceiling.

"I've rung Roberta," said Alice.

Then she searched around for a clean nightie or something, found pyjamas, fetched hot water and cloths. She and Philip stripped Faye. They peeled off her soaked sleeping bag, lifted off blankets, and slid away the foam-rubber mattress, which was filled with blood like a sponge. Then Faye was washed and dressed. Through all this she was limp and meek. But Alice was not deceived. She knew that Faye was waiting for the moment when she and Philip turned their backs, when the strapping would be off those wrists.

Alice's sleeping bag was brought, and more blankets. A hot-water bottle was found in a drawer. It took a long time, but finally Faye was lying clean and tucked into warmth and comfort.

It was well after three.

Alice was thinking: If Roberta was at the hospital, she will have had the message, she will be on her way, she might be here by morning.

Meanwhile, she and Philip must sit up, in case one fell asleep.

No one slept. Faye lay where she had been put, her face like a little ghost's. She did not close her eyes. She did not look at them. She said nothing.

Philip knelt at Faye's feet, and Alice sat at her side. From time to time Alice lifted Faye up and put the cup to her lips and Faye swallowed.

Philip went off to make more of this mixture of salt and sugar and water, and to make tea for himself and Alice. But he did not look at Alice, would not meet her eyes.

He had been so badly shocked by her, by the situation, that he was simply divorcing himself from it.

She thought, defiantly, even mockingly: That defines Philip, then! That's what he's like!

Morning soon came, it being halfway through May. With the prickly, hollow feeling that accompanies exhaustion, Alice listened to the dawn chorus, thinking that she would like to hear it more often; tried to catch Philip's eye, to share this moment of renewal, or promise, with him, but he knelt there, like a little devotee, patient, modest, ready to be useful. And absolutely cut off from her.

At last she said, "If you go and sleep, Philip, I'll make myself stay awake. And then, when I can't stay awake, I'll shout up the stairs." Meaning, I can't leave her, we can't, not for a second. He heard this, understood, nodded, and went out.

Faye slipped off to sleep, or was pretending to sleep—Alice did not know which, but was taking no chances. She sat on, from time to time flicking water onto her own face, slapping her cheeks. When she did this she thought she saw a flicker of something that could be amusement, or at least comment, on Faye's passive face. The sounds of a normal Saturday morning, the milkman, children playing in the street, voices from the gardens. What a lot of sounds there were that she never ordinarily listened to. . . .

The bloodstained pile in the corner was beginning to sicken Alice. But she could not, must not move. She knew Faye was not asleep.

Time passed . . . passed. More than once she had caught herself as she dropped off, even jerking awake. Once when she did this, she saw Faye open her eyes; they exchanged looks. Alice: I'm not going to let you; and Faye: You can't stop me if I want to.

Then, at last, steps bounded up the stairs, the door opened, and Roberta was kneeling by Faye, whose eyes were now open. She said in a voice that mingled passionate love, anger, exasperation, incredulity: "Faye, oh, Faye darling, how could you, how could you!"

Alice stood up, and watched how Roberta gently, tenderly, gathered Faye to her, kissed her, cradled her, then bent down to kiss the wounded wrists, one after the other.

Faye turned her face into the bosom of her friend, and lay there, at home.

Roberta looked at Alice over Faye. Her face was running tears. As well it might, thought Alice.

Roberta said, "My mother's in a coma, so it's all right."

"That's all right, then."

Alice gathered up the stained things and said matter-of-factly, "Philip has been asleep for some hours, so he can come and help when you want help, but I have to sleep now."

She went to her room, where she did not sleep, not for a long time. She was replaying the scene over and over again in her mind, of Roberta's infinite tenderness with Faye, the passion of love in her face as she looked at Alice, Faye's face pressed to her breast.

When she woke, she was determined to leave. It was all enough, it was too much. If Jasper wanted her he would have to come and find her. And, no, she would not be leaving an address. She would have breakfast, then go.

But, of course, it wasn't morning. She had slept through the day. Downstairs she found Philip disposing of the remains of a pot of her soup. She could see in him last night's hostility softened, modified. After all, Faye had lived. Yes, Alice knew Faye might easily not have lived. But at least she had kept Faye out of the hands of Authority.

She waited, indifferently, while he explained something he had been planning to say, probably working on it all day in his mind.

Half listening, her mind on trains for tonight, or tomorrow, and where to, she heard herself sigh, and this brought her attention fully back to Philip.

Yes, he looked awful. Worse than was warranted by not sleeping last night.

Working from eight in the morning till late in the evening, and over weekends, he still had not been able to keep up with what he had promised. The date he had given for finishing was passed, and there was painting still to be done, several days of it. The Greek said he had been tricked by Philip: never would he have employed one person alone to do that big job of conversion and decoration, let alone a sparrow like Philip. If Philip could not finish the job in a couple of days, he—the Greek—would consider it a breach of contract, and Philip would not be paid the second half of the money. (Yes, Philip had been in this position before, but had not expected to be this time.)

What Philip wanted was help from the commune. Reggie wasn't working! What did Reggie do with himself all day? Philip demanded hotly of Alice. He wasn't even trying for a job. He went around salesrooms and auctions, picking up bargains. Did Alice know that the attic was filling with Mary and Reggie's furniture, let alone the room next to the one they slept in? What would it cost Reggie to help Philip for a couple of days?

"But can he paint well enough?" asked Alice, almost mechanically, and Philip's conscious look chimed with the conviction that suddenly came into her: of course, Philip wanted her, Alice, to go down and help. It was she who had painted most of this big house —painted it fast, and very well. They had joked, these communards, that a professional could not have done it better. And, in fact, at this or that time in her past she had done it professionally, and no one had complained.

His dislike of her, which she had felt so strongly last night, was partly that he had been thinking like this for some time: Alice was the one who could solve all his difficulties, and yet she did not seem to see it, refused to recognise his need.

Alice sat there quietly, eyes lowered, shielding herself from Philip, thinking. Why should he expect this? What right had he? The answer was plain enough: he had done all the work on this big house, for wildly inadequate pay. It was Alice who had wanted it; the others hadn't really cared. Now it was Alice who should make it up to him. Oh yes, she could see it all, the logic of it, the justice. But she wanted to leave, to get out and away. This house, for which she had fought, she now felt as a trap, ready to redeliver her back to Jasper, from whom she must escape. (Even if only for a little while, her sad heart hastily added.) Yet she knew she was going to help Philip, because she had to. It was only fair.

She said she would, and saw Philip's whole body, that sparrow's body, convulse briefly with sobs. His face was illuminated, prayerful.

She went with him down the road to look at the premises. They were enormous, not one of these little cubbyholes off the street with a counter over which a few pies or sandwiches were passed. Along the middle of the room ran a broad counter, finished but unpainted, and there was a large area behind that for the cooking and preparation. Stoves, refrigerators, deep freezes had already been delivered and stood waiting to be put in place. But the walls at the back needed plaster. The walls on three sides were not bad, but should be cleaned down before painting. Alice, from Philip's look, knew that he had intended to do more to these walls than he now did. Paint would go on before paint, ideally, should. Philip watched her, waited for her verdict.

But as she hesitated, knowing that if an employer was looking for an excuse not to pay, or to pay less, he would find one here, she heard that someone else was with them in the great empty place, and turned to see the Greek, Philip's employer. At one glance she knew that Philip was going to be cheated, no matter what he did, or how she helped him.

He was a nasty little piece of work, all right. His little black eyes were full of the exaggerated anger that goes with defending a false position, and when he saw her, he shouted, "I said another workman, not your girlfriend!"

Alice said, in her best cold voice, "You are making a mistake. I have done this kind of work often."

"Yes," sneered the Greek, using the sneer with a conscious theatricality, "I suppose you've put a coat of paint on your kitchen."

"In any case," said Alice, "you are grossly underpaying. For the kind of money you are paying for this job, you are not in a position to take that line."

She did not know what Philip was being paid, though, having seen this man, she did know it was not enough. And she knew that with this type of man you had to be as bad a bully.

She turned her back and went to stand in front of a wall, examining it. Philip followed her lead and stood beside her. The Greek pretended to fuss about by the counter, then said, "I'll give you two days." And he went out.

But Alice knew it was hopeless. Yes, because of her, Philip would not be cheated out of as much; but that man had no intention of paying in full.

Therefore, she did not say to Philip that these walls should be properly scraped and cleaned. She said that if Philip had spare overalls, she would start in now; it was only ten o'clock. He went to work on the plastering, and she painted. They worked all night. Twice a pair of policemen, neither of whom Alice knew, went past and looked in. Once the Greek sauntered by, thinking he was not noticed.

By morning Philip had done the plastering. Alice had put a first coat on the three walls and the ceiling.

She knew that the Greek would be in the moment they left and would find fault.

She and Philip went back to number 43; and there were Jasper and Bert, eating bacon and eggs. There was a look to both of them she did not like—this was the first impression, before all of them exploded into smiles and embraces. For, of course, the sight of Jasper melted away everything Alice had felt; she was happy, she was herself, she had been half a person without him. And he was as pleased; he even kissed her, his dry lips light on her cheek, his arms like a circle of bone, but meaning warmth, meaning love.

Philip did not stay, said he must get two hours of sleep. This was the amount he had allowed himself, after two nights and two days of sleeplessness. He imploringly looked at Alice, for she had said that was all she would need before starting in again.

But here was Jasper! Philip, from the door, glanced back at Jasper, and there on his face was the recognition of inevitability, Jasper as doom, for of course now Alice would not keep her word. . . .

But Alice would keep her word, although she knew that this moment, now, when Jasper was just back and the pressures on him from her, which he had to resist, had not yet begun to build, was when she could hear about his adventures—and once the moment had passed, she would get nothing, only curt yeses and noes.

There was something about these two men—a feverishness in their eyes, some bad kind of excitement—what was it? Well, it wasn't to do with Jasper's sex life, for Bert did not share that; but Bert had the same look. Anger, was it? Restlessness, certainly. Only exhaustion? Perhaps. They said the crossing on the boat had been bad, and that they had not slept for some nights. They would go up to sleep now.

Alice explained what she was doing; the conventions of commune or squat life ensured that they would commend her for helping a fellow.

They said nothing about coming to help themselves.

Up the stairs they went together, a pair, a unit, welded by all their experiences, about which they had been prepared to say only that the tour wasn't bad, the Soviet Union's trouble was bureaucracy; if the comrades could sort that out, it might even be a pleasure to go there.

And after the Soviet Union? They had left the tour at Moscow, and gone to Holland. It hadn't stopped raining.

Bert went to his sleeping bag on the other side of the wall from Alice. Jasper found his room upstairs occupied by Jocelin's things. Great crashes and bangs from up there: Jasper was heaving out the furniture from the room next to Mary and Reggie's, onto the landing. Alice knew this was happening, could hear from the noise that Jasper was in one of his rages, when he could shift cupboards and packing cases as if he were ten men. She slept, with her internal alarm set for two hours' time.

And woke again, doleful, desperate; there was no way she could see out of helping Philip, yet she could not really help Philip. And she wanted to be with Jasper.

The Greek's premises were done by midnight. Two coats on everything. Even on the plaster, though it was too soon. Everything, too quick, rushed. Done adequately. Done, as far as Alice was concerned, with no pleasure.

At midnight, the three again stood together under the glaring working lights, this time surrounded by primrose-yellow walls, which the Greek stared at, one after another, despising them.

Everything happened as Alice had known it must.

The work was not up to standard; Alice was only an amateur and Philip a crook. He, the Greek, would have to pay someone else to come in and finish the job. (Of course, all three knew that this was a lie; customers would see only a fresh and charming yellow— which would soon, however, begin to flake.) Philip could go to the police if he liked, but not another penny . . . And so he went on, shouting, putting on theatre, pointing rejecting forefingers at ceilings, at plaster, shrugging shoulders that despaired of the human race, rolling hot bitter little black eyes.

Alice came in with words, cold and hot. They fought. Philip, white as an egg, stutteringly intervened. The end of it was that Philip got two-thirds of what had been contracted.

At one in the morning, Alice and Philip shouldered ladders, trestles out of the shop, knowing that these would be confiscated if they were left. Alice stood guard while little Philip staggered the half mile up the road with a ladder three times his height, and came back with Bert and Jasper, who were helping him because they had to. Bert had been pulled out of his sleeping bag.

Philip's gear was got safely into the downstairs room, Jim's room, and Philip stayed there with it, in a state of angry despair.

Bert went back to bed. Smiling and gentle, like a bride, Alice said to Jasper that it would be nice if he would sit with her while she ate. She had scarcely eaten that day. He said, curtly, yes, there was something he wanted to discuss with her. But tomorrow would do. Off he went upstairs, to sleep.

Without eating, so did Alice; she felt as though she were being dragged over a waterfall, or into an abyss, but did not know why.

Awake early because she was hungry, she was in the kitchen eating when Philip came in. He was red-eyed and beside himself. Mad, Alice judged. Simply not himself.

He probably had not slept but had been awake with thoughts he had been marshalling, ready for presentation the moment he could get her alone.

He sat himself down, but so lightly that he could jump up again on the crest of any wave of the argument. His fists rested side by side before him.

He knew of another job, a shop just opening up. He could get it, but it would have to be within the next day or so. It was no use working by himself. He had to have a partner—Alice could see that for herself, surely? Alice ought to come in with him! They would make a fine team. She was such a good painter, so neat and quick. Between them there was no job they couldn't tackle. After all, Alice wasn't doing anything with her time!

He was shouting at her because he knew she was going to refuse him and the rage of rejection was already in him. He could have been threatening her, instead of suggesting a partnership.

"All you people," he yelled, "never lift a finger, never do any work, parasites, while people like me keep everything going. . . ." It seemed he was going to weep, his voice was so heavy with betrayal. "They talk about all these unemployed everywhere, people wanting work, but where are they? I can't find anyone to work with me. So what about it, Alice?" he demanded, aggressive, accusing.

She, of course, said no.

He then shouted at her that she cared about no one but herself—"just like everybody else." She had got Jim thrown out of his job and had never given a thought to him since. Where was Jim? She didn't know or care. And Monica—oh yes, he knew all about that, he had heard, Monica had been sent off on a wild-goose chase to an empty house—he supposed that was Alice's idea of a joke. Faye could have died, for all the trouble she was prepared to take, wouldn't even call an ambulance. And she didn't care about him, Philip, once she had got all she could out of him, got him working day and night for peanuts, and now she'd got her house, he—Philip—could go to the wall for all she cared about him.

And so he raved on, half weeping, and Alice knew that if she had got up and put her arms about him he would have collapsed into her embrace like a little heap of matchsticks, with, "Alice, I'm sorry, I don't mean it, please come and be my partner."

But she did not, only sat there, thinking that the windows were open, and if Joan Robbins was in the garden she could hear everything.

Philip's fury died into silence, and misery. He sat staring, not at her, at anywhere but her. Then he ran out of the room, and out of the house.

Alice sat waiting for Jasper to wake. It seemed to her a good part of her life had been spent doing this. She thought again: But I'll leave, I'll just go. I must. No, it wouldn't be forever, but I need time by myself.

She found she was on her feet, opening the refrigerator, searching cupboards. She would make one of her soups. But because she had been working with Philip, there was very little in the house. She went down to the shops, bought food, took time over the preparations, sat at the table while her soup evolved. The cat arrived on the window sill, miaowed through the glass; Alice welcomed it in, offered it scraps. But no, the cat was not hungry; probably Joan Robbins or somebody had fed it. The beast wanted company. It would not sit on Alice's lap, but lay on the window sill, and stretched out. The cat looked at Alice with its vagabond's eyes, and let out a little sound, a grunt or miaow of greeting. Alice burst into tears in a passion of gratitude.

The morning went past. When Jasper woke, she would explain it to him: a short break, that was what she needed.

At midday Bert and Jasper came down together, joking about being woken by the smell of Alice's soup. Their mood of rage, or rebellion, or whatever it had been, seemed to have vanished with their exhaustion.

Chatty, companionable, they offered Alice little anecdotes from their trip and praised her soup. She sat listless, watching them. Her mood soon became obvious to them, and they even exchanged "Mummy-is-cross" glances at one point, earning from her a sarcastic smile.

They abandoned attempts at placating her, and Bert said,

"We've decided it is time we had a full discussion on policy, Comrade Alice. No, only the real revolutionaries, not the rubbish." He bared all his lovely white teeth and sneered. Alice let it pass. Jasper, too, leaned towards her, smiling, and said, "We thought tonight. Or tomorrow night at the latest. But the point is, where? Mary and Reggie mustn't know. Or Philip!" He, too, sneered.

The two of them seemed to have acquired a fairly dramatic new style, thought Alice, examining them dispassionately.

She enquired, really interested, "And how are you going to class Faye? Serious or not?"

Their faces seemed to cloud; yes, they knew about the suicide attempt, but had not really been bothered about it.

"Well," said Bert, doubtfully, "I suppose she'll be fit enough to join in, won't she?"

Alice laughed. It was a laugh that surprised herself, sounding so natural and even merry. She was finding these two funny, because they were so stupid.

She said indifferently, "If you want a meeting convened, then why don't you convene it." She got up and attended to the cauldron of soup, adding some more split peas, salt, then water. Jasper's and Bert's appetites had not diminished, she noted.

When she turned, they were sitting disconsolate, opposite to but not looking at each other. Or at her. They were reflecting, she could see, that her anger with them had justification, that they had been foolish not to take it into account. And, too, that they felt her rejection as another in a succession of rejections.

Her heart almost melted. She said to Jasper, "I am sorry. You go off like that, all kinds of lies. Then you just turn up. . . . I'm sorry."

She went towards the door, and Jasper was beside her. She felt his frantic grip on her wrist; it was all he knew to bring her back to him. She shook off his hand quite easily, and said, "I'm sorry, Jasper." And went out.

From outside the door, she relented a little and said, "Let me know when you have convened the meeting."

She was on her way up, thinking that she would sleep, and then perhaps ring her old commune in Halifax. A few days there and she would be herself again.

But there was a knock, loud and urgent, at the front door, and she went to it, ready for the police, but it was a woman she did not know, who said quickly, "I am Felicity, you know, from round the corner. Philip's friend. They telephoned from hospital. Philip was in an accident. They want some of his things taken up."

She was already turning away on a smile, duty done, but Alice said, "Aren't you going up?" Meaning, Isn't this your responsibility?

"Yes, I'll be up to see him," said Felicity, vaguely enough. "But not now. His things are here, aren't they?"

She had been an extension of number 43 all this time, but no one would think so from her manner. She was a small, brisk, authoritative woman, every bit as competent as Alice in holding her own. She was saying that she did not intend Philip to be her responsibility.

Alice thought of Philip that morning, raging and pitiful. She said, "Oh, very well. Is he bad?"

"He's not dead. He could have been. He was lucky. Broken bones." She smiled and hastened off.

Alice went upstairs to Philip's room. On nicely painted shelves were his clothes, tidily arranged. She found three pairs of clean pyjamas, green, blue, and brown, stacked on top of one another; a dressing gown on a hanger behind the door; toothbrush and a flannel spread to dry on the window sill; soap, electric razor. She set off, only saying through the kitchen door to Jasper and Bert that she was going to the hospital, not mentioning Philip. She did not want to hear either of them dismiss this accident as they had Faye's wrist cutting. It was appalling, and she knew it. This meant some kind of an end for Philip. Of course he had got himself run over, or whatever had happened, because he needed to underline his situation. Make himself helpless: make his helplessness visible.

But in the hospital Alice found it was worse than Felicity had said. Broken shoulder. Broken kneecap. Fractured left wrist. Bruises. But he also had a fractured skull. He was being taken down to the operating theatre again in a few minutes. They suspected internal damage. Meanwhile, he was unconscious. Because Alice said that as far as she knew Philip didn't have a family, or if so, she couldn't supply an address, the ward sister had put her down on the form as "next of kin." Telephone number? But Alice, determined that Felicity should not slide out altogether, said Felicity must be rung in emergencies. Anyway, number 43 had no telephone.

She then stood in a doorway, not knowing what to expect, because she had not visualised anything, and saw in the middle of a room a high slanting contraption like a machine with pulleys and levers and wheels and tubes, and on this, half sitting up but collapsed and limp, was Philip, all bandages and wrappings. His face was really all that was visible: dead white, blue veins fluttering on waxen lids, white lips that seemed to have some sort of dried pink dye at the corners. More than ever he seemed like a small elf, an inhuman creature, and Alice, standing there helpless, with the ward sister just behind her, could not move. She was thinking that this is what happened to marginal people, people clinging on but only just. They made one slip; something apparently quite slight happened, like the Greek, but it was part of some downward curve in a life, and that was that—they lost their hold and fell. Philip had lost his hold.

Alice turned such a shocked face on the ward sister that she said, "Are you all right?" Deliberately perfunctory, because she did not want to cope with Alice. "Go and get yourself a cup of tea downstairs," said the sister. "Sit down a bit."

Her look indicated that she was prepared to be concerned about Alice if she produced symptoms that warranted it, but Alice said, "It's all right." She watched the sister go to stand by Philip, looking down carefully at him for about a minute. For some reason this long close look told Alice everything. She turned and ran away down the corridors and stood waiting for the lift, and then went down in the lift, but she did not know she was doing these things. She was whimpering steadily, her eyes fixed in front of her—on Philip's dying face.

And now came the thought: Philip was a long way down on that curve before he asked if he could live with us. What we thought we saw was somebody at the beginning of a curve up, with a new business, everything in front of him, but it wasn't like that at all. Probably it wasn't even the Greek who did him in, made him lose hold—it was when Felicity threw him out. (Alice knew now that this was what had happened, from Felicity's manner.) Perhaps long before that? Suddenly Alice knew. All of it was perfectly clear, like a graph. It was not a question of Philip's having "lost hold." He had never grasped hold. Something had not happened that should have happened: a teacher, or someone, should have said: This one, Philip Fowler, he must be a craftsman, do something small, and delicate and intricate; we must get him trained for that. Look how perfectly he does things! He can't fold a shirt or arrange some chips and a piece of fish on a plate without making a picture of it.

It had not happened. And Philip began to work for a building firm, like everyone who hasn't a training. A painter in a building firm, losing one job after another until he said: I'll start my own business.

The relentlessness of it. The fucking shitty awfulness of it . . .

She did not afterwards remember how she got back from the hospital. In the kitchen Roberta took one look at her and produced her remedy: brandy was poured into Alice, and Roberta put her arm around her, helped the sodden heavy girl upstairs, got her into her sleeping bag, drew curtains.

Alice slept through the two events of that evening.

The first was that the vicious policeman from the station came in with a policewoman, on some business to do with a stolen car. Jasper and Bert were there, and things didn't go well, would certainly have ended in violence and arrests, only luckily Mary and Reggie appeared, and dealt with the police in their own language, on their own terms. But Mary and Reggie were afterwards cold, were disapproving, saying that there was really no need for trouble with the police if people knew how to handle them. "And, of course, if they behave themselves," was implicit.

They went upstairs, but Reggie came down again almost at once to ask whether in fact Jasper and Bert knew anything about the stolen car?

"We are revolutionaries," said Bert, furious. "Not crooks."

Then, late, after twelve, Felicity came again to say the hospital had telephoned. Philip was dead. She was very upset, so Alice was told next day. She had had to be asked in, fed Alice's soup and Roberta's brandy.

None of this Alice knew till next day. Mid-morning. They were all in the kitchen, the sun coming in, the cat on the window sill.

She said, first, "He went under fast, didn't he?"—mentally seeing a small broken thing, like a bird or an insect, trying to clutch hold of a straw, a twig, and failing. The others did not understand, but Faye, with a cold smile, said, "Lucky Philip." Mary said that Philip had struck her as unstable.

Alice remarked that if the police had got this house in their minds as the place to come and have a bit of fun, then it wouldn't be worth living here. The others of course stared at her, curious: the indifference with which she said it, that was the thing.

Then Alice got up and went upstairs, put Philip's ladder in position, climbed into the attic, and stood under the great rotten beams, keeping the light of the torch on them. She was thinking— or trying to think, to make her mind, or her comprehension, accept it—that Philip had tackled everything else in the house, all the threats and dangers. But this threat, the main one, he had not dealt with, could not. Because—simply—of his size. Because there was nothing to him but a handful of frail bones and a skim of flesh. Alice could see in her mind's eye the sort of man who could have pulled down these two rotten beams, then put in others. A large bale of a man (she could see him), shouldering the beams into place. Effortlessly. Humbled but uncomprehending because of the arbitrariness, the frivolity, of life, she went downstairs again, and remarked that if those beams were not dealt with, the house would start falling in, from the top. She sat in the chair she had been in before going upstairs to the beams, at the side of the table. At head and foot, like mother and father, sat Mary and Reggie. They radiated disapproval. They knew they did, but not that they were full of panic as well.

"The beams are obviously going to have to be put right," said Mary.

Jasper and Bert, Faye and Roberta, who had been observing Alice put things right for weeks, all looked at her, waiting for her to say, perhaps, "It is all right, I have fixed everything." Jocelin and Caroline were uninvolved.

Alice remarked, "Oh, so you have found yourself a flat, then?"

Startled, even affronted, Mary said, "Yes, but how did you . . . ?" And Reggie, "But we haven't told anybody yet; it's not final."

"And so," said Alice, "this house is back on the list, is it?"

"Not for demolition," said Mary. "It was agreed a mistake was made. Both this house and number forty-five will be converted. But, at any rate, nothing will happen immediately. The point is, there will be plenty of time for you to find somewhere else."

"Find another squat," said Reggie kindly.

Again the others looked at Alice, who had put so much into this house, and again seemed surprised that she was unconcerned.

She was examining Mary, examining Reggie, quite frankly, for she needed to know what happened. She could see the two, sitting up side by side in their marriage bed, discussing them all, with identical looks of scandalised criticism. Jim. Faye's suicide attempt. Now Philip. Alice saw that they must have felt trapped among lunatics. Well, never mind, these two good houses were saved, and a lot of people had found shelter for a time.

"Have you got a job?" asked Alice, sure that Reggie had.

Again, annoyance; because, of course, the middle classes did not like to be so transparent.

"As it happens, yes," said Reggie. "It's a new firm, in Guildford. Of course, it'll be a risk, the failure rate with new firms at the moment being what it is. But it's an interesting venture; it may succeed."

The fact that he didn't say what it was meant, Alice thought, that the "venture" was something they, the others, would criticise.

Chemicals; Reggie was a chemist. Well, she couldn't be bothered to be interested.

Reggie got up. Mary got up. Smiles all around. But relief was what they felt. Body language. Written all over them. They had felt, Mary and Reggie, that they should sit for a while with the others, because of Philip's death, and now that was enough, they could go back upstairs and get on with their own, sensible lives. *They* wouldn't lose hold of life and slip down and away, to be washed into some gutter.

Funny, thought Alice. Sitting around this table, let's say three weeks ago, all of us. You'd not have said that Philip was due to lose hold. Jim? Yes. And Faye . . . ? Alice was careful not to look at Faye, feeling that a look at this moment would be like a doom or a sentence. To her, Alice, the room seemed full of ghosts, and her heart ached for poor little Philip, who had tried so hard, been so gallant. *It wasn't fair.*

Well, with Reggie and Mary off soon, there wouldn't be many left here. Jasper and Bert and herself. Caroline and Jocelin. Faye and Roberta. Seven.

Pat, gone. Jim, gone. Philip, gone. Comrade Andrew—disappeared somewhere. Even the goose-girl seemed to Alice, in this mood, like some good old friend, taken from her. Very well, let them take this house away. Why not? She wasn't going to care. She knew she had her look: she could feel Jasper's eyes on her. To avoid them, she got up and began preparations for another cauldron of soup.

"Comrade Alice," said Bert in his political voice, "we are all here. We had decided to have a meeting when Reggie and Mary crashed in."

"Oh, were you going to bother to call me?" asked Alice. But she came back to her seat, noting that Bert and Jasper had put themselves at the head and the foot of the table.

Mid-afternoon. Sunshine. Joan Robbins was cutting her hedge with old-fashioned shears. Clack, clack, clack, with irregular intervals that kept the ears straining. In the jug on the stool were some early roses. Yellow. The cat lay on the window sill outside the glass, looking in.

Bert began, "In view of our observations in Moscow and subsequent discussions, Jasper and I agree that we should formulate a new policy. Of course it will have to be discussed fully in its implications, but, just to indicate where our conclusions are pointing, we have a tentative formulation. That the comrades present see no reason to accept directives from Moscow."

"Or from any other extraneous source," added Jasper.

Bert leaned forward, and looked at them all challengingly.

"Right on," said Caroline. She was peeling an orange and licking the juice off her fingers. "I agree, absolutely."

"Me, too," said Jocelin at once.

"Well, yes," said Roberta, "but it certainly wasn't our idea, was it? I mean, Faye's and mine?"

"Bloody well right," said Faye. "Whose idea was it to get us all involved with shitty Comrade Andrew and his works? It was yours, Comrade Bert, and yours, Comrade Jasper." She was using her proper BBC voice, and this, as always, came as a shock after her usual coquettings with the language. She sounded cold and full of hate.

Bert and Jasper were disconcerted. The fury of their disappointment in Moscow had been soothed away by discussions on policy, on "formulations," and they had lost sight of recent history in theorising. Alice could see that they were really having to make an effort to remember.

Bert was not prepared to relinquish the pleasures of the "implications," and he said, "But it is essential to analyse the situation. Advisable, at any rate," he amended, lamely.

"Why?" said Jocelin. And "Why?" asked Faye.

A silence.

Alice said diplomatically, "There are certain things I'd like to know before we drop the subject."

Faye sighed. Exaggeratedly. She was making an effort to sit here with them at all. She was very pale. There seemed to be life only in her bright hair, which made its pretty ringlets and curls around her emptied face.

"I'd like to know how next door, how number forty-five, got involved with the bloody Russians," said Faye.

"Good question," said Caroline, making little piles of orange peel with her solid white fingers, which had rings gleaming on them.

"Does anybody know?" Alice persisted.

"Jocelin knows," said Caroline.

Jocelin shrugged, as if irritated by the whole thing.

They all looked at Jocelin. She was not easy to look at. This was not because of her appearance, which was unremarkable. She was a blonde, whose ordinariness was pointed by pretty Faye, so delicate and fine, always presenting herself this way and that. Jocelin did not care whether she was admired, or even seen. Cold green eyes observed everything, and she was angry all the time, as if a generalised anger had taken her over at some point and she had come to believe that this was how one experienced the world. Not easy to withstand that hostility; and people tended to look not at her face, but at her hands, which were fine, with long clever fingers, or at her clothes, hoping to find something of interest there. But she wore, always, jeans and a jersey.

"This is what happened," said Jocelin. "As far as I know. There was a house over in Neasden, which worked very well as an exchange point, for some weeks. No one expects to use a place for longer than weeks. But suddenly the police were on to it. There was an informer. Or something."

She lit a cigarette, and Alice could see this was to give her time to work out exactly how much she wanted to say.

Alice prompted, "Exchange what, exactly?"

"What was going through next door—at forty-five. Propaganda material mostly. But also *matériel*."

This businesslike word caused, as Alice could see, agreeable *frissons* in Bert and Jasper, who both, not knowing they did, leaned forward intently to stare at Jocelin. And then, realising what they were doing, looked away, uncomfortable.

"It was a question of finding somewhere, quickly. Very quickly. Someone said that forty-five was empty. All that was needed was a place for two days. So it was thought."

"*Who* needed it?" said Bert, clumsily.

"Obviously, Comrade Andrew," said Caroline, crisp and disapproving.

"Yes," said Jocelin. "He had been organising propaganda material. Mostly for the IRA. Printed in Holland, mostly. And . . . other things. Some of it tricky stuff. Very." Here she smiled coldly at them, but with closed lips, and they all smiled uneasily and averted their eyes.

"But the house wasn't empty," said Caroline. "I was only away for a few days. I came back and found two rooms stacked with stuff. And then Comrade Muriel appeared, then Comrade Andrew." Caroline laughed, genuinely, and, relieved, they all laughed. Not, however, Jocelin, who turned her green eyes on them, one after another, waiting to go on.

"It seems it was not easy to find another suitable house," said Jocelin. "Nothing really safe. Meanwhile, they went on with forty-five. They had all kinds of makeshifts. Once there were four dustbins full of pamphlets covered with rubbish in the garden. They had plastic rubbish sacks with *matériel* more than once. But it couldn't go on like that. Next, most of the comrades left all at once from this house, and Comrade Alice moved in." She smiled, but her eyes were like lumps of green stone. "Comrade Alice's combination of remarkable talents were a godsend. It seems that Comrade Muriel and Comrade Andrew were about to follow your example into getting forty-five an agreed tenancy with the Council. But they had second thoughts: that it would risk all kinds of visits from the Council, and the stuff kept arriving, any odd time of the day or night, and being taken off again, too. No, they decided that it was enough that such perfect respectability existed next door. And there was a Council official, too. Mary Williams moved in. And then there was even a CCU Congress." She laughed, making it clear what she thought of the CCU. And of them?

"But how did you get involved in all this," demanded Faye. "You didn't like Comrade Andrew any more than we did."

"I didn't say I didn't like him," said Jocelin. "*Like*—who cares about all that? I was not involved with Comrade Andrew, or any of his doings. I decided to move in here because I was told by Muriel that you wanted to work with the IRA."

And now she looked at them again, slowly, one after another, taking her time about it. She said softly, "That is my interest. But about Moscow, the KGB and all that, I'm not interested—but that's all history, isn't it, now that Andrew has gone. Wherever he has gone. And I wouldn't like to be in his shoes."

"No," said Caroline. "No."

Alice felt hurt for Comrade Andrew. It seemed something was softly whimpering away in there, in her chest. That was the end of Comrade Andrew, then? They didn't care what happened to him! Or if they never saw him again!

Jasper was saying, "Why? What? I don't know what you mean?"

And Bert, "What did he do?"

Nobody answered. *They couldn't be bothered.* Comrade Andrew was not worth the effort. Gone. Disappeared.

Jasper said hotly—it came bursting out—"Bert and I went to Ireland. We saw the comrades. They weren't all that interested."

"So I heard," said Jocelin calmly. "Yes, I heard about that. But what of it? Who are the IRA to tell us what to do in our own country?"

This struck them all with the force of some obvious and ineluctable truth that inexplicably had not been seen by them till this moment. Of course! Who *were* the IRA, to tell them what to do?

Bert laughed softly, and his white teeth showed. Jasper laughed—and Alice suffered on hearing it, for she could measure by it how hurt he had been, how put down, by the refusal in Moscow to take him seriously, after the refusal in Ireland. Jasper's laugh was scornful and proud, and confidence was rushing back into him, and he looked about at them all, justified.

"Right on," said Faye. "At last. As far as I am concerned, you've all just seen the light. *We* have to decide what to do, and *we* will carry it out. We don't have to ask permission of foreigners." She was still using her cold, correct voice.

"Absolutely," said Roberta.

"Then that's that," said Alice. "All we have to do now is to make a plan."

At this point, a knock on the front door. Alice went, and came back in with Felicity. It was a question, since Alice was Philip's "next of kin," of her going to the hospital for the formalities.

Felicity did not want to sit down; did not want, as they all saw, to be forced into taking on Philip's affairs.

Alice said angrily, "Why me, Felicity? Why not you?"

"Look," said Felicity. "Philip came to stay in my place because he was stuck. Desperate. As far as I was concerned, he was just someone without a place to live."

"But he must have a family, or someone?"

"He has a sister, somewhere."

"But where?"

"How do I know? He never said."

The two women faced each other, as if in a bitter quarrel. Seeing how they must look, they became apologetic.

Felicity said, "When I said Philip could stay, I thought it was for the weekend, a week. He was with me for over a year."

Alice saw that it was she who was going to have to do it, and she said, bitterly, "Oh, very well." Now she had got her way, Felicity became "nice," and refused a cup of tea with many hurried apologies, and fussed her way out of the house.

"Poor Alice," said Roberta. "I'll come with you." Alice began to cry. They all looked at her in amazement.

"Of course she is crying," said Roberta. "Of course she is. She is *tired*." She put her arm around Alice and took her to the door. "Don't do anything we wouldn't do when we've gone," she said facetiously to them all, but her eyes were on Faye, who, betrayed, tossed her head and would not look at Roberta; she had suddenly again become a cockney maiden.

The two women were at the hospital for some hours, signing forms, seeing appropriate officials. Alice agreed to get a death certificate. She arranged to go through Philip's possessions with a Council representative, who would come tomorrow.

At midnight, Roberta tucked her up with a cup of hot chocolate, making it clear that that was it: she did not feel obliged to do more for Philip, though she would if Faye were not so needful.

Alice spent the morning over the death certificate and the afternoon going through Philip's possessions, with the official. It was an awful, painful business. Philip owned a few clothes, and about five hundred pounds in the post office, which would go to pay for his funeral.

As for his ladders and equipment, Alice said nothing about them, so they, at least, would not be sold to some dealer for a tenth of their value. They—in number 43—now at least owned their own ladders, trestles, and tools. For what that was worth; for as long as that was worth anything.

Because of Alice's preoccupation with the disposition of Philip, the household marked time. Rather, all did save Jocelin, who was at work in an upstairs room on a variety of devices that she was concocting out of the books she referred to as "recipe books," which gave admirable and concise advice about making explosive devices. She had purloined some of the *matériel* on its way through number 45. Alice, with the others, saw these devices, on Jocelin's invitation. They were ranged on one of Philip's trestles in a locked room— locked because of Mary and Reggie, who, though moving out in a few days, were not yet gone. What struck Alice about the things Jocelin had made was that they looked so unimportant and even flimsy, were mere assemblages of bits of this and that. Electronic devices that Jocelin was clearly proud of seemed no more portentous than those fragments of minuscule circuitry that appear when the insides of a transistor radio are broken apart.

There were also paper clips, drawing pins, a couple of cheap watches, bits of wire, household chemicals, copper tubing of various sizes, ball bearings, tin tacks, packets of plastic explosive, old-fashioned dynamite, reels of thick cotton, string.

While Jocelin worked with relish ("enjoyment" was not a word for Jocelin) at these little toys, and Alice wept over Philip—for she felt now as if she had lost an old friend, even a brother—Jasper and Bert went to some demonstrations, admonished by the others on no account to get themselves arrested, for there was important work to be done; and Roberta took Faye to stay with a friend at Brighton, because the sea air would do Faye some good. Roberta's mother was still in a coma.

A day passed slowly. The house seemed empty. Alice found herself thinking that Roberta and Faye probably would be back that night. Would they like to be welcomed by a real meal, even a feast? While she worried about this, sitting in the kitchen with the cat, Caroline came in with carrier bags full of food. She was smooth and sleek with pleasure; she said she felt like cooking a real meal; no, Alice must sit where she was and for once allow herself to be waited on.

Until then only Alice had brought in food. Real food, that is, not a pizza or some portions of chips. Only Alice had trudged in with loads of fruit, of vegetables, had stacked the refrigerator with butter and milk, piled a cupboard with pastas and pulses. Now she sat gratefully watching Caroline, who worked smiling, full of a rich secret contentment that seemed to spill out over her, like candlelight. Alice felt meagre, dry; she did these things, cooked and fed and nurtured, but it was out of having to, a duty. She had never in her life felt what she saw brimming over in Caroline, who, as she licked a spoon to test a sauce, looked at Alice over it as though she were sharing some pleasure with her that only the rare, the initiated, of the world could even suspect. And then she lifted a spoon over to Alice, carefully, guarding—it seemed—some essence or distillation, and watched, her eyes glistening, as Alice tasted and said, "Yes, fantastic, wonderful."

"I am a great *cook*," sang or purred Caroline. "This is what I ought to be doing. . . ." And, because she was reminded of what she was doing, how employed, a bleakness came over her for a moment, and she was silent.

She told Alice her history. A good daughter of the middle classes, as she described herself, she saw the light—that is, that the System was rotten and needed a radical overthrow—when she was eighteen. She was in love with a young Che Guevara from the LSE, but he turned respectable on her and settled for the Labour Party. Nevertheless, he was the love of her life. When she visited him—"Absolute anguish, my dear, why do I do it?"—she knew that this was the man for her. "But how could I live like that? I couldn't! One weekend is enough. Then we weep, we quarrel, and we part. Until next time." So she chattered, becoming flushed, seeming to loosen and soften from the heat in the kitchen, flour on her cheek, sleeves rolled up, her large white hands in control of everything. She looked plump, soft, content, full of secret and unscrupulous satisfactions.

Jasper and Bert came back, ready for hot baths and food. They had gone down to Nottingham to join the pickets in a miners' strike. It had rained and was cold. Roberta and Faye were starving, they said when they returned. Faye had colour in her cheeks again; she had rejoined the living, and was amusingly and enliveningly her cockney self. Roberta, so happy that her love was better, showed a side of herself they had not seen. She sang, very well, in a full, controlled contralto, first some workers' songs, then a whole range of songs from the Portuguese, from Spanish, from Russian. It turned out that she had been trained to sing, but she had found her niche with the revolution.

There was enough wine, and everyone got tight. Mary and Reggie did not appear.

They were all going up to bed, at about two in the morning, when there was a low, hurried knock at the front door.

"My God, the police," shrieked Alice and rushed to confront them. But it was not the police. Two young men shouldering large packages stood there, smiling, bent sideways from the weight.

"What's that? You can't bring those here," said Alice, knowing what was happening, all her pleasure in the evening gone, feeling chilled and apprehensive.

"Come on, now," said one, Irish as they make them. "We were told to leave these here."

"It's a mistake," said Alice.

But he had slid the package onto the hall floor and gone off, while his fellow, grinning bashfully, let his load slide off.

"You have to take them back," said Alice. "Do you understand?" They had both gone down the path, and she could see them standing by a small shabby van. They were conferring, turning to check the house number with a piece of paper. Alice arrived beside them and said, "You haven't understood. This stuff shouldn't be left here! You must take it away again."

"Ah, well now, but that's easily said," said the one who had spoken before. He sounded injured. More, afraid. He even glanced around into the shadowy gardens, and then out into the main road, where the traffic was thinner but still moving. It was a dark night, damp. The three stood close together under the street light and argued.

Alice said that this was the wrong house, and the house they wanted, number 45, was no longer safe to leave anything at.

They said that they had been told number 43.

"You have got to take them away."

"And we will not!"

She imagined that she heard a window going up behind her and turned to stare up into the darkened top of the house opposite Joan Robbins, and while she did this the two men took the opportunity to nip into the van. She had to stand aside quickly to avoid being run over.

"Oh no," she wailed into the dark, watching the little van dart off to the corner and turn out of sight. "No, it simply isn't *on*. It's not *fair*."

She stood there, helpless, feeling that things had gone out of control. Then thought that she should go in, in case any nosy neighbour was awake and interested. Slowly she went indoors. The two cartons, as smooth and bland as two brown pebbles, stood there in the hall with nothing on them to announce their contents.

On the stairs stood Jasper and Bert, staring, disconsolate. Also, rather drunk. Above them, Jocelin. Roberta and Faye had gone off into their room. Caroline was still clearing up in the kitchen.

"We can't have these here," appealed Alice, to the men, but it was Jocelin who leaped down past them, and said only, "Up into the attic." As the two women laboured up past the men on the stairs, they came to and helped. First one very heavy carton and then the other were stowed in a far corner of the attic.

Jocelin said she would find out what was there in the morning. Perhaps even tonight: she didn't feel sleepy.

"Don't blow us all up," said Jasper, and she did not reply. She did not think much of Jasper, and showed it. She seemed to like Bert, however. Bert, for his part, was attracted by Caroline, who either had not noticed this or had decided to ignore it.

Alice went back into the kitchen, tidied up this and that, listening for sounds of some or all of them coming back to talk it over. For she had understood that something bad had happened. It was not just another little harassment, like a visit from the police! When she realised that no one was coming, which meant they had not seen what by now they should, she sat down at the head of the table and lapsed into a numbed condition. Numbed feelings, not thought, for her mind was active.

No one had said anything to them about number 43's becoming a collection point. Comrade Muriel would certainly have mentioned it, had she known. Caroline and Jocelin had not expected it. Comrade Andrew had not even approached the subject. (Here the thought of the money, the five hundred pounds, presented itself, and Alice contemplated it, as it were, without prejudice.) Number 43 couldn't have people just dumping stuff here, and others whisking it off again, any time of the day or night! It simply wasn't on! But who could Alice contact to announce this? It occurred to her that she had no means of reaching Pat, or Muriel; let alone Comrade Andrew. The unreality of it, that these people had been so vivid, so *there*, in this house and in the next house, for weeks—comrades, you could say intimates— and then not to be there, and so absolutely gone, lost, rubbed out that she could not even send them a postcard . . . This thought deepened her numbness, like a blank area slowly spreading through her.

And there was another thing. (But this was certainly not a new thought.) Here they were, committed to "doing something real at last," all ready for it—you could say that number 43 was now quivering on the edge, like people in a little boat on the verge of a waterfall (here Alice painfully shook her head, like a dog clearing its ears of water)—yet they did not really have much confidence in one another. (Alice was replaying, as it were, the look on Jocelin's face as she saw that Jasper and Bert lolled on the stairs, while she, Jocelin, ran down to help carry the big packages.) No, Jocelin did not admire Jasper! What did she think of Faye? Well, it was not hard to imagine. Almost certainly, though, she must approve of Roberta? Caroline? You could hardly imagine a greater contrast between the indolent, sensual woman and the cold, functional Jocelin. And herself, Alice? Did she despise her, too?

It occurred to her that she was using Jocelin as a touchstone, a judgement point. As though Jocelin were the key to everything? Well, it was she who was at work on the bombs, or whatever.

Alice went up to the top of the house, saw that light showed beneath the door of Jocelin's workroom, knocked, heard a low "Come in."

Jocelin looked up from where she sat behind her trestle, her hands intricately engaged with a length of copper wire. Close by her stood packages of various household chemicals, looking reassuring in their bright packaging.

Jocelin went on looking at Alice, waiting for her to explain herself. She was formidable and frightening, Alice thought. Yet what could be more ordinary than Jocelin? A stranger would see a rather slatternly blonde, strands of pale hair falling over her face, smears of some sort of white powder on her old grey sweater. But it was her concentration, her focussing of herself behind what she did . . .

Alice said feebly, "Hello," and Jocelin did not respond, but went on working, pouring white grains from an old saucepan into a copper pipe.

"I didn't like what happened down there," said Alice, sounding ineffective even to herself, and Jocelin nodded and said, "No, neither did I. But I don't see that we can do anything but go on. We must get the job done quickly, and then scatter."

There was nowhere in the room to sit, only the trestle and behind it the stool on which Jocelin sat. Windows showed a greying sky. The birds would start soon. Alice stood in front of Jocelin like a schoolgirl in front of a teacher, and said, "Have you thought yet what we should do?"

"Yes, of course. What we blow up depends on our means,

doesn't it. I've got a pretty good idea of what the capacity of these things is. But we have to discuss it."

"Have you . . . I mean . . . you've . . ."

"No, I haven't done this before. But it's a question of using your common sense," said Jocelin briskly. She set aside one copper tube, which was about ten inches long and presumably had reached some stage of readiness, and took up another. She nodded sideways at the "recipe book," which lay open. This production shared the same qualities as the devices made according to its recipes. It was not printed, but photographed, which gave it a technical, ugly look. It was on bad paper. It had a yellowish plastic cover, like a cheap cookery book. Everything on that trestle looked cheap, makeshift, sharp-edged, and for some reason unfinished. Everything, that is, except the clever packets of chemicals, which seemed glossy with the amount of thought and expertise that had gone into them.

"And it wouldn't be a bad idea if we had a practice run," said Jocelin, smiling. It was, as might be expected, a cold, off-putting smile.

"Right on," said Alice. "Of course."

"We could choose something that deserves to be blown up."

Alice came to life with, "*Yes*. Something absolutely shitty . . . something revolting, yes."

Jocelin looked at her curiously, because of this sudden animation. "Have you anything in mind? I want something defined, if you know what I mean. Something definite, not too big; and solid. So that I can check quantities."

Alice was reviewing in her mind's eye things she would enjoy seeing blown up. She had to discard the high corrugated iron fences around the former market where everyone had had such a good time; which, all through the week, and particularly on Saturdays and Sundays, had been like a festival. A fence was not "defined." It went on and on.

"Not a telephone box," said Jocelin. "It says here exactly how much one needs to do one of those in."

"A car?"

"Yes, we might have to use a car, because of the difficulty of access. Of being seen. But I know what a car would need. Something else."

Alice smiled. "I know what." A passion of loathing had taken her over, so that she felt quite shaky with it. "Oh God, yes," she breathed. "I'll show you. It's not far."

"Right." Jocelin left her post and was beside Alice as they went silently down the stairs. The hall was not dark, but grey. Daylight. There would soon be people in the streets, the early workers.

They had only to walk half a mile, to an area of small streets that had been built before the invention of the motorcar. Now lorries trundled there all day, crunching backwards around corners, passing one another with inches to spare. The pavements, built so that two people could pass each other, were narrow, and in two of these little streets, at right angles to each other, the pavement had been widened on one side, thus further narrowing the streets by about a yard. This piece of official brilliance was dazzling enough, but in addition, to make it all totally incomprehensible to the ordinary mind, having gained this extra yard or so of pavement for the comfort and satisfaction of the citizens, the Council had then stuck all along the reclaimed edge of pavement cement stanchions or bollards of a peculiarly ugly grey-brown, about a yard tall, and round, like teeth. These hideous and pointless and obstructive objects, twenty or so around each corner at either end of the afflicted street, which Alice passed whenever she went to the Underground, provoked in her the all-too-familiar helpless rage, useless, violent, and unappeasable. She would stand there, examining this scene as she had done when seeing how the Council workmen had filled in lavatories with cement, smashed pipes, vandalised whole houses, saying to herself, People did this. First, in some office, they thought it up, and then they made a plan, and then they instructed workmen to do this, and then workmen did it. It was all incomprehensible. It was frightening, like some kind of invincible stupidity made evident and visible. Like modern university buildings.

Side by side on the pavement, which was, because of the

cement teeth, as narrow as it had been before the widening, Alice and Jocelin looked at the scene. A reversing or too narrowly turning lorry had knocked one of the teeth sideways. Their bases were stained with dog urine and shit. Under the low grey dawn sky, the still-sleeping houses held the people who would be insulted by these pavements, these cement teeth, every time they came out of doors. The houses seemed tender and innocent, the sky pure and sad. Then began the dawn chorus.

Alice was weeping with rage.

Jocelin sighed, and said, "Right. I see what you mean. But this isn't an easy location. There must be people around most times of the day and night."

"There are none now."

"But there are always night owls looking out of windows, or women up with their babies."

Alice was comforted by this evidence of the ordinary in Jocelin, but said, "But that is true of everywhere, all the time, isn't it?"

Jocelin did not answer. She was looking at the knocked-askew tooth. Without guiltily glancing around, or looking along the rows of windows, she went quickly to this stanchion and tried to lift it. It moved a little. Alice joined her, and together, with difficulty, they raised it to the perpendicular and let it go again.

Swiftly, Jocelin examined the gap at the base of this tooth, where there were some thin metal wires, and said, "This will do. I'll put the charge under it. Then make it stand upright. All I want to know is how much I need to use of something. Tomorrow. We'll do it tomorrow. About an hour earlier than this."

It was getting on for five.

They had been standing there for a good ten minutes, but not a soul had appeared. Yet they were surrounded by windows and, possibly, eyes. A familiar feeling of recklessness, excitement, was stealing through Alice. Her awful lethargy had gone. The dim, grey numb feeling like a poison—gone!

And as they turned the corner to their street, she broke into a run, and sprinted, from sheer excess energy, up to their gate, and vaulted over it, and then up the path, to be brought to a halt by the door, which after all had to be opened. With a key.

Jocelin, arriving calmly, said, "One has to be very together for this job. Calm. Not excitable." Alice muttered something apologetic.

They went up to bed.

Alice did not sleep much; she was thrilling with excitement, with anticipation. Coming downstairs in a sleeping house, she made herself walk sedately, because of what Jocelin had said.

She sat in the kitchen and thought, Well, here I am again, waiting for people to wake up. She drank tea, ate wholemeal toast and honey, then remembered the packages in the attic. At once her whole self seemed afflicted with confusion, with division. What was needed was a car . . . but there was no car at 45. . . . How to get hold of a car? Checking that it wasn't too late—about eight, time to get her before she went to work—Alice walked as fast as she could to Felicity's place.

Felicity was just coming out of the gate, and when she saw Alice, wary annoyance possessed her. But Alice gave her no time to develop this. She went straight up and said, "Philip's affairs are more or less sorted out. But they are looking for his sister. If they don't find her in a couple of days, they'll fix the funeral for Monday or Tuesday anyway." Felicity, as expected and as she ought, looked embarrassed, if impatient, and said, "Thanks, it's good of you to take it on."

"I had no alternative," Alice reminded her crisply.

The two women stood facing each other, but Felicity looked as though she were in a game of trying to dodge past someone without being touched. Alice said, "Can I borrow your car for a few hours?"

At this Felicity sighed and said, "But I'm using it this morning." Felicity was a social worker.

"I need it," said Alice simply.

Felicity thought, and said, "You could have it tomorrow morning until lunchtime." She could not have said more clearly: And that is all you are getting from me as *quid pro quo!* Alice answered this with, "Fine. We'll consider accounts settled, then." Hearing it put into words made Felicity blush, but she said, "I'm in a hurry. Same time tomorrow?" And almost ran to her car, a

Datsun, which stood parked with all the other conforming, obedient cars along the pavement's edge.

That's done, thought Alice, and put all thoughts of the dangerous packages out of her head. Tomorrow she would take them to the municipal rubbish tip, and that would be that. And if any more turned up, they would be got rid of.

Outside her front door stood a man, in a neat grey suit and a tie, so much the official that she thought, Oh no, not the Council again, and put on her competent, I-am-coping-with-everything face.

But it was in an American accent that he said, or stated, "Alice Mellings?"

"That's right"—and she knew that this forthcoming encounter was one she would need all her wits for. Her excited blood told her so.

"Can I come in?"

Without speaking, she opened the door, and went in front of him to the kitchen, and indicated that he should sit in the chair at the end of the table. She put on the kettle and sat at the head.

He looked younger than herself. But he was the type to look young. He had a smooth face, attentive and polite, like an old-fashioned student. He had rather nice brown eyes, at the moment devoted to her every movement, eyes that examined her as closely as she did him. He had well-cared-for hands. But his most remarkable feature was his featurelessness. There was nothing, but nothing, to fasten on to in him. A clerk; someone essentially indoor, weathered at the worst by a draught or too-cold air from a left-open window. He might have taken an exam in how to be ordinary! Yet there was something excessive in it. . . . Of course, she, Alice, was only likely to meet nonconformists—or, as her mother in her old-fashioned way put it, bohemians; and, of course, in England in these days, particularly London, no one gave a fuck, but all the same . . .

It was he who broke the silence with, "Comrade Mellings, I was informed early this morning that you were reluctant to accept a consignment of *matériel*."

Alice stared. The use of the word *matériel* now, in this context, was not thrilling her at all. In this situation (one she wanted to shake off and be rid of), the word *matériel* was too portentous; it was a word that insisted on being taken seriously.

He said, "Is that true, Comrade Mellings? I would like some kind of explanation." He spoke as it were abstractly, his own personality removed, but the words he used were enough, and she was suddenly furious. Who the fuck did he think . . .

"It certainly is true," she said calmly, and coldly. "It was quite out of order to bring it here. No arrangement has ever been made that any sort of stuff should be sent here." She deliberately used the word "stuff," which sounded unimportant.

He licked his lips, and his eyes were slightly narrowed as he stared.

"That is not possible," he observed, at last. But she could see he was nonplussed, was trying to find some thread or loose end to guide him in.

"Oh yes, it is," she asserted herself. "All kinds of things were dumped next door and picked up again. But that had nothing to do with us in this house. This is a quite different situation."

There were sounds from the kettle that enabled her briskly to rise and go to it. Her back to him, she stirred powdered coffee into two mugs. Slowly. Something about him bothered her. He was rather like those large, smooth, shiny bales upstairs, with not a mark on them, and with God knows what inside.

An American? Well . . .

She took her time in turning, in setting the mug down in front of him. She had not asked what he would drink. Then she surprised herself by yawning, a deep, irresistible yawn. After all, she had hardly slept. He glanced at her, covertly, surprised. This glance was not, as it were, on the agenda; and she felt suddenly in control.

She calmly sat down, and when he seemed to be looking about for milk, or sugar, she pushed a half-empty bottle of milk towards him, and a quite pretty old cup with sugar in it. She could see that these domestic arrangements did not meet with his approval.

She waited, her mind at work on what it was about him that disturbed her.

"The American revolutionaries depend on this liaison, so that their aid can reach the Irish revolutionaries," he said.

"What American revolutionaries?"

"As you know, Comrade Mellings, large numbers of honest Americans wish to aid the Irish in their fight against the British oppressor."

"Yes, but most of them are just ordinary people; they aren't revolutionaries." There was considerable contempt in this for him— for his inexactness.

He was now staring down at his mug, as if examining her was not yielding him the information he needed, and the mug might provide inspiration.

"Just let's get this clear," she said. "You are supposed to be an American supplying the Irish comrades with *matériel?*" She had not meant to sound so raw and derisive.

He said, still looking at his mug, "Yes, I am an American, Gordon O'Leary. Third-generation American. An old Irish-American family. Like the Kennedys." He laughed, for the first time. The laugh offered her this joke like a present, and he looked full at her, with confidence.

"And Comrade Andrew is an American too?" she enquired, her voice quite stifled with derision.

"Yes, he is an American. Of course. But I think his family came from Germany."

"Oh, for shit's sake," she said. "Comrade Andrew is about as American as . . ." She looked straight at him, with the full force of her essential innocence, her candour, and said, "And you are not an American. You couldn't be an American, not in a thousand years."

His pale, obedient cheeks coloured, and his breathing changed as he dropped his dangerously angry gaze. Regaining control, he said, "But I can assure you I am. Why shouldn't I be?"

"You are Russian. Like Andrew. Oh, you speak perfect American, of course." Alice laughed, from nervousness. But she was fuelled by the most sincere anger. She had never been able to stand being treated like a fool. She was being treated like one now.

He made some internal adjustment or other, sighed, sat up straight in his chair, as if reminded by an inward monitor that one didn't slump in a chair, and looked at her. He said, mildly enough, "Comrade Mellings, as it happens I am an American. From Michigan. I am an engineer, and when I have finished certain little assignments here, that is what I shall return to do. Do you understand?" He waited for her to reply, but while she was listening to him, her gaze fixed on his face, the gaze was a little glassy, because her mind was hard at work. Why could he not be an American? His accent was perfect, better than Andrew's! No, it was his style. It was something about him. What were Americans, then? (She even shut her eyes, allowing Americans she had known to appear in her mind's eye, for examination.) All the ones she had met— which, she reminded herself, were mostly young and belonging to the network of international wanderers and explorers but, nevertheless, real Americans—were quite different. There was a quality— what was it? Yes, there was a largeness, an openness, a looseness . . . there was a freedom, yes, that was the word. Whereas this man here (and she opened her eyes to make comparisons with what she had been examining on her inner screen, to see him most curiously watching her) was tight and controlled, and looked as if he couldn't make a spontaneous movement if he tried. He looked, even though he sat "relaxed"—presumably that was meant to be an informal pose—as if he wore an invisible straitjacket and had never been without it, ever, in his life. His very molecules had got into the habit of being on guard.

"You are not American," she concluded. "But I don't care anyway. You are not to bring any more of that stuff here. We won't take it in."

"You will do as you have contracted to do. As was understood," he said, very soft, very threatening. She felt this way of conveying threat had been taught to him: method 53 for intimidating the subject. The contempt she felt for his obviousness was putting her out of his reach.

"I told you, we haven't contracted for anything."

"You have! You have, Comrade Mellings!"

"When did I? It was never even mentioned. It wasn't mentioned once."

"How could it not have been mentioned? Did you or did you not accept money from us, Comrade Mellings?"

This did set her back a bit, and she frowned, but said, "I didn't ask for the money. It was simply given to me."

"It was just given to you," he said, with polite derision, mild, to match his general style.

"Yes. All I knew about it was when Comrade Muriel, you know, the woman who looks like a goose, handed me a packet with five hundred pounds, just before she went off to her spy course in Lithuania or wherever."

This time he went properly red, a raw beef red, and he did actually glare at her, before recovering himself. Again he sat himself up straight, reminded, perhaps by his anger, that even when one was sitting relaxed at a table, nevertheless one's knees should be set together and one should at the most have one elbow on it.

"If Comrade Andrew or anyone else said anything about spy schools anywhere at all, then it's just a pack of nonsense."

She thought about this, taking her time. "I don't think it was nonsense. Where have Muriel and Pat gone to? They've gone off somewhere for training. Well, I don't care anyway. I'm not interested in America or Czechoslovakia or Russia or Lithuania. None of us are. We are English revolutionaries and we shall make our own policies and act according to the English tradition. Our own tradition."

He said cautiously, after a considerable pause, "It is of course understandable that you owe first loyalty to your own situation. But we are dealing with a struggle between the growing communist forces in the world, and capitalism in its death throes. That is an international situation, which means that policies must be formulated from an international point of view. This is a world struggle, comrade."

"I don't think you quite understand," said Alice. "We are not taking orders from you or from anyone else. Not from *anybody*," she added.

"It's not a question," he said slowly, emphasising each word, "of what you have or have not decided, comrade. You cannot renege on agreements already made."

She completed the circular argument by repeating, "But not by us."

His violently hostile eyes were hastily shielded from her, as he lowered his gaze.

The silence went on for a time, and Alice remarked, quite in her good-hostess manner, putting people at their ease, "It seems to me that your Comrade Andrew has goofed things up. Isn't that it? And you are sorting it all out?"

She heard his breathing come too loud. Then slow and regular as he controlled it. His eyes were not available for inspection. Everything about him was tight, clenched, even his hand, where it lay on the table. "Well, don't get so uptight about it. With so many in the KGB—millions of you, aren't there?—yes, I know that is for the whole of Russia, only some of you are out keeping an eye on us—well, there are bound to be some inefficient ones." His glance upwards at her did quite frighten her for a second, and she continued bravely, even kindly, for now she genuinely wanted to set him at his ease, if possible, having won the advantage and made him accept her point of view: "I am sure the same is true of our lot. I mean, what a shitty lot, that is, if even half of what you read in the papers is true. . . ." This last part of the sentence was her mother, straight; and Alice wondered that her mother should be speaking so authoritatively and naturally from Alice's own mouth. Not that Alice minded. Dorothy Mellings's voice sounded quite appropriate, really, in this situation. "Getting caught the way they do all the time. Well, I suppose we wouldn't be likely to hear about yours: you'd just rub them out. I mean, that's one thing about having a free press."

Now he moved his position, apparently trying to relax, though he had a fist set upright on the table in front of him. His look at her was steady, his breathing normal; some turning point had occurred in the conversation, if conversation was the word for it. Some decision had probably been taken. Well, so, that was all right. He'd go off in a moment and that would be that.

But he showed no signs of moving yet.

Well, let him sit on there, then. What she really wanted to
think about was not him, or why he was here, but tonight, and the
adventure that awaited her with Jocelin, with whom, at this
moment, she felt an almost sisterly bond, in contrast to the murky
complicated feeling she had about this Russian. This *foreigner*.

She remarked, "I do think that part of our problem—I mean,
now, between you and me—is what is referred to as a culture clash!"
Here she laughed, as Dorothy Mellings would have done. "Your
traditions are so very different from ours. In this country you really
cannot turn up and tell people what to do or think. It's not *on*.
We have a democracy. We have had a democratic tradition now
for so long it is in our bones," she concluded, kindly and smiling.

What was happening with him now was that he was thinking—
as, after all, happens not so rarely in conversations—But this person
is mad! Bonkers! Round the twist! Daft! Demented! Loco! Completely insane, poor thing. How was it I didn't see it before?

At such moments, rapid and total readjustments have to take
place. For instance, the whole of a previous conversation must be
reviewed in this new, unhappy light, and assessments must be made,
such as that this person is really beyond it, or perhaps is showing
only a rather stimulating eccentricity, which, however, is not appropriate for this particular situation.

Alice had no suspicion that any such thoughts were in his
mind; she was happily afloat, all kinds of reassuring and apt phrases
offering themselves to her as though off a tape coiled in her mind
that she did not know was there at all. If, however, she could have
seen her own face, that might have been a different matter; for the
upper part of it, brows and forehead, had a worried and even
slightly frantic look, as if wondering at what she was saying, while
her mouth smilingly went on producing words.

"And I think that was probably Comrade Andrew's problem."
(Here the scene on the bed came into her mind, and she actually
gave her head a good sharp shake to get rid of it.) "He seemed to
have a good deal of difficulty in understanding Western culture
patterns. I hope you don't think too badly of him. I thought very
highly of him."

"So you did, did you," he remarked, not enquired, in a quite good-humoured way. Everything about him said he would get up and go.

"Yes. He seemed to me a fine person. A really good human being."

"Well, I am glad to hear that," said Comrade Gordon O'Leary from Michigan or Smolensk or somewhere, who now did in fact get up, but in slow motion. Or perhaps that was how Alice saw it, for there was no doubt she was not feeling herself. Lack of sleep, that was it!

"Someone will come for the *matériel* tonight," he said.

"It's not here," improvised Alice smoothly. They couldn't have this Russian, this foreigner, creeping all over their house. Not with all those bombs and things upstairs. The next thing, he'd be telling them what to do with them. Giving them orders! Well, he'd never understand; he was a Russian; they had this history of authoritarianism.

"Where is it?" He whipped about on her, standing very close. She had stood up, holding on to the back of her chair. Now he didn't look smooth and clerkly and *nothing*. All the terror that she might reasonably have felt during the last half hour swooped down into her. She could hardly stand. He seemed enormous and dark and powerful looming over her, and his eyes were like guns.

"It's on the rubbish tip at Barstone. You know, the local rubbish dump, the municipal dump." Her knees seemed to be melting. She was cold, and wanted to shiver. She had understood, but really, that this was indeed a serious situation, and that somewhere she had gone wrong. Without meaning to. It was not her fault! But the way this man was looking at her—nothing like this had ever happened to her before. She had not known that there could be a situation where one felt helpless.

He was so angry. Ought he to be so angry? He was white, not red, a leaden white, with the effort—she supposed—of holding himself in, the effort of not hitting her. Of not killing her. She knew that was it.

She should not have said, in that casual way, "rubbish dump," that the stuff was on the rubbish tip. Yes, that had been foolish. Hasty. Perhaps even now she should say, No, I was joking, the cases are upstairs. But if she did, he would go upstairs and find Jocelin at work, and then . . .

She felt she might faint, or even begin to weep. She could feel tears filling her, beginning to press and exude everywhere over her body.

He said, "I am by myself. I have a car. I need someone—better, two people—to go out to this place and get the packages."

"Oh," she said, breathlessly, her voice sounding weak and silly. "I shouldn't do that. Not in full daylight. There might be people there. Rubbish vans emptying rubbish, for a start. It would be dangerous."

"It would be dangerous?" he enquired. Again she felt he might easily kill her, do something he could not stop himself from doing. "We can't have that lying around on a rubbish dump," he said.

"Why not? Have you ever seen one? It's full of all kinds of stuff. Acres of it. A couple of ordinary brown packages wouldn't be noticed much." She was beginning to feel better again, she noted.

"Two new, large, unopened packages?" he enquired, his face close to hers, eyes quite dislocated with anger.

"All the same, I'd wait till tonight."

"I'm not waiting till tonight. Get two people down here. Men. There are men in the house, aren't there?"

She said, cold, almost herself again, "I and another girl carried the cases"—she was going to say "upstairs," but caught herself in time—"to the car."

"Then two women. It doesn't matter."

"Yes, it does matter," she informed him. "Don't give us orders. Don't you understand, you can't give us orders, we aren't Russians."

Her eyes were shut, not so much because she did not feel well (in fact, she felt better) as because she could sense his hatred for her enclose her. Well, that was it, she was going to be killed. A movement, the sounds of footsteps; she opened her eyes and saw him going off. But at the door he stopped and turned and said very quietly, with an extraordinary intensity of contempt, of personal dislike, "Don't imagine that this is the end of it, Comrade Mellings. It is not the end, far from it. You can't play little games with us like that, you'll see, *Comrade* Mellings." And his face convulsed briefly, in that movement of cheeks and tongue which if continued would have ended in the action of spitting. And he stood with eyes narrowed, staring at her, determined to mark her, force her down, with the strength of what he felt.

And now this was the man himself, absolutely what he was. She knew this, knew she saw *him*. This was not the smoothie, the conforming spy who had been taught to control every movement, gesture, look; but something behind that. This was power. Not fantasies about power, little games with it, envy of it, but power itself. He embodied the certitudes of strength, of being utterly and completely in the right. He knew himself to be superior, dominant, in control. Above all, in the right.

He went out, shutting the door—she noted—gently. No loud bangs that might alert neighbours.

She went swiftly to the sink and was sick.

Tidily she swirled away all that nastiness, scrubbing and cleaning, though she had to hold on with one hand, her knees were so weak. She took herself, actually staggering, to the lavatory, for terror, it seemed, sat in her bowels. She came back, holding on to door edges and door handles, to the kitchen, where she collapsed on the table, face down, arms sprawled out, limp as a rag. She had never before felt anything like this physical weakness. She lay there for perhaps half an hour, while strength slowly returned.

Then Jocelin came in, hardly glanced at her—so she couldn't be so obviously in a ruinous state—and said that she must have strong coffee: not sleeping did not suit her. If she started now, she was sure she could get ready the appropriate explosive device for their work tonight. She spoke in an abstracted way, but with the cold relish that was her way of showing the excitement that, Alice knew, would shortly again be restoring herself. To hasten the healing process, she went up with Jocelin to her workroom, taking a chair with her this time, and watched those careful, intelligent hands at work. And soon she did feel so much better she had almost forgotten Comrade

Gordon O'Leary. She thought vaguely: We'll have to decide about whether to take those packages to the rubbish tip or not. As things are, he'll believe they have already been found and taken off somewhere. So far behind her now did her real terror seem that she actually thought: Well, that'll give him a bad moment or two. Serve him right. She told Jocelin about him as if he had been some sort of importunate salesman she had sent packing.

"Who the hell do they think they are?" Jocelin agreed.

Their elation began to fill the whole house, like the aromas of one of Alice's soups, and for a while they were all up there, watching Jocelin at work, joking about how they would like to use this bomb or that. Tower blocks of flats. Police-computer information storage. Any information storage systems, for that matter. Certain housing estates. Any nuclear shelters that had been built anywhere, for it was only the rich who would benefit from them. Nuclear power stations.

This game got wilder and noisier, until Caroline pointed out that Reggie and Mary would be in soon. Jocelin was left to her work, and the others dispersed about the house, but kept meeting on landings, or in the kitchen, for today it was hard not to be in one another's company, to share this tide of excitement, of power.

Everything went well that night, which was a Thursday. Reggie and Mary came in long enough to collect a few things; they were off for the weekend. A stroke of luck: it meant they could all spend that evening together. They gathered in the kitchen, laughing, joking, as if they were drunk. But no one drank. And Jocelin was quiet, self-absorbed, set apart from them by the necessities of her task.

She decided that it would be better if there were three in all, not two, because of lifting that heavy cement post. They competed for the honour, and Jocelin chose Bert. Faye was disappointed, and a little bitchy. Roberta said, "Never mind, there'll be other times."

At a quarter to four, Jocelin, Bert, and Alice quietly left the house. All the windows in the little street were dark. In the main road the lamps seemed to be withdrawing light back into themselves; their yellow was thickening as a cool abstract grey stole into the sky. Along the pavements between the lamps it was dark. Low down in front of them this darkness agitated itself, and became a small black-and-white dog, trotting with a modest and thoughtful air from somewhere to somewhere. There were no people in this street, and no one in the little street where they had to do their work. The whole business took a minute, with Alice and Bert heaving up the bollard, and Jocelin placing the bomb under it. The bollard stayed upright. They did not run off, but walked slowly to a corner, then walked fast. Some minutes after they reached home, and were in the kitchen drinking chocolate, they heard the thud of the bomb. It was louder than they expected.

They sat around, not joking now, but tense, even irritable, longing to go and see, but Bert said that criminals always tried to visit the scene of the crime and the police counted on that.

Jocelin actually went off to bed. Then so did Faye and Roberta. The others could not. At about nine Caroline strolled down, through busy streets, found the area roped off with red and yellow tapes "like a street fair," she said, and the police all over the place. There seemed to be quite a bit of damage. Windows blown in, for instance. They woke Jocelin to tell her this. She was upset; she had intended to fragment the bollard and a certain area of the pavement. She, too, went down to look, and came back gloomy. Her calculations had not been correct. She returned to her workroom, saying she wanted to be alone to think.

Alice remembered that this morning was when she had the car to dispose of the bales, or packages. She was bad-tempered, and even bitter: that she should have to deal with this, on such a morning, on a day when surely she should be allowed to be with the others, without problems!

They discussed it. Should they go out now, mid-morning, and find some place to dump the packages? Caroline said lazily that they shouldn't bother—everyone would be gone from the house quite soon anyway. Let the next lot of squatters deal with the problem.

Bert and Jasper said no. Alice, reluctantly, agreed.

The four got the packages down out of the attic, with difficulty, and much bumping. The noise brought Jocelin out. She said she wanted to see what was in there; after all, it might come in useful. The bands of plastic webbing were easily cut. The wrappings were of thick waxed paper. Under that, a heavy cardboard. Inside, thick wads of coarse oily wool-waste. Within this nest were parts of guns. The five conspirators were bent over the opened package, staring in. Their hearts thudded, and their eyes dazzled. They straightened themselves, slowly, to breathe more easily. Caroline's hand, which was resting on the package's edge, was shaking, and she quickly removed it. The five of them stood there upright around the half-buried gun parts, which gleamed dully in the inadequate light. Their breathing rasped and sighed, and they heard one another swallow, and Bert said, laughing, "You'd think we were scared shit-less—and I believe I am. Suddenly, it's all for real. . . ." They all laughed, except for Alice, who was standing with both hands loosely fisted, covering her half-open mouth. Her eyes stared tragically over her knuckles at Jocelin. Jocelin gave her an impatient look and said, "Come on, let's get moving," and started to push back the packaging.

"No!" shouted Jasper, coming to life. In a fury of energy he began removing parts of guns, and assembling them as he thought they should go, working on top of the other parts still half buried in the waste.

"No," said Jocelin, cold and quiet—much to Alice's relief; and she chimed in with, "No, Jasper, don't."

Bert was already trying to help Jasper, but he was slow and clumsy compared with him.

Although Jasper was so neatly and competently sliding the parts together, taking them apart, trying other ways to fit them, he was not achieving anything like a complete weapon.

"Are they machine guns?" asked Alice, almost weeping.

"Stop it," said Jocelin directly to Jasper. "If you did manage to assemble one, what would you do with it?"

"Oh, we'll find a use for it, all right," said Bert, all his white teeth gleaming, trying hard to be as skilful as Jasper, who had nearly got together a black, shining, sinister-looking thing that was like the weapons you see in children's space films.

"Now you've got fingerprints all over it," said Jocelin, with such contempt that first Bert and then Jasper let go the guns and fell back. "Stupid fool," said Jocelin, her cold eyes demolishing Jasper, showing exactly what she really did think of him. "You *fool*. What do you think you are going to do? Have them just lying around, I suppose, in case one of them came in handy for some little job or other?" She pushed the two men back with her elbows, and began work herself. First she swiftly and cleverly pulled apart the half-assembled weapons (showing them all that she knew exactly what she was doing, she was familiar with them) and then took up handfuls of the waste, with which she cleaned off the fingerprints, holding the parts carefully with fingers gloved in waste.

Caroline remarked, "Probably just rubbing the marks off like that won't be much good—not with the methods they use these days."

"Probably not," said Jocelin, "but it's too late to think of that now, isn't it? We've got to get rid of these things—just get rid of them."

"Why don't we bury them in the garden?" suggested Bert, sounding like a deprived small boy, and she said, "In *this* garden, I suppose you mean, what a brilliant idea!" And then, as she snuggled back the gun parts into their nest, she said, "If you have in mind any little jobs that actually have to be done, something *concrete*—that is, within a proper context, properly organised—then weapons are available. Surely you know that?"

Bert was looking at her with resentment, but also with admiration that relinquished to her the right to take command. His eyes burned with excitement, and he could not stop smiling: teeth, eyes, his red lips, flashed and shone.

Jasper was containing himself, eyes shielded by his lids, so as not to show how furious he was—which Alice knew him to be. She was seeing Jasper, Bert as she had not done before—soldiers, real soldiers, in a war. She was thinking, Why, they'd love it, particularly Jasper. He'd enjoy every minute of it. . . . This thought made her even more dismayed, and she took a few steps back from the scene, the knuckles of both hands again at her mouth.

Jocelin was taking in her condition very well, despite her preoccupation with closing up the package. "Alice, have you never seen guns before?"

"No."

"You are overreacting."

"Yes, she is," said Jasper at once, coming to life in open fury at Alice. "Look at her, you'd think she'd seen a ghost." And here he became, suddenly, like a child in a playground trying to scare another. "Woooo-o-o," he wailed, flapping his hands at her, "Alice has seen a ghost. . . ."

"Oh, for Christ's *sake*," shouted Jocelin, losing her temper. "We've got a serious job to do—remember? And I'm going back up to work. Take those cases out somewhere and dump them and forget about them. They're nothing but trouble." With which she went upstairs, in her slow, determined way, not looking back at them. She was—they knew—furious with herself for losing control.

They all watched her, silent, till she was out of sight, and the atmosphere eased.

"Come on, let's get going," said Bert.

Indecision. With Jocelin, the real boss of the scene, absent, for a moment no one could act. Then Alice came to life, saying, "I'll go and get the car." She ran off.

The car keys had been left downstairs with Felicity's neighbour, because—she said crossly, demonstrating Felicity's annoyance for her—Felicity had waited for Alice to arrive when she had said she would. Apologies and smiles. Alice drove the car back to number 43. The four of them got the packages out to the car. No wonder they were so heavy.

They stood around debating where to take the packages. The rubbish dump? No, not at that hour of the day. Down to the river? No, they would be observed. Better drive out to some leafy suburb like Wimbledon or Greenwich, and see what they could find. They were on their way through Chiswick, crawling through heavy traffic, when they saw, in a side street, big corrugated iron gates and the sign: "Warwick & Sons, Scrap Metal Merchants." They turned out of the traffic and round the block and past the gates. The place seemed deserted. Alice double-parked while Bert went in, coolly, like a customer, and hung about for a bit. But no one came. He sprinted back, face flushed, eyes reddened, white teeth and red lips flashing in his black beard. Jasper caught the fever at once. Alice, admiring them both, backed the car between the great gates and stopped. It was a large yard. In this part of London, capacious plots of ground accommodated large houses and big gardens. But this place had some ramshackle brick-and-corrugated-iron sheds at the back with heavy locks on them, and otherwise everywhere were heaps of metal pipes, bits of cars, rusting iron bars, bent and torn corrugated iron. Brass and copper gleamed unexpectedly, and stacks of milky plastic roofing showed that these merchants dealt in more than metal. There were ancient beams piled near the gates, oak from the look of them (two of these would be just the thing for the roof of poor 43) and, all around these beams, an area where every kind of rubbish had found a place, including a lot of cardboard cartons, rapidly disintegrating, that had in them more metal, and plastic bottles, plastic cups. This was it. Jasper and Caroline were out of the car in a moment, and they and Bert wrestled the packages out of the car, and let them fall near the pile of beams. Alice's eyes seemed to be bursting; black waves beat through her. But she had to keep the car running. Through her fever she saw how Bert had already stood up, looking around, the job done; how Caroline had come back to the car, was getting in; while Jasper, deadly, swift, efficient, was rubbing soil into the smooth professional surfaces of the packages, and scarring them with a bit of iron he had snatched up from a heap, working in a fury of precise intention and achievement. That was Jasper! Alice thought, proud of him, her pride singing through her. No one who had not seen Jasper like this, at such a moment, could have any idea! Why, beside him Bert was a peasant, slowly coming to himself and seeing what Jasper was doing, and then joining in when Jasper had virtually finished the job. Those two packages did not look anything like the sleek brown monsters of a few minutes before, were already just like all the other rubbish lying around, would easily be overlooked.

Jasper and Bert flung themselves in and Alice drove off. As far as they knew, no one had seen them.

They drove back towards the centre of London, and into a pub at Shepherds' Bush. It was about half past twelve. They positioned themselves where they could see the television, and sat drinking and eating. They were ravenous, all of them. There was nothing on the news, and the minute it was over, they left the pub and went home. They were all still hungry, and ready to drop with sleep. They bought a lot more take-away and ate it round the kitchen table with Faye, with Roberta, with Jocelin. There was a feeling of anticlimax. But they did not want to part; they needed one another, and to be together. They began drinking. Jasper and Bert, Alice and Caroline went off for a couple of hours' sleep, at different times, but all felt, when alone in their rooms, a strong pull from the others to come back down. They drank steadily through the evening and then the night, not elated now but, rather, depressed. Not that they confessed it; though Faye was tearful, once or twice.

As soon as the Underground was open, Jasper sprinted off to get the newspapers. He came back with them all, from the *Times* to the *Sun*. The kitchen was suddenly flapping with sheets of newsprint, which were turning more and more wildly.

There was nothing there about their exploit! Not a word. They were furious. At last Faye found a little paragraph in the *Guardian* that said some hooligans had blown up the corner of a street in West Rowan Road, Bilstead.

"Hooligans," said Jocelin, cold and deadly and punishing, her eyes glinting. And she did not say—and there was no need, for it was in all their minds—We'll show them.

And so they went to bed. Saturday morning. Six o'clock.

They slept through the day, and woke with that pleasantly abstracted feeling that comes after going without sleep and then enjoying long, restoring sleep.

They discussed what was to be the scene of their next attempt. Various possibilities, but Jocelin said she needed more time to be sure of her means. Besides, Alice said, Philip would probably be buried on Monday or Tuesday; they should get that over first. She knew, from the silence that followed, from how they did not look at her—at least, not at once—that it had occurred to no one to go to Philip's funeral. She said in the polite, indifferent voice she used at her most hurt, most betrayed, "I am going, if no one else is." Jasper knew that voice, and said that he would go with her. He was pleased and even bashful, like a boy, at the grateful look she gave him. Faye said she loathed funerals, had never been to one. When people were dead, they were dead, she said. Caroline pointed out she had scarcely known Philip. Jocelin agreed.

Somebody going out to buy cigarettes came back with the local *Advertiser*—the sheets given away on the streets or put through letter boxes or under doors. In it they found this piece:

A bomb exploded at the corner of West Rowan Road early on Friday morning. A cement post was destroyed and another chipped. The blast damaged the brickwork of nearby houses, and blew the windows out of four of them. Mrs. Murray, a widow of 87, said she was sitting by her upstairs window and had seen three youths near the cement post. It was not yet light, and she could not see them properly. She thought they were having a bit of a lark. She went to lie on her bed, still dressed.

"I sleep badly these days," she said. She heard the explosion, and glass flying into her room. "Lucky I wasn't still sitting at the window," she confided to our reporter. Mrs. Murray sustained minor injuries from the glass and was treated for shock.

"Oh, poor old thing," quavered Alice. She did not look at Jocelin, for she knew the look would be reproachful.

"Silly old cow," said Faye. "Pity we didn't do her in properly. We'd have done 'er a favour, we would. These old crones, their life isn't worth living. 'Alf dead with boredom, they are, years before they go."

They decided to laugh, to placate her. Faye was in the grip of one of her violent, reminiscent moods—but provoked by what?

They never knew. She only sat and trembled a little defiantly, not looking at them, not looking even at Roberta, who was sitting rather hunched, her silvered poll lowered, eyes down, suffering for her.

"Well," said Jocelin, "I think I know what to do. I'll get it right this time."

She sounded angry, even bitter. They were all bitter with frustration. A paragraph in the local *Advertiser!* They felt it was a snub of them, another in a long series of belittlings of what they really were, of their real capacities, that had begun—like Faye's violences—so long ago they could not remember. They were murderous with the need to impose themselves, prove their power.

They went on drinking. Alice was sober, as usual, and apprehensive. It was Saturday, after all. And at eleven o'clock, as she had half expected, there was a loud knocking at the front door. She was up at once, sliding out of her seat, and at the kitchen door before the others had come to. She said to Jasper, "Keep out of sight, d'you hear? Don't you come out, *don't*. . . ." To Bert, "Keep Jasper here. Don't let him come out." To Jocelin, "Is there anything they can find?" Jocelin ran past her and up the stairs. "It's that little fascist. I knew he'd come back. He's come to pay us back. I knew he would."

The knocking went on. She opened the door, saying crisply, using all her resources to be in command, to be Miss Mellings, "You'll wake everyone in the street."

It was he, the fair, vicious young man, with cold baby eyes, the fluffy moustache. He was grinning and sadistic. He held something behind him, and there was a disgusting smell.

Alice had some idea of what was coming, knew that nothing could be done to stop him. But the main thing was that Jasper should not come out, not in the mood he was in—there would be a fight, she knew it.

Behind the policeman stood another. Both had schoolboy sniggers on their faces; neither looked at Alice—a bad sign.

She said, "What do you want?"

"It's what you want," said the little pig, and at this he and his colleague both guffawed, actually holding their hands to their mouths, like stage comedians.

"It's what you fancy," said the second policeman, in a strong Scottish accent.

"A little of what you fancy does you good," said Alice's enemy. Oh, how she loathed him, how she knew him, through and through! Oh, she knew what went on in police cells when he had someone helpless and at his mercy. But it mustn't be Jasper.

To provoke him, to draw his fire, she allowed herself to say in a weak, quavering girlish voice, "Oh, please, please go away. . . ." It was enough. It was just right.

"This is what you like, isn't it?" guffawed the little fascist, and flung, in a strong underarm action, a filled plastic bag into the hall.

"Shit to shit," said the other.

The smell filled the hall, filled the house, as they ran away, laughing.

Of course, it was everywhere, had splashed all over the place. The main thing was, Jasper had stayed inside.

Stepping delicately, she went to the kitchen door, said, "If I were you I'd stay exactly where you are."

But they did not, appeared in a noisy, raging group, full of imprecations and threats. Jasper would go up to the police station now. He would kill that fascist. He would burn down the police station. He would blow the place up.

Faye was retching into the kitchen sink, aided by Roberta. Jocelin appeared on the landing, stood looking down, like a figure of Judgement or something, thought Alice, sick of them all. She knew who was going to clear up.

"Shut up," she said. "You don't understand. This is good, it isn't bad. He was going to get his own back for being made to look a fool the other day. We are lucky he's done this. He could have come in and smashed everything up, couldn't he? We've all seen that done before!"

"She's right," said Jocelin. She, too, retched, and controlled herself. She went back into the room.

Alice had already got a pail, water, and newspapers. She stood for a moment looking at the three, Jasper, Caroline, Bert, who were all still in the doorway, staring at her.

She knelt down at the very edge of the hall, and began on her task of slowly washing the carpet, every inch of it. When she had finished she would get Bert and Jasper to carry it out to the rubbish bins.

"Why are you wasting time washing that for?" demanded Caroline. "Throw it out."

She had expected someone to say just that. She said coldly, "If we put it out like this into the garden it will stink, and there'll be complaints, and an excuse for the police to come back."

"Yeah. That's right," said Jasper.

She went on with her task. She was full of a cold fury. She could have killed, not only the policemen, but Jasper, Bert, and even the good-natured Caroline, whose shocked face peering out of the door seemed to say that one couldn't credit the stupidity and malice of the world.

"Don't go to bed," Alice ordered Jasper. "When I've done this, you and Bert can carry it out."

It took her an hour or so to do the carpet. They carried it, heavy with water and detergent, smelling now of chemicals, out to the dustbins.

"I suppose some night owl will be up and watching, as usual," said Alice, bitter and very tired, standing carefully in the very middle of the hall floor.

Faye said she was going to bed. Roberta took her up, then came back and got another pail and helped with washing down the wood-work and the walls. All the others went to bed.

As Roberta worked, she swore steadily in her other voice, the rough, clumsy, labouring voice of her upbringing, not the slow, easy, comfortable voice of the everyday Roberta they knew. She did not swear loudly, but only just audibly: a steady quiet stream of hatred against the police, the world, God; on her own behalf, on Faye's.

When they had finished, both women took baths. Then Roberta went out for the Sunday papers. But there was nothing in the Sundays, not a word.

Alice and Roberta slept for some hours. Faye, awake at mid-morning, was angry with Roberta for "getting herself involved." To pay her out, she went up to talk to Jocelin, at work on her bombs. First, as apprentice, she helped Jocelin; then, it turning out she had a real aptitude, she tried out a tricky little number on her own account. She came down for a cup of tea and brought her instruction manual with her. At the same moment, Reggie and Mary returned from work on their new flat. It was an awful mess, they said: but, having seen Alice at work, they knew what could be done with chaos. The way they said this told the others that they were determined to be "nice" for as long as they had to stay there. Then Mary picked up from the table *The Use of Explosives in an Urban Environment* and leafed through it, first casually, then slowly, taking her time. She handed it to Reggie with a look that was far from "nice." In the kitchen at that stage were Caroline, Jasper, Bert, and Faye, and suddenly they were all tense, determined not to look at one another, trying to appear indifferent. Reggie studied the manual, and then laid it on the table. He had not looked at the others, sat thinking. Next he and Mary had a long eye-consultation, and he said that they had decided to move into the new flat, ready or not, at once. Only a few moments before, Mary had been saying that they would be here until their flat at least had hot water.

The couple went upstairs, leaving half-finished cups of tea.

"That wasn't very clever, comrade," said Bert to Faye, showing a lot of his white teeth.

Faye tossed her head. She was breathing fast, smiling and frowning and biting her lips. "It doesn't matter," she stated. "Once they are rid of us, they'll never want to think of us again. We're just shit to them, that's all."

"All the same," said Bert, making an effort to be severe, as the occasion demanded, "that was stooo-pid!" He laughed, as at a joke. She laughed wildly, eyeing him with resentment. Then she scrambled up out of her chair and ran upstairs to Roberta. They could hear, over their heads, Robert's low maternal voice, Faye's angry raucousness; her complaints to Roberta were being made in her "other" voice, that of her upbringing; Roberta answered in her everyday voice.

The three sat on uneasily. Then Jasper said, laughing, "I don't see why Alice should sleep all day," and went up to wake her. Which he did by banging on the door of the room she slept in, where he had slept but now would not. No response. He stepped delicately in, saw the huddled bundle that was Alice turned to the wall, and, finding the dark of the room unlikable, sharply dragged back the curtains. Alice shot up in her bag, eyes screwed up because of the afternoon glare. She saw a black spiky menacing figure outlined against the light, and screamed.

"For fuck's sake," he said, disgusted with her.

"Oh, it's you." She lay down, as she had before, back to him.

He could not stand this. He knelt by her, at her back, and saw sandy eyelashes tremble on her freckled creamy skin.

"Alice," he said, quite politely, but firmly. "You do have to wake up. Something has happened."

She opened her eyes. Did not say, "What?" They remained in that position for quite a time, more than a minute. It was as if, for her, getting up on his order and coming downstairs was going to commit her more than she wanted, commit her *again*, when she had made a decision.

At her back knelt Jasper. She could feel his warmth on her shoulders, felt in that warmth the determination of his need for her.

She muttered, sounding indifferent, "All right, I'll be down in a moment."

He stayed a bit, hoping she would turn and smile. But she looked at the wall, waiting for him to go. He got up off his knees and went out, quietly shutting the door.

"Oh *no*," said Alice, breathless, to the wall. "Oh no, I *can't*." But she suddenly got up, dragged on her jeans and jersey, and went down.

Around the table now were Jasper and Bert, Caroline. Jocelin had been summoned from above.

Alice made herself tea, silent, taking her time. She sat down. She listened to what had happened. Then she said, confirming Faye, "It doesn't matter. They'll never want to think about us again, once they are gone. Anyway, there's no reason to connect anything that happens with us. Lots of people have these how-to-be-a-terrorist books." She did not put this into inverted commas, a joke, as it had been in this house till now. The joke had been worn into ordinariness.

"But they are such bloody law-lovers," said Caroline. "They'll probably think it's their bloody duty to inform, when they connect one thing with another."

There was a bad moment, during which they looked at one another, acknowledging the truth of it. But Bert dismissed it, laughing. "Connect what with *what*? We haven't even decided."

"This is as good a time as any to talk it over," said Jocelin.

"We'll have to call down Roberta and Faye, then," said Jasper, uneasily. He involuntarily looked up at the ceiling, immediately beyond which Roberta and Faye, presumably reconciled, lay or sat. At any rate, silently.

"Perhaps it isn't the right time," said Bert. From his grimace Alice deduced that Faye was in one of her moods.

She said vaguely, "Perhaps we should do it without Faye."

They all looked at her, ready to be censorious. All, however, were thinking, as she could see, that there was something in what she said.

It was Jocelin, who had been working with Faye for some hours that day, who remarked, "But she's very clever. And she's got some good ideas about where."

"Where?" asked Bert, laughing again. "Tell us. She hasn't patented her thoughts on the subject."

Jocelin said seriously, "I agree with you that Faye is emotional. But I got the impression this morning that she'd be good in an emergency."

"Who is going up to call them down?" said Jasper, facetiously.

They all looked at Alice.

Alice did not move, but stirred her tea.

"Well, what's wrong with you, then?" demanded Jasper.

"I'm tired," she said.

She got up, in a way that seemed both impulsive and mechanical. She seemed surprised she had got up and was going to the door. Jasper was after her and had her by the wrist. "Where are you going?"

"I'm going for a walk," she said.

"But we're discussing whether to have a regular meeting or not. A meeting to decide what venue we are going to use."

Again, it was like the moment when he had knelt behind her as she lay in her sleeping bag. A long pause, and she came back to her chair, went on stirring her tea as if she had not left.

"I'm going to call Faye and Roberta," said Jocelin, and she went upstairs decisively.

They could hear a little descant of voices, Faye shrill, Roberta full and positive, Jocelin coming in like a response. Jocelin had the last word. She came down, announced that it was all right. They waited for half an hour, being humorous about it.

Then they were all together. It went on for hours. They discussed the merits of railway stations, restaurants, public monuments. The Albert Memorial was favourite for a few minutes, and then Faye said no, she adored it; she wouldn't harm a hair of its head. Hotels. Number 10. The Home Office. MI-5's information computer. The War Office.

It went on. As when a group of people are choosing the name for something among many possibilities, the suggestions became wilder and more imaginative, became funnier; the whole thing turned into comedy. From time to time, one of them would say that they must be serious, but it seemed that seriousness was not on the agenda. They were all weak with laughter when they finally decided where. And were restored to seriousness by Faye's imperious demand that it was she who should actually place the explosives. It was her turn, she said. Alice and Jocelin and Bert had had all the fun last time.

The decision was taken that "the real thing" would be conducted by Faye, Jasper, and Jocelin as mistress of explosives, the others assisting. The meeting broke up at about eight. They celebrating by going to the Indian restaurant. Then Faye and Roberta went to the pictures. Bert and Jasper and Caroline—Bert wanted Alice to come, too—went to visit the South London squat. Jocelin had some last finishing touches to make.

Alice said no, she was all right, she wanted to go for a walk. Yes, she did want to go walking; she didn't understand why they made such a fuss. She liked walking by herself.

This was the first time some of them had heard about this proclivity of Alice's, and jocular remarks ensued.

She set off, frowning, into the dark streets. She stopped after a hundred yards or so and stood looking into a garden where only the outlines of flowers, a shrub, were visible, all colour drained from them. She came to herself with a sigh and walked towards her mother's flat. There she briskly rang the bell, almost at once rang it again, and said when she heard her mother's voice, "It's Alice." A pause. "It's *Alice*," she said, peremptory, peevish.

Another pause. A long one. Then the door buzzed and Alice rushed up the bare ugly stairway. It seemed that she expected, when her mother opened the door, to enter the pleasant large room of the Mellingses' old house, for she charged in as if into a big room and had to pull herself up short in front of her mother, who stood with her back to the armchair she had obviously just left. It was a quite decent little room, but Alice thought it paltry and ugly. The two armchairs, on either side of the little gas fire, which had in the old house had so much space around them, now were like too-large, shabby prisoners, made to face each other. They needed re-covering; Alice had not noticed it before.

She said in a scandalised, hostile voice, "What do you think you are doing, in this place?"

The room was chilly. Alice did not mind this, but Dorothy was wearing a thick jersey and woollen stockings, winter clothes. Alice knew that baggy yellow sweater and the full brown skirt. They were old. Her mother's hair, quite white now, was in an untidy chignon. Her haggard, handsome face, unsmiling, confronted Alice in a frown that showed no signs of softening.

As always when Alice was actually with her mother, pleasant and kindly emotions took over from the angry ones she felt when she was away from her.

The suffering and aggressive face she had brought in with her was already gone, and she smiled. It was the timid, anxious-to-please smile of the good daughter. She looked to see whether she might sit down. The armchair her mother had been in had books stacked up beside it to the level of the arm. On the shelf above the gas fire was a bottle of whisky and a glass, a third full.

The armchair opposite her mother had had someone in it. Alice even looked sharply around to see if this person was hiding somewhere. The cushions of the chair were pressed in, with a look of long and intimate occupancy. There was an empty teacup on the floor by this chair. Alice suddenly imagined Zoë Devlin and her mother sitting opposite each other, and heard their strong, relishing laughter, which seemed to exclude everyone else. A sharp pain went through her, and her look at her mother was again all resentment.

"Why are you bundled up like this? Are you ill?"

A pause. Dorothy said carefully, still frowning, "As you know, I feel the cold. Unlike you."

"Then why don't you light the gas fire?"

A pause. "As you might have been able to work out for yourself, I have to be careful with money."

She spoke in a wary, almost hushed voice, afraid of what a tone of voice, a wrong movement, might provoke. Rather like a nurse with an intractable patient.

"I don't know what you mean," cried Alice. "It can't be so bad that you can't afford to have the fire on if you are cold."

Dorothy Mellings sighed. She turned away. Not to the two armchairs, which now seemed a promise of a long friendly talk that was owed to Alice, but to a small oblong table against the wall, where it seemed she ate her meals. There was a plate on it with one apple and one banana. Alice let out a furious exclamation, and rushed to the small refrigerator in the cooking recess that called itself a kitchen. In the refrigerator was a bottle of milk, some cheese, four eggs, half a loaf of white bread.

Alice whirled round on her mother, but before she could say anything, Dorothy said, "Alice, are you going to want tea or something? Are you hungry?"

"No, I am not hungry," said Alice, sounding accusing.

Dorothy sat down on one of the chairs at the small table, indicating that Alice should sit opposite, but Alice could not bring herself to acknowledge the rights of that petty little table in her mother's life, and she sat on the arm of the chair that had had her mother's friend in it.

"Has Zoë Devlin been here?"

"No, she hasn't. As you know, Alice, we aren't getting on all that well at the moment."

"Oh, don't be so bloody ridiculous. You've known her forever."

"*As you know,* we quarrelled."

"Well, has Theresa been?"

"Not yet."

"Don't tell me you've quarrelled with Theresa?"

"There is no reason why I should tell you anything at all," said Dorothy. She half got up—she did not need to do more—reached over for her glass of whisky, and took a firm ration of it, her mouth a bit twisted. Grant's whisky. Oh yes, Dorothy might be poor, thought Alice bitterly, but she wasn't going to drink anything but her brand of Scotch.

Alice was looking anxiously at that stern face, which seemed as if it had been set forever into a frown, the brows pulled together.

Alice felt she did not know her mother. Dorothy Mellings, in the good old days, the days that could fill Alice's memory for hours at a time, had been a tall, striking woman with reddish-gold hair in a chignon, creamy, delicately freckled skin, greeny-blue eyes. Rather pre-Raphaelite, really, they had used to joke, all of them. But since Dorothy never lolled or languished or rolled her eyes about, the comparison did not go far. Now she was a tall, strong, elderly woman with all that untidy white hair. Her eyes were like squarish lumps of green stone. When she was with other people—Zoë Devlin, for instance—she was all vitality and laughter.

"Who's been here visiting you, then?"

"Mrs. Wood from downstairs."

Alice stood up, stared, sat down again. "Mrs. Wood! What do you mean, Mrs. Wood! Why, she's . . ."

"Are you suggesting she isn't good enough for me?"

"But . . ." Alice was literally unable to speak. All that splendour of hospitality, the big house, the people coming in and out, the meals, the . . . "Mrs. Wood," she stammered.

"I didn't know you knew her."

"But you can't . . ."

"You mean that she's working-class? Surely, Alice, you can't hold that against her? As for me, I've reverted to my proper level. And who is it that boasts all the time about her working-class grandfather?" Dorothy, for the first time this evening, was smiling, was really looking at Alice, those greenish eyes cold, angry. "Or is it that you think she's not intelligent enough for me?"

"But you have nothing in common—she's never read anything in her life, for a start, I bet."

"A sudden reverence for literature?" she enquired. And took another mouthful of whisky. "I can tell you, I find the company of Mrs. Wood just as rewarding as . . . a good many people I might mention. She's not all full of rubbish and pretensions."

This, reminding Alice of that inexplicable movement of her mother towards savage criticism of things she had held dear all her life, filled her eyes with tears, and she thought: It's all been too much for her; oh, how awful, poor thing. She cried out, "You should simply never have said you'd leave home. You should have said you wouldn't go. Then you wouldn't have had to come here."

This sounded like an appeal, as if her mother might even now say, "Yes, it was all a mistake," and go back to her own house.

Dorothy was looking surprised. Then the cautious look was back, with the frown.

"But, Alice, you know what happened."

"What does it matter, what happened? What is going to happen now, that's the point?"

"Well, I do rather despair of talking to you lot about . . . necessity. It's no use. You've all had it so easy all your lives, you simply do not understand. If you want something, then you take it for granted you can have it. . . ." Alice let out a little protesting sound, meaning to say that as far as she was concerned, her mother had gone off the point entirely. But Dorothy went on, "I know it is no use. I have been thinking hard about you, Alice. And I have come to one simple conclusion. You're all spoiled rotten. You're rotten. And Zoë's children are the same."

This was said without emotion. Almost indifferently. All passion spent.

Alice let this go by her, as part of Dorothy's new *persona*, or craziness. It was best ignored. Would go away, probably, like this nonsense over living here.

"I think you should tell Cedric that you won't live here; he must give you more money."

Dorothy sighed, shifted about on her hard little chair, seemed to want to droop away from sheer weariness, pulled herself together, sat up.

"Listen, Alice. And this is for the last time. I don't know why you don't seem able to take it in. It's not very complicated." She now leaned forward, eyes fixed on Alice's pudgy, pathetic, protesting face, and spoke slowly, spelling it all out.

"When your father left me, he said I could stay in the house. I was to have the top floor converted into a self-contained flat. I would let the flat and it would pay expenses. Rates. Electricity. Gas." Alice nodded at this, connecting with what was being said. Encouraged, Dorothy went on, "But instead I took in you and Jasper. You wrote asking if you could come home for a bit."

"I don't remember anything like that. You wrote to me and said why didn't I come home for a bit?"

"Well. Very well, Alice. As you like. I'm not going to argue. There's no point. However it happened, you did come home. I took you and Jasper in. I told your father some people needed a long time to grow up—I was talking about you, of course. I don't care about Jasper."

A chill of rejection afflicted Alice. She strengthened herself, as she had done so often, to take the burden of it, on Jasper's behalf.

"Your father kept on saying, 'Throw them out. They are old enough to fend for themselves. I don't see why I should have to keep that pair of scroungers.' But I couldn't. I couldn't, Alice." This last was said in a different voice, the first "nice" voice Alice had heard from her mother that evening. It was low, hurt, an appeal.

Alice felt strengthened by it and said, "Well, of course, that big house and only you in it, and your cronies coming in and out."

Dorothy was again surprised by Alice. She peered at her daughter, the frown well established.

"It's funny," she said, "how you simply don't seem to be able to take it in." If Alice seemed unable to grasp an essential point about the situation, then Dorothy was unable to take in an essential fact about Alice. "Why can't you?" she enquired, not of Alice but of the room, the air, something or other. "I simply cannot make you see . . . The point is, I would be there now, at home, if it weren't for you and Jasper. No, Alice, I am not blaming you, I am blaming myself." Another good gulp of Scotch. At this rate she would be tight soon. Then Alice would simply leave! She hated her mother tight; it was then she began saying all those negative things.

"And so that's it, Alice. Though why I bother to say it all again, I can't imagine. You are not my favourite person, Alice. I don't particularly want to see you."

Alice was wrestling with a difficult thought. Her face was screwed up. She bit her pink lips. She looked offended, as if Dorothy had said, "I don't like the blouse you are wearing."

"But when Jasper and I left, why didn't you get the flat converted then, and let it?"

"Because," Dorothy spelled it out, "I had spent the money Cedric gave me for converting the flat. On you. That means on Jasper, of course. Besides, since the only way I could get rid of you seemed to be to move, I had already arranged everything with the estate agent. *As you know,* since you were making the telephone calls . . ." She stopped herself, sighed. "No, of course it wasn't that. Your father said he had had enough. That was the reason. Cedric said: Enough! And I don't blame him."

"Wait a minute," said Alice, "what do you mean, *I* made the telephone calls?"

"Well, of course you did. You took it all on, didn't you? Being helpful. As only you know how to be."

"*I* made the calls?"

Alice could remember nothing of that. Dorothy could not believe Alice did not remember. For the thousandth time the situation was recurring where Alice said, "I don't remember, no, you're wrong," thinking that her mother maliciously made things up, while Dorothy sighed and pursued interesting thoughts about the pathology of lying.

"In any case, you could have said you had changed your mind."

This time Dorothy's sigh was elaborate and histrionic. "In the normal world, Alice—but you wouldn't know anything about that—there are such things as contracts."

"Oh, shit," said Alice.

"Quite so. Shit. But there were two reasons I wouldn't have changed my mind, even if Cedric had changed his. For one thing, I wanted to be rid of all that. You did me a great service, Alice. There was a time I could have wrung your neck—I felt like a visitor in my own house; I could hardly go into my own kitchen—then suddenly I thought, My God, what a release! I am free of all that. Who said I had to spend my life buying food and cooking it? Years, years of my life I've spent, staggering around with loads of food and cooking it and serving it to a lot of greedy-guts who eat too much anyway."

Here Alice's sound of protest was like a moan, and she stared with frantic eyes at her mother: stop, please stop, before you destroy everything, even the memories of our lovely house.

But this dangerous, destructive force that was now her mother did not hear her, or decided to take no notice, for she was going on, in a hard, cold, but amused voice, as if nothing, but nothing, was to be taken seriously. "And the other reason was, there was this fantastic deal: those Germans—what's their name? You know, you spoke to them—wanted to buy the house as it stood with carpets and curtains—the lot. But I had to get out fast to fit their schedule. And you and Jasper wouldn't get out, no matter what I said." Here Dorothy Mellings put her head back and laughed, while Alice, eyes wide, knuckles of her left hand between her teeth—she would have toothmarks there—sat looking as if she would simply dissolve in front of her mother's eyes in a puddle of tears. "Then Cedric rang Jasper up and said if he didn't get out, the police would be called in. Then, thank God, you left, and I had the estate agent hounding me to get the place ready. The next thing was, as soon as the house was cleaned up, some joker got in and stole every stitch of curtain." She rocked with laughter. It was the kind of laughter she shared with Zoë Devlin, certainly, but it was not being shared with Alice. "Not a bloody curtain left. With the what's-their-names coming in in four days. They were livid. They had contracted for curtains, and curtains they were going to have! The deal was off!" Here Dorothy had another good swallow of Scotch. "I lost the flat I was going into: I had to tell them what had happened. They were nice about it, but they couldn't wait. It was a good flat, but actually I am pleased. It was too big for me. I really need something this size. I wanted to be done with it all."

Hearing, correctly, "I wanted to be done with *you*," Alice felt her eyes at last fill with tears which ran down her face.

"Some people from Yorkshire took the house, without curtains. For two thousand less, but by then I was past caring. This flat was available. It's fine. The simpler the better. When I think, the years of my life I've spent *fussing*."

Alice said in a doleful little voice, "I am sorry I took the rug."

"Oh yes, so you did. Well, as it happens, it doesn't matter. I don't have room for it anyway, so you might as well have it."

Alice snuffled and sniffed, and then said, "I am sorry I called you a fascist."

"Wha-a-at?" Dorothy seemed incredulous. "A fascist, did you? Well, well. And what about all the other things. A fascist. Who cares about your naughty little swearwords."

"What did I say? I didn't . . ." Somewhere at the back of Alice's mind there still reverberated that parting scene when she had screamed abuse at her mother, and so had Jasper. Incandescent, she had been. Molten with rage.

"Are you still with Jasper?" demanded Dorothy.

Another Alice, all rectitude and certainty, banished the snuffling child. "Of course. I am *with* Jasper. You know that."

"Oh, God, Alice," said Dorothy Mellings, suddenly offering her daughter the simple warm sincerity that was what Alice remembered of her mother, particularly of the last four years in her house, and for which she had been starving. "Oh, *God*, why don't you get a job? Do something?"

"You seem to have overlooked the fact that we have over three million unemployed," said Alice self-righteously.

"Oh, rubbish. You got a better degree than most of your mates. All my friends' children of your age got jobs and have careers. You could have done, too, if you had wanted. You didn't even try. Well, you could start now—your father could help. Have you seen Cedric?"

"No, I don't want to," said Alice. "I'm not going to live that kind of life. I'm not going to sit in an office nine to five."

Suddenly wild with exasperation, with loss, with incomprehension, Dorothy cried out, "Oh, I did so want something decent for you, Alice. I had no proper education, as you know—God knows I dinned it into you. . . . I was married when I was nineteen. There should be a law against it. And then I just kept house and looked after you and your brother and cooked and cooked and cooked. I am unemployable. I used to sit there, when you and your brother were babies, thinking how my friends were all making something of themselves. And I was stuck. Do you remember Rosemary Holmes? Did you know she's at Bart's? She's a world specialist, in something to do with the liver. There you are, I am so ignorant, I don't even know what. We were at school together. But she went to university."

This wild loose emotion of her mother's was having the effect of tightening Alice up, making her feel prim and disapproving. Seeing her mother getting tight, at parties or otherwise, was the main reason why Alice never drank. There had always been a point, when Dorothy drank, where some awful malevolence spilled out of her, like a vicious chemical, burning everything it touched. But the destructiveness that once had jetted out of her only when she was drunk, as if from an overpressured container kept in some corner deep inside her, seemed now to have taken her over, so that nothing was safe from her sarcastic hostility: not her children, her friends, her former husband, or anything in her past.

Alice thought, as she watched Dorothy staring with heavy sorrowful eyes into some lost opportunity or other, Well, what does she think she should have been, then?

Dorothy said, "I would have been a good doctor, I know. You know what you would have been good at. I'd have been a good farmer, too. And an explorer."

"An explorer!" jeered Alice feebly, and Dorothy said, "Yes, an explorer." Her glass was empty. She got up, went to the shelf, poured another liberal dose of whisky, sat down. She was not looking at Alice. "I haven't done anything with my life." She was even smiling, contemptuous, as she negated Alice in this way. "I used to look at you when you were little, and I thought, Well, at least I'll make sure that Alice gets educated, she'll be equipped. I won't have Alice stuck in my position, no qualifications for anything. But it turned out that you spend your life exactly as I did. Cooking and nannying for other people. An all-purpose female drudge." She laughed bitterly, demolishing all the lovely years Alice thought about so longingly, killing the old Dorothy Mellings who shed warmth everywhere, people coming to her, surrounding her, wanting what she had—the gift of filling everything about her with life.

Alice was hurt beyond speaking, sat in a dwarfed, shrinking position, listening as her mother went on: "This world is run by people who know how to do things. They know how things work. They are *equipped*. Up there, there's a layer of people who run everything. But we—we're just peasants. We don't understand what's going on, and we can't do anything."

Alice found she was becoming herself again. "Don't be silly, we can do anything we like."

"Oh, you, running about playing at revolutions, playing little games, thinking you're important. You're just peasants, you'll never *do* anything."

"You don't understand, Mother," said Alice, calm and confident. "We are going to pull everything *down*. All of it. This shitty rubbish we live in. It's all coming *down*. And then you'll see."

This brought Dorothy back to herself. Her dry watchfulness returned, she set a distance between herself and her daughter; her green eyes again seemed like stones, and she said, "And then you are going to build it all up again in your own image! What a prospect." She laughed. And as Alice began to go red, rising to her feet, "Oh, don't misunderstand me, you probably will. With so many of you around, with only one thought in your minds, how to get power for yourselves . . ." She was laughing loudly, her half-drunk laugh, which Alice so hated. "Yes, I can see it all. Jasper will probably be Minister of Culture—he's the type for it. He loathes anything decent, and he once wrote a terrible novel he couldn't get published. And you'll be his willing aide."

Alice was going to burst, she was so furious, standing there, fists clenched, face working and red.

"Oh, God, Alice," said Dorothy Mellings, "do go away. I'm just fed up with you, can't you see that? I just can't be bothered with you."

Alice shrieked, "You'll see, you shitty old fascist. You and your fascist friends. That's all you care about. . . ." She was incoherent, panting, sweating. "But you just wait. Everything is *rotten*. It's all *undermined*. But you're so dozy and stupid and you can't even see it. We are going to pull it all *down*." And she even came over to her mother and gave her a push on the shoulder, so that Dorothy had to hold on to the table edge. "You'll all see," Alice yelled finally, and ran out of the room, slamming the door.

Fuelled by an anguish of rage, Alice dashed down the stairs and then the street, turned a corner, and became part of the thin late crowd dispersing from the Underground. A block away, two strolling policemen approached, and Alice became at once the good citizen coming home after an evening's fun. She knew one of the policemen. He had been on that very first raid. He did not know her. She nodded at him, and smiled, ratepayer who paid his wages. He said, "Good evening."

Well, they had orders to fraternise, thought Alice, allowing her face, her body, to scorn him, once safely past. But her real anger had gone into her pounding race along the pavement. Now she was thinking of her mother with a strong protective pity. Two shitty little rooms! Dorothy looked so big in that sitting room; if she turned too quickly she might knock a wall down. Spending her evenings talking to Zoë Devlin and reading books! Alice now examined, from a stored mental picture, titles from the two tidy little strips of shelves up the walls, and from the pile of books on the floor by the big chair. What did she want to read that kind of book for! She might just as well still be at school. When Zoë Devlin came to spend the evening they sat opposite each other and talked about life. No. About books. No, of course, they had that row. Well, that was ridiculous; they'd have to make it up; they'd been like sisters; they said so themselves. A stupid shitty row . . . well, quite a lot of quarrels, really.

Alice was standing on the pavement, like a child playing statues, apparently waiting for a taxi or to be given a lift. She was—unwillingly—seeing the scene of that dreadful final row between her mother and Zoë. It was in the old sitting room, on the first floor, which stretched from front to back and from side to side of the old house, windows all round, and through the windows views of garden and trees. Dorothy Mellings and Zoë faced each other, pale, too serious to shout or insult each other, as they had done before, but then always made it up, laughing. Two tall strong handsome elderly women, with the lovely room stretching away all around them to the windows, and, beyond them, the gardens.

Alice's vision seemed to shift. Two old women. *Ancient.* They both looked so battered and beaten. Alice felt their being old as an affront to her. How had they got like this so quickly? Why had they? Why had they let it happen? Why didn't they care? Didn't they see how ridiculous they were, taking themselves so seriously?

Three days before that, these two women had broken off an argument, saying that if they did not, they would start hitting each other.

On that occasion, Dorothy had said, "You and I met on the Aldermaston marches. We met because of our political attitudes. That is what we had in common."

Zoë had said, "Oh, all the rest didn't count, of course! We've been friends for twenty years!"

"Zoë, do you realise that I have to censor everything I say to you now? I can't talk to you about anything I am really thinking?"

"Well, there's plenty to talk about."

"No, there isn't. I'm not wasting my time gossiping and talking about whether we should eat butter and bacon or not. Or start making our own pasta. That's what we talk about."

"You've got so bloody reactionary, that's the trouble."

"Don't stick bloody stupid labels on me. You're back in the

nineteenth century, all of you. Weeping about the Tolpuddle Martyrs and singing the Red Flag. You are a bad joke."

"You used not to think it was a joke."

"No. I do now. Do you realise I have to think twice before I invite you here? You can't be invited with anyone who has a different political opinion on anything, because you start calling them fascists! You won't meet anyone, even, who reads a right-wing newspaper. You've become a dreary bigot, Zoë, do you know that?"

"And you are a fascist! Not far off one. Reading books about the KGB, and seeing Reds under every bed."

"There are Reds under every bed," said Dorothy seriously. "God, when I think it used to be a joke, do you remember? The funny thing was, we *were* the Reds under the beds." And Dorothy had started to laugh. Zoë had remained serious, fiercely accusing: "The next thing, you'll be supporting Reagan's and Thatcher's foreign policies."

"I've been wondering whether I shouldn't. After all, forty years ago it wasn't fascist to fight for the bad against the worse. Why is it now?"

"I'm just going to leave, Dorothy. If I didn't, I think I'd hit you."

"Yes, I think you'd better."

That had been three days before. Neither woman had made any move towards the other. Then Zoë arrived one morning. Jasper was in the kitchen, eating breakfast cooked by Alice. Dorothy Mellings was on the telephone in the sitting room, having taken herself well out of the way of Jasper, as Alice appreciated.

Zoë went into the sitting room, looking through Alice, who was doing the flowers for her mother. She stood in the middle of the room, gazing dramatically at Dorothy. Who took her time ending the telephone conversation, in order—as both Alice and Zoë could see—to prepare herself for the confrontation with Zoë. A confrontation it was going to have to be—Zoë's face and body said so. It was evident to Alice that Zoë had come to provoke a quarrel. She wanted some kind of noisy showdown with Dorothy; there was something self-consciously accusing about her. She had prepared all kinds of things to say and how to say them.

Dorothy slowly got up and went to stand opposite Zoë, as if accepting a challenge to fight. But now the moment had come, both were very pale and serious, and—much worse than shouting, which anyway usually ended in laughter—spoke in low voices that were breathless because of the awfulness of what was happening.

"Listen, Dorothy. I've got to say this and you've got to listen. Even if you start hating me for it. I mean, even more than you do already."

"Rubbish," said Dorothy, impatient.

"Well, it amounts to that, doesn't it? If everything I do or think is stupid in your eyes?"

"Do you want to talk about that? I mean, *seriously?* People with different political opinions being stupid? That is what I used to think, certainly."

"Dorothy, don't sidetrack me. I *want* to say this. Do you realise what you are doing, Dorothy? Because Cedric has left you . . ."

"Five years ago now."

"Let me say it. Cedric left you, and you have to leave this house. And it's all so awful, you just have to burn your boats, scorched-earth policy—just destroy everything as you leave. Because it won't hurt so much if you do."

Here Zoë stood waiting—expectant, it seemed, of Dorothy's grateful acceptance of her diagnosis.

"You can't be serious!" said Dorothy, keeping her voice low, though it sounded bitterly scornful. "You've come here to say that?"

"Yes, I have. It's important. You've got so extraordinary. . . ."

"Strange as it might seem, the idea had occurred to me. You know, that psychotherapy of yours has made you very dim-witted, Zoë. You come out with something absolutely obvious as if it's some revelation."

Zoë stood vibrating with anger. But she was not going to let her voice rise, either. "If it's so obvious, then why do you go on doing it?"

"There might be different ways of looking at it? Can you conceive there might be different ways of looking at a thing? I doubt it, the way you are. . . . Can't even meet someone who reads a different newspaper. . . . Listen. My life has to change. Right? Strange as it might seem, I had taken all that into account, what you said. But I am doing a stock-taking—do you understand? I am *thinking*—do you see? I'm *thinking* about my life. That means I am examining a lot of things."

Dorothy and Zoë stood opposite each other, standing straight, like soldiers told to stand at ease, or a couple about to start the steps of an intricate dance.

"And all you can see about me," said Zoë, "is that we've got nothing in common. Is that all? Twenty years of being friends."

"What have we got in common now? We've been cooking meals and talking about our bloody children and discussing cholesterol and the body beautiful, and going on demonstrations."

"I haven't noticed you going on any recently."

"No, not since I understood that demos and all that are just for *fun*."

"For fun, are they?"

"Yes, that's right. People go on demos because they get a kick out of it. Like picnics."

"You can't be serious, Dorothy."

"Of course I'm serious. No one bothers to ask any longer if it achieves anything, going on marches or demos. They talk about how they feel. That's what they care about. It's for kicks. It's for *fun*."

"Dorothy, that's simply perverse."

"Why is it perverse if it's true? You've just got to use your eyes and look—people picketing, or marching or demonstrating, they are having a marvellous time. And if they are beaten up by the police, so much the better."

A silence. Zoë was staring at Dorothy, bewildered. She really could not believe Dorothy meant it. As for Alice, who was standing there transfixed with flowers in her hands, staring at the two, and praying inwardly, "Oh, don't, don't, please don't, please, please stop," her mother had gone over the edge into destructiveness, and there was no point in even listening to her. Better take no notice.

"I'll tell you something, Zoë. All you people, marching up and down and waving banners and singing pathetic little songs—'All You Need Is Love'—you are just a joke. To the people who really run this world, you are a joke. They watch you at it and think: Good, that's keeping them busy."

"I just don't believe you mean it."

"I don't know why not: I keep saying it."

"You want to smash things up, you want to break with all your friends."

"Well, I just can't talk to you any more. When I say anything I really think, you start weeping and wailing."

"Well, I care about our friendship ending, if you don't."

"I haven't the energy for all these rows and little scenes," said Dorothy.

Then Zoë had run out of the room, muttering something furious —but not loudly; not once had the voices of the two women risen. And Dorothy, with a pale, listless, dreary look, had gone back to the telephone and sat down, ready to make another call. But had not dialled at once. She had sat, head on hand, looking at the wall.

"Shall I make you a cup of tea?" Alice had brightly offered.

"No, thank you, Alice dear."

But she had gone into the kitchen, made tea, taken her mother a cup, put it by her where she still sat, not moving, head in her hand.

Alice thought (standing on the pavement's edge, though she did not know she was, not yet): She needs someone to look after her, she really does! No food to speak of in the refrigerator, drinking away there by herself. It's not on. No, better if she came to live with us, at number 43. She could have those two big rooms upstairs, when Reggie and Mary move out. Through Alice's mind floated the thought, immediately censored: Then I would have someone to talk to.

Alice saw herself and her mother at that table in the big kitchen, newspapers and books all over the place. Dorothy would talk about the books, and Alice would listen to news about that world she herself could not for some reason bring herself to enter.

This idea died a swift natural death.

Alice came to herself, on the pavement's edge. It was chilly. Overhead a sky full of hazy stars. Opposite, a yellow street lamp.

It was about midnight now. Jasper and Bert and Caroline would not be home tonight; she had known that when they went off. And Bert and Caroline would be humping and bumping away together; all those flashing eye exchanges and atmospheres hadn't been for nothing. And Jasper would (if he could) be in the room next to them. . . .

Alice put this last thought out of her mind and entered the house quietly, not wanting to see Faye and Roberta, or Reggie and Mary. But no one was at home, except for Jocelin, still at work. Alice knocked, polite, and went in on a gruff sound that presumably was a "Come in." On the long table in front of Jocelin were four nasty little devices, identical, ranged side by side, and looking rather like outsize and complicated sardine tins. Everywhere on the trestle were parts of bombs, now dismantled, and some white kitchen bowls holding the household chemicals. Presumably waiting to be returned to their proper packets in the kitchen? Jocelin was sorting items into little piles. She nodded at Alice, not smiling. She looked like a factory worker bending over an assembly bench, but no factory worker would get away with those stray pieces of pale greasy-looking hair falling over her face, and the old stained jersey with the hole in the elbow.

"I'm going to bury these," said Jocelin. "We can get them when we need them next." She allowed Alice a smile. "No policeman is going to come digging around in this garden for a bit."

"Are those four enough?" Alice asked, but only to show she marvelled at Jocelin for planning to accomplish so much with so little, and Jocelin nodded, looking at the four items with a satisfied proprietorial air.

She went to the window and stood with her back to Alice, arms akimbo, and turned to say, "It is dark enough. Come on."

The collection of components were swept—carelessly, since they were not dangerous now—into a plastic bag, enclosed in another and then another, and they crept out into the night, not making a sound.

They stood for a minute over the place where the police had started to dig, both thinking that that would be the safest place, but could not face it. A lilac bush near Joan Robbins's fence was still heavy with scent, though its blossoms, black in this light, had gone bruised and blotched. It had some soft soil around it. No lights were on anywhere. Dark houses stood all about, eyeless for once. Making no noise, using a trowel, Alice dug out a good-sized hole, Jocelin slid the bundle in, together they covered it over, and in a moment they were inside the house, feeling warm towards each other, successful accomplices.

In the kitchen, Jocelin said, "I forgot, there's a message. Two, in fact. First, those Irishmen came back." She sounded unworried, but Alice knew something very bad indeed had happened.

"The ones that brought that . . . *matériel?*"

"Right. They wanted to know whereabout on the rubbish tip the two cases were put."

"What did you say?"

"I said I didn't know."

As far as Jocelin was concerned, it seemed, that was enough; she sat stirring sugar into her coffee, her mind probably on her handiwork, still ranged neatly side by side, on the trestle upstairs.

"And then?"

" 'Well, now, lady, that isn't enough for us, is it? You can see that for yourself! We have our orders, and that's a fact! The lady we saw last time we came, she must accompany us to the rubbish tip, and show us where the things were placed.' " This Jocelin delivered in an Irish accent, perfect, as far as Alice was concerned—so accurate that she was thinking: Irish? Is she? And if so, what does it mean? Does it matter? Here is another of us with a false voice!

Jocelin went on, "And I said to them, 'Are you coming back, then?' They said: 'And indeed we shall. Tomorrow morning, and that's a fact.' " In her ordinary voice, Jocelin said, and as if all this had nothing to do with her, "So I suppose they will."

"Then I shan't be here," said Alice, sounding calm, yet feeling sick with panic. She had thought that their trip out to drop those packages had been the end of it all.

"And the other thing was, Felicity came in. She said they have found Philip's sister, and the funeral is on Wednesday."

"Then we can't do what we planned on Wednesday." They had decided that Wednesday was the best day for their feat of arms.

Jocelin said, sounding critical, "First things first."

"But somebody must be at his funeral."

"You go. You aren't essential for the plan."

"But I want to be there!"

Jocelin shrugged. She lifted her mug, stood up, said "Good night," and went upstairs. Probably to perfect the four explosive devices.

Alice was going to bed when Mary and Reggie came in to say that they were moving out on Wednesday; they would hire a remover's van.

Alice was ready to laugh at the remover's van, but remembered that two rooms and part of the attic and most of their bedroom were piled with furniture, and simply said, "Right. Will you need help?"

"Won't say no," said Reggie, and off the two went upstairs. So it can't be on Wednesday, said Alice to herself. She, too, went to bed. She woke early and left a note on the table saying that if the Irishmen turned up, they must be told that she, Alice, was away, and that no one knew where the packages were on the rubbish tip; they had probably been covered over long ago under new rubbish. She went out, thinking that presumably that Russian had told them to come. Well, she had sent him packing, hadn't she? They would soon all get tired of coming; it was simply a question of sticking it out. She pushed her anxiety down and out of sight.

It was a pleasant morning, sunny, not cold. She walked around the streets, found it was only ten, sat for a long time in a little restaurant, eating a breakfast she did not really want. Eleven-thirty. She thought of dropping in to see her mother again, actually got to the door, and then, realising she would see that meagre little sitting room and her mother boxed into it, with the two shabby, once-splendid armchairs, lost heart and went off across London to visit a squat where lived a girl she had known in Birmingham. The girl had been at the CCU Congress. They talked about having another one, perhaps next month. The house was perfect for a Congress. Alice thought, her heart cold, that in a month they would all be gone from that house: it had been taken for granted everyone would scatter. Who knew where they would all be?

She got back at five. Jasper and Bert and Caroline were in the kitchen, eating take-away. One glance was enough to tell Alice that she had been right: Bert and Caroline could now be considered a couple. But Alice decided not to care.

The Irishmen, she was told, had not been again.

Faye and Roberta had come in, and the six—Jasper, Bert, Caroline, with Jocelin—had decided that the job was to go ahead as planned, on Wednesday afternoon. In the morning they would help Mary and Reggie with loading the removal van. Alice could go to the funeral.

"But I don't know if the funeral is morning or afternoon," said Alice.

No one answered. It was not important. Alice thought it would be just like that if she left the squat: she would never be mentioned, would be forgotten, like Jim, like Pat. Like Philip. No, Jasper would be after her, she knew that; the others might forget her, but Jasper could not.

On Tuesday they all went down to the scene of the crime— their joke—and walked around and about the great hotel, part of the crowds. Of course, they took trouble to dress the part. Jocelin, it seemed, did possess more than her jeans and sweater. She wore a dress of pinkish linen that looked as if it had been bought in Knightsbridge. Caroline, similarly, acquired the protective colouring of a beige well-cut skirt and a yellow shirt. Roberta, out of principle, refused to change, but looked unremarkable in her dark-blue boiler suit. Faye had on a fluffy white blouse and jeans, and was noticeable not only because she was so pretty, but because she was aflame with secret triumph, which made her chatter and display herself. She was the essence of her cockney self, witty and outrageous, but while they laughed, they kept saying to her, "Calm down, be quiet," and so on, while Roberta was anxiously in attendance on her. Jasper, too, had a look of elation which made him, thought Alice, rather beautiful. He seemed serenely above the scene of thronging shoppers and tourists, superior to everything; was in a daze of imaginings about how—and so soon—they would prove themselves here, in this shameless, luxurious scene. After their successful reconnaissance, they all went in to have tea.

Then they took a taxi to Hammersmith, where they saw *Diva*, a film some of them had seen already more than once. They had supper together in their Indian restaurant near home, agreeing they must go to bed early. They told Reggie and Mary it was because of all the hard work they meant to do tomorrow hefting furniture—this, they could see, seemed reasonable to the couple, for whom the business of moving their furniture, reinstalling their furniture, arranging their furniture was the only thing worthy to occupy their minds. Though Mary did remark, almost absent-mindedly, that this house was on the agenda for next week, and there was a recommendation from Bob Hood that "matters should be expedited." It was a shame, remarked Mary, that these lovely houses were not being used.

Alice became suddenly so angry that she was hardly able to bring out, "What a pity that the Council was prepared to leave them *empty* for six years."

Mary could have flared up, as Alice had done. She went red, while the official and the human being fought inside her, and then she said, with a laugh that was both apologetic and offended, "Yes, I know, it was awful letting things slide for so long."

"But it will be all right now," said Alice, not at all mollified. "There will be some *people* living in them."

Mary hesitated, then went out of the kitchen, followed by Reggie. Written all over him was, Thank God, I'll be out of here tomorrow!

Philip's funeral was at ten o'clock on Wednesday. At nine, leaving the others boisterously loading furniture into a van that seemed to fill the street, Alice went to Felicity's, where she found two other people who had liked Philip when he lived there. The four went to the crematorium, in Felicity's car. Philip's sister was there with her husband. They had come down, it seemed, from Aberdeen. Philip was Scottish, a fact that till this moment had not emerged.

The sister was a pale thin little thing, with a dogged look to her, like Philip: determined not to be blown away by the hostile winds of life. Her husband was a small, pale young man with weak blue eyes and a straggly moustache. They both had strong Scottish accents. This couple seemed anxious to avoid Philip's four friends, or at least spoke as little as possible, then, politeness satisfied, went to sit by themselves in the "chapel." It was a proper religious service. Neither Felicity nor Alice, nor the other two, a young man and a girl who had once helped Philip paint out a living room, knew whether Philip had been religious. Perhaps this was only bureaucracy taking its course. And the sister and her husband did not enlighten them. The coffin, large, brown, and shiny, which had to make anyone who had known Philip think of how his frail little body must be lying, like a dead moth, within it, stood full in their view, while a Church of England clergyman did his best to give life to these words that he intoned so often.

And that was that. Philip's sister said a hurried good-bye. Her eyes were red. Her husband only nodded from a distance. The four drove back. The van stood again outside number 43, having made the journey once and returned. "We had no idea we had so much stuff," called Mary gaily, standing in the back of the van, her arms loaded with a carton of china bought by Reggie in a house sale.

"Well, we did," said Bert, loud and jolly and false, and the antagonism that was the truth of what they felt for each other— Mary and Reggie for them, they for Mary and Reggie—was on the surface, and they all knew it, and their hostile faces showed it. Briefly. The smiles and good will set in again.

"Whew," said Bert, as the good-byes were being said. "I'm for a bath and a kip. That's done me in."

"I'm for a bath," said Faye daintily, looking at Roberta, who would scrub her back and dry her afterwards.

"Well, good-bye, all you lot," cried Reggie, cried Mary, jumping into the front of the van with many smiles and waves, and they drove off, leaving behind the reassuring picture of the group waving to them from the garden.

Of course they had paid, before leaving, the exact amount they owed, down to the last greasy penny piece.

And then, almost hysterical with suppressed laughter, the others raced into the kitchen, for tea, for sandwiches. It was one o'clock. Just the right time. Precisely and accurately correct.

Everything was going so well. Had gone well, events slotting into place, luck almost ostentatiously on their side: that the Council should have decided to bury Philip this morning; that Mary and Reggie should have chosen today for moving—the comrades could not have wished for better. And then the car: at the other squat, someone had mentioned—she could not have known how fortuitously—that the man in the next house had gone on holiday with his family, and that the car, an Escort, had been standing outside the house for a week, with another week to go. "He's asking for it," she had remarked. Of course the car was locked, but to Jasper— it was one of his talents—this was no obstacle.

Late last night, after coming back from *Diva* and the Indian restaurant, Bert and Jasper and Jocelin had slipped out of 43, and had gone by Underground back to the other squat. Not inside it: they did not want to involve any more people in this enterprise. Of course, they took the chance that their friends might be coming back from somewhere and see them. But three of them were away; they had said they would be. To open the car, start it, and drive off had taken Jasper and Bert a minute. They drove around Pimlico and Victoria, but did not find anything they liked the look of. They needed a safe place where they could fit in the explosives. They were watching the level of petrol: less than half a tank, and they did not want to have to go into a petrol station. At last, farther away from "the scene of the crime" than they wanted, they found a street of semidetached houses, and one of them was being modernised and rebuilt; at any rate, there were "For Sale" notices, and builders' equipment. In front of each house was a garden, crammed with shrubs, and a shallow drive, not much more than a place to park. The three discussed this place while they drove around and about the streets. It wasn't ideal, but they hadn't seen anything better. The house that was the twin of the one they had in mind was presumably occupied, and although it was by then three in the morning, as usual there was this problem of insomniacs and night owls. Not to mention patrolling policemen. But it would soon be getting light. . . . Jocelin remarked that it was a pity they couldn't wait until winter: a long dark night was just what they needed. They even suffered a low moment, thinking that the whole enterprise was misconceived, or at least being too hastily executed. Everything was so improvised! But it was precisely this quality that seemed to be aiding them—and which appealed to them, adding to their secret, rising excitement, making them want to laugh for no particular reason, and to make jokes, the sillier the better.

In the end this mood of theirs triumphed, and they drove back into the street, and turned into the little "drive" in front of the empty house. Jocelin needed about twenty minutes to insert the explosives into the car. Jasper ran to one end of the street, Bert to the other, to keep watch for the police. Jocelin was in fact concealed by shrubs from the street, if not from the higher windows of the occupied house. But its windows continued dark; she could not see anyone up there. She inserted the four devices, neatly, precisely, in their allotted places. She was listening for any signal from Bert and Jasper, but none came. She felt, as she worked, a good-natured contempt for these careless citizens, who could be so easily tricked, fooled.

At the end of twenty minutes, Jasper and Bert appeared again; she had not heard them come, though they were breathing heavily from running. In a moment the car was out of the shelter of the shrubs, and back at large in the streets. There wasn't much traffic now. The sky was beginning to lighten. There didn't seem to be a place to park the car anywhere. Cars filled every inch along the pavements' edges, and again they had to drive about more than they wanted. The gauge showed well below the halfway mark. How were they to know whether it was accurate? Bert remarked that once he had for months a car with a gauge that showed nearly full when it was almost empty. At last a space, again farther away than they had hoped. They parked, and stood for a few seconds looking at the unremarkable car that was, potentially, a bomb.

They had then gone into an all-night café and eaten a meal together, though prudence should have said no: they were a noisy, noticeable group. "To hell with it," had said Jocelin, and "Fuck that," had said Bert.

They had come home in full daylight, at about five. No, Mary and Reggie were not yet up, which was the one thing they had been afraid of; luck stayed with them, they could not do wrong!

All this Alice learned now, while they ate her soup and some good wholemeal toast, because she had not woken until eight, and by then Mary and Reggie were up, and in the kitchen.

She felt as if she were not really a participant in this great enterprise, not considered a partner. Yet she could not say this, or even suggest it, for there was nothing specific she could take hold of to complain about. But as the six sat around that table, telling the story of the past night, or early morning, she noticed they scarcely looked at her. They were giving one another attention exactly in accordance with the roles each played: Faye and Jasper, Jocelin and Bert. Then Roberta, who was nearly as much on the outside as she, Alice, was.

Alice heard that it was Jasper who was going to drive the car into position. This did frighten her. He was not a good driver, tending to panic in an emergency. She had been taking it for granted, for some reason, that she would drive the car. She was a good driver, modest and skilful. At the least she wanted to say, "No, not Jasper, he shouldn't do it; why not Faye? why not Roberta?" Both of them were good drivers. But her situation on the periphery of events seemed to bar her from this.

Everything had been decided, it seemed, that morning, while Mary and Reggie were out of the house fetching their van and she was at the funeral.

Jasper would drive the car. Faye would be with him because— so it seemed to Alice—she had demanded it as her right. Jocelin would go down with them now, to where the car was parked in the side street, and set the devices to go off at a time that would be chosen then, when she did it. For they were not to know exactly how long it would take them to get there, nor yet the state of the traffic. A quarter to five, they thought.

It was now that Alice learned that the bombs would be timed to go off, not set off by some electronic control. She was appalled. Every previous discussion had been in terms of Jocelin's being some-where close by and—able to see the state of affairs in the street and on the pavement—choosing an exact moment.

Alice asked, almost timidly, certainly having to make herself break into an animated, jokey exchange between Faye and Jasper, "But if the bombs just go off, then we aren't going to know who's going to be around, are we?"

At once each assumed a severe, dedicated look. She could see that this thought was in their minds, behind all the exhilaration, but that it was being suppressed, kept in its place.

Bert said, showing a lot of his white teeth, " 'Morality has to be subdued to the needs of Revolution.' V. I. Lenin." Everybody laughed, and Alice saw from the way they were suddenly not allowing their eyes to meet that they were uncomfortable.

"Anyway," said Faye, "it serves them right."

This was one of "her" remarks, which they all habitually covered over, ignored, or—like Roberta now—soothed away.

"Faye, dear," she said. "That's not very nice."

Faye tittered and tossed her head. Her eyes were glittering, her cheeks flushed.

Alice said stubbornly, "I don't think it's right. It's not what we decided."

Jocelin said soberly, taking her seriously, "You weren't here when it was discussed. The thing is, these electronic controls aren't absolutely reliable. Not the things I've got, anyway. Of course, there are good ones, but don't forget, I've just put this and that together."

"Then why not set them to go off in the middle of the night, not when people are around?"

"We did think about that. But it's a question of how to make the greatest impact. A few windows in the middle of the night—and so what? But this way, it'll be front page in all the papers tomorrow, and on the news tonight."

Jocelin, having said, or pronounced this, looked away from Alice; and none of them looked at her. She understood now that she felt excluded not only because she had not been here at the crucial discussion, but because the crucial discussion had taken place "behind her back"—as she felt it—so that she could not be there to say things they did not want to hear. They had known—felt, if not thought—that she would protest, say no, say it was wrong; then they would have been forced to listen, to think. And so, without anyone's actually planning it, the five had discussed it when she was well out of the way.

And where was Caroline?

It turned out that Caroline, learning that the bombs would be set to go off at a certain time regardless of possible casualties, had said she would have nothing to do with it.

It was Jocelin who told Alice this, in a nonjudging voice, but cold with disapproval. Cold, Alice thought, because of the need to put a distance between her and what she had felt when Caroline had said that. Oh yes, Alice knew what had happened; she could reconstruct the moment, from what was on all their faces now. The plan had nearly been given up, because of Caroline's decisiveness. Now, as they remembered that argument—which they were all doing—their faces had identical looks of cold uneasiness.

If only I had been there, thought Alice, I could have backed Caroline up; between us we could have swung things the other way.

Alice sneaked a look—she did not dare more—at Bert, who knew she was likely to be looking at him! This was a repetition of Pat! Pat had said Bert was an amateur, at that meeting when the decision was first made to "join the IRA," when a lot of the inhabitants of this house had simply left. Since then she had sometimes, affectionately, called him an amateur. Probably Caroline too had called him "amateur."

Alice thought: Pat, Jim, Philip, and now Caroline. She was my friend, she was my real friend.

Already they were talking again. At two o'clock Jocelin, Faye, and Jasper would go off to the Underground, to the car, which there was no reason to believe would not be exactly where it had been left this morning. To set the explosives to go off would take Jocelin five minutes, Faye aiding her with her quick, clever fingers. No one need take any notice of three people with the bonnet of the car briefly up, making minor adjustments to something, re-arranging the contents of the boot, checking the set of a wheel.

Jocelin was saying that there was no need for the others to be at the scene at all. There was nothing for them to do. Redundant. Adding to the danger. She suggested that Bert and Roberta and Alice should stay here, and put the kettle on at five-thirty. And how about Alice making some of her soup; they would all be dead with hunger by then.

"No," said Faye, smiling, all her sharp little teeth showing. "Absolutely no." Charming and pettish, spoiled and whimsical, she swam her eyes at Roberta, then at them, and said, "I must have my Roberta. I *must*. I must!"

"Absolutely," said Bert, hearty. "And I and Alice will be there, too. No argument! Vote taken! That's it, then."

Laughter, even from Alice, who felt again one of the family.

Two o'clock. Off went Jocelin and Faye and Jasper.

Jasper did not remember to give Alice a smile or a look. He was in animated talk that looked like a flirtation—with Faye. They were all laughing loudly as they went off.

Roberta sat in a huddle at the table, silent, morose. Now it could be seen how much she did not like this, had not wanted Faye in this danger.

With the three gone, the remaining three were edgy, quiet, far from elated. They had to wait.

It would take Faye, Jasper, Jocelin ten minutes to get to the Underground. Then probably half an hour, depending on how the trains were running, to reach the car. Say three-quarters of an hour; there were two changes. Ten minutes from the Underground to the car. Then it was hard to judge exactly how long it would take to drive the car to the scene of the crime. The rush hour would not have started. But there might be a lot of traffic; who could tell? That journey could take fifteen minutes or, with bad luck, take forty. Somewhere between half past three and four o'clock, Jasper and Faye—not Jocelin; she would have been dropped off along the route—would be looking for a parking place outside the great hotel. They might have to drive round and round it for some time. There was also the question of traffic wardens. If they appeared, while Jasper and Faye were still driving about looking, then they would go away for a few minutes and come back after the wardens had gone. If the wardens appeared after the car was parked, it didn't matter; the worst that could happen—Faye had said—was that they would be too close when the car exploded.

The bombs would have been set to go off at a quarter to five, later only if the traffic looked particularly bad.

There would be no point in Alice, Bert, and Roberta's leaving until three, they thought, but at half past two they could not bear to wait even one more moment. As they got up from the table, there was a knock on the front door. A civilised knock, not the police.

"I'll go," said Alice. "It's probably Felicity with something she's giving me from Philip." In Felicity's house had been left a little marquetry table made by Philip, and she had said she would bring it round, for Alice. This was partly, as Alice knew, a need to rid herself of everything that reminded herself of Philip and the complex emotions that he evoked, and partly a generous impulse: she said that she felt Philip would have liked Alice to have it.

At the door stood a man Alice did not know. Having expected only Felicity and a table and a brief emotional moment, being literally ill with apprehension and excitement, she was not prepared to ask him in, or to deal with him or with any situation he was bringing.

"Is Miss Mellings in?" he enquired, and she automatically made the usual assessments from his voice: middle-class, British, an official of some kind, probably.

"I am Alice Mellings," she said, "but, excuse me, I am in a very great hurry."

"If you will be kind enough to give me a moment," he said.

Oh, Christ, she was thinking, oh, shit, we have to *leave*: for now that the decision had been taken to go, she felt that not one more second should be wasted. "Well, can't you come back?"

"Yes, I can come back. I certainly will. But in the meantime, you could assist me with some information."

Alice thought that this might have something to do with the Council's decision to do up the two houses; he might be someone from the Council. She was not really thinking at all. A flash of recognition, or of warning, that this man's manner, his style, his way of talking were not appropriate to the Council situation, but to another one altogether, went past her.

"What?" she said hurriedly. "What is it?"

"Have you any information about a man called Andrew Connors?"

She stared at him, a wild inappropriate laughter threatening her. She said, with a sudden derisiveness, like a jeer, "Don't tell me that you are still another phony bloody American? No"—she caught herself up—"of course not; English accent; well, what's in an accent?"

Her visitor looked startled, not surprisingly, and took his time in answering. At last he said, with a certain quiet authority that was not unlike Gordon O'Leary's, "I agree, Miss Mellings, that accents are not always what they seem. But about Andrew Connors —I need some information about him."

In her normal condition Alice at this point would have said: "Indeed? And who are you"—that kind of thing—but as it was she itched with the need for him to be gone, so that she and the others could leave. She was in a fever, a rage, of impatience. She said, "Well, what sort of information? I don't know anything much. Anyway, why don't you ask Gordon O'Leary, he seems to know everything."

A pause. If she had had her wits about her, she might not have liked the way this man suddenly focussed on her: narrowed eyes; a close, expert inspection.

"Well, perhaps I will," he remarked.

"Yes, and he can tell you about it all. Look, I do have to go in, I am so sorry. . . ." She was about to go in, shutting the door on him, when "niceness," the hospitable person in Alice who could never bear to disappoint, or seem unfriendly, caused her to add, disastrously, "And when you see him, just tell him from me that if any other little consignment of *matériel* or anything else turns up here, we are going to throw it straight back into the street and leave it there." She said this quite brightly, even smiling, as if she had said, "When you see him, say hello from me."

She had turned away, was about to go in.

"Just a minute, Miss Mellings."

"Oh, God," she cried, "oh, please, I have to *go*."

"All right. So you have said. But there is something I have to discuss with you."

"Then let's discuss it, but not now. Anyway, I have already discussed it. I keep saying, we are not taking orders from Russians or anybody else. You don't seem to understand that, comrade . . . You didn't tell me your name."

"My name is Peter Cecil," he said.

"Peter Cecil?" she said, and might have laughed again. "Well, your accent is really perfect. Bloody marvellous. Congratulations." She did give a little laugh here, girlish and merry, and though she did not really take him in, because of her pounding heart, her general overstimulation, she looked at him enough to see that he really did seem the essence of an Englishman, to match his name.

"Thank you," he said, pleasantly. "Perhaps you would care to have lunch?"

"Yes. But I was going to say, you don't seem able to take it in, but we are British, you understand? British communists." She hesitated and added, since the situation seemed to demand elucidation: "Freeborn British communists."

"Ah," he said. "Well, where can we meet? Tomorrow?"

"Tomorrow? Well, why not? Tomorrow's all right. Do you know the Taj Mahal? That restaurant in the High Street?"

"Very good. Tomorrow. At one. Thank you for your time, Miss Mellings."

"Not at all," said she, forgetting him entirely, as she ran in to the others, who were saying: "For God's sake, Alice, come *on*, will you. We've got to go. Get a move on."

It was twenty to three. At the station they waited ten minutes for a train, much longer than they expected. At Baker Street they sat in the train, the doors open, with people drifting in, taking their time, for another seven. They joked they could not remember waiting for so long before. At Green Park they waited again. They were frantic with suspense; felt like bombs themselves, which could go off. Coming out of the Underground at three-thirty, Bert burst into a run, and the other two ran after him, to slow him down. "Stop it," said Roberta, irritable. "We have to be unnoticed, remember."

No one looking at Roberta was likely not to notice her.

She was very pale, was sweating, her face was tragic with seriousness.

They walked rapidly round the hotel, past the people on the pavements. The three did not look at one another or, very much, at the possible victims. Alice was thinking: But people might be *killed*. . . . Oh no, that couldn't happen! Inside her chest, however, a pressure was building up, painful, like a cry—but she could not let it be heard. Like the howl of a beast in despair, but she could not reach it, to comfort it.

What were the others thinking? Roberta—well, that was easy, she thought only of Faye. Bert? He seemed not much different from his genial self; but surely he must be wondering, like Alice, Will this girl be killed? This old woman? Perhaps this one, or that one?

There was no sign of Jasper and Faye. Having circumambulated the hotel twice, Roberta said, "There's no point in this. And we shouldn't be together." Without even looking at them, she walked off by herself and stood on the opposite pavement, from which she could see the side of the hotel in front of her, and on her left the street along which Faye and Jasper could reasonably be expected to drive.

Bert went off, without looking at Alice, to stand on the pavement opposite the front of the hotel. Alice, then, logically, could have gone to stand on the side where Roberta was not, but decided that the front was best, and stood near Bert.

It was a quarter to four.

No sign of the car.

A bus very slowly went by. Jocelin sat downstairs near the window, looking at them. She mouthed at them, "A—quarter—to—five." Then she briefly held up her left hand with its five fingers spread, lowered it, held it up again, this time with four fingers showing, bent down the forefinger, quickly again mouthed, "A—quarter—to—five," and then stared ahead of her.

"I think," said Bert facetiously, "that it will be a quarter to five."

Four o'clock.

The great hotel, with its look of sedate luxury, brooded massively there with people teeming about it. Alice thought, Well, perhaps something has gone wrong and they won't come. It'll be all right.

"Shall we tell Roberta it'll be a quarter to five?" she asked Bert. He said, "No, we can't draw attention to ourselves." Then he changed his mind and ran across the street, in and out of the traffic. Roberta was standing on the very edge of the pavement, absolutely still. Alice watched Bert go up to her, say something, then take her by the arm, apparently urging her to stand in a less noticeable place. Roberta shook off his hand on her arm, and stayed exactly where she was. Bert stood beside her for a minute, then slowly came back, this time waiting for the lights to change.

Alice could see his face clearly. She had not seen him like this, not ever. Would not, perhaps, have recognised him. He had about him a look of isolation, separateness; as if nothing could bridge the distance between him and the people who streamed with him across the road, as if he were cursed or cast out. He had a leaden, sickly colour, like a corpse.

The howl, or cry, in Alice's chest forced itself out of her mouth in a yelp, and she found she was dashing off away from Bert and into the hotel. She was looking for a telephone. Two booths, back to back; and one was empty. She thought: Oh my God, if the right directory isn't here! But it was, and she found the Samaritans' number and dialled it, while the little whimpering yelping cries came out of her, uncontrollably, as though the animal lodged inside her were being beaten.

The friendly, nonjudging Samaritan voice.

Alice said, "Oh, quick, quick, there's a bomb, it's going to go off, come quickly, it's going to be in a car."

"Where is this car?" enquired the Samaritan, in no way discomposed. When Alice did not at once answer, "You must tell us. We can't get someone there until you tell us."

Alice was thinking: But the car isn't even there yet. How do I know it will get there at all? Then she thought of those people, all those poor people, and she said despondently, "Well, perhaps it will be too late, anyway."

"But where? The address, do tell us the address?"

Alice could not bring herself to give the address. "It's in Knightsbridge," she said. She was going to ring off, and added, as an afterthought, "It's the IRA. Freedom for Ireland! For a united Ireland and peace to all mankind!" She rang off.

Alice started to run back, then walked. She went straight up to Bert, so that he could turn that face towards her, and she could see that it was normal. But when he did look at her she saw a dead, awful face; and then he winked at her, slowly, and the wink dislodged that other vision of him as a corpse, and he became his ordinary self, a bit pale and tense, but that was all.

It's not too late to stop, she was thinking. It's all a mistake. We should plan it all more carefully. Perhaps Faye and Jasper have decided to call it off. They have disconnected the bombs. That is why they are late.

Four-fifteen.

In all that time there had been only three spaces available for parking.

And then Alice saw that Bert was standing facing away from her, very still, staring, Presumably it was the car. A white Escort went past Bert and then Alice, with Jasper and Faye in front, Faye driving. They looked exalted, but scared. The rear mudguard on the side nearest the pavement was bashed in. That was why they were late. She went up to Bert, and he agreed with her diagnosis.

There was no parking place anywhere. The car, confined by traffic, turned right, slowly, and crawled round down the side street, where cars were almost stationary, vanished for a while round the back, came into view again, and, rather faster, drove up past Roberta, who, unable to stop herself, raised her arms as Faye went past, but dropped them slowly, presumably when the couple in the car took no notice of her. That they could have that much sense comforted Alice. The white Escort went past Bert and Alice again. It was four-twenty-five. No traffic wardens; that was something.

They had not discussed what should be done in the event of there being no parking places. Presumably as the time ran out the two would find somewhere to park and just run?

This time Faye did not turn to drive up the side street by the hotel, but went on for another block and then turned. Inexplicably. While the car was out of sight, two cars drove away in that side street next to the hotel, leaving quite a long empty space. Would Faye see this when she came back into position again, at the far end of the hotel?

When Faye did reappear, it was after half past.

By then Alice was sick with tension, with misery. She knew that she was sniffling and snuffling, but she couldn't help it.

Faye was driving again past Roberta, who this time did not move, only stood. Despair. People were noticing her.

As the car passed Bert he signalled, pointing to the empty space. Faye and Jasper looked like two blocks of wax with eyes fixed in them. At first they did not look at Bert; then Jasper glanced at him, and tugged at Faye's arm.

Just in time, Faye turned to drive into the side street.

As she did, a car slid into the empty space from the other direction, but leaving quite enough room for Faye to park. Cars were already behind her. In order for her to park, she had to hold up the traffic, looking for a way through, to get to the other side of the street. The car, others hooting at it, waited, then forced its way across the flow of traffic, to a chorus of hoots and shouts. Faye inserted the car in the space on the diagonal and, it seemed, was ready to leave it, for her door opened, but it shut again, and she drove the Escort violently up on the pavement. A long pause, then the car reversed hastily, so that it was better parked, but not much.

The other cars were still hooting.

Roberta, seeing from Bert's and Alice's rigid, attentive poses and how they stared that Faye was parking, came hastening across to join them. Oblivious of any previous decisions not to stand together so as not to make themselves conspicuous, the three stood in a tight group, staring at the delinquent car. Now, however, it could be said that they were people censorious of a bit of very bad parking.

"For God's sake," Roberta was saying, in a harsh, sick, loud voice, "for God's sake, move. Get *out*."

Jasper got out of the car, opening the door against the flow of the traffic, and stood inside the half-opened door, bending down to look into the car and at Faye.

"For God's *sake*," prayed Roberta.

Then Jasper straightened, shut the door, and came away down the side of the car, meaning to go round it, onto the pavement, and to open the door for Faye. At least, that was how it seemed to the three who watched. For there was no reason at all, if the door was not jammed in some way, for Faye's not opening it, and just as quickly as she could. Time was running out. There were five minutes to go. But time had run out, for then came the explosion, and it seemed that the windows of all the world were crashing in, while the car flew apart.

"Faye, Faye," Roberta was sobbing, as she ran across the street, not looking to see whether there were cars or not; and "Jasper," whimpered Alice, running after her.

All down the side of the hotel, it was a scene of disaster; bodies on the pavement, some lying still, some struggling to sit or rise; bits of metal, of shattered glass, handbags, masonry, blood.

When Alice got to the scene, Jasper was not there. Then she saw him running away down the other side of the street, hands to his head. Blood was all over him.

Idiot, she was thinking. Don't run away, much better wait here, there are a lot of people hurt; you'd just be one of the hurt people.

Roberta was standing among the bodies, staring at the wreck of the car, which seemed to have sunk into itself; a low tangle of metal.

Roberta, moaning, turned away from the car, and, bending, began to peer into the faces of the wounded and—as Alice had just realised —the dead on the pavement.

Suddenly, Roberta cried out, and was sitting on the pavement, cradling a bloody mess that, Alice reasoned, could only be Faye. Yes, she could see an arm, white, pretty, whole, with a tangle of coloured bangles on the wrist.

Alice stepped up to Roberta and said, "Stop it. There's nothing you can do, you know. We have to get out."

Roberta, her eyes not seeing Alice, or anything, stared at Alice, then down at the red bundle. She was sobbing, in a dry, breathless, frantic way.

"Roberta," said Alice again, reasonably, and even managed a companionable, persuasive smile. "Please get up."

And at this moment, into this scene of disorder, of destruction, which had remained more or less the same for the last five minutes since the explosion, erupted Society, erupted Law and Order, in the shape of a wailing of ambulance sirens, and the police, who suddenly were everywhere, hundreds of them, it seemed. The ambulances, parked nose to tail up the street, began their sober, careful job of collecting casualties and corpses from the pavement. But the police were in a state of panic, out of control, rushing about, shouting orders, hustling the onlookers, who of course had arrived by now, and who were generally adding to the confusion.

To the ambulance man who bent over Roberta, Alice said, "She's not hurt, I don't think. But *she*"—for some reason Alice could not bring herself to use Faye's name of this mess of blood and flesh—"*she* was right in the way of the explosion."

"And where were you?" asked the ambulance man, gently assisting poor Roberta to her feet.

"I was over there, on that pavement," said Alice truthfully. "No, I'm not hurt."

By now two of them were crouching beside Faye, and Roberta and Alice stood upright, Alice holding Roberta.

"She's dead," Alice said reasonably to Roberta.

"Yes, I know," said Roberta in a normal voice.

At this point a policeman charged up and ordered, "What are you doing here, are you hurt? Then move along."

Alice put her arm round Roberta and walked her away. She did not want the policeman to come to his senses and start questioning Roberta, who, on casual inspection, did not look abnormal, though she was soaked with blood from the waist down.

She had not thought what she would do with Roberta, blood-soaked and in a state, away from the crowds and the police; but they were stopped by another policeman, this time in control of himself, who said that Roberta looked as if she needed attention.

"She's in shock," said Alice.

"Then get her into the ambulance," said the policeman, turning away to join with others in pushing away onlookers.

There was nothing for it. Alice went with Roberta in the ambulance, together with ten others, all of them shocked or slightly hurt. The badly wounded were being loaded into other ambulances.

Theirs was one of the first away. Alice and Roberta were silent, listening to people who wept, who complained, or who excitedly told their stories; how they were peacefully going along the street, or in or out of the hotel, and then . . .

Cut faces and arms, possible fractures, bruises. One woman had had her clothes torn off her by the blast and was wrapped in a blanket. Another had been flung right through the window that at that moment had been in the process of shattering. She was covered with small deep cuts and seemed the worst off.

They were in the hospital in a few minutes.

Roberta was examined and pronounced unharmed.

Alice explained to a sympathetic policeman that Roberta and she had been going into the hotel when it happened. They got into a taxi and were driven home. The taxi man said it was a shocking thing; probably those Arabs again; they had no sense of the sacredness of life, not like the Westerners; if he had his way he would stop the Arabs from coming here.

Roberta and Alice said nothing.

It was seven when they reached home. In the kitchen was Bert, attending to Jasper, who had a great many cuts on his face and his head, but was otherwise all right. Bert said he should get the cuts stitched up; some of them were deep. Jasper said no. And Jasper was right. He should have stayed, instead of running away, Jocelin argued, and then he could have told some story and got himself stitched up with the others in hospital. Now, he must on no account go near a hospital, or even a doctor. But one of the women in the squat in South London had been a nurse; it would be all right to go down there.

"I don't think it would be all right," said Jasper. "The fewer people involved, the better."

Alice thought this was sensible, and tried to examine the cuts. He shook her off. They didn't seem too bad to her; perhaps they wouldn't leave scars. Well, there was always plastic surgery.

The five of them finally sat round the table.

Jasper told them, in a businesslike, formal way, how, as he had turned the car out of the street where it had been left, he had misjudged a distance and scraped the front mudguard of a parked car. He would have driven off, but now there was a car immediately blocking his way, and a man who had seen the incident from a first-floor window came running out to say that Jasper need not think he was just going to escape and get away with it. Jasper had said that no such thought had been in his mind. The man said he was lying. They had had quite a little shouting match before they reached the point of exchanging insurance companies: Jasper, of course, had had to say he would supply the address of his later. Then it turned out that the dented mudguard was pressing on the back wheel, and they had to get out of the car and use a heavy spanner to hit the mudguard until it was free of the wheel. The man from the house was standing over them, as if they were criminals who had to be watched. To reach the dent in the mudguard, Jasper had to lie full-length in the road, and hit it from below, and at an angle. It was awkward and took time, and they were holding up the traffic.

When they at last got into the stream of traffic again, they were so late they thought of calling the whole thing off. Faye could easily disconnect the bombs, but the trouble was that this time the work would be in full view of all the people in the cars and the passers-by on the pavement. Besides, said Faye, do or die; she was game. A pity to have gone to all this trouble and give up.

When Faye had turned, the second time, not immediately up past the hotel but on the next turning, it was because they had not seen any parking places, had decided to stop the car anywhere they could find a place so that, regardless of who was watching, Faye could wrench the connections off the bombs. They then had only twelve minutes to go. But there were no parking places anywhere along that street.

"No," Faye had said gallantly, "there's nothing for it," and had tried to drive faster, but was hemmed in by traffic.

And when Jasper had got out but Faye had not, was it that Faye's door had jammed? Had he been going to help her with the door?

This was Roberta, and she sounded accusing.

Jasper hesitated. Alice knew it was because he was trying to think how not to say something. When he looked like this, very pale but luminous, with a candid, suffering, helpless look, it meant he was going to lie. Or wanted to. He began to stutter, checked himself, and said simply, "When Faye drove into the empty space, she went too fast up onto the pavement, and then braked. She did not have on her seat belt. We did not have our seat belts on, you see."

"Of course not," said Roberta, severely.

"But she was jerked forward, and the driving wheel got the pit of her stomach. She didn't have any breath, you see?" he said gently to Roberta. Alice was thinking, There, he's kind, Jasper's kind, he didn't want to tell Roberta any of this. . . .

Roberta was staring at Jasper, her mouth was open, and she was breathing badly. She was thinking, they all knew, that her Faye had been killed because of some silly little thing, something ridiculous; for the rest of her life Roberta would be thinking, incredulous, that Faye died because she drove too fast and too hard up onto a pavement.

"I could see she couldn't move," said Jasper. "I got the car into reverse—I stretched my feet over, and did it. Then I said she must get out quickly. But she did not move. I think she was too sick to move. I got out to drag her out of the car from the driving side. And then the bomb went off."

"Five minutes too early," said Roberta, this time accusing Jocelin. Who, like Jasper, had sat quiet, hesitating. There was something she did not want to say.

Roberta asked quickly, "Who set the timing? Faye?"

"Yes."

Roberta shook her head, as if saying *No, no, no*—to all of it— but then sat heavily silent, saying yes to tea, yes to sugar in it, yes to a biscuit. But she did not eat, or drink.

Roberta, they all knew, would at some point come out of this passive state.

Jasper was beginning to hurt, very badly. Bert ran upstairs, fetched painkillers for Jasper, sedatives for Roberta, and a radio.

They listened to the news.

"Five people have been killed, and twenty-three injured, some seriously, this afternoon, when a car exploded outside the Kubla Khan hotel, breaking all the windows down that side and damaging several parked cars. This monstrous and callous crime illustrated yet again the total lack of ordinary feeling by the IRA, who had claimed responsibility for the crime."

"Well, what about that," said Jocelin. "What a fucking nerve."

"Absolutely," said Alice, not connecting her telephone call with this development. Then, after a few minutes, listening to the indignation, the frustration of the others, she did connect it, and she realised that she could never tell them what she had done. Never. She never would be trusted again.

Suppose Bert remembered that she had been gone off that pavement near to him for what must have been a good five minutes?

It seemed he did not.

At about ten o'clock Caroline came back. She was distant, even cold. She said she wouldn't sit down; she was tired and wanted to sleep.

She had heard the news, she said, when it seemed that Jasper was about to start the story.

She made herself coffee, drank it standing, not looking at them.

"Where's Faye?" she asked, and they realised there was no possible way she could know.

Roberta said, "Faye's dead," and began to cry. At first it was quiet, helpless weeping, and then she began to wail and moan.

"Well, that was due," said Bert, briskly.

"Was she in the car, then?" asked Caroline, but she didn't want to sound interested.

Roberta began to howl, a sound like that which Alice seemed to carry about with her, in her chest; a raw, dismal sound.

They checked that the windows were shut. They gave Roberta yet another sedative pill, and Jocelin and Alice assisted her upstairs. She was heavy, almost inert. They had to push her, support her, even order her to move her legs. Alice ran into the room first to make sure the windows were tight shut. Too late, when Roberta was already lying in the cosy heap of flowered stuffs and cushions that she had shared with Faye, did they remember that another room would have been better. They left her there, hoping that sleep would soon silence that awful weeping.

When the two women returned to the kitchen, they joined Bert and Jasper at the table. Caroline sat on the window sill, keeping her distance from them. They were silent, trying not to be affected by that terrible noise just over their heads. Roberta was howling now, and didn't sound human. They could have believed it was an animal up there: a wounded animal, or a dying one.

They were all pale, and tense. Bert's forehead had beads of sweat on it. On Jasper's face was a cold little smile. Caroline seemed ill. Jocelin was the least disturbed of them.

Bert kept sending appealing looks at Caroline, who would not look at him. Suddenly he pulled out of his top pocket, where it had been buttoned in over his heart, a piece of much-folded paper that had words scribbled on it. They all knew what the words were, for Bert had made sure they had the benefit of them, more than once. Now, having looked at each of them, one after another, carefully, to claim their attention—but Caroline still would not respond—he read, "The law should not abolish terror; to promise that would be self-delusion or deception; it should be substantiated and legalised in principle, clearly, without evasion or embellishment. The para-

graph on terror should be formulated as widely as possible, since
only revolutionary consciousness of justice and revolutionary conscience can determine the conditions of its application in practice."
A silence. They were not looking at him. "Lenin," said Bert.
"Lenin," he insisted, with confidence.

Alice had been watching him as he read, interested to see if
that vision of him she had had outside the hotel would reappear—
the leaden-faced corpselike Bert; but, on the contrary, the reading
strengthened him, and he smiled as he read, his white teeth showing between healthy red lips.

Jocelin said, "Thanks," as a matter of form, but she was listening to Roberta. She lit a cigarette, and her hands were shaking.
Seeing that they noticed this, she muttered, "Reaction, that's all."

Jasper continued to smile. He might have been listening to
distant music. Alice knew he was controlling the need to be sick.
She thought he looked like a wounded soldier, with his bloodstained bandages.

Then Caroline got off the window sill and said, "What has
Russia's Criminal Code got to do with us? Or Lenin, for that
matter," she added, daring them. "All amateur rubbish, if you ask
me," she said, angrily, and to Alice, "There was a message for you.
A man came this afternoon. An American. He said he would be
back to see you tomorrow. About four. Gordon O'Leary."

She did not look at Bert, but went out, without saying
good-bye.

"Gordon O'Leary again," remarked Jocelin, as if it didn't
matter very much.

"Bloody cheek," said Alice mechanically, thinking she was in
for a busy day, lunch with Peter Cecil, and then Gordon O'Leary in
the afternoon.

No one else said anything.

Then Bert said, "I'm off, too. No point in hanging around."

"Me, too," said Jasper.

"You're *leaving*?" said Alice, incredulously, to Jasper.

"But we said we were going, the moment it was done," said
Jasper, not looking at her.

She thought, Surely he can't be planning to go off with Bert?

Why, the moment Bert gets another woman, he'll be a spare part again.

She said nothing, and this made Jasper uneasy. Truculent, he asked her, "Well, how about you? Coming?"

"I don't think I'm going to leave," she said, vaguely.

"But you'll have to. Mary said this house was on the agenda again."

"Oh, they are always saying that," said Alice.

"Don't be so bloody stupid," said Jasper. "If not this month, then next, or the month after."

"Well, in the meantime, I'll stay. And someone has to stay with Roberta."

This being unarguable, Jasper was silent for a little, and then, overcome again by Alice's intransigence, he said, amazed, scandalised at her, "But, Alice, we agreed to scatter. It was a unanimous decision." And he even grasped her wrist in the old bony urgent grip, and bent to stare into her face.

That grip told her that she would not be without him for long. She smiled tranquilly up at that face, with its blue eyes in the creamy shallow lakes where the tiny blond freckles were, and said, "Let me know where you are, and we'll keep in touch. Anyway, does anyone know where Roberta's relatives are? She does have some, doesn't she?"

They knew only the hospital where Roberta's mother was dying.

"She won't stay here," said Jocelin, and Alice knew she was right.

Bert went up to get his canvas sack with clothes in it, and some books. Jasper fetched his belongings. He had even less than Bert.

Alice sat listlessly at the table, thinking of this house, this home she had made, deserted, empty, and the Council builders coming in.

Jocelin said she would leave in the morning. Said she thought the bag full of explosive components would be safe enough until they were needed. Laughed. Went upstairs.

Bert and Jasper lingered about the kitchen, at this last moment not wanting to leave. Not wanting to leave her, or the comfort she had made for them all? She did not choose to think about that. She remarked that she thought Roberta was quietening down.

And certainly the howling from overhead was less. It stopped. The house was silent.

Jasper bent quickly, and darted a kiss onto Alice's cheek, as in a game of "last touch." "See you," he said, and went out, not looking to see if Bert was following. It wasn't easy for him to leave her, thought Alice gratefully.

Alice was alone in the kitchen.

She listened to the news again. Well, they certainly were getting enough coverage; they had made their mark, all right.

Five dead. Another one, a girl of fifteen, seemed likely to die. Over twenty injured.

The midnight news devoted more than five minutes to the story.

Alice slept, sitting at the table, head on her arms.

She woke at about six, to see Roberta, shaky, sick, and awful, making herself tea.

Roberta said she would pack her things and be off. She would go to see her mother. She should have gone before, of course, but Faye . . . Her voice shook, she bit her lips, controlled herself, and drank her tea. She went upstairs to pack, came down with various addresses where Alice could reach her, pencilled neatly on a slip of paper. At least Roberta was not floating out of her life forever.

Roberta, unlike the others, owned a lot of things. She would abandon the actual furniture, but keep curtains, hangings, coverlets, pillows, mirrors, blankets. These were made into two great bundles, and she took them away in a taxi to the station.

Alice listened to the 8:00 a.m. news.

The IRA (in Ireland) said they had had nothing to do with yesterday's bombing, and they would kneecap those who committed such acts in their name. They did not—said the IRA (in Ireland)— go in for murdering innocent people.

Well, thought Alice, fancy that. And actually giggled. At the ludicrousness of it.

Well, it didn't matter what the IRA said; it was not for them to decide what comrades in this country did.

Alice sat wondering if it was worthwhile making a trip over to Ireland so as to explain to the Irish comrades the English comrades' point of view?

This speculation was stopped by Jocelin's coming down, with a backpack and a suitcase. She, too, drank tea, and heard that Roberta had departed without commenting, or even asking whether Roberta had asked her to keep in touch. She did not mention Bert and Jasper. About Caroline, Jocelin said that she was a good comrade but did not understand that sacrifices had to be made. She said this standing—she had not sat down—holding a mug of tea between both her hands, staring over it with red-rimmed eyes. Alice thought that she might very well have been crying.

Jocelin departed, and Alice was alone in the house.

She listened to the news again, and thought she would go out and get the newspapers. No, she would buy them when she went out to have lunch with Peter Cecil. Peter Cecil! The poor Russians, they didn't have enough sense not to choose such an obvious name. It was almost like a joke, as if they were sending themselves up. (Here, deep inside Alice, there stirred a little uneasiness, a doubt, but she could not pin it down to anything, so suppressed it.)

It was too early to leave for the restaurant.

She sat on quietly there by herself in the silent house. In the *betrayed* house . . . She allowed her mind to move from room to room in it, praising her achievements, as if someone else had accomplished all that, but the work had not been properly acknowledged, and so she was doing it as something due to justice. The house might have been a wounded animal whose many hurts she had one by one cleaned and bandaged, and now it was well, and whole, and she was stroking it, pleased with it and herself. . . . Not quite whole, however; but she wasn't going to think about what went on in the rafters. Poor house, she thought, full of tenderness, I hope someone is going to love it one day and look after it. When I leave here . . . It was silly to stay here, Jasper was right, but she would not leave yet, she would stay on a little longer: she felt that she could pull the walls of this house, her house, around her like a blanket, where she could snuggle, where she could feel safe.

She really did feel very peculiar, not herself at all! Well, that was only natural. She needed to go for a good long walk, or perhaps drop over for a little chat with Joan Robbins? No, there'd only be a lot of silly talk about the IRA and the bombing. Ordinary people simply didn't understand, and it was no good expecting them to. . . . Here the tenderness that had been washing around the place, inside and outside her, not knowing where it belonged, fastened itself on these ordinary people, and Alice sat with tears in her eyes, thinking, "Poor things, poor things, they simply don't understand!"—as if she had her arms around all the poor silly ordinary people in the world.

Now she began to think, but very carefully, about her parents. First, her father: no, he was too awful to waste time on, she wasn't ever going to think about him again. Her mother . . . What would Dorothy say if she knew her daughter had been at the bombing? Not that Alice believed that she—Alice—had any real reason to feel bad; she hadn't *really* been part of it. Alice sighed, a long shuddery breath, like a small child. This was something she could never, ever tell Dorothy, and knowing this made her feel severed from her mother as she had not done before: she might have said a final good-bye to her, instead of just having had one of their silly quarrels!

Oh no, it was all too much, it was too difficult. . . . Here Alice got abruptly to her feet: it looked as if she was about to walk right out of the kitchen, and after that the house; but, having stood in a stiff, arrested pose for a minute or so, she sat down again, because she had remembered Peter Cecil. (Peter Cecil, ha ha!) She couldn't go now, because there was this lunch. But perhaps I'll tell him all about it, she thought, he's a professional, I can talk about the bombing without all the rights and wrongs of everything coming into it, just as a job that was done, but was bungled a bit. . . . Funny, she had not thought until this moment that they had messed it up. And had they? After all, if publicity was the aim, then they had certainly achieved that! And Faye? But comrades knew their lives were at risk, the moment they undertook this sort of thing, decided to become terrorists. . . . She could not remember a point where she had said, "I am a terrorist, I don't mind being killed." (Here she was again impelled to get up from her chair, in a trapped panic movement, but again sat down.) I was all the time waiting for something to *start*—she thought; and on her face came a small, scared, incredulous smile at the inappropriateness of it. Had she not believed that the bombing was serious, then? No, not really; she had gone along with it, while feeling it was not right—and behind that was the thought that *serious* work (whatever that might turn out to be) would come later. Well, what would *they* think about the bombing? (Meaning, the Russians.) There was no need to ask what Andrew would say. Or Gordon. She could imagine, only too vividly, their condemning faces.

And Peter Cecil? For some reason, he was different. Of course, I wouldn't give away any names, she thought: I'd just talk very carefully, tell him the story. I'd say I was told by someone in the know, and I wanted to have his opinion.

Here various little warnings that her nerves had registered and were holding banked there till she could attend to them nearly surfaced, but retreated again. Meanwhile, she was thinking that Peter Cecil had a nice face. Yes. (She was looking at him in her mind's eye, as he had stood there yesterday outside the door, she in a frenzy of impatience to be off.) A kind face. Not like those Russians, not at all like them, he was quite different. . . . And here the warnings came back, in a rush, screaming for attention, and she could no longer shut them out.

Of course Peter Cecil was not like those Russians, because he wasn't a Russian. He was . . . he was MI-6 or MI-5 or XYZ or one of those bloody things, it didn't matter. The point was, he was English, *English*.

At this thought, at the word, a soft sweet relief began to run through Alice, so strongly she had to recognise it and be embarrassed by it. And what of it! English or not, he was the enemy, he was—worse than the Russians—he was upper-class (*Cecil*, I ask you!), he was reactionary, he was a fascist. Well, not exactly a fascist, really, that was exaggerating. But English. *One of us.* She sat thinking about his Englishness, and what that meant, what she felt about it—that talking to him would be a very different thing from talking to those Russians, who simply got everything wrong, and that was because they didn't know what we were really like: English. And what was the matter with feeling like this? Had they (the comrades) not decided to have no dealings with Russians, IRA Uncle Tom Cobbley and all, only with *us*?

As she imagined herself talking to Peter Cecil, she knew that many things would not have to be said at all, as they don't between people from the same country, no matter how divided about certain things. (Like politics!)

But what did he want to know? Alice could not remember what had been said yesterday. Her memory was a blank except that he had asked about Andrew. (Andrew *Connors*? Well, why not, perhaps he really was Connors.) But what had she said? Had anything been said? No, she was sure not, everything had been so rushed, she had been in a fever, she had only wanted to get off as fast as she could. The *matériel*? No, was it likely she would mention that? Of course she hadn't!

She sat on, cold, tense, frightened, trying to remember, while at the same time, the thought, *He is English*, was coming to her rescue. She was struggling to make her memory come to heel, to give up what it should, while she thought, He is English, he will understand.

Oh yes, Alice did know that she forgot things, but not how badly, or how often. When her mind started to dazzle and to puzzle, frantically trying to lay hold of something stable, then she always at once allowed herself—as she did now—to slide back into her childhood, where she dwelt pleasurably on some scene or other that she had smoothed and polished and painted over and over again with fresh colour until it was like walking into a story that began, "Once upon a time there was a little girl called Alice, with her mother, Dorothy. One morning Alice was in the kitchen with Dorothy, who was making her favourite pudding, apple with cinnamon and brown sugar and sour cream, and little Alice said, 'Mummy, I am a good girl, aren't I?' "

But today her mind would not stay in this dream, or story; it insisted on coming back into the present, away from her mother, who was finally repudiating Alice because of the bombing.

Alice sat quietly on, while time passed, carrying her towards lunch and Peter Cecil. She was very anxious, and the pit of her stomach hurt, and her heart thudded painfully.

There was no need to tell Peter Cecil anything about it. Why should she? Perhaps she would say a little about Andrew. It would not harm Andrew: she did not even know where he was. "Andrew Connors?" she would say. "Yes, he said he was an American. He sometimes visited the house next door; he was in love with a girl who lived there then, I've forgotten her name. And that's all I know, really."

They would have a nice lunch. Perhaps he would even turn out to be a friend, like Andrew. After all, she counted Andrew as a friend, though she did not now think as well of him as she had. There were always decent people, even among reactionaries. She remembered some comrade or other, saying somewhere or other—in Birmingham, was it? in the Manchester squat?—that it was primitive Marxism to think that as individuals every member of a ruling class was bad. She would just have to watch her tongue; it would be all right. Just have to be careful—and trust to inspiration. It was silly sitting here worrying about what to say; she always did know, when the time came, how to handle things.

And that went for Gordon O'Leary, too. . . . But as she thought about him, Alice felt the anxiety in her stomach becoming a sharp, almost unbearable pain. Oh, shit, she had just understood she must be careful not to mention Gordon to Peter Cecil, or to let Peter Cecil come anywhere near this house after lunch. Never mind, she was sure she could manage that. She would first handle Peter Cecil, and then Gordon O'Leary. But—she suddenly thought—why should she meet Gordon at all? After lunch, she could simply go off for a walk somewhere, and not come back to this house till later. No, that would only be postponing the problem. She would come back in good time from the restaurant, saying good-bye to Peter Cecil there, and pin a note on the door saying . . . No, there couldn't be a note: the neighbours would see it and come to investigate. Much better let everyone think that things were going on normally for as long as possible; and that was why it was a good thing they would at least see her going in and out.

When she got back from the restaurant she would lock the doors and windows—there was only one window that didn't lock, and she would nail it down, now, before she went off—and she would go right up to the top of the house and into the attic, and put a weight on the trap door so that no one could come up into it. Even if Gordon O'Leary got into the house somehow—and he would hardly want to be seen breaking into a house in full daylight—he would not know you could get up into the attic; why should he?

This detailed planning and arranging was making her feel better. It was what she was good at: she felt in command of everything again, and her painful stomach was easing, and she was breathing more quietly.

She was actually looking forward to the meal with Peter Cecil!

Smiling gently, a mug of very strong sweet tea in her hand, looking this morning like a nine-year-old girl who has had, perhaps, a bad dream, the poor baby sat waiting for it to be time to go out and meet the professionals.

A NOTE ON THE TYPE

The text of this book was set in Electra, a Linotype face designed by W. A. Dwiggins (1880–1956). This face cannot be classified as either modern or old style. It is not based on any historical model, nor does it echo any particular period or style. It avoids the extreme contrasts between thick and thin elements that mark most modern faces and attempts to give a feeling of fluidity, power, and speed.

Composed by Maryland Linotype Composition Company, Baltimore, Maryland
Printed and bound by The Haddon Craftsmen, Inc., Scranton, Pennsylvania

Typography and binding design by Tasha Hall